The car stopped.

"Is something wrong?" Jenifer asked.

Eric cleared his throat. "I, er . . . there's something I want to ask you."

What did he want from her? To spend the night? "Just say it, Eric." Her heart had picked up speed.

"One little hint as to where in the hell I am?" His words exploded out of his mouth.

She couldn't believe her ears. "Directions? You want directions?"

He winced. "Look, at least I asked."

Insufferable man. He should have been thinking of kissing her, not asking which way to turn. "Go straight," she said.

He followed her instructions to her house. Once there, he turned toward her. "I know you don't understand my reaction," he said.

Jenifer nodded. "It's only dir—"

He cut her off with a kiss. And then he broke away. "Out."

"What?" She quivered all over.

Eric leaned across her and yanked open the passenger door. "Go home. Get out now before you're lying naked beneath me."

She caught her breath. She didn't understand why he was being so honorable. That was okay, though. There was always tomorrow.

Avon Contemporary Romances by
Hailey North

HAILEY NORTH

Love: Undercover

AVON BOOKS

An Imprint of HarperCollins*Publishers*

This is a work of fiction. Names, characters, places, and incidents are products of the author's imagination or are used fictitiously and are not to be construed as real. Any resemblance to actual events, locales, organizations, or persons, living or dead, is entirely coincidental.

AVON BOOKS
An Imprint of HarperCollins*Publishers*
10 East 53rd Street
New York, New York 10022-5299

Copyright © 2004 by Nancy Wagner
ISBN: 0-06-058230-8
www.avonromance.com

First Avon Books paperback printing: June 2004

Avon Trademark Reg. U.S. Pat. Off. and in Other Countries, Marca Registrada, Hecho en U.S.A.
HarperCollins® is a registered trademark of HarperCollins Publishers Inc.

Printed in the U.S.A.

10 9 8 7 6 5 4 3 2 1

To Mocha and Stanley,
my faithful feline companions who kept me
in good cheer while I wrote this book.
Thanks for not chewing through
all the cables of my computer!

One

$\mathcal{E}$veryone in Doolittle, Arkansas, knew Jenifer Janey Wright didn't need a man.

She'd raised her twins on her own, having sent their father, her college freshman sweetheart, packing when he suggested her pregnancy fell into the category of an obstacle to their career success that could be "dealt with." After all, she planned to be a lawyer and he a doctor. To him, a baby at nineteen was worse than a C in Organic Chemistry.

No, Jenifer didn't need a man.

She'd earned her college degree by correspondence course, completing her homework in between teaching Autumn and Adam to read and hurrying to her job at the Doolittle Public Library. She'd worked there summers during high school, and the aging Mrs. Million was more than happy to have her help. They didn't pay much more than minimum wage, but Jenifer eagerly chose being surrounded by books over wait-

ing tables at the Verandah Restaurant or standing behind the counter at Harolene's Hobby and Crafts. Her
uncle Pete, not really her uncle but her parents' next
door neighbor and best friend, held the post of Chief
of Police of Doolittle. He'd taught her to handle guns
and to shoot the heart out of a target at close, mid-,
and long range, and he almost succeeded in recruiting
her to become the town's first female policeman, but
Jenifer declined.

Her son and daughter needed her, safe and in one
piece.

Not that anything ever happened in Doolittle.

There'd been a flurry of excitement a few years ago
when a handsome young veterinarian had moved to
town. Jenifer's friends, particularly her best pal Pamela,
had urged her to wangle a date with Dr. Mike Halliday.
She declined. Dr. Mike, as everyone soon called him,
was into rescuing people, and Jenifer, as capable as she
was, assumed they'd never mesh. Butt heads maybe.

Besides, she didn't need a man. By then she'd earned
her Master's in Library Science, organized Mrs. Million's retirement party, and taken charge of the library.

No, she didn't need a man.

But that didn't mean, Jenifer thought wistfully, now
and then when no well-meaning friends or family were
within sight, that once in a while she didn't want one.

Especially now that her twins had left for college.

Twenty-nine days ago they'd left for Fayetteville;
Autumn's scholarship courtesy of the track team,
Adam's based on academic merit.

Jenifer sighed and pushed a long strand of hair back
from her cheek. She didn't recommend experiencing

empty nest syndrome all alone. Surely she'd settle down, get used to the quiet in the house.

Even now, perched behind the checkout counter at the Doolittle Public Library, where she'd spent countless contented hours, she felt the restless stirring within that had been stealing over her more and more lately.

She flipped the pages of the *Library Journal*, not focusing on one little word.

Not that she wanted a man to keep. Jenifer was far too used to running her own life to let anyone interfere. But only last night when Pamela, sharing some of the secrets of her life with her third husband, went off on a tangent about experimenting with *Kama Sutra* oils and Gravitron boots and Velcro restraints, Jenifer's mouth had fallen open. People did stuff like that?

No, she wasn't shocked, she assured her friend. More like pea-green envious. She wished—no, she didn't. Yes, she did. She wished she could meet a man who'd be willing to explore the naughty and the unknown with her—the sensible, capable, practical Jenifer Janey Wright—and not insist on putting a ring on her finger.

But where in Doolittle would she meet such a paragon of lasciviousness? Pamela had picked up her latest "eligible" man—if you could call him that—on a trip to Little Rock. Jenifer knew she had picky tastes, but Pamela's number three fell way below her standards.

No, she knew she wouldn't accept just any man to fulfill her fantasies. He'd have to be tall, dark, and handsome, just for starters. He'd possess a worldly air, be rather mysterious, yet able to walk in the rain without fussing about his expensive clothing. He'd have lips that smiled knowingly, making her blush just remembering where those lips had kissed her sated body. He'd be—

What was wrong with her? The town of Doolittle didn't pay her to daydream. Jenifer slammed shut the *Library Journal* and pushed back the high-backed stool. She had books to reshelve.

Only then did she glance up and realize a man stood in front of the checkout counter, gazing at her with an amused expression on his face.

His rather handsome, expressive, chiseled chin, deep-set dark eyes, strong nose, full lips sort of face. A face she'd never seen before.

Jenifer swallowed hard, wondering if it were possible to conjure reality from wishes. Tipping her head to one side, she considered the notion, and the man.

And the rather wicked gleam in his eyes. She felt naked, suddenly, as if he could both read her mind and see through her sensible white blouse. Which was impossible, of course, and even if he could, all he would catch a glimpse of was her sensible white bra.

A bra she would throw away the minute she got home.

She'd been sensible enough for years of her life.

"May I help you?" she said to the man, keeping her voice pleasant and professional.

He nodded, and leaned a hand on the counter. He had a tan—not surprising toward the end of summer— and his shoulders moved beneath his polo shirt with a grace that spoke of either lots of time in the gym or out of doors.

Jenifer smiled. She liked a man who didn't stay cooped up inside all day.

He fixed her with a dark-eyed gaze that made her

feel as if no matter what he asked for, she could provide it. Even if the library didn't carry it, she'd order the request. She grinned, most unprofessionally, knowing it wasn't a book she wanted him to want.

"I'm looking for information," he said, his voice a low-pitched baritone. Very pleasant.

"Ah," Jenifer said, "then you've come to the right place." As soon as she said the words, she felt like an idiot. She should stick to being sensible and leave flirting to the women like Pamela.

"Oh, I think I have," he said, his murmured words almost lost in the smiling way he delivered them, his expression too pointed for her to miss his meaning.

Heck, maybe he knew enough to flirt for two.

Jenifer straightened her shoulders, unconsciously showing off her ample bust, and heard a betraying "pop" as her top blouse button let go of a loose thread and skittered across the counter.

She snatched at it the same time the man did, and his hand came to rest atop hers.

He smiled, and lifted his hand.

Palming the button and forcing herself not to glance down at her blouse to see what damage had been done or how much fabric gaped open, she said, "What kind of information do you need?"

"It's better this way," he said, "less formal. Are you the librarian?"

"Yes, I am." She held out her hand. "I'm Jenifer Wright, Doolittle's librarian."

He took her hand and shook it briefly. His skin was warm and pleasantly dry. A callus or two caught her attention. Nice.

"Eric Hamilton," he said. "You don't look like any librarian I've ever met before."

"I don't know why not," Jenifer said, glancing at her white blouse, gray skirt, nylon-clad legs and sensible pumps, wishing she could squeeze her eyes shut and when she opened them be decked out in a sleek form-fitting black number with diamonds at her wrists and fingers. And underneath, she'd sport silk stockings and garters and her long legs would perch above daring stiletto heels.

"Well, your hair isn't in a bun, and it's this incredible roasted chestnut color. And so shiny." He leaned closer, and lifted a strand of her long hair. "Ginger," he said, letting go of her hair almost as suddenly as he'd reached for it. "Your hair smells like sweet ginger."

Jenifer gaped at him. "That's right. You're very observant."

He shrugged, and his lips tilted upward. "So I'm told."

This man knew too much. Jenifer glanced around the library. It was only about ten minutes till closing time. All the other patrons had left before she'd started her daydreaming under cover of studying the *Library Journal.* So here she stood, alone in the Doolittle Library with the sexiest man she'd ever met. None too sensible. "And what do you do, Mr. Eric Hamilton?"

"A little of this, a little of that," he said.

"Ooh, a man of mystery," she said jokingly. But Jenifer was too pragmatic, and also too curious to accept such a vague answer. She liked facts, all lined up in a row. "So what type of this and that?"

"Potential investments," he said, handing her a business card. It read HAMILTON INVESTMENT INC., with a Virginia address.

"You're a long way from home."

"I'm a bit of a rambling man," he said. "I travel a lot."

"Then that makes us opposites," she said.

"And you know the saying," he replied.

Her pulse did a little skip-jump. Yeah, opposites attract. She moistened her lips with the tip of her tongue and tried to think of some flip comment to make in reply. And then her common sense reasserted itself. Sexy strangers did not wander into the Doolittle Library to flirt with Ms. Jenifer Janey Wright. This man wanted information, and he was plying her with practiced guile in order to soften her up.

And boy did he know how to succeed in doing exactly that!

"I bet you've lived here all your life," he said.

She nodded, then sighed. "But never mind that. The library closes in five minutes," she said, straightening the edge of the *Journal* so that it lay at a forty-five-degree angle to the edge of the countertop. "You may have to come back tomorrow."

"Tomorrow's Sunday," he said.

"Is it?" Her eyes widened, and she quickly caught herself. "Of course it is. The next day, then."

"Maybe you could help me learn what I need over dinner," he said. "I'm new to town and I don't know anyone and even though I'm only going to be here a week or so—"

"You're only here for a week?" Her own daring surprised her. But what the heck, hadn't she been wishing for a fantasy man who'd not be sticking around? Why not grab at the opportunity? Chances are, nothing would happen, but at least she'd met a subject who met her baseline criteria.

"Two or three at the most," he said.

"Until you're ready to ramble on?"

He grinned. "Exactly."

She tucked the business card he'd given her into the edge of the desk blotter. She'd have Uncle Pete check him out to make sure he wasn't a criminal, and then . . .

Jenifer sighed. Pinch me, she thought.

The telephone shrilled and she jumped. Maybe it was her alarm clock and she'd been dreaming. It kept on ringing.

"Go ahead and answer it," the man said. "I'll wait."

Jenifer lifted the receiver. "Doolittle Public—"

"I know it's the library, dang it," came the booming voice over the phone. "Ain't that the number I called?"

Rooster. Jenifer cupped a hand around the receiver, not that the gesture would dampen the decibels much. "Mr. Mayor, what can I do for you?"

"For starters, you can stop calling me by that name. I've been Rooster to you since your mama and daddy brought you into this world."

"Yes, Rooster," Jenifer said, stealing a glance at the sophisticated urbanite leaning ever so casually against the library checkout counter and waiting for her.

"Besides, you might as well be the mayor. We know who gets things done in this town, now don't we?"

Jenifer only nodded. Rooster rarely needed verbal prompting to keep him rolling onward.

"I mean, who got the garbage collection fee passed? And persuaded the council to fund that dang bookmobile? Anyway, there's hope at last for the Horace House. Mrs. Ball claims to have some rich old geezer interested in buying it."

"That's great!" Jenifer couldn't help but be pleased at the news. "Did you get this straight from Mrs. Ball?" Mrs. Ball *was* real estate in Doolittle.

Rooster chortled. "Not exactly."

Jenifer sensed a mystery. Any other day or time she would have pursued it. She might be restless in her small town now that her twins had left for college, but she'd spent her life helping Doolittle be a good place to live. And Doolittle needed economic development. And if someone were planning to reopen the Horace House, she'd want to know about it.

But right now she didn't want to talk to Rooster, not with Eric Hamilton standing in front of her. Well, he had been, but he'd moved away and appeared deep in study of the bulletin board her children's reading group had designed.

"Let me know when he gets to town," Jenifer said.

"I can do better than that," Rooster said, lowering his voice to a conspiratorial whisper. "You come to my office whenever Mrs. Ball arranges the meeting and I'll let you help welcome him to town."

"Okay," Jenifer said. "Let me know when, and if I'm available, I'll be there. I have to close the library now."

"Hell, yes," Rooster bellowed, "no overtime in the city's budget!"

Jenifer put down the phone, shaking her head and smiling in mock exasperation. "Crazy coot," she said.

The man had strolled back to the counter. "Everything okay?"

"Sure," Jenifer said, wondering if he'd bring up going to dinner again.

Dinner.

She couldn't go to dinner with Eric Hamilton.

"Are you sure everything is all right?"

"Town business," Jenifer said. "But I did remember a prior engagement, so I won't be able to accept your invitation to dinner."

"Ah," he said, the murmured syllable a polite speculation.

"I'm not making that up," she said, somewhat defensively.

He smiled. "I wouldn't blame you if you were. After all, I'm a complete stranger. You'd be nuts to go anywhere with anyone you don't know."

Jenifer almost sputtered. "If that's what you think, then why did you ask me?"

He shrugged, and then with a twinkle in his eye, he said, "I'm hungry?"

"You're not very well-mannered," Jenifer said, somewhat crossly. "I ought to call Uncle Pete and have him run your license and then make you take me to dinner tomorrow night."

"It's a deal," the man said, still with that maddening smile in his eyes. He reached into his well-fitting slacks and pulled out a thin wallet.

"Don't you want to know who Uncle Pete is?"

"Well, let's see. The mayor just phoned you, so let me guess. Uncle Pete is the chief of police?"

"If you're so smart, why do you need assistance from a librarian?"

"Maybe it's not information I'm after." He leaned

over the counter and flicked a strand of hair back from her cheek. "I may be smart, but sometimes I'm a little foolish, too."

Just the way he said it, his voice an invitation to share a mystery only he knew the secrets of, melted her knees. She leaned against the edge of the counter, feeling like a cat that wanted to be scratched under its chin. One more dark-eyed glance, another murmured innuendo, another appreciative gaze up and down her body, and she would be purring.

"So why can't you have dinner with me tonight?" he asked.

"It's family cookout night."

"And?"

She could inhale him, all the way down her throat and into her lungs. Breathing in his scent, she lifted her head and said, "It's my mother's birthday and it's the first one since—" She paused and said the words carefully. "—since my father died."

"I'm sorry," he said. "Maybe tomorrow, then?"

His voice had grown more distant. Jenifer studied him, puzzled. Perhaps he had suffered a loss, too, and didn't know how to deal with being reminded of the pain.

"Would you like to come? Tonight?"

He kept staring at her, as if she'd said something extraordinary, and she blushed a little.

"To the cookout," she added.

"Oh, I'd probably just be in the way," he said, backing off a step or two. "Family and all."

"Oh, it's family, but our cookouts are much bigger than that," Jenifer said. "They're famous in Doolittle, as a matter of fact."

"Hmm," the man said. "That sounds interesting."

And safer, Jenifer suspected. "Don't worry, you won't have to hold the hand of dotty grandparents or change diapers."

He laughed. "Mind reader, are you?"

She smiled, pleased that he'd relaxed again. "So you'll come?"

Eric nodded, more than satisfied with the way the meeting had turned out. Despite her gorgeous looks, this small-town librarian would be far more at ease around her family than dining tête-à-tête with a man she'd just met. He didn't care for family gatherings, but any means to an end would serve his purposes.

When he'd said he was scouting investments, he'd fed her his cover story. That purpose existed to explain his presence in Doolittle. He was very much employed—as an undercover agent of a special federal unit whose job it was to track down, infiltrate, and arrest counterfeiters. He'd stopped at the library to follow up on surveillance photos taken of her with two known low-level functionaries of an international criminal ring.

Jenifer Wright more than lived up to the surveillance photos his boss Chester Huey had shown him back in D.C. In black and white she'd set his blood humming, and in person she jacked up more than his interest. None of the thorough background research he'd done on her had prepared him for her impact on him. The facts showed a quiet life, the only blip in her otherwise placid existence the anomaly of her single parenthood. But underneath those sensible librarian togs, she sizzled. He'd bet on that. He was far surer of her sex appeal than the report that she had something to do with the men he was keeping an eye on.

He'd volunteered to make a solo recon trip to Arkansas to check out the presence of the two criminals—and Jenifer Wright's potential involvement—knowing full well it was the woman who intrigued him.

"I have to close up now," she said, watching him and not moving from behind the checkout desk.

"Want some help?" One thing Eric always got right was how to charm a woman.

"Oh, you don't have to do that," she said, looking pleased despite her words.

Exactly the effect he had intended. He sometimes wondered if he ever uttered any words without knowing in advance the desired results, calculating bastard he knew himself to be. "Let me. You're probably anxious to get home and prepare for the party."

"Cookout," she said. "Charlotte—that's my mother—hates birthday parties, so we just call it our cookout."

"Obliging of you," Eric said, wondering what she'd do if he leaned over and touched her hair again. "You have the most beautiful hair," he said.

Her cheeks turned a delicate pink. "You've flattered me enough for one afternoon," she replied, and reached beneath the counter. "Here, you can take out the trash." She dragged out a wastebasket and handed it over the counter.

"Don't you have a janitor?"

She shrugged. "I'd rather spend the money on books."

"Doolittle is lucky to have you."

He stood there holding the wastebasket, watching her, admiring her.

"That's nice 'cause I was born and raised here, literally. Evidently I wouldn't wait for my parents to make it to the hospital in the next county, so I first opened my eyes in the back of Uncle Pete's squad car right in front of the courthouse square."

"But you went away to college, surely?" He knew the answer from his research, but he was curious to see how she'd characterize having earned her degree via correspondence courses. Eric admired that determination. His own college education had been handed to him on a silver platter.

Her face clouded, only for a moment, but he spotted the telltale reaction. "Of course," she said, and pointed a finger past the stacks that stood to her right. "The Dumpster is through the back door."

Subject closed. Interesting. Eric always made note of the topics people didn't want to discuss. Those were often more telling than the ones they chose to ramble on about.

"Be right back," he said, and headed to perform his assigned task. He walked past orderly book-lined shelves, noting the decorated bulletin boards in the children's section, and moved past the doors marked MEN and WOMEN. He hoped the cleaning of those wasn't included in the end-of-day checklist.

Though no doubt Miss Perky the librarian would gladly scrub a toilet if it meant one extra volume of literature. Eric pushed open the exit door, reflecting that his boss had to be wrong. This woman could not be in league with the type of bad guys he spent his days and nights apprehending on behalf of the United States Treasury Department.

Yet the photos had shown her quite cozy with Lars and Franco, the men he was watching. In one shot, they'd been in front of a Wal-Mart. In another, taken on a different day, they'd been chatting away over mugs of coffee.

It had been sheer luck that a vacationing agent had spotted the trio, while she was en route from New Orleans to Eureka Springs, Arkansas.

Eric lifted the Dumpster lid, holding his breath against the smell, until he noticed the container was amazingly clean. He grinned and let his lungs function normally. Jenifer Wright personified the spic and span type. He lifted the wastebasket and shook the contents out. A few sheets of paper stuck in the bottom, and mindful of the librarian's neatness standards, he reached in the can and snagged them.

An image on one of the sheets caught his eye. He smoothed the crumpled paper and let out a low whistle. The page had been printed from an Internet site. The information detailed the paper content of U.S. Treasury notes, with notations on techniques used in the paper production to make it as difficult as possible to counterfeit the new colored twenty-dollar bills.

Frowning, he folded the paper and slipped it into his pants pocket. Perhaps the sexy brunette wasn't as perkily innocent as she appeared. It was a good thing he was here to keep an eye on her, not that that responsibility fell into a hazardous duty category.

He strolled back into the building, empty wastebasket in hand. He found her balancing on top of a ladder, wrestling with a large brightly colored papier-mâché object. Her blouse had slipped free from the prim waistline of her gray skirt and the skirt had hiked up, treating Eric to a delightful view of long slim legs and a wisp of white. She would wear white panties, he thought, grinning for a reason he couldn't understand. She'd kicked off her shoes and her toes, curled around the rungs of the ladder, were highlighted with cherry red polish.

"Darn it," she said as she missed the ceiling hook with the end of the bright yellow string.

"Let me," Eric said, hating to ruin his view, but mindful of his plan to win her confidence.

She didn't even turn around. "I can do this," she said, the words squeezing out from gritted teeth. "I hang the decorations every time we change them. Today is no different from any other day."

"I don't mind assisting," Eric said. He stepped beside the ladder and placed one hand on it to stabilize it. "See, isn't that better?"

Jenifer looked down. She hated to admit it, but the ladder had quit rocking. "Yes, thank you," she managed. "It's just that I'm used to doing things by myself. And I don't need a man in order to manage." There, she'd said it. Declared it out loud. While he'd gone outside to dump the wastebasket, she had realized that she'd practically thrown herself at this stranger. He'd be thinking she was some helpless female on the prowl for a man, or worse, a husband. She had to set the record straight. If she wanted to avail herself of Eric Hamilton's presence in Doolittle, it was for one thing and one thing only.

He placed his other hand on the ladder and gazed up at her with an expression that looked very close to satisfaction. Now what could she have said to make him look so smug?

"As long as I'm here," he said, "you might as well finish the job."

That was sensible. Jenifer nodded. "Quite right," she said. She eased around till her fanny faced him, then suddenly realized what his view must be. Getting warmer by the second, Jenifer looped the end of the string around the ceiling hook. The piñata had to be in place for next week, for the buildup to Doolittle's sesquicentennial-year celebration.

She tipped her head back to study the knot, and the ladder wobbled. She snatched at the ceiling and missed, her shoulders swinging backward over her center of gravity.

Two hands caught her derriere and saved her from falling. She grabbed the top of the ladder. "Wow," she said.

"Wow," Eric Hamilton said, his hands sliding up to her waist.

A surge of heat threatened to melt her off the darn ladder. Jenifer tipped her chin downward and said, "Thank you. You may let go now."

He dropped one hand. "Sure you're okay?"

She nodded. Anything but okay, she could have said. She was behaving like a woman who'd never been touched by a guy, let alone a to-die-for sexy hunk like Eric Hamilton.

Jenifer felt his other hand slowly leave her body, but she could swear she felt his breath on the backs of her legs. Well, he'd had to move close to save her from falling. She gave a tug to the piñata to make sure it was secure, and then edged her way down the ladder.

Facing him, she noted that the smug look was gone from his face. His eyes appeared even darker, and he watched her the same way Tigger did when he was about to lunge for a mockingbird.

"Thank you for your assistance," Jenifer said, wondering what her friend Pamela would do. No doubt she'd fling herself at him and invite him into the washroom for kinky sex. Jenifer tugged at her blouse, smoothed her skirt, and said nothing.

"Tell me where it goes and I'll put away the ladder," he said. "I know you don't need a man, but we do have our uses."

Surely he couldn't read her mind. Blushing slightly, and still feeling the heat of his hands cupped around her fanny, she pointed to the supply closet. As he returned the ladder, she locked the desk drawer where they kept the change for overdue books and collected her purse.

"All done," he said, back at her side.

"Are you always this helpful?" The way he switched from sexy and pursuing to Boy Scout puzzled her. She didn't like to be kept off base so much.

He grinned. "Only when I want something."

Two

"Jeni, he's cute." Pamela looked up from her emery board and the acrylic nail she'd been trying to rescue. "No, he's more than cute, he's . . ."

"Mysterious? Magnetic? Ravishing?" Jenifer pulled another bowl mounded high with potatoes glistening with Hellman's out from Uncle Pete's refrigerator. For all the family cookouts she could remember, Uncle Pete, whose house stood between her mother's house and her own bungalow, inherited from Granny Wright, made the potato salad.

"Guys aren't ravishing," Pamela corrected, then giggled. "But they can and do ravish. At least the ones worth keeping."

"He's only in town for a couple of weeks." Jenifer tugged the plastic wrap from the bowl. "Which is perfect." The kitchen door slammed and she glanced up to see who'd interrupted their girlfriend talk.

"Mom says I have to offer to help." One of Jenifer's

several nieces stood there, a towel tied around the waist of her bathing suit, an expression of resignation on her face.

"Thank you, Bonnie," Jenifer said. "You've offered, now go and tell your mom everything is under control and swim a lap for me."

"Yahoo! Aunt Jenifer, you're the best!" The ten-year-old raced back outside, the door slapping against the frame.

Pamela peered at her nail, then tossed her blond hair from her shoulders and wiggled her body suggestively. "Surely you can figure out how to keep Mr. Good Looking around longer than a week or two."

"Honestly, Pamela, I just met the man."

Pamela seemed to consider the comment. "Come on, admit it, you're just as interested in the opposite sex as I am, but you're afraid. You've buried yourself behind that 'putting your kids first' routine. You've used that like a chastity belt, and now that the twins have gone, what do you have?"

Tears welled in Jenifer's eyes. She smarted as if a wasp had stung her heart. "Not so," she said, the words mixing with a sniffle. Despite her protest, she feared that her best friend had just sized up the situation with a hundred percent accuracy.

Pamela opened her arms and drew Jenifer into a hug, the potato salad bowl caught between them. She smacked a kiss on Jenifer's hair and said, "What are friends for if not for helping you face the awful truth?"

Jenifer hugged her back and giggled as she placed the bowl on the counter. "*The Awful Truth*, 1937. Irene

Dunne, Cary Grant, and Ralph Bellamy. Leo McCarey won the Oscar for Best Director."

"Facts are cold comfort on a lonely night," Pamela said. "Pamela Jarvis. September the twenty-first, Doolittle, Arkansas." She placed her hands on her shapely hips. "Now, look, skidoo, the man is sexy, he is in your backyard—or at least Uncle Pete's backyard—and he's obviously attracted to you or he wouldn't have accepted this invitation. I mean, it's a family cookout, for Pete's sake!"

A burst of laughter and hearty splashes sounded from the yard. Uncle Pete's cheery face appeared in the doorway. "Hurry up, you two. The chicken's done!"

"Be right there," Jenifer said. To Pamela, she said, "Pete looks happy again, doesn't he? Mother seems to have recovered from her loss, but I still miss my dad so much." She sighed. "He should be here, too."

Pamela picked up the bowl of potato salad. "He is. He's in your smile and your heart and in the way your family is so wonderful, even to us scalawags."

Jenifer grinned. "You're no scalawag. Shocking sometimes, maybe."

Her friend put a hand on the screen door and looked back. "Aren't you coming out?"

Jenifer stubbed one thong-clad foot on the aging linoleum. "It's safe in here."

Pamela rolled her eyes, grabbed Jenifer with her free hand, and thrust her out the door. "Would you get a grip?" She whispered into her ear, "If you don't go after him, I will."

"You do know how to motivate," Jenifer said, pausing to survey the scene. Youngsters of all ages splashed and leaped into the aboveground pool. Jenifer's three brothers and their wives and Uncle Pete's three daughters and their husbands were grouped by gender under the shade of the porch overhang. Charlotte, Jenifer's mother, maintained a relaxed supervision of the water activities, chatting with Pamela's husband Ace, as he liked to be called. Uncle Pete presided over the grill, naturally, and appeared to be explaining his technique to a politely interested Eric.

Almost everyone made up a couple, Jenifer reflected. Except for Uncle Pete, whose wife had passed away only six months ago, and her mother, who'd been widowed for the past year.

And Jenifer.

And Eric.

He glanced up and smiled at her, and she wondered just why she'd holed up in the kitchen for so long. Uncle Pete looked up from the grill long enough to catch their exchange of glances. Jenifer gave him a cheeky wave and called, "Need a platter?"

Uncle Pete shook his head and said something to Eric, who headed toward the house. Jenifer hesitated, not wanting to move away, not wanting to look as if she were lying in wait.

"I've been sent after a platter," Eric said. "Be my guide?"

Uncle Pete had been playing matchmaker for Jenifer for as long as she could remember, and he didn't know the meaning of subtle. "This way," Jenifer said, and stepped back into the house with Eric close behind.

"Quite the family you have," he said.

She wasn't sure how to interpret his remark. He must have seen the question in her eyes.

"Lively, and they make me feel as if I've been in town for years, not a few hours."

Jenifer nodded. "Just wait. By the time the apple pie and ice cream are on the table, they'll have your entire life history out of you."

He grinned. "Inquisition-style?"

She kneeled in front of a lower cabinet, swinging the door open. "Nah, but you have to remember that Uncle Pete's a policeman and so are two of my brothers and one of his daughter's."

"Really?" He sounded very interested in that fact.

Jenifer tugged on a large ceramic platter, and one of the sauce pans clattered onto the floor.

Eric hunched down beside her and scooped it up. His face close to hers, he said, "I thought of becoming a policeman."

"Instead of doing some of the 'this and that,' which you never did define, what do you do?" She hoped she didn't sound too nosy, but she was curious.

"Hamilton Investments specializes in the shoe business."

"Making them?"

"Import-export. Primarily import. The Italians, you know, have a way with shoes."

Jenifer glanced down at her thongs crowned with a floppy straw flower. "So does Kmart," she said, somewhat wryly.

He tucked the saucepan into a stack of other dishes. "Hand me the platter."

She gave it to him, and they rose together in one

flowing motion she couldn't help but notice. And admire. "So how did you get into that line of work?"

"My parents and before them my father's parents ran the company."

"So who's taking care of the business now?" She took the platter back, deciding to rinse it. Since Uncle Pete's wife had died, he hadn't paid too much attention to housekeeping.

Eric leaned over and flicked on the faucet. He always stood so close to her. Normally she preferred to keep her distance, as at the library where she maintained her presence behind the checkout desk much of the time. But somehow Eric didn't bother her.

He flustered her, though. She dropped the sponge twice.

"My parents left the business to me, and someone else does the hands-on management," he said, reaching for the sponge and placing it in her hand.

"Oh, so what do you do?"

"You could call it strategic planning." His face pretty much a mask, he added, "I have plenty to keep me occupied."

Charlotte knocked on the door. "You two putting the clay for that platter on the potter's wheel?"

Jenifer smiled. "My mother has a way with words." She rinsed the oversized platter and dried it. "Take this out," she said, as if she did these everyday actions with Eric all the time. "There's another one in the hall closet."

"Sure thing," Eric said. He felt like some kind of criminal, invading Jenifer's world under false pretenses. He needed to get close enough to investigate her possible involvement with Lars and Franco, not close enough to experience these twinges of conscience so unlike him.

Most of the work he did he thought of as cut and dried. There were bad guys. He tracked them down, outsmarted them, and made sure they got locked up. He moved from quarry to quarry, adrift in the various roles he played. He appreciated the movement, knowing he would have felt stifled in a more typical nine-to-five job. The independence was in contrast to the lives of his parents, who had not only lived with each other, but worked together. Early on he'd seen their arrangement as a prescription for misery. Not for him to be tied down.

So as he played out his various roles, he linked up with women who satisfied his momentary needs. Finding a woman was easy; meeting one he was willing to risk committing to staying with—well, that had never happened. When he wanted a woman, he sought one out. He'd play until either the sex grew boring or the woman too demanding, and then move on.

Eric, the consummate rolling stone, gathered none of the moss of long-term relationships.

"Those are some serious thoughts chasing their tails in your head," said a soft voice beside him.

Eric blinked. Jenifer's mother tapped him on the forehead. "The Wright and the Simon clans can be a bit much to absorb," she said. "I'll take the platter to Pete. Why don't you sit down here with the boys and grab a soda?"

"Sure thing," he said, doing as she suggested. He needed to cut his time here shorter than he'd planned or he'd find himself getting too comfortable—or too close to a possible suspect. He'd check in with the real estate agent soon, in keeping with his cover identity. In the meantime, he'd have to be patient until his contact in Miami came through, and set up a meeting with Lars and Franco. By the time they'd made it to the dessert course, he should be able to discover from someone in this gathering whether any strangers other than himself had come to town recently. After all, most of Doolittle's police force had to be right here, lounging in the early evening warmth.

He reached in the ice chest and pulled out a Pepsi. Funny how with all these he-men, there wasn't any beer. Just as well; he was technically on duty, and perhaps some of the family members were, too. He liked that feeling, that he was part of a brotherhood. He worked alone so much, he seldom felt that connection.

He not only worked alone, he lived his life alone.

One of the women, round with child, circled one hand slowly over her swollen belly. A youngster skipped over to her, asked a question Eric didn't hear, then raced back to the pool.

Eric observed their interaction, the murmur of voices all around him. Living alone made it easy to forget about wanting what he'd never had.

He chugged his Pepsi, his jaw knotting with a tension that caught him off guard.

Hell, he'd chosen to be a loner.

Or had he simply been afraid of failing at Relationships 101 so he'd never put himself at risk?

Jenifer reappeared, carrying another platter. He leaped up to help her, and his lawn chair tipped backward. The man sitting next to him laughed and said something to the guy next to him, and they both turned friendly faces to him. One righted the chair, and said, "It's okay, man, we all fall hard when we fall."

"I'm not sure what you mean," Eric said.

The two men exchanged knowing glances. "Yeah, right, buddy."

Dignity in action, Eric stalked over to Jenifer. "I'll carry that," he said, snatching the tray from her grasp. No wonder she wasn't married; her male relatives had probably scared all the prospective bridegrooms away.

He had to believe she must have a lot of guys after her. Every single man in town—and knowing human nature, no doubt one or two married ones as well—had to be hot on her trail. Tray tucked against his hips, he said, "So why aren't you married?"

Jenifer looked at him as if he'd said there was a cockroach perched on her nose. "That's for me to know and you to . . . no, *not* for you to find out," she said primly, and sashayed past him toward the pool.

"Everybody out," Jenifer called. "Dinner's ready."

"Five more minutes! Five more minutes!" A chorus of children's voices mingled with splashing water.

Shaking his head, Eric retreated to the lawn chair. He'd bungled that one. He knew better than to storm an objective head on. But her answer had also intrigued him. What was she hiding?

The brother, or was it brother-in-law, who'd righted his chair when he tipped it over, said, "She's a tough nut to crack."

"Is that right?"

"I'm Shane," the man said. "Jenifer's oldest brother.

I'm impressed that she invited you over. She doesn't do that often, though she did drag a couple of cowboys over to LeDru's Coffee Shop two weeks ago."

"Cowboys?"

Shane laughed. "Not literally. Traveling salesman in lumber products she met outside of Wal-Mart. Seems he and his buddy were passing through and asking where to get a good cup of joe."

"And she asked two perfect strangers to join her for coffee?"

Shane eyed him, a little too knowing for Eric's comfort level. "How long were you in the library before she invited you to the cookout?"

"Not long," Eric said. "But I, er, had suggested having dinner first."

"Mutual attraction, then," Shane said, turning to his sidekicks. "Hey, guys, want to pony up some bets?"

A few hoots and hollers sounded but no one took Shane up on the offer.

"I like you a long sight better than those other two," Shane said. "I can sniff a loser a mile away."

"You're one of the police officers?"

Shane shook his head. "Nah, I sell insurance. Do pretty well at it, too."

Eric nodded, his face showing how impressive he found that, while his mind considered the two strangers. "So you met the guys Jenifer had coffee with?"

"My office is on the Courthouse Square, across the way from LeDru's. Busby—that's my kid brother there—called me from his squad car from the Wal-Mart parking lot and I picked up the trail."

"Not much goes unnoticed," Eric murmured.

"Jenifer's special," Shane said, giving him a tough-eyed look.

Eric glanced over to the pool, where Jenifer had lured one, two, three, four, five—no, six—youngsters from the water. In her trim capris and sleeveless knit top, wearing those goofy floral thongs, her hair pulled into a clip at the top of her head, he thought she looked more like she belonged with the kids than the grown-ups. She bent forward to help the littlest one towel dry, and treated Eric to a view of the lush swell of the tops of her breasts, and Eric abandoned that whimsical notion.

Jenifer Wright was all woman.

"Yes, she is special," Eric agreed, distracted, as he treated himself to another glance.

"She says one of the reasons she doesn't need a man is because she has brothers," Shane said.

"Makes sense," Eric agreed absentmindedly, watching as the youngster threw her arms around Jenifer's thighs and gave her a big hug.

"For instance," Shane said, "we happen to know you're staying at the Highway Express off the interstate." He turned toward the other men and said, "What's the room number, Busby?"

"Two eighteen," Busby said.

"You guys are good," Eric said, impressed. "I guess you've run my plates by now?" He referred to his car tags.

"You don't think you'd still be sitting here if we'd gotten back any negatives, do you?" Shane grinned and gave him a friendly jab to the shoulder.

Interesting that one of the rare times he'd come on

assignment as "himself," he'd fallen into a nest of police officers. But their powers of observation could come in handy. "So these other guys, how'd their plates check out?"

Shane scowled. "Something funny about those two. Car belonged to someone else, registration not clean, vehicle identification mucked up, no current insurance."

"So I guess you and your brothers hustled Jenifer out of that coffee shop before she stirred sugar into her cup?"

"We would have," Shane said, "but Busby got an emergency call. And darned if Jenifer didn't talk to one of them again after that." He frowned. "She hasn't been herself since her twins left for college."

"Twins?" Eric almost spit out the swallow of soda he'd taken. "Jenifer has college-age children?" That had to be biologically impossible, surely? He'd known from his background check on her she had children, but the ages hadn't registered. He did the math in his head and realized why she'd been so touchy when he'd asked about her college experience. No doubt the pregnancy had interrupted her freshman year.

"They're great kids," Shane said. "Anyway, you seem pretty interested in these good-for-nothing salesmen. Don't worry about them as competition. They told her they were only in this territory every so often, so we shouldn't see them again for a while. And even if we did"—he cracked his knuckles—"it wouldn't do them any good."

Eric nodded. Pursuing the subject further would make it stand out too much. If Shane didn't think he was asking only out of jealousy for Jenifer's attentions, he'd already be asking himself what Eric's interests were. Lars and Franco knew him by name only, at the moment, as big-money player Troy King, and he didn't want those paths or those identities to cross one another.

"Chow's on," Pete called out.

While he'd been talking, or more accurately, running the gauntlet of the Wright brothers, the women had laid places along a spacious picnic table. Eric and the others rose. He stood, uncertain of the order of things, observing the others in order to fit in.

Jenifer scooted over to his side, the young girl skipping and holding her hand.

"Do you swim?" the child asked Eric.

"Yes."

"Will you go in the pool with us after dinner?"

The question seemed very important to her. Eric had no clue how to talk to anyone that young. He turned to Jenifer, knowing he appeared lost.

She flashed him a bright smile, one that made him want to forget about investigating her as a suspect and woo her into his bed, even if all he had at his disposal was the rock-hard full-size mattress provided by the Highway Express.

"Mr. Hamilton doesn't have any swim trunks," Jenifer said.

"He can borrow Daddy's," the girl said.

Eric relied on an answer he remembered hearing over and over again in his own childhood. "We'll see," he said.

"Gather around," Pete said, his voice carrying over the many other conversations. "We're here to celebrate Charlotte's birthday. And we know that isn't her favorite holiday, but heck, any excuse to get this gang together works for me."

"Thank you, Pete," Charlotte said, smiling softly at him and, Eric realized, effectively cutting off any further fuss over her birthday. "Let's say the blessing and eat."

Blessing? Eric glanced around as everyone, including even the rough-and-tumble Ace, held out their hands to the person next to him or her. Jenifer slipped her hand into his and he belatedly offered his to the little girl who had invited him swimming. Jenifer smiled at him, looking very much like her mother as she'd smiled at Pete, and Eric shuffled his feet in place. All this touchy-feely stuff made him nervous.

"Dear Lord," Pete began, and as everyone else bowed their heads, Eric stared at his own restless feet. "Thank you for the many blessings of family, and for another year of Charlotte's life as she serves you here on earth. And bless those of us who are no longer here in our backyard, but with You." Pete cleared his throat, and went on, "Most particularly Arlene, the best helpmate a man ever had, and Shane."

Jenifer's hand tightened around his, and Eric gave her a comforting squeeze. No doubt Shane was Shane Senior, Jenifer's father.

"And bless Pickle and Autumn and Adam and keep them strong in Your ways. And we thank You for the bounty of food and love You have blessed us with, and rejoice in sharing it with the strangers amongst us, knowing that with Your love and guidance, all good things are possible. In Jesus' name, amen."

Whew. Eric thought the prayer would go on forever,

certainly longer than the first course at any fancy restaurant. Still, despite the foreignness of the ceremony, he felt a sense of comforting togetherness that surprised him.

And Jenifer still held his hand.

Jenifer glanced down at their joined hands, thinking how odd it seemed to be holding the hand of a man during grace when she'd invited him to dinner in order to entice him into sexual adventuring. How confusing. She wanted very much to explore the many things she'd never experienced, but at this moment she couldn't imagine a better feeling than the connection of palm to palm.

Feeling shy, she stole a peek at him and saw he was looking as bemused as she felt. Then she remembered the way he'd shuffled his feet, and realized he probably felt nothing but awkwardness. Man of the world that he appeared to be, this hokey family cookout probably bored him stiff.

She tugged her hand from his.

"Who's Pickle?" he asked.

"My sister." She tucked the hand he'd held into her pants pocket. "She lives in Tampa or she'd be here tonight."

"And is she half as cute as you?"

He had to be joking. "I am not cute," Jenifer said sternly. "Librarians," she said, "are not cute."

"Would you two quit yakking and grab a plate?" Uncle Pete called to them from the grill. "Slaving away in the kitchen all day, and does anyone appreciate me?" He put a hand on one hip and the other against his forehead.

"You're such a ham," Charlotte said. "I'll take a drumstick."

The others filled their plates, and Jenifer and Eric joined them along the trestle table Uncle Pete had built years ago. Jenifer was sure it had stood in the yard when she was the age of the child she'd dried from the pool. So many things stayed the same in her life. Doolittle changed almost not at all. No wonder she felt the loss of her father so much, and with her sister and her twins gone, loneliness had not just crept into her life, but come in swinging a big heavy bat.

She had to be careful, she realized, sitting next to Eric, his leg just brushing hers on the bench. She might make choices she'd regret, in order to stave off these unaccustomed feelings of being left out of life. Oh, well, at least Eric had said he'd be here and gone. If she made a fool of herself, he wouldn't be around to remind her that she'd thrown herself at him.

At that moment Eric smiled at her, a look both companionable and charged with sensuality. Suddenly the thought that he'd be gone soon held little consolation.

Three

About an hour later the adults still sat around the table, sipping coffee and scraping the last crumbs of apple pie from their plates. The children had devised a wild game that involved running, jumping, and chasing each other, so they were quite content. Charlotte had a firm rule about not going back into the water until food had been properly digested.

Ace strolled out the kitchen door, making that at least the third time he'd gone into the house and then returned to the table. He sat down beside Pamela, cupping a hand over her breast and giving her a big smooch. Pamela frowned, tugging at his hand. Instead of taking the hint, he left it on her breast and started to toy with one of the buttons of her blouse.

Jenifer knew she could never like Ace. He and Pamela had been married only three months, since she'd met him in Little Rock and impulsively—or so

Jenifer judged it—married a truck driver with whom she had little in common.

Ace fixed Eric with one of his typically belligerent looks. "So, you two up for a little action after we blow this joint?"

Jenifer frowned straight at him. "No, thank you," she said.

He shrugged, but at least he moved his paw to the side of Pamela's neck. "What about you, stranger? Want to see what else there is to do in this hick town?"

"If you don't like it, why don't you leave?" Jenifer said. There, she'd spoken her mind. But one glance at Pamela's embarrassed expression, and Jenifer could have bitten her tongue in two.

"Yeah, well, maybe we will," Ace said. He stood up and tugged on Pamela's arm, none too gently. "I let you come to this thing, but I'm not gonna stick around to be insulted."

Pamela got up, too. She didn't meet Jenifer's eyes when she mumbled, "Sorry, Jeni, I'll call you tomorrow."

"That's what you say," Ace said. "Maybe we have other plans."

A hush had fallen over the table. Charlotte rose, but Uncle Pete said something to her and she sat back down.

"So, Ace," Uncle Pete said, "you're a truck driver, right?"

"Yeah, that's right. Damn proud of it, too."

"No reason not to be," Uncle Pete said, glancing around the table. The others nodded.

"Got that right. I might not have all that college

learning that my little wife here does, but I know a thing or two."

Uncle Pete nodded. "You suppose you know enough to sit back down and stay awhile, nice and polite like?"

"We've got plans," Ace said, his arm wrapped around Pamela's elbow.

"And I've got a Breathalyzer," Uncle Pete said.

"What's that supposed to mean?" Ace dropped Pamela's elbow and advanced toward Uncle Pete.

Jenifer held her breath and grabbed Eric's arm. She couldn't stand to see her best friend so humiliated, especially in front of the entire family. Pamela had practically been raised along with her.

Uncle Pete stood up and beckoned Ace closer. When the man reached his side, Pete put an arm around his shoulders and barreled him into the house.

Pamela stood there, studying her feet. She hunched her shoulders, half turned away from the group at the table.

Jenifer let go of Eric's arm, embarrassed that she'd actually clung to him, and went to her friend. But Pamela shook her off. "I married him, and I'll stand by him," she said.

Jenifer ignored her protest and walked her toward the pool, away from the others. The children continued to dash about, shouting and laughing. "Do you want to stay with me tonight?"

Pamela lifted her head. "Are you nuts?" But she said it wistfully. "Ace would have a fit."

"Well, he'd know you weren't out with another man," Jenifer said, attempting to make her friend smile.

"That wouldn't matter. He's kind of possessive. It was okay at first, but now that school's started and I'm at work and I have after school events, if he's in town he gets pretty grouchy."

"But you're the principal," Jenifer said. "He had to have realized what your schedule and responsibilities would be when he asked you to marry him."

"It was summer and he didn't think about it," Pamela said. "Anyway, it'll work out. Being married to someone new takes adjusting."

"If that's true, then I'm certainly glad I've never gone to the altar," Jenifer said.

Pamela shrugged. "It's different for everyone." She laughed, somewhat shakily. "I should know. This is my third time."

And not exactly a charm, Jenifer thought, but this time wisely kept her tongue between her teeth.

"I'm going to go splash some water on my face," Pamela said. "Thanks for everything."

Jenifer gave her a hug. "If you change your mind, the sleepover offer is there anytime."

Pamela nodded and slipped into the house.

Jenifer swung herself up and sat on the edge of the swimming pool decking. After a few minutes she looked up to see Eric standing by her side.

"Feel like company?"

She nodded. "Sure."

"Pretty tough watching your friend with that guy."

"You can say that again." Jenifer met his eyes. "And I'm not known for my tact around him, either, as I guess you could tell. Pamela deserves someone so much better."

"Not exactly a match of equals."

"Pamela can't stand being alone," Jenifer said. "She got her heart broken in high school and married on the rebound when she was eighteen. That husband was actually a pretty nice guy at first, but she didn't want children and he wanted to start a family."

"So they got divorced instead of him waiting till she was ready?"

"Yep. He got someone else pregnant and that was that. And right afterward she married again, someone from out of town, but he moved here and we all liked him. He died in a car accident, the same one that killed Uncle Pete's wife. Well, Uncle Pete hasn't remarried, but Pamela couldn't stand it. She waited only a couple of months and showed up with Ace, ring on her finger and all."

"Does she need to be married? I mean, financially?"

"She's the principal of Doolittle High," Jenifer said. "She has money from her second husband's insurance, not to mention the lawsuit. . . ." Her voice trailed off. "Oh, man, that snake!" She jumped down and would have run into the house if Eric hadn't caught her by the hand.

She glanced up, wondering why he'd stopped her when he must have guessed she was hell-bent on warning her friend against the obviously money-grubbing husband. "I've got to get to Pamela now," she said.

"Is now the best time?"

"Don't you get it?" Jenifer couldn't believe he could be so obtuse. He seemed so quick on the uptake. "Ace will hang around making her life miserable until she's collected the settlement, then empty the bank account and slither off like the reptile he is."

"And if you tell her that right now, will she listen to you?" Eric spoke softly. "That man is no good, anyone can see that. But he's been drinking and she's going home with him, and if she throws this in his face, he's likely to take it out on her."

"He wouldn't hit her!" Jenifer shrank at the very idea of someone hurting her friend.

Eric's mouth tightened into a grim line. "He has all the signs of a bully. Just ask your uncle Pete."

"Well, he can't have been drinking," Jenifer said. "Uncle Pete only serves sodas."

"Did you notice how many times he disappeared inside?"

Jenifer's eyes widened. "You're right. He must have brought his own liquor and stashed it. What a jerk. You're very observant," she said.

He shrugged. "Pete tipped me off when he threatened the Breathalyzer. He saw it all before I put two and two together."

"You should have become a policeman," Jenifer said. "The business world is a waste of your talents."

Eric grinned. "Maybe it's not too late."

"No time like the present to start something new," Jenifer said.

Eric felt the grin die from his lips. What would Jenifer think when she knew the truth? That he'd wriggled his way into her family and friends under false pretenses? And then he caught himself up short. She'd never know. He had to remember that until he'd cleared her of any wrongdoing, the woman was under investigation. And once his job was done, no matter the outcome, he'd be on his way to the next job, the next undercover assignment.

And Jenifer and her lively family and friends would be only a memory.

"Hey, what's wrong?" Jenifer's voice sounded distant even though she stood right next to him.

"Nothing," Eric said, giving her a smile. "Shall we go in and check on your friend?"

Jenifer nodded. "I guess you're right about not confronting her with my suspicions right now, but I won't hold off long."

"Pick a time he's not around," Eric suggested.

Pete walked back outside, the kitchen door slamming behind him. He had a look of disgust on his face as he retook his seat beside Charlotte. He leaned over and said something to Busby, and Busby rose, kissed his wife and then Charlotte, and headed into the house.

"He's sending Busby to keep an eye on them," Jenifer said.

"Your family keeps track of things," Eric said.

Jenifer laughed, a happy sound that made Eric smile. "My brothers are famous for that."

"Did they tell you they've already run my plates?"

"No, but I'd be surprised if one of them hadn't," Jenifer said.

"You two come on back over here and join the group," Pete called. "The drama's over for the moment."

Eric followed Jenifer to the picnic table and they both sat down. "Thanks for dinner," Eric said to them, glancing around the table.

Pete patted his stomach, though he didn't have much

of one. The older man clearly kept in shape. "So tell us about your family," he said.

Eric heard the command as much as the invitation. "Well, there's not much to tell," he said, sticking to the truth of his own identity. "My parents passed away last year. I have no siblings."

Silence greeted his words. They all stared at him, eyes wide, sympathy flowing freely.

"Oh, how absolutely lonely," Charlotte said.

"What do you do on holidays?" That was Shane's wife, her blue eyes round with concern.

Eric shrugged. "Oh, I always worked."

Jenifer stared at him along with the rest of the Brady bunch. He shuffled his feet under the table and played with a saltshaker close at hand.

"I'm used to it," he said, knowing he sounded defensive.

"People get used to prison, too," Charlotte said. "And you've never married? If you don't mind me asking."

Little late for that, Eric thought. But these people meant well. They'd opened their home to him, if only for one evening. And he'd taken them up on the offer, in order to gather information, to scope out the librarian and find out what he could about Lars and Franco. Instead, he'd fallen for her charms, and enjoyed himself in the midst of this relaxed yet perceptive group.

Him, surrounded by all these people, having a good time. "No, I've never married," he said.

Pete clapped his hands together. "Well, that's about enough of an interrogation for now. There's only one other thing to discuss."

"What's that?" Eric almost didn't have the nerve to ask, afraid Pete meant to say something about his obvious interest in Jenifer and embarrass them both.

"Why in the name of all that's good and sensible are you staying at the Highway Express when everyone knows the only place worth staying in Doolittle is the Schoolhouse Inn?"

"I'm only passing through," Eric said. "And I spotted the sign from the interstate."

"R.J., the desk clerk at the motel, says you reserved the room for seven nights," Shane said.

Eric stifled a groan. He'd forgotten temporarily how good their sources were. "Right," he said. "Seven nights."

"And what brings you to Doolittle?" Charlotte asked. "I have to confess I missed that part of the story earlier." She smiled, her interest apparently genuine, and Eric wondered if these families often brought strangers home to dine. No doubt they did.

"Scouting the state," Eric said, deciding to leave it at that.

"For investments, you said," Jenifer prompted.

"Right," Eric said. Pete had fixed him with a stern look. He probably kept a lie detector machine along with his Breathalyzer, Eric thought. But for whatever reason, he felt reluctant to go into his cover story about being in town to inspect the historic Horace House Hotel for possible purchase and renovation. This family would take it too much to heart.

"That's okay if he doesn't want to tell," one of the women said, with a grin. "Sooner or later, we'll find out, right?" She winked at him, but Eric knew she was right, at least about the Horace House.

He smiled back. "Don't mean to be mysterious," he said, "but it has to do with a possible investment."

"If you need insurance, you know who to call," Shane said.

"Right," Eric replied.

One of the children raced up and flung herself against him. "Now can we go swimming, and are you coming in, too?"

Saved. "If I had trunks, I'd join you," Eric said. "Sorry."

"We've got a houseful of clothes," Pete said. To one of the women, he said, "Sunny, run in there and see if there isn't something that fits this young man. And, you, Jenifer, you should take a dip, too."

"Oh, no, I'll clean up," Jenifer said.

Eric leaned over and whispered in her ear, "Chicken."

"Am not," she said, hotly enough that he knew he'd pushed a button. She had a body to die for, and he'd be willing to bet she was shy about showing it off. Well, he for one wanted to see that body, preferably without even a swimsuit on.

"Come on," the child said, tugging at Jenifer's hand.

"I'm not sure my dinner has settled," Jenifer said.

"If Grandma Charlotte says it's okay for me, then it has to be okay for you," the girl said.

"Brilliant reasoning," Eric said, grinning at Jenifer. "You can swim, can't you?"

"Of course I can. I can outswim—"

"Outshoot, outrun, and outtalk most anybody," Pete interjected. "Say, you know how to handle a firearm?" he asked Eric.

"Yes," Eric said, almost adding a "sir." "I guess you'd call me an average shot." Yeah, as average as Superman.

"Stick around for the police picnic and we'll see how you stack up."

"That's our annual fund-raiser," Charlotte added. "We've been running it for twelve years now, to help buy new equipment. We also raise money for a scholarship for young people who want to attend the police academy. The whole town comes."

"We're doing something different this year," Jenifer said. "We're adding a new fun thing to do. I hope people like it."

"Now I don't know why you want to go and mess with what works," Pete said, "but if you're running things, we know it'll be a success."

"It's a month from now," Charlotte said. "I don't suppose there's any way the new owner of the Horace House will have it open by then. Maybe by next year. It's such a great setting for a sponsor's reception."

Eric froze. Did they know he was a prospective buyer, and were they waiting for him to reveal it? Or was the comment completely guileless?

"Rooster said he was meeting with the buyer Monday," Jenifer said. "He called me at the library this afternoon and he referred to him as an old geezer, so I doubt if he's going to be moving too fast."

Eric let out his breath. Old geezer? Now how had that impression gotten formed? No matter, it helped him with his split-second decision to stay incognito for the moment.

Later they might wonder why he'd said nothing, but he would worry about that when the time came. He still regretted being talked into using the hotel as a reason for his presence. That kind of home office clever thinking drove him to operate alone as much as he could get away with.

"Well," Charlotte said, "Mrs. Ball's only spoken to the man on the phone. She really has no idea whether he's old or not."

"When I met those two salesmen," Jenifer said, "I thought they might be interested in buying it."

"Those guys?" That was Shane, who broke off one conversation and jumped into this one. "Two bums."

"They seemed to be pretty well off."

Eric could picture the two sticking out like skunks on a subway. Lars never could tone down his look, and Franco never met a gold chain he could resist hanging around his gorilla-size neck. He'd be glad when he had the two of them behind bars. But despite the traps that had been laid for them time and again, the two always managed to evade the law, or if arrested, never ended up with charges pressed against them.

Jenifer wrinkled her nose. "They weren't at all what we're used to in Doolittle."

"And I suppose you went out with them twice just to discuss their investing in Horace House," Shane said.

"Whether I did or not is none of your business," Jenifer said primly.

Shane's brows shot up, his nonverbal challenge loud and clear.

"Children, calm down," Charlotte said. "Jenifer is a grown-up, attractive, single woman, and we should encourage her to look around."

"Sure," Shane said, "but not with those toads."

"Sometimes a girl has to kiss some toads to find a prince," Charlotte said.

"Mother! You told me you never kissed any man other than Daddy. Besides, I am not seeking a prince," Jenifer said. "You all know perfectly well that I don't—"

"Need a man," the entire table of men and women said, finishing the sentence for her.

A blush on her cheeks, Jenifer rose. "Make fun of me if you will, but I prefer independence to misery."

They all stared at her. Charlotte shook her head and shrugged her shoulders, as if to ask, Wherever did she get her ideas?

"Nobody here is miserable," Shane said. Then he grinned. "Except maybe Eric. He seems like a lonely kind of guy."

Eric put up a hand. "Oh, I'm fine," he said.

Charlotte looked at him, then over to Jenifer, and back again. She turned toward Pete, who was sitting beside her, and for a moment Eric had to remind himself that she and Pete weren't also a couple. The two of them seemed to communicate simply by being within reach of each other.

His parents had never been like that.

"I think I'll go next door and change," Jenifer said, in a very dignified voice.

"It's about time," the child said, a sentiment Eric shared. "Can I go with you?"

Jenifer held out her hand. "Sure," she said, her glance meeting Eric's.

He should have had the smarts to ask that question, he thought, and smiled at her, his look meant to tell her he envied the child.

She got it, too, or at least he was pretty sure she did, because she tossed her hair over her shoulder and gave him a saucy look.

Eric shifted in his chair in time to hear Charlotte say, "What about you, Eric? Are you looking for a new place to settle down?"

"I, er, well, possibly." He nodded, hoping she'd leave it at that, but certain she would not.

"Horace House would be a good investment, if that other buyer doesn't come through. And to have a deal in place in time for Doolittle's sesquicentennial—my, that would be lovely."

"Yes, well, I guess we'll have to leave that to the old geezer," Eric said jokingly, mentally crossing his fingers.

"If the papers aren't signed, the property is still up for grabs," Shane said.

"And Mrs. Ball—she's the realtor—has been awfully close-mouthed about this buyer. I sure hope it's not some out-of-state corporation coming in to mess with the way we do things here," Pete said.

"I'm from out of state," Eric said. He lived in Virginia, outside of the District of Columbia.

"That's different," Shane said.

Eric thought of asking why he thought that, but then Sunny returned. He'd almost forgotten she'd gone to find him some swimwear. She waved a Speedo about the size of a doll's diaper. "Here you go, Eric. This ought to fit you real nice." She smoothed her other hand over her very pregnant belly and winked at him as she tossed it to him.

Now he'd done it. By teasing Jenifer into swimming,

he faced getting half naked in front of her entire family. He'd better hop into the pool before Jenifer returned. He rose and headed into the house to change, the scrap of spandex wadded into a ball in one hand.

Just thinking about Jenifer clad only in a slick wet bikini got him hot all over. And one thing was for darn sure—this Speedo wasn't going to cover his reaction to that delicious body.

Four

"Are you going to marry Mr. Eric?"

Jenifer dropped the two-piece swimsuit she'd been contemplating, wondering whether she had the nerve to parade in front of Eric in the candy red bikini. She wasn't sure how much to flaunt the charms that usually stayed tucked beneath her sensible librarian clothing. She turned toward her six-year-old niece Kimberley. "What makes you ask that question?"

"Duh," the girl said, making a face. "Like who wouldn't ask? He likes you and you like him."

"Is that what they teach you in first grade?"

Kimberley giggled. "I have a boyfriend."

Jenifer sighed. "Does your mother know?"

"Sure. She said she'd worry about me if I didn't. She said she knew when she sat next to my daddy in kindergarten she was gonna marry him when she grew up."

Her sister-in-law was a traitor to feminism, Jenifer

thought. "Well, not everyone has that same experience, and it's good to be open to possibilities," she said.

Kimberley wrinkled her pert little nose, and Jenifer waited to hear what the child would torture her with next. In the meantime, she dropped the bikini and dug around in her drawer in search of a one-piece suit.

"I know what possibilities are," Kimberley said. "That's when it might rain or it might not rain."

"That's pretty good," Jenifer said. "And to be more technically correct, a possibility is something that is possible, which means that it's capable of being realized and at the same time it's something that may not happen."

The girl giggled. "You sound like a talking dictionary."

"I do, don't I?" Jenifer dropped the sober black one-piece suit she'd pulled out and picked up the red bikini. Time to live a little; time to open up possibilities. After all, if she were going to entice Eric into becoming the man to assist her in exploring some sensual adventures, she'd better make quite sure she not only caught his attention, but also held it.

"So if it might rain or might not rain," Kimberley said, using the foot of Jenifer's bed as a ballet barre, "that means you might or might not marry Mr. Eric."

Jenifer laughed. "Remind me to tell your mother to make sure you go to law school."

Law school. Exactly what she had intended to do so many years before. Well, things hadn't turned out that way, and there was no point in looking back now. But looking ahead, now that was something she could do. Why not go to law school now? She shook her head, as if to shoo the idea away. Snatching up the bikini, she said, "I'll be right out." She popped into her bathroom. She wasn't shy about changing clothes but didn't need Kimberley reporting that she'd also touched up her makeup, so she hid behind the privacy of her bathroom door. Children were sometimes too honest.

She tossed a pair of shorts and a T-shirt on over her suit, and with Kimberley skipping beside her, returned to Uncle Pete's house. Living so close had its definite pluses, though of course there were no secrets. And her brothers! Why, their protectiveness was worse than ever. Well, maybe not, Jenifer reflected, remembering the one time Lawrence, the father of her twins, had been late with a child support payment. They'd driven to LSU Medical Center in Shreveport, where he'd been doing his medical residency, found him on duty in the E.R., and slapped handcuffs on him. Then they drove him to an ATM and let him loose to take out the cash he owed her.

In fact, she hadn't wanted any money from Lawrence, but her family wouldn't hear of that kind of pointless sacrifice. Anyway, after that embarrassing scene, he'd sent his checks to arrive at least a day ahead of time.

Charlotte and her daughters-in-law were in the kitchen, rinsing and stacking dishes, when Jenifer walked back in. "Let me help," she said, but Kimberley protested, as did Charlotte. "Run on outside and swim with the kids. And I think Eric's in the pool, too."

"If you're sure," Jenifer said, hearing the echo of Eric's voice calling her "chicken."

"Go on, girl," Sunny said. "Show him your stuff." She winked.

"Remember the possibilities," Kimberley said, looking pretty proud of herself.

"Good point," Jenifer muttered under her breath, and headed outside. At least dusk had settled over the yard. She wouldn't have to reveal her choice of bikini and all the body it didn't cover under the bright glare of sunlight. Uncle Pete moved around, lighting citronella candles to ward off the pesky evening mosquitoes.

Eric had joined the youngsters in the pool. They were shouting and leaping, playing what looked like a lively game of water polo. Kimberley covered her nose and ran to the pool, landing with a huge splash. Jenifer followed at a more sedate pace, pausing by a lawn chair to wiggle out of her shorts. She glanced toward the pool and saw Eric holding the ball. His attention appeared to be held by the sport. She tugged her T-shirt off, tossed it onto the chair, and walked to the edge of the pool.

He threw the ball to her. "Now that's what I call a bathing suit," he said, dashing water from his eyes and running his gaze up and down her body. "I think that may give your team an unfair advantage."

She slipped into the water. "And why is that?" She flicked the ball back to him.

He snagged it and grinned. "It's pretty hard to keep my eye on the ball."

"Throw it, Eric!" One of her nephews, dog-paddling, waved one arm.

Eric did, then swam over to Jenifer's side. "I'm going to sit in the penalty box for a few minutes, guys," he said to the kids.

"But you haven't done anything wrong," one of them called.

"No, but I'd like to," Eric said, but only loud enough for Jenifer to hear.

Eric trod water for a moment or so, watching Jenifer. She seemed self-conscious, but she had nothing to be ashamed of in the bathing beauty category. The scrap of a bikini top barely held her breasts from spilling free. Yeah, and right into his hands, he wished silently. The cool water had hardened her nipples, and left little to his overheated imagination. Lucky his lower body was underwater. He had to control himself. There were children in the pool.

"Keep looking at me like that," Jenifer said, "and you will find yourself in trouble."

Her words were an invitation, an invitation to pleasure, to plunder her body. Eric counted silently to ten, backward, in German. The ball bonked him in the head and he fell into the water, dousing him, and he came up shaking himself like a dog.

Jenifer laughed and snatched the ball from him. She dunked him playfully under the water, and Eric paid her back in kind.

The kids got into the act, and pretty soon there was more water splashing through the air than left in the pool, or so it seemed to Eric.

"Horsey," the youngest child called out. "Let's play horsey."

Eric looked questioningly at Jenifer. She flipped her wet hair from her face, and said, "You know the game, don't you? We pair off, with one person on another's shoulders, and the last team with the rider still on top is the winner."

"Love it," Eric said. "I'll be your horse."

Kimberley clapped her hands. Someone else said, "No fair, you two are bigger than the rest of us."

"Oh, but much clumsier," Eric said.

"Speak for yourself," Jenifer said.

She did love to compete. Eric patted his shoulders. "Up you go."

The look on her face was priceless. Too late, she realized just how intimately she'd be positioned, with her bare legs wrapped around his neck. If it were the two of them alone in the pool, Eric would have reversed her body and buried his face in the front of her tempting little bikini bottom.

"Maybe it is unfair," she said, playing with her lower lip with one damp finger.

"The others are already scrambling," Eric said, showing her no mercy. He wanted her legs wrapped around him. Oh, yeah. He'd been working way too much lately, and hadn't had a woman in his life since he'd broken off with Maggie, er, Margie, last year. "We don't want to lose by default."

"Here we come, Aunt Jen," cried two of the boys, already partnered up and ready for action.

That did it. Jenifer closed her eyes and leaped onto Eric's shoulders. His gut clenched from the effort it took him not to react to the sweet feel of her slippery bare skin, the heat of her fanny through the wet bikini, the weight of her breasts as she leaned around his neck and shoulders. "I think I've died and gone to heaven," he said, surprised into speaking his thoughts out loud.

She laughed. "Oh, no, that comes later. Now, go, horsey!" She reached with one hand and stroked his back.

Fortunately for the G-rating of the situation, Eric had to concentrate on the two young boys challenging them, rather than on the beauty riding his shoulders. She locked hands with one of the kids and they seesawed back and forth. Eric dipped and swayed in the water, lowering Jenifer so she was level with the children. Every move he took caused that red scrap of bikini to brush against him and remind him what cradled the nape of his neck. As the boys attempted to topple her, she kept tightening her grasp on his neck and shoulders, till the sweet opening of her body nestled as close to the back of his head as it possibly could without entering his brain.

Which quite possibly it already had.

Certainly he felt possessed by her.

That thought caught him unawares and he lost his balance and fell into the water, Jenifer splashing down beside him. The two boys crowed with laughter, proclaiming victory.

Jenifer came up sputtering. "How did that happen? We were about to take them out," she said, wiping water from her face.

"Don't we get a second chance?" He wanted her body pressed up against him again. Now.

"Nope. The rules are the rules. Once you've been dumped, you have to sit out."

Darn. "I blew it," he said.

"Did you trip?"

"Must have," he said, eyeing her bikini top. The tie had loosened and one side had come almost uncovered. "Er, you might want to straighten that out," he said, glancing at the kids, who were still involved in the game he'd flunked out of.

"What?"

He flicked water toward her chest.

Jenifer looked down and saw she was practically naked. She tugged the fabric into place and tightened the tie around her neck. She couldn't help but feel a surge of heat. If he hadn't been staring at her breasts, he wouldn't have noticed, would he? She licked her lips. But for the life of her, she couldn't think of one lighthearted, flirtatious comment to make.

So she lifted her wet hair from her shoulders and fanned it out a bit. Eric usually had a ready line or two. She'd wait for him to say something.

But he just kept watching her.

As if he could eat her up.

"Oh, my," she said.

"Yeah," Eric said. "What are you—"

"Hey, Eric, what are you doing about church tomorrow?" Uncle Pete's voice carried easily across the lawn.

Jenifer glanced at Eric, wondering what he'd been about to ask her.

"Church?" Eric said the word as if Uncle Pete were speaking Swahili or some other lesser-taught language.

She watched as he literally tore his gaze away from her breasts and turned toward Uncle Pete, who'd ambled up to the side of the pool after asking the question.

"I hadn't thought about it," he said.

"You can come with us if you'd like," Uncle Pete said.

Eric glanced from him and over to Jenifer. "I don't think I packed a suit."

"You don't need a suit," Uncle Pete said. "You can wear what you wore tonight."

"Well . . ."

"I'm only the police chief," Uncle Pete said, "not the morality cop. Whether or not you go to church back home is your business, but here in Doolittle, you might as well be driving around with a sign on your car that says you're a heathen. Now, be here by nine." He smiled. "Look at it this way, there's nothing else open in town on Sunday morning."

Eric knew when to cease his objections. When in Rome . . . "Okay."

Uncle Pete nodded. "You'll like it. We have a sensible minister, not one of those sanctimonious hypocrite types." He turned toward the pool. "Come on, kids, time to get out and dry off. We're going to sing 'Happy Birthday' to Charlotte when she comes out of the kitchen, whether she likes to acknowledge her day or not."

"Five more minutes!" they all called in chorus.

Uncle Pete winked. "They always say that."

Eric stood at the edge of the pool, staring at Uncle Pete. Jenifer couldn't help but grin. "It won't hurt you," she said. "You can be anywhere in your mind. I visit all sorts of imaginary places during church."

"Really?"

She nodded. "It's soothing, the music, the ritual. I don't know if I'm religious or not, but I appreciate the sense of peace. It frees my mind."

"I thought the point of being there was to listen to the preacher telling you what God wants you to do."

"No wonder you avoid it," Jenifer said. "I've heard everything Pastor Roemer could ever think up to say. And he never berates us about what God wants or about being sinners. He asks us to ask ourselves what the right thing to do is and then do it, instead of sitting around jawing over it."

"Sounds pretty radical for a small town," Eric said.

Jenifer splashed water at him with her palm. "You city slickers aren't as smart as you're cracked up to be. I mean, who wants to live all jumbled on top of one another in concrete towers and spend an hour in the car just to go to the store and back to buy milk? In Doolittle you can keep a goat in your backyard and milk it yourself."

"D.C.'s not that bad," Eric said, laughing. "And you don't have to figure out how to get rid of the manure!"

"I've seen pictures," Jenifer said. "All those interstates and cars zipping around . . . I've been pretty restless lately and I'm itching to get out of Doolittle, but I've got more sense than to go from the frying pan into the fire. Hey, you said you're from Virginia, so why'd you say D.C.?"

"Must be your body. I can't think straight." He splashed water back at her. "I live across the river from D.C. Different state, same freeway."

Jenifer eyed him, not sure whether to be flattered or worry over whether she should accept his explanation. She'd known this man less than twelve hours, after all. And despite the yummy way her body reacted to his presence, she knew better than to get herself into danger. It hadn't taken her long at all to figure out that the two guys she'd had coffee with couldn't be trusted alone in a room with a nun. "We'd better get out and dry off."

Uncle Pete was rounding up the youngsters from the

pool. Jenifer hopped out, tugging at her bikini bottom, but there wasn't much coverage there despite her efforts. She grabbed a towel from the bunch someone had left on a chair and turned to hand one to Eric as he climbed out of the water.

She halted, both towels clutched to her breasts. That Speedo left nothing to the imagination. There just wasn't enough fabric to go around. She swallowed, hard.

He grinned at her, no doubt knowing full well that she was looking her fill of him.

He moved closer, helped himself to one of the towels and whispered in her ear, "Maybe we ought to go skinny-dipping next time."

She blushed and pulled her T-shirt on over her bikini. Immediately it soaked through, the effect outlining her breasts in a way even the bikini hadn't. Eric stood there, drying his arms and chest ever so slowly, his eyes on her. She shivered, as much from his attentions as the night air wafting over her damp skin. As soon as they sang "Happy Birthday," she needed to run home and change. Face it, Jenifer, she told herself, you need a time out before you make a fool of yourself.

"What I was going to ask you a few minutes ago," Eric said, rubbing his thick dark hair with a towel, "was if you'd like to go out after the party breaks up."

She'd like nothing more. But she wasn't going to let him know that. She might not have dated in more than a decade, but her instincts were sure. Easy come, easy go. Better to whet his appetite. So she fluttered her damp lashes and said, "I'd love to, but I can't."

His disappointed expression surprised and pleased

her, almost enough to cause her to relent. But she knew better. Pamela might have gone with him, had she been single. Yeah, and had a ring on her finger by the next day. But she didn't want to operate the way her best friend did, nor did she want a man permanently in her life. What she wanted was adventure, and with that, she wanted to savor the anticipation and build the tease.

Not that she could have said precisely why a slow buildup would make things even more sensational. Jeez, when her legs had been wrapped around his shoulders and her body was pressed against his so intimately, she'd been wishing the two of them were alone. Alone and completely naked, nothing but skin touching skin.

Eric toweled one lean, muscled thigh, then switched to his other leg. Jenifer couldn't force her gaze to settle anywhere but on his body.

"Sure I can't change your mind?" His voice was an intimate whisper, designed to tempt her.

Successfully so.

Jenifer parted her lips, yearning to take the towel from him and trace the ridges of his thigh to the edge of his Speedo, then slip beneath the edge of the damp fabric that advertised a magnificent form. "I don't think so," she managed to say.

"Aunt Jen?"

Jenifer and Eric both jerked at the sound of Kimberley's voice. Everyone except she and Eric had gathered in a semicircle next to the long table.

Eric grinned. "Don't look now, but everyone is staring at us."

She flashed a smile at him. "There's no such thing as

a secret in this family." To the others she said, "Be right over."

Eric wrapped the towel around his waist. "I'm going to run inside and change. You can tell me later if you'd like to go out."

He turned so quickly, walking with a rapid stride to the house, that Jenifer didn't have time to assure him she had no intention of changing her mind. Cocky man!

She stepped toward the others gathered around the table. "Sorry," she said. "I wasn't paying attention."

Shane hooted. "Oh yes you were, sis," he said. "Just not to the rest of us."

Jenifer blushed. Everyone was smiling, way too broadly. Thank goodness Eric walked so quickly. She hoped he'd made it into the house before Shane got off his teasing comment.

Charlotte walked outside, accompanied by Shane's wife. Soon after, Eric reappeared, fully clothed. He walked around the others, making straight for her side, joining in the chorus of "Happy Birthday" in a rich baritone.

Jenifer felt a rush of pleasure at his attention. At that moment, with Eric close by her side, she had an insight as to how it might feel to be half of a couple, and she realized she'd been fighting something that might just be the sweetest experience possible.

The strength of that emotion scared her. She edged away as Uncle Pete put his arms around her mother and kissed her on the cheek. She watched the two of them, her head cocked to one side. There was nothing unusual in the embrace. The Wrights and the Simons were both touchy-feely families. But something about the way the two of them looked at one another set off an alarm in her head.

Uncle Pete stepped back, but stayed close to Charlotte. He glanced around at the assembled relatives and said, "Both Charlotte and I and our loving spouses who have now gone to heaven have been blessed with wonderful families. I couldn't have made it through the past six months without the love and support of everyone here. And I know losing Shane Senior was the hardest thing Charlotte ever had to endure."

Jenifer couldn't swallow around the lump in her throat. She missed her dad so much.

Eric reached out and offered her his hand. He'd seen the clenching of her jaw when Pete spoke of their losses. He didn't have any right to comfort her, he told himself. Hell, he didn't belong in this world he'd stumbled into, but he knew the right thing to do was to offer his touch and show he recognized Jenifer's pain.

She accepted his hand, curling her fingers around his. Meanwhile, she kept looking straight ahead, watching Pete and Charlotte with an intense expression he chalked up to sorrow.

"So when I was thinking of what to get Charlotte for her birthday," Pete was saying, "I decided the thing to do was to take her away to be thoroughly and completely pampered." He pulled an envelope out of his pocket. "Charlotte, here are tickets to a cruise that leaves from New Orleans just after Christmas."

"Pete Simon, I can't believe you did that!" Charlotte fanned her face with her hand, but she looked extraordinarily pleased.

"Happy birthday," Pete said, kissing her on the cheek.

"Can I go with you, Grandma?" Kimberley shimmied to her side, inspecting the contents of the envelope. "There are two tickets in here."

"I think your mother needs a chaperone," Pete said, a jovial smile on his face. "So I'm going to make sure she has a good, safe trip."

Charlotte fanned her face even more. "Are you really?"

Pete nodded. "If it's all right with you."

Charlotte's happy expression was answer enough to his reply.

Eric realized that Jenifer was clenching his hand. He glanced at her face, noting her brows were drawn together as she watched the discussion about the cruise. He didn't understand Jenifer's tension. If her mother and her dead husband's best friend wanted to get up close and personal, wouldn't that be a happy thing? But Jenifer didn't look as if the idea set well with her at all, if indeed those were the thoughts chasing through her mind. Should he ask her? Was it any of his business? After all, just because he lusted after her body didn't mean he needed to get involved with her family situation. Unless, of course, it related to any possible crossing over to the wrong side of the law.

Still, he found the words sliding over his lips. "Want to tell me what's bothering you?" he asked, easing her grip on his hand and nudging her gently to the edge of the circle of family and friends.

Jenifer followed his lead, drawing away from the lights of the covered table area, to two chairs next to the now-smoldering barbecue grill.

"So, what is it?" he prompted, leaning forward, his

hands on his knees, wanting to touch her but somehow knowing this moment didn't call for contact.

She sniffed once, then said, "Nothing. Nothing's wrong."

Aha. He knew how to interpret that response! Woe to the man who accepted that negative at face value. He could still remember the time he'd overheard his dad ask his sobbing mother that question. When she'd said nothing was wrong, his dad's response had been, "Good. When's dinner?" She'd cried out, "You never care about my feelings!" and flung her favorite Waterford candy dish at his dad's retreating back.

Eric waited. He'd been trained in the subtle art of getting people to open up to him, to spill their guts, confess secrets of the darkest type. He knew when to wait and when to push. What he didn't know, he realized now, watching this beautiful, emotional, compelling woman, was how to genuinely convey his concern for what she was feeling.

He might as well have been an emotional quadriplegic, he thought.

"Jeni," he said, calling her by the nickname he'd heard Pamela use, "let me in."

She lifted her face, her eyes seeking his, asking for . . . what? Reassurance?

"I'm sincere," he said, hoping his words didn't sound too corny. "I can tell you're upset, and I'd like to help."

She dabbed at the corner of an eye and then smiled, the hurt look disappearing from her face. "I believe you mean that," she said.

He nodded.

She rose. "Walk me home and I'll answer your question."

He stood up and offered her his hand. Damn if she hadn't gotten under his skin. He not only wanted her body, he wanted to see inside her mind and look into her heart.

She nodded. "I'll get my things," she said. "And say good night to Mother."

Five

Tigger leaped up the minute Jenifer stepped onto the porch. He liked to sleep in a basket she kept for him beside the front door. As soon as her cat saw she had come home with someone in tow, the yellow tom arched his back and hissed.

"It's okay, Tigger," Jenifer said. "Let me introduce you to Eric." She motioned to him to squat down and offer his fingertips for the cat to sniff.

Looking amused, he performed on cue. The cat relaxed and curled himself around Jenifer's calves.

"He's got you well-trained," Eric said, his voice just behind her right ear as Jenifer fumbled with the doorknob. It wasn't locked. As far as she knew, no one in Doolittle locked their doors. Another reason, she reflected with honesty, not to look elsewhere for some other place to live simply because she'd had ants in her pants ever since the twins left for college. But she had been thinking of visiting her sister in Tampa—until she'd hit upon the more appealing idea of satisfying her restlessness by pursuing an adventure with Eric, and the potentially life-changing course of finally realizing her dream of becoming a lawyer.

She dropped her hand from the doorknob. "Let's sit on the porch," she said. She'd been about to let him follow her into her house. So much for playing hard to get. So much for being sensible, too. Funny how being sexy and being sensible warred within her. Well, she'd save the analysis for later. Right now she'd enjoy the evening and leave both of them wanting more.

'Cause she could tell he liked her.

As she turned around, she bumped into him. A nervous giggle passed her lips before she could corral it.

"It is a nice evening," he said, smiling at her and taking a seat in one of the two oversized wicker chairs. "And this is a nice porch."

"Thanks," she said, settling into the other chair. Her hair had almost dried before she left Uncle Pete's house, and the bikini bottom and top underneath her shorts and shirt were only slightly damp now.

Tigger strolled over, marched past her, and jumped into Eric's lap. He began kneading his paws as if performing a nightly ritual rather than meeting him for the first time.

"He likes you," Jenifer said.

Eric scratched his ears. "Yeah, most cats do," he said. "Don't know why. I've never had a cat."

"Dogs?"

He shook his head. "I'm never home enough to take care of a pet."

"You must have traveled a lot in your business," Jenifer said, deciding to steer him away from asking why she'd reacted so poorly to the interaction between her mother and Uncle Pete. If the two of them went on a cruise, what was it to her? "I bet you have seen every exotic place I've always dreamed of visiting."

"Try me," Eric said.

"Well, first off, there's Italy. You have to know it like the back of your hand, or should I say the last of a shoe."

" 'Last,' " he said, and smiled. "Very good. Not everyone would have that term on the tip of their tongue."

Jenifer looked at him. "There are very few terms I can't define."

"Really?"

She nodded. "It's an obnoxious trait, actually, but there you have it, it's the way I am." No point in telling him she used to hand-copy words from the dictionary when she'd been in high school and striving to make the best score possible on her college entrance exams.

"So if I said to you, oh, for example, 'prestidigitation,' you could define it."

She laughed. "I'm afraid so. But let me pull a sleight of conversational hand and change the topic—can we talk about something else?"

Eric smiled as he stroked Tigger's back, running his hand the length of the cat's body, and all along his tail till his fingers reached the tip. "Sure."

Jenifer stared at the soothing motion, wishing his hands were performing their magic on her body. "Jealous of a cat," she murmured, then caught herself.

"They do have a way of savoring the moment, don't they?" Eric returned to rubbing Tigger's ears.

"No wonder cats like you," she blurted.

He laughed out loud. "Scoot your chair over here and I'll rub behind your ears."

She cocked her head to one side. Eric held her gaze, wondering whether she'd take him up on the invitation. He'd love to run his fingers down her neck, wrap his arms around her, pull her close, and taste the tempting skin of her throat. Maybe she'd loosen up enough to share what was going on inside that pretty head of hers. He stirred in the chair and said, "I'm pretty good at massage."

She didn't budge an inch. Instead, she crossed her legs at the ankles, regarding him with a most serious and fervent expression.

"Yes, Jenifer Wright," he said, leaning toward her, evoking an annoyed meow from Tigger as he did so, "I am trying to seduce you."

"Oh," she said, surprised at his directness. "I mean, that's good." But suddenly she felt confused. She'd imagined an approach much more . . . romantic? She thought she wanted uncomplicated sex, but she still wanted to be romanced. "A good try," she added, smiling sweetly.

Eric shook his head. He'd said that just to throw her off guard. Women liked the open approach because so few men knew how to use it. Most guys would try clever lines or say something about how blue or green or brown their eyes were, and then move in for a quick hit. Eric considered himself a connoisseur, a master of subtle seduction. When he wanted a woman to melt, he knew she would. It wasn't bragging; he'd racked up the statistics to prove his skills. However, this situation remained more complicated than most. If she seemed more of a guilty suspect, he'd be more inclined to use her in whatever way he could to discover truth—but she seemed an innocent, and thus his scruples warned him away. "Not even," he said. "If I were trying, you wouldn't know it."

Her disappointed expression satisfied him immensely. He had the fish on the lure, so it was time to throw her off guard. "I enjoyed the cookout," he said. "Thanks for inviting me."

She nodded, apparently lost in thought, so Eric took advantage of the pause to appreciate the picture Jenifer presented. The low-cut T-shirt still clung to the line of her bikini top. Her nipples pushed against the thin cotton, and even in the dim light of the overhead porch lamp, they created an image he wanted to explore with his fingertips before tasting them with his tongue. He shifted in his chair, and Tigger meowed loudly. He wanted to complain, too. Jeez, but Jenifer had an effect on him!

"I happen to know a thing or two about men," Jenifer said, "and I know when someone is interested in someone as a friend versus a sexual partner."

Eric jerked his thoughts from her swollen nipples. "Er, is that so?" At that moment, he didn't want to ask how she defined his reasons for sitting on her porch on a Saturday evening, stroking her cat when he'd far rather be fondling her body.

"Yes, and I can tell when sentiments are the other way around, too. For instance, there was something different about Uncle Pete tonight." Jenifer leaned forward, treating Eric to cleavage that kept his thoughts on nipples, not on uncles.

"Mmm," he murmured. As long as he pretended to be listening, she'd keep talking. And he'd build his fantasies. And his fantasies weren't the only thing growing. Thankfully, he'd traded in the Speedo for his street clothes, or he'd have to hold that cat on his lap until he walked to his car.

Or got lucky.

"He and Mother have been friends forever. I don't know how she would have gotten through Daddy's cancer and his death and the terrible time afterward if it hadn't been for Pete and his wife. And then when she got killed, Mother carried him through, too. But they're *friends*."

"Mmm," Eric offered, thinking that perhaps friends made the best foundation for long-term relationships. If his parents had liked each other, maybe they wouldn't have fought all the years of their married lives. He suspected the two of them had been lovers and gotten married because it was expected, especially as he'd calculated how close to their wedding anniversary he'd arrived as their little bundle of joy. He thrust those memories from his head and focused on the beauty sitting next to him. Though he wasn't looking for any relationship, he did want to know what Jenifer's lips tasted like. Still he was pleased that she'd decided to share what had troubled her about Pete and Charlotte.

"They need to keep it that way, too," she said fiercely.

Eric tore his gaze from her T-shirt and saw the anguished look in her eyes. He couldn't be sure, but he thought he also detected the glimmer of a tear. He nudged the cat from his lap and moved so he knelt beside the arm of her chair. He smoothed her hair, and said, "That's it. Tell me what's bothering you."

To his surprise, she said in a cross voice, "Nothing. I'm being ridiculous."

He knew better than to agree with that statement, no matter how sensible she might appear.

"Besides, I don't even know you," she said, swiping at her eyes. "And I'm crying on your shoulder about something I'm probably imagining anyway."

He patted his shoulder and eased her face into the curve of his neck and shoulders. She tucked the side of her head against his cheek and sighed.

Eric stroked her hair. It smelled more like chlorine than ginger now, but he inhaled deeply anyway. She felt right, nestled against his shoulder, and he wanted to open his arms and embrace all of her.

But knowing women as he did, he realized he'd score more points being sympathetic to her tears than zeroing in for a kiss. Even as that thought cleared the synapses of his brain, he acknowledged how terribly cynical he'd become. Yeah, hit, score, and run—that had been his modus operandi with women since he'd enticed the captain of the cheerleading squad into the backseat of her dad's Impala when he hadn't been old enough to legally get behind a wheel.

Jenifer sighed and just managed to keep from sniffling. So much for enticing Eric Hamilton into playing out her sexual fantasies, she thought. Now he'd think of her as a crybaby. And she hated the way her eyes turned puffy if she even grew misty-eyed. She didn't understand what had come over her. One minute she'd been flirting, savoring the sexual current that flashed and hummed between Eric and her, and the next she started boo-hooing.

"I'm sorry," she said at last, mumbling the words against the side of his neck. "I'll be fine in a moment."

"Everything's okay," he said. "Take your time." He stroked her hair, and the soothing gesture made Jenifer want to keep her head right there.

"Feels good," she said. "You're very comforting." He couldn't be very comfortable, though, hunched beside her chair. She glanced down, her gaze halting when it reached the front of his trousers. Either his pants were all bunched up or tears turned him on!

She realized she must have gasped, because he said, "What's wrong?"

"Did I do that to you?"

Eric pulled back slowly, lifting her head from his shoulder. He followed her line of sight and grinned. He rose, and stood there looking at her. "Think I should go next door and jump in the pool again?"

"Oh, no," she said, then blushed. "I mean . . ." She trailed off. What could she say? She stretched her arms over her head, nice and slow, watching the effect the sensuous movements had on Eric. He hadn't stepped away from her, and he leaned over her now, one hand on each arm of the porch chair.

Would he kiss her? One kiss. Just one kiss. She wanted to experience the touch of his lips on hers, his breath against her cheek, the sweet scent of his skin close enough to taste.

She hadn't been kissed by a man in so very long.

Surely he wanted to kiss her. Yes, of course! He'd lifted a stray length of her hair and tucked it gently behind her ear. Oh, yes, he definitely wanted to kiss her.

"So soft," he murmured.

So hard, she almost said, thinking of how worked up he was and how much she relished knowing she'd caused that manly reaction. But at least she didn't blurt the words out.

He took her hand and pulled her easily up from the chair, till their bodies stood toe-to-toe. Jenifer moistened her lips, and they parted slightly, though she was scarcely aware of her subconscious and inviting gesture.

"I think I was meant to visit the library today," he said, his voice low and deep and almost a kiss all unto itself.

"Oh, yes," she breathed.

He touched her chin with the barest pressure, and then, in the midst of her sensual dream taking shape into on-her-very-own-front-porch reality, a most practical thought entered her mind. "You never did tell me what information you needed," she said.

"What's that?" He clearly hadn't been listening. No wonder, when she could tell by the rapid rise of his chest beneath his polo shirt that his body had taken over for his mental functions.

"The information," she said, her mind almost disappearing the way his had.

Eric tipped her chin upward, one finger skimming the satiny surface of her cheek. She couldn't be asking a sensible question at this moment. Not now. Not when he'd actually forgotten what story he'd concocted in his head before pushing open the door of the Doolittle Public Library. "You," he said. "I was looking for you."

"That's silly," she said, but with a flirty giggle. "You didn't even know I existed."

"Oh, but I did," he said, crossing his fingers mentally and hoping the gods of the afterlife understood that sometimes a guy just had to say what he had to say in order to score. "In my dreams," he finished. What did his boss always say to him? He heard the dry voice rasping in his head. *As long as you don't break the law, violate the agency's rules, or blow your cover, I don't care how many hearts you break.* Yeah, Chester, you should be proud of your protégé right now.

"Well, that is romantic," she said.

He heard the way her voice relaxed, and he reached out and put his arms around her. He'd forgotten all about not rushing his fences. Something about Jenifer got him so worked up, he'd gone well along the road to wrecking his legendary self-control.

He felt her stiffen when he embraced her. A less

observant guy wouldn't have noticed. She pulled back and was looking at him with that frank stare. He realized he enjoyed waiting for what she might say next.

"Yes, it's romantic," she said slowly, as if mulling over her word choice, "but you don't need to perjure yourself, Eric."

"What do you mean?"

"You're a man. I'm a woman. You want to kiss me, right? I want you to kiss me, so let's do it. You don't have to make up some silly story. Sooner or later you'll tell me why you came to the library, and I'll help you with what you need to know. Right now, dammit, I just want you to kiss me."

He felt like a rider whose horse had shied at a water jump and sent him tumbling over his bridle and into the pond. "Kissing is not like flipping a circuit breaker," he said. "It's not just A plus B equals C. It's more art than science, and doesn't come into being on demand." Dammit, he wanted to call the shots here.

She sighed and the pouty way her lips moved almost made him move to shut her up with a long, swift, hard, delicious, blood-pounding kiss.

"That's rather opinionated," she said.

He threw up his hands. "It's impossible to kiss and analyze the feeling at the same time."

"I don't see why," she said.

"Maybe I'll stick around town long enough to explain it to you," Eric said, stepping back. The only thing to do now was scram. Unless he kissed her to shut her up, of course. But he didn't want her talking and calculating when he tasted her lips. He wanted her whimpering and writhing with passion. Not thinking, only feeling.

"You're not going, are you?"

She sounded disappointed. Good. She'd be a heck of a lot less analytical after a horny night's sleep. And he'd be even more—

A phone shrilled once, the sound coming from inside her house, filtered only by the screened windows that opened onto the front porch. As quickly as it rang, it cut off. And then rang again, quit, and rang once more.

Jenifer swung around, pushed open the door and raced inside.

Noting that she hadn't had the door locked, Eric hesitated only a moment before following her into the house. He'd interpreted the three short rings as a signal. From whom? he wondered as he glanced around a small and tidy entryway. Jenifer stood to his right in a cozy living room, her back to him.

Was she up to something she shouldn't be? He thought of the page he'd skimmed from the library trash and frowned.

She turned around and caught his expression. "I'll be right there," she said into the receiver, and put the phone down. "Oh, I thought you left."

He cocked a brow. "Leave a damsel in distress?"

She smiled then, if only for a second. "It's Pamela. I'm going over there."

"Husband problems?" He pictured Ace's bulky body. "I'll go with you."

She looked at him, then nodded. "Thank you," she said. "Pamela didn't want me to tell Uncle Pete or my brothers." She grabbed her purse and car keys from a table by the door. She paused, studying him for a long moment. "I guess it's okay if you go with me as long as you swear you won't repeat anything you see."

Eric raised his right hand. "My lips are sealed," he said, following her out, thinking Pamela couldn't be in too much turmoil or she would have called the police. And surely she wouldn't have asked Jenifer to race over if she would be putting her in danger. Or would she?

When Jenifer flew down the front steps, he kept pace, then steered her gently from her car toward his rental parked in front of her house. "I'll drive," he said, thinking of the two handguns he had stashed in his car.

She jumped in without arguing over it, and he did the same. "Directions," he said. "Then tell me what happened."

"Go straight for three blocks," she said.

"How badly did he beat her up?" He figured he might as well get to the point. From the interactions of those two at the cookout, he had no doubt that's what had happened.

He could tell he'd surprised her by the way she quickly swung her head toward him. "It's not that," she said.

"Oh," Eric said, relieved, but feeling foolish over his knight-errantry if there'd been no need.

"Turn right here," she said. "I mean, they were arguing, but it's Pamela. Right again at the stop sign. No, I mean it's Ace. Pamela thinks she's killed him."

Eric hit the brake. He turned toward Jenifer. "And that's why she didn't call the police?"

Jenifer nodded.

"And exactly what are you supposed to do? Provide an alibi?"

"Would you please drive or get out from behind the wheel?"

"It's my car," Eric said.

"And you can sit inside it when we get to the house if you're afraid."

"I am not afraid," Eric said from between his teeth. "But I see no reason for you to become involved in illegal activities."

"Don't be such a moralist," Jenifer said. "Friends help friends and ask questions later. Besides, if you had half an ounce of sense in your head, even from knowing me less than one day, you could tell I wouldn't do anything wrong without good reason."

He'd started the car moving again, but that one almost caused him to take his foot off the accelerator. "Of all the confused logic," he said.

"It's a good thing this happened before you kissed me," Jenifer said, prissily.

"Yeah, I don't kiss accessories after the fact," Eric said. He couldn't understand why she'd gotten him so mad, except that he wanted her to be one of the good guys. Girls. Women.

"And I don't kiss men who rush to judgment," she said, now sounding downright haughty. "If you please, slow down and park in front of the corner house."

"If I please?" Eric almost laughed. He pulled over and yanked the key from the ignition. "This house?" He pointed toward the two-story Colonial that would have looked at home in suburban Virginia.

"Would I park in front of the wrong one?"

"Jeez, lady, you might."

Halfway out of the car, she paused and said, "Why ever would I do that?"

"So your brothers wouldn't see this car here, so the neighbors wouldn't report it later, so if Ace isn't dead and comes gunning out the door, he won't know you dropped by for tea. Shall I go on?"

She jumped from the car, and he could tell she wanted very much to slam the door shut, by the way she caught her arm in motion and then closed the door quietly. "So maybe I'm not as smart as I think," she mumbled.

"Let's take care of business," Eric said. "We can argue more later."

She actually grinned. She started up the sidewalk.

"Wait for me before you go in," he said.

"Well, hurry up."

"I've got to get something," he said. Returning to the car, he fished in the glove box and pulled out the hammerless revolver he often wore in an ankle holster, rejecting his Beretta as overkill in the situation. He also grabbed a flashlight, showing only that object to Jenifer as he joined her on the sidewalk. No need for her to know he'd armed himself. Despite what her family said about her being a good shot, guns on a range were quite a different matter from weapons in tight quarters with excitable and possibly violent people. He also didn't want to explain why he happened to have a weapon in his car.

Jenifer put her hand on the doorknob.

In a whispered voice, Eric said, "I suppose she doesn't lock her doors, either?"

"Why should she?" Jenifer looked surprised. "Nothing ever happens in Doolittle."

"Right," Eric said. He nudged the door open with his foot. "Where's Ace?"

"Pam said they were in the kitchen when she knocked him out."

"And your friend?"

"She locked herself in the bedroom upstairs. She's not coming out till she knows we're here."

Noting the irony of the need to lock the door within the house, Eric positioned the flashlight in a two-handed grip, the way he'd normally support a weapon during entry into a hostile room. He slipped inside, hugging the wall, and looked left and right swiftly. They stood in a formal entryway, much larger and more polished than Jenifer's cozy cottage. Pamela had some dough, he reflected.

Jenifer pointed down the entry hall. "The kitchen is this way."

She started to go first, but he caught her by the shoulder and motioned that he'd lead.

"Bossy," she said under her breath, but loud enough so Eric heard.

"I'll take that as a compliment," he said.

"What an ego," Jenifer whispered.

Even as she said the words, Jenifer acknowledged to herself how much she appreciated Eric's presence. He seemed to know exactly what to do, too, moving through the house like a cop on a television show. She'd have to ask him where he learned to do that.

They reached the kitchen doorway and Eric halted abruptly, holding up his right hand. She just missed bumping into him, not that she'd mind the brush of bodies, a silly thing to be thinking of at a time like this. Then she heard what he must have heard, a man's voice moaning in pain.

"Stay here," he said softly.

As much as she hated to, she held back as Eric slipped into the kitchen, hands extended, flashlight wielded as a weapon. Good thing he'd had that handy. Too bad he'd shown an insufferable side of himself, because he certainly had some fine points. She counted to five, and when Eric didn't reappear, she inched through the doorway.

Six

Ace lay sprawled on the kitchen floor faceup, his eyes closed. He'd fallen between the breakfast table and the cooking island, in a spot Jenifer had stood more times than she could count, visiting with Pamela and her second husband, Conway, before and after dinner parties. But those convivial times seemed a thing of the past. Ace found most of Pamela's friends boring.

Shards of pottery, clumps of what looked suspiciously like potting soil, and leafy brackets of dieffenbachia decorated his bullish face. Edging farther into the room, Jenifer spotted the rest of the clay pot on the far side of the island.

"Wow," she said, still keeping her voice low. "She bonked him with a flower pot."

Eric turned from where he stood next to Ace's feet. "I thought I said wait in the hall."

"Oh, yes, you did, but someone has to watch your

back." She treated him to a wide-eyed stare of innocence. "Handling Ace is a big job for a guy who sells shoes." Ouch. Even to her own ears, that line came out as a bit of a low blow, but she'd had it with his implication that she couldn't handle a situation simply because she was a woman.

She could handle anything.

"Right," Eric said dryly, looking her up and down. "And it's a piece of cake for a five-foot-five librarian."

She stood a little straighter. "Five-five and three-quarters."

Ace groaned.

"Let's argue later," Eric said.

Too sensible to argue with. Darn. "Hey, why do you get that line?"

He grinned. "Because I thought of it first? Tell you what. Go see where Pamela is hiding and have her come here and tell me exactly what happened."

"Tell us, you mean."

"Right," he said again, shifting his position till he knelt beside Ace's head.

"If you're sure . . ."

He nodded. She had to admit that Eric looked pretty comfortable with the situation. Very in charge, in a he-man sort of way, too. He had loosened the collar of Ace's shirt, and seemed to be checking the pulse in his neck. If Ace had been dead, Eric would have known exactly what to do, Jenifer concluded, standing there staring at him. She'd never met a businessman like Eric Hamilton.

Forget the business part. She'd never met *any* man

like Eric Hamilton. She watched him, wondering dimly why she didn't move away and go find Pamela. Her friend had been so hysterical on the phone, she could barely understand a word Pamela had said. Yet here she stood, her mind on this man. Friends first, she reminded herself sternly, swinging around abruptly and stepping into the hall.

And smack into Pamela.

"Jeni," she cried, and flung herself into Jenifer's arms.

One glance at her friend had stunned Jenifer. Pamela wore a black peignoir, the frothiest, sheerest, most utterly feminine lingerie Jenifer had ever seen. Not only was it gorgeous, it was practically transparent.

She patted her friend on the shoulder, her heart sinking. After one look at Pamela, Eric would forget he'd ever wanted to kiss Jenifer Janey Wright.

"Thank you for coming," Pamela said, still clutching her and sobbing lightly. "I don't know what I'd do without you."

Those words made Jenifer feel guilty for her shallow thoughts. "It's okay, Pammy," she said. "Everything's going to be okay."

Lifting her head slightly, Pamela said, her words breaking on a sob, "Is he d-dead?"

"No," Eric said, his voice carrying loud and clear from the next room.

Pamela broke free and looked around Jenifer, into the kitchen. She took a step, and Jenifer moved with her, standing in front of her, in what she recognized as a pathetic attempt to hide the peignoir from Eric's line of sight.

"Though you might have wanted to make sure of that a bit sooner," Eric added.

"Ooh," Pamela said, "I think I interrupted something when I called. He sounds quite grouchy."

Pamela moved into the kitchen and stood staring down at Eric and her husband. Jenifer watched her and knew exactly what her friend had running through her single-track mind. She'd put two and two together and come up with eight.

Pamela put one hand on her hip, no doubt knowing just how provocative the gesture appeared in the getup she wore. "I must say, you are just what the doctor ordered for Jenifer. A woman can only go so long without a man."

Jenifer choked and blushed to the roots of her hair. "Pamela!"

Eric stared at her friend, no doubt taking in every curve of her body, highlighted by the black satin and lace. "Yes, well, I agree with that statement," he said, "but perhaps we should focus on our immediate predicament."

Another groan issued from Ace's mouth. His lips moved and his tongue appeared.

Jenifer almost wished Ace would speak. That would at least take the attention off Pamela's comments about her sex life, or the lack thereof. "Tell us what happened," Jenifer said.

"Before we get into that," Eric said, rising, "I think we should call a doctor. Or an ambulance."

"Oh, no," Pamela said, shaking her head. Her long blond curls danced as she did, and Jenifer's heart dropped again. She hated that she could be so shallow at a time like this. She'd never competed with her friend, and she sure didn't want to start now.

"We can't call Dr. Wilkinson," Jenifer said, pulling out chairs from the breakfast table and guiding Pamela into one of them, thinking her robe would be less transparent sitting rather than standing with the light shining through.

"And why is that?" Eric rose, and took the chair closest to Ace's supine form. "Or are you hoping Ace bites the dust, so to speak?" He waved the flashlight at the remains of the potted plant.

"I don't know how you can joke about that," Jenifer said. "Of course Pamela doesn't want her husband to die." She turned to her friend, "Do you, Pammy?"

"Don't be silly," Pamela said. "As hard as men are to come by in Doolittle, why would I bump off a perfectly virile sample?"

Eric grinned. Jenifer could have sworn his gaze had become fixated on the expanse of cleavage Pamela's outfit revealed.

"Maybe I should settle down here," he said. "But seriously, ladies, why can't we call your Dr. Wilkinson?"

"His receptionist is married to the football coach," Jenifer said. "And the nurse is the sister of the school superintendent's second cousin." She spoke slowly, explaining it so that even someone from another planet would understand.

"And?" Clearly Eric didn't get it.

"Dr. Wilkinson might not tell, but the word would leak. Everyone in Doolittle would be whispering that Pamela tried to kill Ace, and as the principal of the high school, she can't afford that type of scandal."

"I love my job," Pamela said. "And unfortunately there is a faction who feel I'm not the best person for it."

Jenifer leaned over and patted her friend's hand. "That's because they only look on the outside."

Eric had to hold back a grin. He'd fallen into a wacky situation comedy; if he looked around, he might spy the hidden camera. Talk about seeing the outside! A blind man would be able to behold Pamela's charms. The woman oozed sensuality. Nah, more like she waved it like a flag, or possibly a weapon. But even as he acknowledged her charms, he realized he preferred Jenifer's quieter and calmer beauty. "All right, ladies," he said, as Ace's groaning sounded in another, louder eruption, "if we're not calling the cops or a doctor, then how about we see if we can bring him around?"

"Shouldn't we have Pamela tell us what happened first?"

He shot her a glance. Hard to object when he'd already said that. "Okay, shoot." He winced at his word choice. Pamela didn't appear to notice, but Jenifer did. He could tell because she grinned. She did have a sense of the ridiculous, a trait he admired almost as much as the scent and texture of her hair and the way her breasts rose and fell when he'd leaned over her, about to kiss her.

Kiss her? Damn, what was he thinking? They had a half-dead man at their feet.

"We were having tea," Pamela said, motioning to the mugs that still adorned the breakfast table.

"Nice mugs," Eric said. If Pamela moved her arm one more time, that sexy black number would slip off her shoulder completely.

Jenifer glared at him. Apparently she could read minds.

"And?" Eric prompted her, because she'd started staring at Ace and getting teary-eyed.

"He wanted to have sex outside on the porch. I said okay as long as it was the back porch, but he said no, what was the fun if it wasn't daring?"

Jenifer's eyes had practically jumped out of her head.

"But I'm already being watched like a hawk at school, because of marrying a truck driver," Pamela said, tossing her head as if indignant at the very idea of such discrimination. "So I said I didn't feel comfortable with that, but I'd do . . ." She glanced over at Jenifer, and finished with, "Well, something else instead."

"It's not like you to hold back on the details," Jenifer said acidly.

Pamela shrugged. "Some things are private."

"I'm your best friend! You tell me everything."

Now that was interesting, Eric thought. Did Jenifer get her sex ed from the high school principal slash vamp? That concept intrigued him. Exploring those possibilities would be worth getting detention in Doolittle. He'd sit in study hall with Jenifer any day.

"Later," Pamela said, as Ace groaned again and his eyelids flickered. "Anyway, we were arguing and he started telling me how I wouldn't have to be the principal much longer because he was coming into real money, money that would make me forget about my stinking ex-husband and that crummy school." Pamela's voice cranked up. "And I laughed and said the only way he'd make more money was if he got a job driving for

ABF instead of that hokey outfit that had him running logs to the paper mill."

"ABF is one of the largest trucking companies in America," Jenifer said. "It's headquartered in Fort Smith, Arkansas."

"And you just happen to know that," Eric said.

She nodded. "I also know—"

"Honey, you can recite the company's P and L later, okay?" Pamela said. "Ace is going to be madder than a razorback stuck by a longhorn when he comes up off that floor."

"Did that bum hit you first? And that's why you conked him with the plant?" Jenifer looked fierce.

Pamela glanced down at her hands, twisting her rings. "Ace would never really hurt me. And it's not as if I hit him on purpose," she said. "We were only arguing, and I said since he didn't want what I had to offer, I'd water the plants and go off to bed. I got up to do the ones in the kitchen and spilled water on the floor, and he slipped and I screamed and I dropped the plant, right on top of his head!"

"You mean this whole thing was an accident?" Jenifer clearly couldn't believe her ears.

Pamela shrugged and stared at her hands.

So she wouldn't blow the whistle on her husband. Eric knew when Pamela veered from truth to falsehood. She didn't want to admit that Ace had attacked her and she'd struck back in self-defense, not even to her best friend. But Eric had spotted the bruises already darkening on her wrist when she reached out and pointed to the mugs. The way her long hair hung forward, he couldn't tell for sure, but he thought he'd spotted the similar telltale marks on her neck.

"So he's expecting a big payoff?" Eric said, wanting to know more about that tidbit.

Pamela shrugged. "It's stupid. I didn't marry him for money. And the things he said made me . . . well, uncomfortable, because they didn't sound quite legitimate. I mean, he spoke of making money, and winked, like there was some hidden secret or joke that I should understand. But the only way I know to make money is to earn it. Or to marry it," she added.

"Or inherit it," Jenifer said. "I guess Ace stands to take all if you die."

"I'm not dying," Pamela said drolly. "Just ask the school board. I'm a tough broad to bump off. Besides, I wouldn't give those biddies who hate me that satisfaction."

Eric smiled, his mind busy with the information Pamela had inadvertently given him. It was a darn sight too coincidental that Ace spoke of "making money" when Lars and Franco were operating in the vicinity. Add to it that Ace drove to and from a paper mill, and Eric suspected that something had to be afoot.

Jenifer had a funny look on her face, as if she'd eaten too many Kastle Burgers. He couldn't think what she could be reacting to—unless she'd caught the funny money reference, too. And knew more than she should.

"Let's get Ace back to consciousness," he said, rising briskly. He had work to do, and he'd been acting like a guy on vacation instead of a Treasury agent on assignment.

Suddenly the groaning shifted gears and noisy, shuddering snores erupted from Ace's mouth.

"Oh, God," Pamela said, and dropped her head into her hands.

"What's wrong?" Jenifer stroked her friend's hair.

"I didn't even hurt him," she said. "He's just passed out drunk. I am so embarrassed."

"He's the one who should be embarrassed," Jenifer said hotly. "Sneaking drinks at Uncle Pete's cookout, trying to get you to have sex on the front porch! What gets into men, anyway?"

"It's me," Pamela said, sniffling. "I drove him to it. He didn't want to go to your mother's birthday party. He wanted to stay home and watch NASCAR on TV and then go to Lesslie's bar to play pool. I said we could do that next weekend but your mother's birthday came only once a year."

"Perfectly sensible," Jenifer said.

"Ace doesn't like not getting his way," Pamela said. "If I'd only known that before . . ."

Jenifer lifted her friend's face from the table and dried her cheeks with the edge of · the tablecloth. "There there, we'll go see what's-her-name the lawyer, you know, the one who was Dr. Mike's first wife, on Monday, and get you out of this marriage."

A louder snore ripped through the room. Eric stood there, between Ace's big body and the kitchen sink, wondering what to do. He wanted to ask Ace some questions while the man was off guard, but on the other hand if he woke him up and then he started beating on Pamela again after Jenifer and he left, he'd feel responsible. He compromised by wetting the dishcloth sitting beside the sink and laying it over Ace's face. He'd try waking him up only a fraction, enough to get him to talk in his sleep, so to speak.

"That doesn't seem very sanitary," Jenifer said.

"Good." Eric despised men who beat up on their women. "Maybe he'll catch some streptococcus."

Pamela dashed at her eyes. "I can't get divorced. Not now, when the school board is voting on my contract."

"When's the vote?" Eric asked, slapping Ace lightly on both cheeks.

"They meet the last Monday of the month," Jenifer said. "They use the board room at the library."

"So that gives you about two weeks," Eric said, doing the math.

"You can stay with me until then," Jenifer said. "Let's go pack some things."

Pamela didn't budge. That didn't surprise Eric. He'd bet good money that it would take more than one domestic disturbance to convince Pamela to give up her X-chromosome vibrator. And people said men were dense!

Jenifer stared at her friend, unable or unwilling to believe she wouldn't do the sensible and safe thing and accept her offer to stay with her. She found Pamela's explanation about the accident pretty fishy, but Ace had been slapping away some liquor so perhaps it had happened the way Pammy described. Nah. Her friend hadn't wanted to tell the truth in front of Eric. Feminine pride, no doubt. Nobody wanted to admit they'd fallen for a cad.

Jenifer knew all about that. She'd gotten over it, but

for years she'd smarted with shame over her gullibility and stupidity in the matter of her high school boyfriend, the man who unwittingly, unthinkingly, and with great irresponsibility, became the father of her twins. The man who hadn't wanted her to give birth to them. No, no woman wanted to admit she'd made that stupid a choice.

So she patted her friend's shoulder and said, "It'll be okay. You don't have to make any decisions at all right now."

"Who the hell are you?" Ace sat up swinging.

Eric dodged the right jab easily and said in a calm voice, "Eric. We met at the cookout. Jenifer and I dropped by for a nightcap. Right, Jenifer?" His look had that command to it, the air of authority that both riled and pleased her.

"Hi, Ace," Jenifer said, wiggling two fingers at him. "Hope we didn't come by at an inconvenient time."

"Babe, get me off the floor and get our guests a drink. And clean up this mess," Ace said, staggering to rise and slumping back to the tile surface. He would have hit his head if Eric hadn't caught his shoulders.

Rather than helping him rise, Eric swung him around so he rested against the kitchen counter beneath the sink. Ace's head drooped and Eric sat down beside him.

"So, long day?" Eric asked the question in a conversational tone.

Jenifer couldn't believe her ears. "You're going to sit there and have a tea party?"

"Good idea," Eric said. "Why don't you put water on to boil?"

"I'll do it," Pamela said, jumping up. The swirls of her negligee danced around, treating them to a pair of shapely legs.

"Bitchin', babe," Ace said. "Man, my head hurts." He looked around, eyes narrowing. "Say, what am I doing on the floor?"

"Tea party," Eric said. "Always sit on the floor. It's the way they do it in Japan."

Jenifer took the hint and joined them, cross-legged, on the tile.

"No reason for us to do it that way," Ace said. "Bunch of squint—"

"Let's not show our xenophobia, Ace," Jenifer said, sounding as much like a schoolmarm as a librarian.

"Nice vocabulary," Eric said.

"Thank you," Jenifer said. She wished she could go home and think. Ace's reference to making money disturbed her. She'd been so taken with Eric, she'd forgotten about the twenty-dollar bill she'd accepted in payment for some overdue library fines. Intrigued by the redesigned twenty-dollar bill with the peach, blue, and mint watermark, she'd swapped out one of her old-fashioned green ones and taken the bill home with her a few days ago. It was funny how the bill was so much the same yet seemed different, with the pastel tones, offset image of Andrew Jackson, and the patterns of 20, 20, 20 in gold. The bills had been circulating for a while, but they were still fairly uncommon in Doolittle. She'd done an Internet search to learn the reasons for the changes, and that's when she discovered that the one she'd taken home didn't match up to the official descriptions. It was missing the vertical bars that showed when the bill was held up to the light. She'd forgotten all about it when the sexy and compelling Mr. Eric Hamilton had strolled into the library that afternoon.

Now she'd have to wait until they made sure Pamela was safe staying with Ace tonight before she could go home and analyze what to do about the question of the possibly funny money.

"Green tea good for everyone?" Pamela asked.

Jenifer nodded.

"Whiskey," Ace muttered. "Tea is for sissies. Right, Eric?"

"Damn straight," Eric said, jabbing Ace in the ribs like they were old bar buddies. "Set me up, Pamela."

Pamela rolled her eyes and shook her head, but she disappeared into another room and came back carrying a bottle of Jack Daniel's Black Label and two shot glasses.

"Do you think that's a good idea?" Jenifer asked.

"Fine idea," Eric said.

Ace looked at him sideways. "You're a better man than I took you for," he said.

Eric reached up and relieved Pamela of the bottle and glasses and filled them. "Thank you, Ace," he said. "Bottoms up."

"Men," Jenifer said, getting up from the floor. She wasn't going to pretend they were having a Japanese tea party if Eric intended to get Ace even drunker. "Let's go upstairs, Pamela."

Pamela flipped off the burner where the teakettle had started to whistle. "Really! Can't you see he's had enough to drink?"

Eric nodded. "Trust me," he said, clinking glasses with Ace.

"Hmmph," Pamela said. "Come on, Jeni, let's go to my dressing room and talk."

"Your keys," Jenifer said, standing over Eric.

"My keys?"

"Give me your car keys, please," she said, one word at a time, as in give-me-your-damn-car-keys, only she politely omitted the curse word.

"I'm not getting drunk," he said.

"Boys will be boys," she said sweetly, her hand held out.

"All right," he said, grumbling. He reached into his pants pocket and metal clanged against metal. A guilty look crossed his face, and Jenifer could see why when a tiny handgun slipped from his pocket onto the floor. He stuffed it back into his pocket and handed her the keys.

"Aren't we full of surprises," she said.

"Give me another shot," Ace mumbled.

Keys in hand, Jenifer marched out of the room, Pamela in tow.

Eric watched her go, relieved she'd taken off in a huff. He'd explain it later, or as much as he could, but he wanted Ace talking freely and he didn't want anyone else to hear what Ace might say or, more specifically, what he planned to ask Ace. And he had to work fast; once the new alcohol took effect, Ace would be out for the night.

"So, I'm new in town," Eric said conversationally. "What's a guy do for fun?"

Ace waved his glass in front of his chest. "Drinking and sex. Better get yourself some ass or you'll be bored as a split rail in this dump of a town."

"Heard you play pool," Eric said, cradling his shot glass. Ace probably wouldn't notice he hadn't tossed his liquor down the hatch.

"That's right." Ace's head bobbed, first right, then left.

"Also heard you're a man who knows a good business deal when he sees it," Eric said.

Ace laughed. "Yeah, but try telling that to my wife. She thinks I'm an idiot. That all I can do is drive a truck. Well, I'll show her."

"So you're getting into a new business?" Eric knew better than to press too hard on the point he wanted most to know about, but he feared that Ace either would lose consciousness or that the women would come back into the kitchen.

"Yep."

"I sure could use some business leads, too," Eric said, shaking his head. "I've got bills up the wazoo."

Ace snorted, and without him asking, Eric waved the bottle over his glass. "You could marry the librarian," he said. "She hasn't had a man between her legs in half a lifetime. Reckon she'd be grateful. She's got a steady paycheck, too."

Eric forced himself to concentrate on the information he needed, but the image of slipping between Jenifer's sweet thighs filled his mind, even though he wanted to smash Ace's teeth in for speaking of Jenifer in those terms. "Yeah, but a man likes to have his own cash," he said. "You wouldn't be willing to let someone else in on your latest deal, would you?" He lifted his glass and tossed the contents down, belching in manly fashion.

Ace laughed. "Well, there might be enough work to go around. Tell you what. Let me ask my p-pals." His head bobbed, this time bouncing to his chest.

"I can't hang out too long," Eric said. "You have any idea when that'll be?"

A soft snore issued from Ace's lips. Eric leaned over and slapped him on the cheek. "Ace, man, wake up, you've got whiskey left in your glass."

"Huh! Huh, I'm not sleeping," Ace said, his head jerking upright.

"Your pals," Eric said, "Going to meet with them soon?"

"Shink so," Ace said, his voice slurring. "Shink it's Tuesday night. They said they'd be playing pool."

"Bet they can't beat you," Eric said, very jolly.

Ace's shot glass fell to the floor, and that fast, he was snoring. Eric reached down, grappling with the man's weight, and hoisted him to his feet. "Come on, buddy, take a few steps for me," he said.

"Yeah, I'm gonna make some money now," Ace mumbled.

Eric guided him from the room, stumbling and swaying until they reached the sofa in the living room. He let go and Ace tumbled to the cushions. Eric figured he'd be easier for Pamela to deal with the next day if he woke up there rather than on the cold tile of the kitchen floor. He'd prefer for her to stay with Jenifer, but he'd heard and seen enough to know the woman wouldn't change her mind. He hoped she'd learn to live without the jerk before Ace ended up doing serious harm to her.

He looked around the formal living room, so at odds with Ace's persona, sad for Pamela but pleased with what he'd been able to get out of Ace. Sometimes the universe had a way of handing out solutions. He'd collect Jenifer, drive her home, and head to the motel to file a report.

Heck, maybe he'd even manage a good-night kiss.

Seven

"Okay, what really happened?" Jenifer demanded the minute she thought she and Pamela were out of earshot. It had taken every smidgen of patience she possessed to wait till they were halfway up the staircase.

"You've been my best friend since you gave Wally Santos a bloody nose when he stuck bubble gum in my tutu at dance recital in first grade," Pamela said. "And that means more to me than I can say."

"Yeah, well, I may have overreacted a teeny bit with Wally," Jenifer said, "but lay out the facts on Ace. I promise I won't go to extremes."

"I cannot lie to you," Pamela said, "but this is one problem I need to keep to myself."

Jenifer stumbled and caught her shin smack against the edge of the top step. "That practically means the same thing as lying!"

"Shhh. I don't want Ace or Eric to hear us," Pamela said.

They walked down the carpeted hallway to one of the house's four bedrooms, the one Pamela referred to as her dressing room.

Jenifer placed her hands on her hips and looked her friend square in her emerald-green eyes. "Okay, I get the message. Wild horses won't drag the truth from you means only one thing. So tell me, is this the first time he's gotten violent?"

Instead of answering, Pamela turned and opened the doors to one of the wall-to-wall walk-in closets. Over her shoulder she said, "I know you don't have one sexy thing to wear, and it's important to keep some clothes on at first. It adds to the mystery, the sensual allure of the unknown potential."

"Would you stop?" Jenifer flopped down on one of the comfy armchairs. "You're trying to change the subject."

"What I'm trying to change," Pamela said, reaching for a wall switch inside the closet door, "is your abominable lack of male companionship." She flipped the switch, and the clothes, cleverly arranged on a dry-cleaner-style automated rack installed by her doting second husband, crawled forward.

"I'd rather be alone than be miserable," Jenifer said, stubbing the toe of her shoe against Pamela's thick carpet.

"We're talking about sex, not relationships," Pamela said. Garments kept whirring past.

"Where do you buy all your clothes?" Jenifer couldn't help but be distracted by the display of wardrobe.

"Mostly on-line," Pamela said. "I can find anything I

like at the touch of a mouse. And of course Conway and I used to travel during the summer."

"I know you must miss him terribly," Jenifer said softly.

Pamela turned around, gave her a sad smile, and slapped the switch to halt the forward movement of the rack. The fabrics danced as forward motion stalled. It was like watching the clothing come alive, Jenifer thought, entranced as always by the display as the line halted. She'd never known anyone like Pamela.

Even now she respected her decision not to talk about Ace. She didn't agree with it, of course. "One more thing and I'll shut up about the topic for now," she said. "Why did you use our signal if you didn't want to tell me what's going on with you two?" Since they'd been kids, the two of them had used those three rings to summon each other.

Pamela shook her head, hugging her arms to her chest.

"Pammy, this is me, Jen."

Her friend smiled, sad but sweet. "Of course you'd know. But you don't think Eric figured it out?"

"Oh, no," Jenifer said. "He doesn't have a clue." She wrinkled her nose. "I mean, he's down there drinking with Ace, for Pete's sake!"

"True," Pamela said. "I don't want anyone talking. I can't afford it."

"He won't say anything," Jenifer said. "Besides, he's only in town for a week or two."

"Then what are we doing wasting time?" Pamela plucked two items from her array of clothing. One piece was elegance itself, a slender column of turquoise satin, cut low in front and dipping deep in back. The other item, a wisp of sheer black chiffon, screamed sex kitten.

Jenifer shook her head. "Oh, I won't be needing either of those. And I don't know how you can urge me on when you're dealing with Ace in this situation."

"Don't be silly," Pamela said. "We're talking about your life. Take advantage of the opportunity. You've got a tiger by the tail. Eric's obviously attracted to you, and what man wouldn't go for you? And so what if his behavior isn't perfect? His body, hon, is delicious." She tipped her head to one side and tapped her cheek with a slender finger. "If you don't want him, let me know."

"You're married," Jenifer reminded her. "That is, until you let me help you get a divorce."

She might as well have not said the D word, because Pamela rolled right on about Eric, adding, "Nah, he's not my type, but listen, just because you're too stubborn to marry anyone doesn't mean you can't expand your sexual horizons. I think it's about time you came back into the world with the rest of us sensory beings."

Jenifer sniffed. "I have plenty of sensations. And I know all about coming, too. One doesn't need a man for that."

Pamela laughed, a gurgle that sounded almost as if she'd snorted water up her nose. Jenifer knew that sound; it conveyed both disbelief and amusement. "If I've told you once I've told you a hundred times, it's not the same when you do it on your own."

Jenifer rolled her eyes. "Yeah yeah. You know, I still can't believe you're talking about sex after what you've been through tonight."

Pamela shrugged. "Oh, Ace just lost his temper. I'll be more careful next time I tell him no."

"Hmmph," Jenifer said. "You're not supposed to have to be careful around your *husband*." She emphasized the word.

"Jeni, not everyone has your strength," Pamela said, very softly. "I don't like being all by myself. After Conway died, I walked around this house like a zombie, pacing the floor. I tried drinking to make the ghosts go away but I realized in less than a week that would never do 'cause I don't like the taste and I'd gained two pounds."

"You could have called me," Jenifer said. "I would have been over here every evening."

"Oh, I know, and I appreciate it, but I feel better with a man around. It makes me feel whole."

Jenifer started to argue, then clamped her lips shut. She'd pick another time to try to convert Pamela to her own more independent ways, though she had to admit, nothing either one of them had said to the other over the past decade plus had had any effect. They remained friends; she single and Pamela attached.

"You've had a rough night, Pammy," she said, "so why don't I go break up the love fest downstairs and let you get some rest."

Pamela nodded, then that mulish look came over her face. "Only if you pick at least one outfit to take with you."

"Okay, okay." Since she'd never get to wear it and she saw no harm in humoring her friend, she pointed to the sexy black number.

"And try it on first," Pamela said. "So I can make sure it's the right image for you."

"No. Not now."

"Yes. Now." Pamela stared her down.

"Oh, all right," Jenifer said. Getting up, she took the black baby doll by its padded hanger and stalked into the walk-in closet. "I hope the school board gives you extra points for bossiness."

Outside the open door of the bedroom, Eric continued to stand stock still, almost holding his breath. He'd been treated to quite an interesting earful since tiptoeing up the stairs and along the carpeted hallway, figuring anything he overheard fell into the category of fair game.

He suppressed a grin as he considered some of the gems the two women had delivered. Women held very little back. They discussed sex much more openly than men did. Men bragged, of course, usually about their prowess. But women got down to brass tacks.

Or battery packs, as it were.

A vision of Jenifer pleasuring herself bloomed and heated his imagination, not to mention his blood. He pictured her on a four-poster bed, surrounded by mounds of satin pillows, her head propped up, her dark hair spread against the satin backdrop, her eyes dark and wide as she slipped one hand from her breast to—

Shit. What was he doing? His breath had started coming in ragged bursts. Easy, guy, he told himself. Pay attention to the job at hand. He edged forward and peered into the room. Pamela sat in a comfy-looking overstuffed chair, her back to him. He didn't see Jenifer, but he heard her voice, loud, clear, and fascinating.

"Not even a streetwalker could carry off this thingamajig."

"Ooh, Jeni, you look good enough to eat."

"Pamela!"

Pamela giggled. "Joke," she said. "It fits you superbly. Take it. Keep it. My gift to you for rescuing me tonight."

"It still has the tags on," Jenifer said. "I can't take this."

"Frederick's was having a buy one get one free sale."

Where the heck had Jenifer gone? Eric crept closer to the doorway, very much wanting to catch a glimpse of the topic of discussion.

"Come out the rest of the way," Pamela said. "You don't have to be shy when it's just me."

Jenifer stepped out of the closet. If his blood had gone wild from his imagination alone, the reality about did him in. The sight of her long legs going up-up-up to where a ruffle of sheer black chiffon skimmed and mingled with her dark pubic hair took his breath away. The fabric moved with her body, the swell of her breasts rising from the teeniest of crisscrossed silky straps.

"Mules," Pamela said. "That's not something a woman should wear barefooted."

"Right," Jenifer mumbled. "Why don't I pick up a pair at Wal-Mart along with my box of Trojans?"

"Good thinking about the condoms," Pamela said, "but I don't think they'd have quite the right thing in slippers." She got up from the chair.

"I'm taking this thing off," Jenifer said, turning around. "I feel silly."

"You look fabulous," Pamela said.

And boy did she! Eric backed away from the door, heading back to the top of the stairs. He counted to ten, willing his overheated body to calm itself. He already knew Jenifer checked for hard-ons, and he wanted to keep his front row seat to that private fashion show his own secret.

The next time she wore that little black item, she wouldn't feel silly at all. He'd make sure of that. But it would do his cause no good at all if she knew he'd been standing there watching, and listening to her insecurities.

Because insecurities they were. Funny, for a woman as voluptuous and brainy as Jenifer, she sure possessed a sense of vulnerability about her feminine side. Nothing like some great sex to cure that insecurity, he thought, smiling. Jenifer would model that delicious negligee for him before he departed Doolittle, or his name wasn't Eric Jay Hamilton II. He whistled softly and started treading noisily in place on the top stair before he moved down the hallway, calling, "Jenifer? Pamela?"

"It's him!" Jenifer jumped and grabbed for her shorts, tugging them on under the nightie.

"You surprise me," Pamela said. "Your grammar is normally impeccably correct."

" 'Him' *is* correct," Jenifer replied, as she began swapping the sexy black outfit for her bikini top and serviceable T-shirt, not wanting to be caught by Eric when she was getting vamp lessons from Pamela. Her friend stepped into the closet and pushed her out into the room just as a knock rapped on the open door. "Go ahead and change," Pamela said. "I'll find some mules and put all this in a shopping bag for you."

"Pick one that doesn't say Frederick's, okay?" Jenifer halted in the middle of the bedroom as Eric stuck his head into the room.

Gosh but he looked sexy.

"Am I interrupting?" he said.

Jenifer shrugged. "No, of course not. Where's Ace?"

"With luck, passed out for a long, long time. I hauled him to the couch in the living room."

Pamela joined them, a Dillard's shopping bag on her arm. "That was thoughtful of you," she said.

"I figured he'd be easier to deal with in the morning that way," Eric said.

"Do you have a lot of experience with hangovers?" Jenifer asked politely.

He flashed her a grin that left her curling her bare toes into the carpet. "No more or less than most guys, I guess." He glanced down. "What happened to your shoes?"

"She took them off," Pamela said quickly. "She's funny that way. Jenifer never has liked to wear shoes, have you?"

"No, just one of my quirks." Jenifer had left them in the closet while trying on the negligee.

"Country girl thing?"

Jenifer nodded. "There's nothing like trudging through the fields with muddy red-orange clay squishing up between my toes." Ridiculous! As if she'd ever done such a thing.

"Here they are," Pamela said, handing her shoes to her after retrieving them from the closet. "So you think Ace will be asleep for a while?"

Eric nodded. "I poured a few more shots into him. Not enough to kill him, just enough to make him wish he were dead." He sounded pretty grim.

Jenifer looked at him, appraising his clearly sober

condition. "Hmm," she said, "you're more devious than I thought."

"Why, thank you, ma'am," he said, bowing and holding the door. "After you."

They headed downstairs. By the time they reached the bottom of the staircase, thunderous snoring assaulted their ears. Jenifer winced. "Is he always that loud?"

Pamela shook her head. "Only when he drinks too much."

"Good thing. I can't stand a man who snores," Jenifer said.

"I guess you put that on all your job applications," Eric said.

She cocked a brow at him.

"You know, when men apply for your attentions," he said.

Pamela giggled. "It sure didn't take you long to get her number," she said. "Thank you both for coming over tonight and I'm sorry I interrupted your evening." She handed the Dillard's bag to Jenifer as they reached the front door.

Jenifer picked up her purse from where she'd dropped it inside the door and fished Eric's car keys from her shorts' pocket. She handed them to him, hoping he'd understand the gesture as a token of silent apology. She should have known he wouldn't drink and drive. He just didn't seem the type.

"You sure you don't want us to stay?" Eric asked. "If you'd feel safer, just say the word. Right, Jenifer?"

She looked up at him, pleased that he'd offered. "Of course, Pamela. Absolutely."

"That is so sweet." Pamela stood on tiptoe and kissed Eric on the cheek. "I feel as if I've known you a long time," she said, and then turned to Jenifer and hugged her. Into her ear she said, "You're a fool if you let this guy get away."

"Right," Jenifer said. "Call if you need me."

"Me, too," Eric said.

Another burst of snoring sounded from the living room. Jenifer stepped out onto the porch and Eric followed. Pamela stood in the doorway, watching them as they crossed the yard and got into Eric's car.

Jenifer waved at her as they pulled away. "She looks sad," she said, feeling sorry for her friend's situation yet irritated with her for making excuses for Ace.

"She'll be okay," Eric said. "Ace can't possibly wake up anytime soon, and chances are when he does he won't remember a thing."

"And knowing Pamela, she'll feed him a story about what great sex they had on the front porch," Jenifer said, unable to keep an acerbic tone from her voice.

"Now why would she do that? Wouldn't that just bring up the same situation all over again?"

"Oh, no," Jenifer said, looking carefully out the side window, wishing she'd thought before she started this train of conversation. "Pamela says they never do it the same way twice."

"Is that so?" Eric sounded intrigued. "How long have they known each other?"

"Too long," Jenifer said. "They've been married three months, and they'd only dated a couple of weeks before they ran off to Hot Springs and tied the knot."

"I take it you're a believer in long engagements?"

"I'm not a believer in marriage," Jenifer said.

"Have you ever tried it?"

"No, but so what?"

"Well, if someone asked you do you like sushi and you'd never tasted it, how could you say whether you liked it or not?"

"I know what you're trying to do," Jenifer said, "but logic doesn't apply to the topic of men and women."

Eric stopped at a stop sign. He turned left and said, "Now how did you come to that conclusion?"

She smiled. "Eric, didn't you just make a left turn?"

"Yes."

"Well, did it occur to you to ask me, a native of Doolittle, whether to turn left at that corner or right?"

"Of course not. I have a perfect sense of direction. I didn't need to ask."

"Ah," Jenifer said, smugly crossing her arms over her chest. "That pretty much proves that logic doesn't apply to the topic of men and women."

"It doesn't prove anything," Eric said, slowing at a T-intersection and glancing to the left and to the right. "We're talking about directions here."

Jenifer swallowed a grin and barely kept from pointing out to him if he'd turned right instead of left he wouldn't be facing an unfamiliar corner. And that if he'd been a woman instead of a man, he would have asked her what to do, but if he weren't a man, she wouldn't want to kiss him—even when he drove her nuts. "Thank you for coming to Pamela's with me," she said. "Men and women may be from different planets, as the famous book proclaims, but there are times when it's nice to have a guy along."

"You're welcome," Eric muttered. "Hey, did you pick up my flashlight?"

"No."

He frowned. "I left it in the kitchen."

"I hope you didn't leave that piece you're carrying in the kitchen," Jenifer said.

"Good point," Eric said, pulling to the side of the street. He pulled the snub-nosed revolver from his pants pocket, leaned over and put it in the glove compartment.

"That's a very small gun," Jenifer said. "Hammerless, too. I bet it would fit real sweet in an ankle holster."

"Very observant," Eric said, making no move to swing back onto the road. "It's nice that you're not afraid of handguns."

"Now that's a compliment I can appreciate," Jenifer said. "I take it you have a permit to carry a concealed weapon?"

He nodded and smiled and stretched out his right arm along the back of the seat. "You're a different sort of woman, you know that?"

"Mmm," Jenifer said, unwilling to agree or disagree. His fingertips grazed the top of her shoulder.

He'd stopped about seven blocks from Pamela's house, heading out of town, rather than going back to her house, due to the wrong turn he'd taken. She glanced out the window and recognized the sprawling oak and tree swing that had adorned the front of Mrs. Kirtley's house since she had first bicycled down these streets as a gap-toothed six-year-old. Well, sad to say, but these days Mrs. Kirtley had little hearing or sight left, so if Eric intended to kiss her, parked in front of this particular house, he'd picked a pretty good spot. By accident, of course.

"So how long have you known Ace?"

The question came from left field. She swung her head back toward Eric. Wouldn't you know it, she sat there drooling and he wanted to talk about Ace. Pamela said she had sex appeal, and her friend seemed a good judge, but at this moment she had to doubt her friend's perception. Why, if it had been Pamela, Eric probably would have had his arm all the way around her shoulder by now, pulling her close, tipping her chin up, smiling into her eyes.

"Did you meet him before the wedding or after the blessed event?" Eric prompted, curious as to the answer, feeling his way through the coincidences he'd begun to note.

"After," she said, making a face. "Pamela knew I would have tied her down rather than let her walk to the altar with him."

"Is it because he drives a truck?" He didn't think that would be her answer.

"I have nothing but respect for hardworking truck drivers," Jenifer said. "Do you know that trucks carry seventy-one percent of goods moved within the United States?"

"I didn't know that," Eric said gravely. If Jenifer wanted a new career, she could apply in Washington. She could probably recite half the contents of the Library of Congress.

"Well, it's true. At least as of two weeks ago, when I

checked the statistics. My problem with Ace stems from his lack of grace."

"That's an interesting expression. What does it mean?" He circled his fingertips along the line where her shoulder rounded into the curve of her upper arm, skimming, scarcely touching. He didn't want to scare her away.

"Remember what Justice Potter Stewart said about obscenity; that he couldn't define it but he knew it when he saw it. It's like that. I know grace when I see it and I know when I don't see it."

"To say you're different doesn't do you justice, Jenifer," Eric said. "Fascinating."

She laughed lightly, as if shrugging off the compliment. "Librarians have a lot of time to read."

"Reading alone doesn't create perception."

"Ooh, well, I do agree with that."

She couldn't be involved with Lars and Franco, he thought. She'd know in two seconds flat neither one of them possessed an ounce of grace. So why two meetings with them? Why not brush them off with a polite nod? She'd said it had to do with finding a buyer for the Horace House. He'd get to know her better and the truth would reveal itself. "So Ms. Wright, tell me more about being a librarian."

She'd tipped her head back against the leather cushion of the headrest. Her eyes had half closed. "Come in on Monday and I'll let you spend the day," she said.

"What, no facts on file on your fingertips?" He smiled as he asked the question, shifting closer. He'd intended to drive her straight home, but since he'd gotten turned around driving and didn't feel like admitting it, it seemed a much preferred course to park and see how things progressed.

"Oh, I have them right here," she said, tapping one finger against her forehead. "For once I don't feel like reciting them."

Eric lifted his hand from her shoulder and traced a line across her forehead. He shifted so he could kiss her easily by dipping his chin. "Always thinking," he murmured. "Too beautiful to wear out your pretty little head."

Her eyes flashed open. "Thinking doesn't wear me out. A mind isn't like a tire; it doesn't lose tread from mileage."

He kept up his gentle stroking of the smooth skin of her face. "Maybe not, but there are some things that are good for it, just the way changing oil and getting a tune-up are good for a car."

"Well, that's logical," she said. "Like what?"

"Mmm," Eric said, "let me see . . . massage, for one." He circled her temples, now using both his hands, rotating his thumbs gently and stroking the sides of her head with his fingertips.

"Ah," Jenifer sighed. "My mind feels better already. What else is on your prescription pad?"

He could kiss her now. The feel and scent of her had him hungry for much more. He traced the line of her jaw with his thumb, gently outlining her lips.

They parted. Her eyes drifted closed and she tipped her face upward.

Eric lowered his mouth—

"Get out of the car now! With your hands up!" The voice echoed from a megaphone, careening from outside the car, coming from the direction of the yard with the huge tree.

"Jesus!" Eric leaped back. "Is that one of your brothers?"

"You two little twerps had better do what I tell you to," the voice demanded.

Jenifer shook her head, and lifting her hands over her head, said, "That's Mrs. Kirtley! I thought she couldn't see or hear enough to notice we were parked in front of her house. But she wouldn't hesitate to shoot an intruder. We'd better do exactly as she says!"

Eight

Jenifer stepped out of Eric's car, torn between cursing Mrs. Kirtley for her untimely interruption and blessing her for stopping her before she made a fool out of herself. She held her arms raised above her shoulders, glancing around the hood of the car to see if Eric had taken the elderly woman's instructions to heart.

He walked forward as boldly as you please, his hands at his sides.

"Eric!" Jenifer stage-whispered his name, jerking her head to where the octogenarian stood beside the picturesque tree swing, weaving from side to side as she wrestled with the weight of a BB gun in one hand and an ear trumpet in the other.

"It's only a pellet gun," he said, in a conversational tone. "Did you say she's deaf?"

"Speak up," Mrs. Kirtley cried.

Lights in the houses on either side flickered on. A door opened across the street.

"Now we're done for," Jenifer said with a groan. "Mrs. Kirtley, it's Jenifer Wright!" she yelled.

"Is that so?" Mrs. Kirtley called. She lowered the trumpet and adjusted the glasses perched on the end of her nose. From down the street a dog barked, then a hound bayed, and another dog somewhere in the distance joined in with a howl, till Jenifer felt like someone must have opened the doors to the brand new Doolittle Animal Shelter.

"Yes, Mrs. Kirtley," Jenifer called, her hands still raised. She glared at Eric, who was leaning against the hood of the car, a huge grin on his face.

"You won't think it's so funny when she puts some of those BB's in your butt," she said.

"If you're Jeni Wright, then which one of your brothers is that with you?" The older woman weaved and bobbed, as if trying to focus on Eric.

"Uh, he's not my brother," Jenifer answered.

"Eh? I can't hear you."

Eric snickered. "And to think I thought I'd be bored silly in Arkansas," he murmured.

"Oh, you did, did you?" Jenifer dropped her arms and whirled on him. "Well, I'll have you know that none of this would have happened if you had asked for directions."

"What are you talking about?"

"Back there on Persimmon Street, when you turned left and you should have turned right. I saw you hesitate, but no. Oh no, you had to act as if you knew right from left and then you took us the wrong way and pulled over 'cause no doubt you didn't want to admit you had no idea in the heck where you were, and then you—you—started to kiss me!"

"And if this crazy old lady wasn't holding a gun on us, I would have gone on kissing you!" Eric crossed his arms on his chest. "Do you have a problem with that?"

Jenifer touched her lips with her fingertips. Did she? "Yes. No. I mean—"

"Which one is it?" His voice was practically a growl. "Maybe I should kiss you again to help you decide."

Darn if she didn't almost pucker up, despite the presence of the gun-toting Mrs. Kirtley. Then she noticed he'd tilted his head, lowered his chin, obviously ready to kiss her.

He assumed she wanted him to.

And he was right.

But what came easy, she thought, just might not be appreciated. Stifling her desire, she said primly, "I think we should pay attention to Mrs. Kirtley, don't you?"

Before he could answer, Mrs. Kirtley demanded their notice. "That can't be Jennie Wright if you're with a man and he's not your brother," the old lady said, "and I know he's not your father 'cause I went to his funeral, so who in the blue blazes are you?" Mrs. Kirtley raised the rifle, and yelled, "I've called the cops, so don't try and run."

"Great," Jenifer muttered. She started walking forward, moving up the sidewalk that led to the picket fence surrounding the yard of Mrs. Kirtley's house. What was taking a pellet compared to serving as the laughingstock of the Doolittle police force, which consisted of two of her brothers, her uncle Pete, one of Uncle Pete's daughters, and one second cousin twice removed? "It's Jenifer," she yelled again. "You used to teach my Sunday school class! You taught us the be-attitudes." Wondering what Eric would think of this recitation, she called out, "Blessed are the poor in spirit! Blessed are the meek! Blessed are the merciful! Blessed are the pure in heart! Blessed are the peace-makers! Blessed are they which are persecuted! See, Mrs. Kirtley, it has to be Jenifer Wright. Nobody else would remember Matthew 5:3-10."

Eric was looking at her as if she'd started speaking in tongues—which to him, Jenifer realized, she probably had.

The rifle dropped to the grass. "Well, thank goodness," Mrs. Kirtley said. "I sometimes wonder if any of my children paid attention all those years. And I thought you and that man were a house invader. Terrible people, not blessed at all. Come in and sit a spell."

Jenifer glanced around. Eric, to give him credit, had followed her up the sidewalk, no doubt prepared to fling himself in front of her should Mrs. Kirtley have tried to empty the chamber of her BB gun into her tender body.

"What is that megaphone?" he asked, covering one of his ears.

"It's an ear trumpet," Jenifer said. "Rather old-fashioned, but fairly effective. Thomas Edison invented the modern version, though someone made one for Beethoven. They've pretty much fallen out of use, with the advent of modern hearing aid technology."

"Which no doubt you can provide a lecture describing," Eric said.

"Speak up," commanded Mrs. Kirtley. "Or use my foghorn." She chuckled. "Jeni Wright. I can't believe you actually came to call. I don't get many visitors anymore." She waved the ear trumpet. "People think I can't hear. It drives 'em nuts. Thing is, they're probably nuts anyway. I just help them see their reflection."

"Very wise," Jenifer shouted.

"Everything okay over there?" called a voice from across the street.

"Sure," Eric called.

"Let me hear from Mrs. Kirtley," yelled the neighbor.

"Mrs. Kirtley?" Jenifer prompted. "Your neighbor wants to make sure we're friendly visitors and not burglars."

"Why'd you go and say that?" Eric whispered.

"Why not? Mrs. Kirtley said it first," Jenifer answered.

Jenifer heard a siren, not too far in the distance. Way, way too close for comfort. "Yell out that you're fine, Mrs. Kirtley, okay?"

"Okay, Jeni," she said. "I am fine, Mr. Hubert," she hollered across the yard. "Thank you for caring. May the Good Lord bless you!"

"Let's go in the house," Jenifer said loudly. Thankfully, the siren had ceased abruptly. No doubt another concerned neighbor had called off the patrol officer. Since she risked a good chance of being embarrassed in front of a relative, Jenifer could only feel relief.

"Good idea," Mrs. Kirtley said. "I made a batch of elderberry wine that's just itching to be tasted." She clumped up the sidewalk and up the stairs to her front porch. Jenifer walked on one side and Eric on the other. At the front door, Eric said, "She left the gun on the grass. I'll go get it."

"What's that?" Mrs. Kirtley said.

"I'll be right back," Eric shouted.

"I still can't place which brother of yours that is," Mrs. Kirtley said as Jenifer followed her into the house. "Did you have one who skipped Sunday school?"

Eric retreated to the sanity of the front yard. Most of the lights that had been turned on had gone to black. Retracing Mrs. Kirtley's path, he found the BB gun lying in the dewy grass. He opened the chamber to check it for ammunition, and as he did, felt the unmistakable shape of a gun barrel pressing against his fifth cervical vertebra.

"Drop it." The voice was a high-pitched tenor, and vaguely familiar.

Eric complied, glancing to the house as he did.

"Don't even think of running inside that old lady's house," the man behind his head said. "I've got you dead in my aim."

"I can explain," Eric said, his tone mild, considering the circumstances. He figured the officers in Doolittle didn't shoot to kill, and the male relatives of Jenifer's whom he'd met earlier that day seemed fairly levelheaded. But if the barrel stayed etched against his neck much longer, he stood to have bruises to rival Pamela's.

"That your car in front of this house?"

Eric started to nod but thought better of it. "Yes, sir," he said. "Say, which one of Jenifer's relations are you?"

"Which Jenifer? I know a couple. Let's see, there's Jenifer Graham and Jenifer Gordon and Jenifer Thiel."

"Wright," Eric said.

"I'm not related to Jenifer Thiel. I am friends with her sons, though." The barrel prodded his flesh. "Are you aiming to distract me?"

"Wright, I mean, no, wrong. You know, W-R-I-G-H-T. Are you related to Jenifer Wright?"

"Oh, her," the voice said. "Yeah, but we call her Miss Jenifer Janey."

"Good," Eric said, curious about it, but not prepared to inquire right now. "I've dropped the gun, and if you like, I can even kick it away from my reach."

"Now don't get smart with me," the man said. "Some people may say I'm wet behind the ears, but I know a man caught in the act when I see one. What have you done with Jenifer Janey?"

"I haven't done anything with her," Eric said, reflecting that that sad state of affairs wasn't due to lack of trying. "We were on a date, parking, if you must know."

"Ho ho! Now I've caught you red-handed smack in a lie," the man said. "Everyone in Doolittle knows Miss Jenifer doesn't date anyone. I'm taking you in."

Several of the neighboring porch lights had snapped back on, including, Eric saw from the corner of his eye, one belonging to the esteemed Mrs. Kirtley. Jenifer appeared on the porch illuminated by the yellow bug light, and he thought he'd never seen a more beautiful sight. She shaded her eyes with her hand, and Eric realized she couldn't clearly see the scenario unfolding in front of her. Either that or she found it hard to believe.

"Hurry up, Eric," she said. "Mrs. Kirtley needs to get to bed."

"Yeah, well, so do I," Eric muttered. "Can't you see I'm deep in conversation?"

Fortunately, his sarcastic comment goaded her into advancing toward the porch steps.

"Randy Robert McDougal, what in the blazes do you think you're doing?" Her voice grew as she approached.

At least he'd drop the gun now, Eric thought.

Only he didn't. "What do you think I am doing, Miss Jenifer? I am detaining a prowler." He enunciated each word as if he'd practiced it many times.

"Randy Robert, I changed your diapers when you were ankle high to a grasshopper, and I want you to remember that when I tell you this man is not a prowler."

"Oh, darn."

The barrel unleashed its grip on the flesh of his neck. Eric listened carefully, and not until he heard the scrape of gun metal against leather holster did he slowly turn around. When he did, he stood toe-to-toe with the most baby-faced officer he'd ever seen in uniform. The officer rose two inches taller than his own six feet. Looking up at him, Eric couldn't quite get his mind around the image of Jenifer viewing this man's privates, even as an infant. "Thank you for the timely arrival, Tante Jenifer," Eric said.

"You're welcome," she said. "Surely the two of you could have worked out this situation without me."

"It's my first week on the force," Randy said. "I was thinking how cool it would be to catch a criminal. I'd be a hero."

"You're more likely to get fired for pulling your

weapon without sufficient justification to warrant the use of force," Jenifer said.

Eric lifted a brow. "Listen to the lady lawyer." He said it sarcastically, but she'd impressed him.

"I'm a librarian, not a lawyer," she snapped at him. "Now Randy, you'd best get back in your car and write a brief no-incident report, then continue on patrol."

"Yes, Miss Jenifer Janey," he said. To Eric, he said, "No hard feelings or nothing, right?"

Eric rubbed his neck. "Nah," he said. "Judgment grows with experience."

Randy pulled a small spiral notebook out of his pants pocket. "That sounds like something I ought to write down and study," he said. "Could you repeat that for me?"

Eric humored him. Jenifer stood there watching him, practically tapping her toe. As soon as he finished spelling *experience* for Officer Randy, he asked permission to retrieve the BB gun, which Randy granted with a wave of his hand as he reread what he'd written.

Eric and Jenifer walked toward the house at last. Eric said in a low voice, "You changed his diapers?"

She shrugged. "He's the same age as my twins. I baby-sat him from the time he was six months old till about age three 'cause his mom had to go back to work on the night shift at the paper mill. And let me tell you, when it comes to the environment versus heredity question, I come down hard on the side of heredity." She sighed. "He means well, but neither one of his parents were the sharpest pencils in the jar."

Eric smiled. "You have a way with words," he said, holding open the screen door for her.

"And you! 'Judgment comes with experience.'" She smiled, and said, "Thanks for not cussing him out. Most men who'd had a gun plastered in the back of their neck would have ripped him up one side and down the other."

"Yeah, after they knew they were safe," Eric said. "No point. I know what it's like to be young and unsure of oneself."

"I can't even picture that," she said.

"Picture tube?" Mrs. Kirtley said, coming around a corner and into the front room. "There's nothing on the TV this time of night. Believe me, I know." She carried a small tray that held three crystal dessert glasses. "Now where did I put the wine?" She looked around, knocked into the coffee table, and then settled the tray there. "Be right back," she said. "Sit yourselves down."

Jenifer sneaked a sideways look at Eric. She hated to disappoint Mrs. Kirtley, yet found it hard to believe Eric really wanted to sit in this stuffy room crammed with the relics of the years Mrs. Kirtley had reigned over the Sunday school classes at Doolittle Community Church.

He appeared to be fascinated by the dimly lit room, staring around him like a six-year-old at Toys 'R' Us. Walking around a curved-leg side table, he passed another table, supported by legs with snarling gryphons, and approached the mantel of the marble fireplace. "Would you look at these?"

Jenifer tiptoed over, careful not to bump into the stacks of hymnals and vinyl records piled against the high-backed sofa.

Eric pointed to a clutter of snow globes, each filled

with a different scene. "My grandmother had a lot of these," he said. "Look at this one. It's a miniature zoo. See the house of reptiles squeezed in next to the elephants?"

His fascination with the globes intrigued Jenifer. And the fact that when they'd asked about his family, he hadn't mentioned a grandmother, which told Jenifer she had passed away. "Do you miss your grandmother?" she asked.

"Hmm?" He swiveled his head, a distant look in his dark eyes. "I do," he said softly. "Grandmother Hamilton collected these globes. My happiest childhood memories are my visits to see her."

"Did she live close by?"

He shook his head. "Oh, now this one is amazing." He bent his head toward the mantel. "It's a desert scene with sand instead of snow."

"That's a crèche," Jenifer said. "Don't forget, Mrs. Kirtley is religious."

"Now where have I heard that term before?" Eric cast his expression toward the flocked wallpaper on the wall above the mantel. "Crash, cresh . . ."

"A crèche is a representation of the Nativity scene in Bethlehem," Jenifer said severely. "Though to be accurate, it can also mean a nursery."

Eric transferred his stare from the wallpaper to her face. "I'm kidding," he said gently.

"Oh," Jenifer said. "Right, I knew you were kidding. I mean, who doesn't know a crèche from a crash?"

In the distance a distinctive crash, of glass and crockery, sounded.

"Oh, dear," Jenifer said. "Let me go help Mrs. Kirtley."

"I'll go, too," he said.

She'd already turned and stepped over a basket filled with skeins of yarn. "I wonder if she sees better than she lets on," Jenifer murmured.

Eric reached down, picked up the pale blue yarn on top, ran his eye over it and said, "Nope."

"Now how can you tell by looking at the yarn?" Jenifer stopped, hands on hips, and Eric stepped over until he stood by her side.

"Look," he said, touching her shoulder. She savored the warmth of his hand for that fleeting moment. "The price tag," he said. "If I'm not mistaken, Kresge's went out of business years ago, and it's been a while since yarn cost twenty-nine cents a skein. There's also a layer of dust on the whole thing, so chances are that she's done no knitting for a number of years. And there's a magnifying glass next to the large print Bible."

"I'm impressed," she said. "You have some excellent deductive reasoning skills."

He grinned. "So I've been told."

Another crash sounded, and Jenifer hurried toward it. With Eric right behind her, she cleared the living room, dashed past the dining room, then halted in the doorway of the kitchen.

"Well, if that don't beat all," Mrs. Kirtley said. She stared from a spreading pool of a deep, sweet purple-black liquid to a welter of broken dishes scattered over the counter next to the stove. "All I did was open the cupboard and it all fell out." She sighed and turned vaguely in the direction of Jenifer and Eric. "I reckon my grandchildren are right. This house is just too much for me to keep up."

She turned, and if Eric hadn't moved with the speed of a sprinter and caught her gently by the arm, Mrs. Kirtley would have stepped into the wine seeping its way across the graying linoleum floor.

"Do your grandchildren live in Doolittle, Mrs. Kirtley?" He spoke loudly, and as he asked the question, he pulled out a vinyl-covered kitchen chair from a wobbly looking metal table packed with old newspapers and *Guidepost* magazines. Atop the stack sat a faded red leather Bible.

"Not anymore," she said. "They both went off to Houston."

Jenifer glanced around in search of paper towels or rags to stanch the flow of the elderberry wine. Not seeing any, she helped herself to some old issues of *Ladies Home Journal*. She hoped they weren't a collectors' item, but right now she needed to do something about the mess.

"Houston?" Eric shook his head, as if saddened by the treachery of her grandchildren.

He must have said exactly the right thing, because Mrs. Kirtley smiled and patted him on the arm.

"Never been there myself," she said, folding her hands in her lap. "Don't think I'd like it."

Leaving Eric to entertain their hostess, Jenifer fashioned a dam out of the pages of the *Journal* and used some other pages to scoop as much as she could up and into the sink. Her hands grew sticky and stained with purple, as Eric, leaning against the kitchen table, favored Mrs. Kirtley with everything wrong with the state of Texas, its chief flaw being the cities were so big that it took so long to get from work to home that grandchildren never could find time to drive all the way to Arkansas.

Jenifer's heart went out to the elderly woman. Her faded cotton dress looked as if she'd slept in it, but despite the late hour, Mrs. Kirtley was not only garbed in street clothing, but also wore stockings and lace-up black shoes. It was almost as if she'd been sitting there, waiting for someone to visit.

As much as she sympathized with Mrs. Kirtley, she admired Eric's skillful handling of her even more. His deep voice carried easily when he raised it so Mrs. Kirtley could hear him, and he seemed to know just what to say. Jenifer didn't begrudge her job as the clean-up crew one whit, not while watching Eric leaning forward, his eyes intent on Mrs. Kirtley, practically doting on her, making her happy for one evening.

He had magic about him. Just as he was doing with Mrs. Kirtley, he'd made her feel special, and he hadn't done more than talk, and listen, and almost, almost, almost kiss her.

Jenifer sighed and dropped a wad of magazine pages into a trashcan crammed under the kitchen sink. She'd speak to the ladies at the Community Church about offering to come clean on a regular basis for Mrs. Kirtley.

"What's your recipe?" Eric was asking.

"No, I don't need a receipt," Mrs. Kirtley said.

"Rec-i-pe," Eric said, slowly and a little louder. "For the wine."

She slapped him lightly on the arm and wagged a finger at him. "Oh, no you don't, young man. No one's wangled my secret out of me in all these years, and not even your sweet-talking ways can pull it out of me." She smiled, and patted the bun at the back of her neck. "Not that I don't thank you for asking. An old lady likes to be flattered almost as much as a young one." She looked around, her eyes darting this way and that. "Jenifer Janey Wright, where have you run off to?"

"Right here, Mrs. Kirtley," Jenifer shouted, now down on her hands and knees. She'd found a shriveled fossil of a sponge under the sink. She swiped the sticky linoleum and rinsed the sponge in the sink, cleaning one section of the faded floor at a time.

"Come sit with your brother and me," Mrs. Kirtley said. "He's awful nice for a young man who skipped Sunday school. I reckon your mama must be proud of him."

Eric smiled down at Mrs. Kirtley. "I'm actually going to church tomorrow," he said.

"You're what?"

"Tomorrow I'm going to church."

She shook her head. "No, not tomorrow you're not."

Eric looked surprised.

Jenifer stifled a grin. Mrs. Kirtley had a way of getting Eric all wrapped around his words. She rose and rinsed the sponge one last time. "Mrs. Kirtley," she said, approaching the woman, "he is going to church tomorrow."

Mrs. Kirtley started laughing and shaking her head. "Oh, no," she said, "'cause tomorrow never comes!"

Eric laughed along with the elderly woman, then glanced over at Jenifer. He realized his mouth had dropped open, because she was looking at him questioningly. "What's wrong?" she said in a low voice.

She had purple stains on the tip of her nose, and dual splotches on her knees. He smiled, suppressing a laugh, and said, "Nothing."

Mrs. Kirtley stood up. "I'm glad you two youngsters came by tonight, but I can tell it's my bedtime. Maybe past my bedtime, so I'll say good night, if you don't mind. Sorry about the wine but I'll stir up another batch and you can come back over and have a glass with me. That is, if you have time."

She moved closer to Eric and peered up toward his face. "Would you do that?"

He nodded and took her hand, moved by her loneliness and her toughness of spirit in the face of the isolation that so obviously served as her only constant companion. "Just say when," he said.

"When," she said, and laughed at her own joke. "I'll let your sister know. Jenifer Janey, you still running the library?"

"Yes, Mrs. Kirtley."

"Good. Good girl." She leaned over and kissed Jenifer on the top of her head. "Say hi to that mama of yours. Did she tell you I taught her Sunday school, too?" Mrs. Kirtley sat back down in the kitchen chair and folded her hands in her lap.

Eric hesitated. Should they offer to help? Lock up? Jeez, who took care of this forgotten woman? He knew the answer to his question, but it seemed too sad to accept. But when he would have offered to turn out the lights or see her to her bedroom, she lifted a hand, and waved and said, "You two trot on home now."

Eric walked with Jenifer to his car, both of them

quiet. He slid behind the wheel, feeling as if six months had passed since his face had been poised above Jenifer's sweet lips. He looked at her and found her looking at him.

"Well," she said. "Well well." She rubbed the palms of her hands across her wine-stained knees. "That almost broke my heart."

"You and me both," he said softly. "I wouldn't be surprised if she grabbed that gun and came after us with the idea of having some company. She never seemed all that scared."

"Eric, you might be right! It's so sad, when she's taught half this town over several generations, that she's that lonely. But I've never gone to visit her."

"No, we don't, do we," he said, turning the key in the ignition. "Not even when they are our own grandmothers."

"How often did you see your snow globe grandmother?"

He shrugged and took a left at the corner, intending to retrace his moves back to where she'd said he made the wrong turn. "We went to see her every year at Thanksgiving. Grandmother Hamilton got Turkey Day, and Grandmother and Grandfather Willoughby usually came to see us on Christmas."

"And what about visiting your grandmother Hamilton made it the happiest times of your childhood?"

He tipped his head in acknowledgment of her good memory. "It was the only time my parents didn't argue constantly."

"Oh," Jenifer said. "Your parents weren't happy together but they didn't get a divorce?"

He laughed, a remnant of misery from years gone by. "They were both married to the family business. That's why they didn't argue around Grandmother Hamilton. She'd inherited control of the company when Grandpa died, and after one memorable dustup between my parents, she threatened both of them with the loss of the only thing they cared about if they didn't keep the peace."

"She sounds like quite a character."

Eric smiled. "Yes. Sometimes I think I inherited some of my bark from her."

"Oh, no," Jenifer said impishly, "you've no more bark about you than a . . ."

"Couldn't bring yourself to say pussy cat, could you?" He liked teasing her, liked the way she crinkled her forehead and then gave way to a gurgle of laughter.

"Not quite," she said. "It doesn't describe you."

Again he smiled. Darn, he'd done more of that tonight than he had in a long time. And to think all he'd wanted from Jenifer a few hours ago could be wrapped up in a few arousing kisses, a quick build-up of heated sensation till his body screamed with want and need and she moaned in ecstatic satisfaction, and he claimed his own hot, sweet, panting release.

That would have been that. As good as it would be, Eric realized he wanted more. Connection. Intimacy. Respect. He stole a sideways glance at her. She'd fallen quiet, and her eyes were half closed. He knew it was late enough now for anyone in her right mind to be sleepy, but watching her, remembering how she'd cleverly and competently taken care of the mess in Mrs. Kirtley's kitchen, he realized that respect and admiration mingled with his fully stoked desire. "I'm sorry I didn't help you clean up that wine," he said softly.

She shifted her face toward him. "Oh, no, you did the perfect thing. Mrs. Kirtley needed conversation and to be distracted from the loss." Jenifer smiled. "It's funny, but she'll never believe you're not one of my brothers."

He grinned. "As long as you know I'm not, that's all that matters."

Jenifer heard the warm undertone in his voice, and she shivered even as heat raced through her body. Ooh, no need to clarify any confusion on that point. She moistened her lips, remembering how she'd barely been able to breathe as he'd leaned closer and closer, claiming the air around her she'd always found necessary for life. But when he'd been about to kiss her, she'd discovered that all she needed existed within his lips, his tongue, his body pressing close against her own trembling self.

The car stopped.

Jenifer opened her eyes, only then realizing she'd closed them when she slipped into her heated moment of fantasy. "What are you doing?"

He stared straight ahead, his jaw working.

"Is something wrong?"

He cleared his throat, studied his hands gripping the steering wheel. "I, er . . . there's something I want to ask you."

Whatever could it be? Jenifer leaned forward, her body half turned to face him. "What is it, Eric?"

"Could you give me one—"

What did he want from her? To spend the night? To

go back to his hotel? "Just say it, Eric." Her heart had picked up speed. He wanted her, she knew that, and despite her sadness over Mrs. Kirtley's loneliness, and being covered in the sticky residue of elderberry wine, she wanted nothing more than to fling herself at him. Just anticipating that he wanted to ask her to . . . ooh, heaven had paid a visit to earth, right here in Doolittle.

"One little hint as to where in the hell I am?" He said it all in a rush, the words exploding out of his mouth. Then he turned toward her, a lopsided grin on his charming face. "There. I've said it."

She couldn't believe her ears. She tried replaying the last few minutes, wondering which one of them had lost touch with reality. Clearly, she had. "Directions?" She sat up straight, shoulders pressed against the back of the leather seat. "You want directions?"

He nodded.

"Okay, I'll give you directions. Go straight till you reach the next stop sign, and when you have stopped at that intersection, I'll give you more directions." What had happened to kissing?

"Could you not say that word in every sentence?"

She boiled. She fumed. She wore embarrassment in every purple-stained pore of her body. Had he lost interest in her that quickly? "Sure. I'll say 'directions' only in every other sentence."

He winced. "Look, at least I asked."

"Yes, you did," she said, nodding briskly, wondering why she kept making such a fool out of herself over this man—even if all the foolishness did go on inside her head and he didn't have a clue, of course, as to how much she'd built him up as a role player in her very overheated fantasies. "You did ask for directions. No doubt for the first time in your life."

"Damn straight," he said. "I think you'd be more appreciative of the effort it cost me, too."

"Right. I mean, turn right." She made a point of studying the darkened terrain outside the passenger window. "Appreciative?" She muttered the word, then repeated it, louder the second time.

He jerked to a halt at a four-way stop, keeping his eyes fixed on the road ahead.

Jenifer counted to three. Insufferable man. He should have been thinking of kissing her, not swallowing his pride over something so simple as asking which way to turn. "Go straight," she said.

He nodded and followed her instructions, saying not a word during the brief drive to her house.

Once there, he pulled to the curb and turned toward her. "I know you don't understand my reaction," he said.

Jenifer nodded. "It's only dir—"

He cut her off with a kiss. Her gasp of surprise got lost in the heat of his lips on hers. He didn't ask. He took. He claimed. He caught the back of her head and pulled her into his grasp, savaging her mouth.

Jenifer whimpered, then moaned, kissing him back, wrapping her arms around his neck, pressing against the restraint of the seat belt in an effort to get as close to him as possible. This kiss was what she'd wanted for hours. She fumbled for the clasp of her seat belt.

And then he broke away. "Out."

"What?" She quivered all over. She wanted him to kiss her like that all night long. "What did you say?"

Eric leaned across her and yanked open the passenger door. "Go home. Get out. I'd walk you to the door, but I wouldn't stop there." Then he anchored his hands to the steering wheel.

"Of all the rude, insensitive—"

"That's right. Curse me. Just get out now before you're lying naked beneath me."

She caught her breath. Did he mean that? So he wasn't upset over the directions? He wanted Jenifer Janey Wright. She almost leaned over and risked another kiss. She didn't understand why he was being so honorable and not following her inside. That was okay, though. There was always tomorrow.

All dignity, she freed her seat belt and stepped from his car. "Sweet dreams," she said, blowing him a kiss and waltzing up her sidewalk. When she reached her front door, she turned around. The hungry expression on his face did her a great deal of good.

Nine

*E*ric woke up Sunday morning about as grouchy as he could ever remember being. Not only did he still have a hard-on, he'd barely slept. What with tossing and turning as he replayed the sweetness of her lips and her heated response to his kiss in the car, and beating himself up for not speaking up about being the prospective buyer for the Horace House, he couldn't have logged more than a few winks of shut-eye.

Driving toward Pete and Jenifer's houses, her precisely issued directions echoing in his head, Eric decided the best adjective for his mood had to be grouchy. His mood was no doubt most directly attributable to his state of extreme sexual frustration. Arousal alternated with verbal sparring had raw oysters beaten hands down as an aphrodisiac. Sex. He had to quit thinking of sex.

He would not give in to Jenifer Wright even if she were dolled up in that teasing wisp of black chiffon he'd sneaked a peek of at Pamela's house. Just remembering how little that outfit did to conceal the tantalizing flesh and curves and mysteries—and knowing he had every reason in the world to ignore her considerable charms—made Eric even grouchier.

Pulling to the curb in front of Pete's house, he fervently wished he'd never agreed to attend church.

He'd finally slept around dawn, and if not for this appointed hour, he still could be asleep, one of the motel's lumpy pillows plastered across his head to drown out the light that insisted on streaming through the skimpy cheap drapes that didn't quite cover the room's solitary window.

Eric threw the car into park. Pete, coffee mug in hand, waved from his front porch.

No sign of Jenifer. Surely she'd appear? Eric had gotten the impression they would all go to church in one big happy group.

Last night's gathering certainly had pointed out to him the emptiness of his own usual existence. Well, now wasn't the time to psychoanalyze himself. Leaving his car, he waved a greeting to Pete and then joined him on the porch. He welcomed the opportunity to explain that he was the prospective buyer for the Horace House who they'd been discussing the night before. He should have come out with it then and there. Any further delay and they'd look at him askance, wondering why he hadn't been up-front with them.

Undercover 101. Keep your stories straight, Hamilton, he chided himself silently, even as he shook hands with Pete.

"Morning, Eric," Pete said, his cheerful voice ringing out loud enough for Jenifer to hear in the house next door. "Can I get you some coffee?" The man peered at him. "You look like you could use some caffeine."

Eric grinned. "Yes, sir, I could."

"Long night?" Pete asked, opening the door and motioning Eric into the house.

His voice was just a mite too casual. Eric shrugged. "Hard to sleep in a strange motel bed."

"They've got feather beds at the Schoolhouse Inn," Pete said. "Let me know if you decide to move. How do you take your coffee?"

"Black, one sugar," Eric said, glancing around the kitchen where he'd been last night with Jenifer. All the mess had been cleaned away. Not a sign of the cookout remained. "Thanks for including me last night. You must have had quite the cleanup crew in here."

Pete set the coffee carafe back onto its stand. "Charlotte and I sent everyone else home, not too long after you left. We took care of it together."

Eric smiled slightly, picturing the two of them kissing and snuggling between rounds of washing and drying dishes. A tinge of envy nipped at him. He wasn't sure he could explain what had started going round and round in his brain, but he wanted what Pete and Charlotte had with one another.

"Let's go outside," Pete said, leading the way. "There's no place like a man's own front porch to sit on a Sunday morning."

Back home in Virginia, Eric didn't have a porch. He

had a balcony, some forty floors above an eight-lane expressway. But it was a good balcony, as he owned one of the penthouse suites in his condominium complex. "Sure," he said, following his host.

"The others will be ready in a few minutes," Pete said, settling onto one of the oversized rocking chairs. "We're close to the church, and I never see much reason to get there much ahead of the preacher."

Eric took one of the other chairs and sipped his coffee. "Makes sense to me. Look, there's something I want to—"

Pete's cell phone rang. He unclipped it from his belt and answered it. After a few words, he closed it. "Sorry about that," he said. "One of the officers had a question about his report from last night."

Eric would have bet Randy Robert had been on the other end of that call, but he refrained from asking.

"How was Jenifer after she left last night?" Pete said.

"How was she about what?"

Pete sighed. "Lord knows I miss my wife, but with a woman who's also one of my best friends, I'd have to be dead to walk away from her. But I know the idea of me and Charlotte doesn't sit well with Jenifer."

"Maybe it just needs more time," Eric said, wondering how they'd gotten into this conversational train when he'd intended to direct the discussion to the Horace House.

"Time's a funny thing," Pete said, a distant look in his eyes. He gazed out over the porch railing, giving Eric the feeling that Pete had forgotten all about his presence. "You think it's endless. That there will always be a tomorrow. And then, bam, the world stops turning and the woman you love isn't there anymore. No time for that vacation you were putting off till the next summer. No time to finish that argument you'd started at the breakfast table." He cleared his throat and turned back toward Eric. "Well, that's sorrow talking, young man. But if I learned one thing from losing my wife like that, I learned tomorrow isn't always there. So, no, I'm not waiting for Jenifer to accept me loving her mother. Acceptance will come or it won't. Now what was that you wanted to say to me?"

Eric stared into his coffee, his jaw working. He lived for tomorrow. Next case, next thrill, next woman to pursue. "It's about the Horace House."

A door opened and closed next door at Charlotte's house. She stepped outside, pretty in a pale blue skirt and jacket. She waved and started walking toward them.

"What about it?" Pete asked the question, but clearly had eyes only for Charlotte. His smile grew broader as she came closer.

"I'm thinking of . . ." Eric trailed off.

Pete wasn't listening. He rose to take Charlotte's hand. He kissed her on the cheek, then offered her his chair. Then Pete leaned against the porch railing, looking every bit like a teenager gazing at his first crush.

"Good morning," Eric said, also rising.

"And good morning to you, too," Charlotte said. "I see Jenifer is the only sleepyhead in the group. Why don't you run next door and see if she's almost ready?"

Well, he might as well, for all the good he was accomplishing on Pete's porch. Eric set his coffee mug on a small table. "Why don't I do that?"

Just then Jenifer stuck her head out her front door. She held a phone in one hand. "I'm running late," she called. "I'm on the phone with Autumn, so why don't you all go on to church without me?"

Without waiting for a response, she disappeared.

Eric sat back down.

"You're welcome to come with us," Charlotte said.

Eric smiled. So Jenifer thought she could sidestep him that easily? "You two run along," he said. "I'll finish my coffee and wait for Jenifer."

"Great idea," Pete said, giving him a man-to-man wink Eric could have done without. "Help yourself if you want more."

"Does anybody in Doolittle lock their doors?"

Pete shook his head. "Probably not. But who's going to break into the house of the chief of police? Would have to be a pretty stupid criminal." He clasped Charlotte's hand. "Ready?"

She smiled at him. They walked down the steps, got into the blue sedan in the driveway, and drove away.

Eric pushed against the porch floor and set his rocker into gentle motion. It was peaceful here on the porch. He sighed. A man could get used to this kind of life. He closed his eyes. Birds chirped in the trees in the yard. A lawn mower sounded in the distance, so at least one Doolittle citizen was playing hooky from church. His breathing deepened. The chair rocked more slowly. Sleep tiptoed in.

Next door, Jenifer told her daughter for the third

time that she loved and missed her. Finally, Autumn had had enough mothering, and laughingly insisted she had to run. She and her friends were playing flag football on the quad.

After putting down the phone, Jenifer stood in her living room, listening to her silent house. She'd not gotten used to the emptiness since her twins had left for school. "Well, what do you expect?" She asked the question out loud. They hadn't been gone a full month.

She gave herself both a physical and mental shake, then ran lightly up the stairs to slip out of her robe and into her dress and pumps. Three minutes and she was ready. Pulling a brush through her long, thick hair, she headed down to the first floor. She'd been late on purpose, as she preferred to go alone, rather than face her mother, Uncle Pete, and Eric Hamilton. The first two caused her such unsettled emotional feelings. And Eric, well, he drove her crazy with both desire and frustration.

Pleased with having sent them on their way, Jenifer collected her purse and keys and stepped outside. She'd made it halfway to her Saturn wagon when she spotted the man on Uncle Pete's porch.

Not just any man.

Eric.

Eric with his eyes closed, his head leaning against the high-backed rocker, the first peaceful expression she'd seen on his handsome face.

Not that she had much to judge by, she reminded herself as she turned away from her car and stepped closer to where Eric sat. She'd met him only the day before, after all.

Funny how it seemed much longer than that.

"Hey," she said softly.

He didn't stir.

Well, well, Jenifer thought, easing into the matching rocking chair. Perhaps he'd gotten as little sleep the night before as she had. Annoying man, kissing her into frenzy, then practically pushing her from the car! She lay her head against the high-backed rocker, thinking how much nicer it was outside on a beautiful fall day like today than being cooped up in the confines of the Doolittle Community Church.

Of course Eric hadn't gone docilely along to church with Uncle Pete and her mother. Oh, no, that would have been too cooperative of him.

Still, instead of being annoyed, she felt a ripple of pleasure. He'd waited for her.

She smiled and let her hands fall to her sides. How nice that he'd thought of her.

"I'm awake," Eric said, his eyes still closed.

She jumped.

He opened his eyes a bit. "Sorry. Didn't mean to frighten you," he said. "But if it looked like I was sleeping, you were mistaken."

"You had your eyes closed and you didn't stir when I walked onto the porch, but you weren't asleep?" Jenifer stared at him, remembering in a rush just how contrarily he'd reacted to her driving directions last night. "Right."

He nodded. "A good man doesn't get caught off guard."

"Or at least he never admits to it?"

Eric grinned, stretching his arms lazily over his head.

What a picture he made. She could feel the strength in his arms by the graceful way he moved, even though he wore a crisp dress shirt and slacks.

He rose, his eyes half smiling down at her, as if he could read her mind. "Time to go?"

She'd rarely felt less like going to church. "I guess so."

"Tell you what," Eric said, standing next to her on the top step. "Why don't you drive?"

"So you won't have to listen to me giving directions?" She smiled as she asked the question.

His answer was another one of those slow grins that she felt from the tips of her toes upward through her body. How did the man do it? Jenifer waved the car keys she held in her hand. "Let's go."

He had to set the passenger seat farther back to make room for his long legs. Glancing around, he said, "You keep a neat car."

"Thank you," she said primly. "I noticed you're driving a rental car. What's your usual set of wheels?"

"A Beemer, and I confess it often looks like a traveling suitcase."

She wondered if he kept changes of clothing in case he got lucky when out on a date. "I find it's easier to put things away before they build up," she said. Gosh, how boring she sounded. She backed the car out of the driveway, searching her brain for something cute to say.

Eric stretched his arm across the seat backs. "I imagine librarians have to think that way."

"It helps." Jeez, the conversation had gone from bad to worse. How was she supposed to tempt this hunk when she acted and sounded like a nerdy maid/house-keeper? Yet, that kiss last night . . . she touched her lips with the tip of one pinky finger.

"Ah," Eric said, "I was wondering if you remembered last night."

She blushed. Jerked to a halt at a stop sign. Looking carefully to the left and then to the right, she saw no traffic, but the gleam in Eric's eyes was unmistakable. Suddenly, Jenifer knew she couldn't go to church, not and sit beside this man. No, she needed to do something out of character, give in to the free-spirited impulses she so rarely heeded.

"I remember," she said. "Would you mind if we don't go to church?"

Eric heard what Jenifer said, but at first thought he'd heard her wrong. He couldn't believe his good luck. But casually, he said, "Fine by me. As long as Pete and Charlotte won't wonder what happened to us." As soon as he said that, he realized those two would have eyes only for one another. Kind of the way he felt about the woman sitting next to him.

Though he had to keep his interest within professional bounds. But the more he got to know her, the better for his investigation. Yeah, right, Hamilton.

"Let's drive to the lake. There's a place there that I think of as my own private church. It's almost a cathedral. And it's such a beautiful day . . ."

Eric touched her on the shoulder. "Jenifer, you don't have to explain so much. Thank you for offering to share it with me."

She nodded, her eyes on the road as she took a turn onto a road leading past the outskirts of town. They drove in silence for a few miles before she broke the companionable quiet with, "Too bad we're not driving your Beemer. You'd probably have a spare pair of shoes and maybe swim trunks."

"Probably a raft or two," he added. "And enough leftover candy bars and trail mix to feed us for at least a day."

She grinned. Her hands on the wheel relaxed. Sunlight streamed into the car. They drove with the windows open, and the mild air whipped Jenifer's hair into a dark cloud.

Eric stretched his legs out and sighed with pleasure. He might be working, but this case was the most pleasant one he'd taken on in a long, long time.

"There's a river that flows into Lake Doolittle," Jenifer said, turning onto another blacktopped road. "It's just ahead, and there's this train bridge that runs overhead. Well, anyway, I'll show it to you when we get there."

"And it's one of your favorite spots?"

"I call it my thinking spot."

"What do you think about when you're there?"

"Knowledge without wisdom isn't enough," she said slowly. "I live my life surrounded by facts, but at the same time I know it's not enough. So when I have a decision to make, I try to remember to get out of the facts and focus on the wisdom." She laughed, a bit nervously. "Not that I'm very good at all of that."

Eric gently tapped the side of her head. "It's hard getting outside this box?"

She nodded. "And I don't even know why I'm telling you this stuff."

"Maybe it's because you recognize the same traits in me," he said, realizing it was true. Chester often told him that more cases were solved by intuition than calculation. Listening to Jenifer, Eric realized just how much he lived by his head and not his heart.

"Maybe," she said, slowing the car to take a sharp turn.

Around the bend, Eric saw the train bridge, elevated by a high trestle over a river that he realized had been running alongside the road, out of sight. Jenifer pulled off the road, scattering bits of gravel as she stopped.

She got out of the car. Eric followed her down the hillside, walking through ankle-high grass, brushing past tangles of underbrush, heading closer to the river below. The sturdy base of the trestle bridge appeared to be formed from hewn blocks of local rock. It arched above them in an inverted U. In the distance Eric saw a matching rock base on the other side of the river.

They reached the base. The stone rose sturdily. Eric saw why she had called it a cathedral, as the two of them stood within the private hideaway formed below the stone archway. Jenifer spread her arms, gesturing around her. "Welcome to my private church," she said.

A train whistle sounded in the distance. Eric glanced upward, to the bridge high overhead. The ground and the trestle hummed. The river danced by alongside the bank. Jenifer stood there, a smile in her eyes.

He stepped closer to her. "Thank you for bringing

me here," he said. He wasn't sure he understood why she'd decided to share it with him, but at that moment he decided the why didn't matter.

Jenifer was an enigma.

"This is a place of peace," she said. "I've been coming here for years now." She sat down on the high grass, wrapping her arms around her knees.

Eric joined her, stretching out beside her, leaning his head on one elbow. The train whistle blew again, closer this time. "When was the first time?"

A shadow crossed her face. "I was eighteen, almost nineteen."

Eric thought he knew what she would say. He reached out and placed a hand over hers.

She nodded. "I sat down and cried. I prayed for guidance. For strength. Being that age and pregnant and alone, well, it's a scary thing, but coming here helped."

"I'm glad," he said, stroking the top of her hand. "You were brave."

"I couldn't not have my babies," she said. "Even if it meant changing everything else I'd planned for my own life."

"You've never regretted that decision, have you?"

She gave him a fierce look. "Absolutely not."

Eric smiled, leaned over and kissed her on the cheek. "I knew you'd say that."

She smiled back.

"What comes next?" He asked the question idly, but his interest in her response was keen. With Chester counseling him to solve cases using his intuition, no time like the present to follow that advice. She couldn't be walking on the wrong side of the law. Not this lady.

She shrugged. "I don't know. I lived by my kids, and now I'm not sure what to do."

"What about the plans you had when you were eighteen?" He knew from his research that she'd managed to finish college by correspondence course and had a Master's in Library Science. With a will that strong, why wouldn't she reclaim whatever those original dreams had been?

She wrinkled up her nose. Overhead, the bridge seemed to hum. The approaching train rumbled onto the bridge. She looked up and waved to the engineer, though he probably couldn't see her. "I was going to be a lawyer," she said. "And Lawrence—the father of my children—was going to be a doctor."

"I'd have to say you'd make a fine attorney," Eric said with a grin.

She plucked a few blades of grass and tossed them at him. "Based on my argumentative nature?"

He tickled her nose with one of the long stems of grass. "You're one smart lady."

The train roared across. They looked into one another's eyes, and before Eric could say what had happened, they were lying next to each other and in one another's arms. He wasn't sure who'd moved first, or if the motion had been choreographed by some unseen spirit that dwelled in Jenifer's personal sanctuary.

But he knew he didn't want to let go of her sweet body, didn't want to lift his lips from hers, or have to pull away and return to the world that waited for them just outside this private paradise.

Jenifer clung to Eric, the breath half crushed from

her. The ground trembled, and even though the logical part of her brain told her that was caused by the vibrations of the train passing overhead, it could have been from the intensity of Eric's kisses.

Then, as suddenly as they found themselves in one another's arms, Eric lifted his head. Looking into her eyes, he said, "Forgive me. I forgot myself."

Jenifer grasped him by the shoulders. "Don't apologize. Please."

"Okay," he said, a faint grin appearing. He kissed her on the tip of her nose. "I thought kissing wasn't allowed in church."

"This is a very special church," she said, trailing her fingers along his arm. Reaching higher, she tapped on the knot of his tie. "Is this uncomfortable?"

"I'm used to it," he said.

"Oh." Well, darn, he wasn't going to take a hint and loosen his tie.

He pulled them both to a sitting position. "Maybe we should head back," he said.

She pouted. Darn it, she knew he wanted her. No man could fake that kind of kiss. Of course, they couldn't do much beyond kiss here anyway. Jenifer perked up. Maybe he wanted to leave so they could find a more private spot? "Okay," she said, brushing some grass off her skirt.

Eric rose in one easy move and reached a hand to Jenifer, pulling her to her feet. She stood there, so close to him, her hand tucked in his, her breasts almost brushing the front of his shirt. He had to show more restraint, but she sure didn't make it easy to hold back.

"So, what do people do in Doolittle after church?"

They walked up the hillside hand in hand. "Sunday dinner always comes first."

"Dinner?"

"It's the main meal of the day, usually eaten around noon, but we call it dinner on Sundays. You get together with friends and family. Sometimes the church hosts a dinner, but there's not one this week."

More communal activities. Doolittle didn't leave people much time to be alone. Or lonely. "And then?"

"Oh, whatever you like after that. Watch football. Mow the yard. Work in the garden. I like to curl up with a good book on my porch."

"Is that what you're doing today?"

Jenifer nodded. "Probably."

He didn't miss the sideways glance she gave him. He'd love to spend the rest of the day with her, but he had some reconnaissance work he needed to do. Knowing she planned to be tucked away at her house helped him. "I've some phone calls to make for business," he said. "Can I call you later?"

"Sure, but you don't know my number."

Oh, but he did. He knew her phone number, her address, the value of her house, the size of her shoes. He'd gathered these facts before coming to town. What he didn't know was what made her so delightful, so desirable, and so determined to maintain her stance that she didn't need a man. They reached her car. "I think I can get it anyway," he said, "but why don't you write it down for me?"

She slid behind the wheel. He climbed in and wasn't at all surprised to find that she pulled a pen and a small notebook from her glove box. She wrote a number on a sheet of paper, tore it off, and handed it to him.

Eric slipped it into his shirt pocket. She turned the car around, heading back to town. They drove in silence, Eric content to watch her expressive face, her glossy hair dancing in the breeze from the window, wondering just when the two of them would end up naked in each other's arms.

Because one thing was certain, that would happen before he left Doolittle.

Ten

Jenifer expected to hear from Eric later that afternoon. The way he kissed her, the looks he gave her, the gentle touch of his hand on her shoulder—all these gestures conveyed only one message. He was interested; he'd be back. So certain was she that he'd call and no doubt come over that she abandoned her plan to curl up with a novel.

Instead, she plucked her brows, applied an apricot facial masque, and freshened the cherry red polish on her toenails.

By six o'clock she'd begun to doubt her conclusion. Three hours later, grumpy and hungry, she fixed a tuna fish sandwich, giving the empty packet to Tigger to lick clean. At least her cat remained a constant companion.

She went to bed at ten, daring him to phone and wake her up. To her disappointment, he didn't call.

By Monday morning, perched behind the checkout

desk at the library, she'd sworn off men entirely. She'd never needed one before and she didn't need one now. Especially not the maddening Eric Hamilton.

By Wednesday, when she still hadn't heard from Eric, she'd composed a litany of pithy remarks to deliver if and when he ever showed his face again. Most of them consisted of clever ways to make sure he knew that she'd never noticed his absence.

At least that day she'd hit on a way to keep her mind occupied. The girls' after-school reading group met on Wednesdays. She greeted the first seven girls as they filed into the library and claimed their usual seats in the circle. One seat remained empty.

Jenifer waited a few minutes to begin, hoping that Andie, the girl who'd paid her fine with the twenty Jenifer suspected to be counterfeit, would appear.

She never did show.

Jenifer concentrated on the circle as best she could, wondering what had happened to Andie. According to the other girls, she'd been in class. Jenifer decided to look up Andie's address and head to her house as soon as she locked up the library.

She'd just turned the key in the front door when the unmistakable voice of Eric Hamilton greeted her. Jenifer whirled around, then remembered she'd intended to be oh-so-cool when he showed his face. "Eric?" She said his name tentatively, as if she'd almost forgotten his identity.

"At your service," he said, looking her up and down. "You look lovely, Jenifer."

Compliments would get him nowhere. She stood there, her back to the door, wishing he didn't have such a devastating effect on her. "Thank you," she said, taking a step away from the door.

"Dinner?" he asked, moving with her.

"I have plans," she said sweetly.

"Ah."

"Ah, what?"

They'd reached her car. He leaned against the hood. "I would have called," he said, "but I was tied up."

"Show me the rope marks if you expect me to believe that," she said, reaching for her door handle.

He held out his wrists. "Can't you see the bruises?"

She fell for it, looking at his hands. Nothing but sinew and muscle and a dusting of sexy dark hair. She wondered in a flash how much hair he had on his chest.

"Seriously," he said, "some work-related things came up and I couldn't call."

"Hmm," she said.

Eric held his breath. He didn't want her to be mad at him. The irony was, he really had been working and unable to call. Franco and Lars had been spotted in southern Arkansas, and he'd hustled over to tail them. The two goons had spent most of their time lounging around a Holiday Inn Express pool in El Dorado, but his patient watch had been rewarded earlier that afternoon when Ace rumbled into the hotel parking lot in a truck loaded with pine logs. Eric watched as Ace unloaded two heavily stuffed duffel bags and delivered them to the room rented to Lars.

Eric had left another agent to baby-sit Lars and Franco and followed Ace at a discreet distance back to Doolittle, where Ace delivered his load of logs to the Tri-Forest Paper Mill. Nothing unusual occurred there,

Ace just hanging around the office while his load was weighed and some paperwork signed.

When the time was right, Eric would contact Lars and Franco, under one of his cover identities, big money dealer Troy King. For now, he'd watch and wait.

And coax Jenifer back into thinking well of him.

"How about later, then?" he asked.

"Later?"

"After dinner?"

"I have bowling."

"Need a scorekeeper?" Eric wagged his brows. "I'm good at math."

She smiled. "Do you bowl?"

He shrugged. "Hit and miss, but I can probably remember how to stick my fingers into those little holes."

"Hmm," she said, a naughty gleam in her eyes.

Eric knew he had her then. "I'll pick you up. What time?"

"Seven."

"Okay." He held her car door for her while she slid behind the wheel, then shut the door.

Eric walked from her car to his, parked nearby in the small lot facing the front of the library. He watched her as she sat there, not starting the engine for a few minutes, wondering what her plans were. He intended to find out.

Finally, she headed out of the lot, turning in the opposite direction from the route to her house. Eric found that interesting, but waited until another two cars went by before he fell in behind her. He followed at a discreet distance, pulling over when he saw her swerve into a corner gas station.

She walked to a phone booth, dialed a number, and talked briefly.

Well well. He'd give more than a dime to know who was on the other end of that conversation.

Jenifer hopped back into her car, having set her mind at rest about Andie's absence from the reading group. After inviting Eric to bowling, she'd thought better of the trip out to Andie's house past the edge of town. She would go another day. She'd been relieved that Andie had a perfectly good explanation for missing the reading group. She had a lot of homework.

She was a few blocks from her house when she realized how easily she had fallen under Eric's charms. She'd been so determined to ignore him for not calling, and what had she done? Invited him to join the Wednesday night bowling group.

That didn't exactly count as ignoring him.

"Face it, you enjoy the cat and mouse," she muttered. He did ignite her senses, keep her on edge, and cause her more than a few hours of lost sleep.

And he made her hornier than she could ever remember being. Just his voice had an effect on her, not to mention his touch . . . or his kiss.

Jenifer shivered pleasantly as she pulled into her driveway, then skipped into her house. She hadn't seen much of Uncle Pete or her mother in the last several days. She hated to admit it, but she'd been avoiding them, unsure of how to react to the undercurrents sparking between the older couple. She was feeling a bit guilty, too, for not having mentioned the odd-looking twenty-dollar bill to Uncle Pete. She'd wanted to solve the mystery herself and had gotten distracted.

She resolved to visit Andie at her home tomorrow and see if the girl knew where she'd gotten the bill. As far behind as she'd been with her overdue fines, Jenifer figured the youngster didn't come across twenty-dollar bills often, so perhaps she would remember.

Eric had continued to tail Jenifer, carefully, leaving plenty of space as the neighborhood grew more residential and there were fewer cars to disguise his presence. Once she turned onto her street, he waited, then made the block, verifying that her car sat in her driveway.

He didn't see any reason to return to his depressing motel room, so he drove slowly around the block twice more. On his second trip he got lucky. Charlotte stood on her porch, watering the potted plants and hanging ferns. Eric slowed his car, enough to catch her attention. She waved, and he returned the gesture, pulling over in front of her house, two doors down from Jenifer's.

He got out and ambled up the sidewalk. Flowers bloomed in beds along the walk and in front of the broad porch. He didn't know much about plants, but he thought these were chrysanthemums, blazing in gold and yellow and rusty orange.

"Hello, Eric," Charlotte said, lowering her watering wand.

"Hi, Mrs. Wright," he said.

"Please, call me Charlotte," she said, with a smile that reminded him so much of Jenifer.

"Okay." She had a lot of Jenifer in her, or perhaps he should say Jenifer resembled her mother, with the same dark eyes and brown, almost black, hair with that hint of auburn when the late afternoon sun caught it just right.

"Are you looking for Jenifer?"

"Oh, now, Charlotte, never tell one woman you're after another," Eric said teasingly.

She shot him a glance that reminded him of her daughter during one of her verbal sparring matches. "Now where did you learn about women?"

"I guess you could call it the school of hard knocks," he said, deciding it was best to change the subject before Charlotte started to psychoanalyze him. He still hadn't clarified his role relative to the Horace House, and since he had a meeting set with Mrs. Ball, the realtor, the next afternoon, he knew he needed to say something. And soon. Word traveled fast in Doolittle.

"Mmm," Charlotte said, eyeing him thoughtfully. "If you don't mind me saying so, you don't seem as if you've had a difficult life, though I know looks can be deceiving."

"I suppose I haven't," Eric said. "At least not in terms of physical comfort, education, travel. You name it, the luxuries were there."

"Poor little rich kid?"

He shrugged. No point in feeling sorry for what he'd never known.

Charlotte tapped her chest. "Your family caused you pain. I remember thinking that when we asked you about your family the other night."

Eric nodded. He didn't want to be reminded of the bleak contrast between his home life and that of Charlotte's and Pete's families. "Never mind all that stuff," he said. "I wanted to let you know—"

He paused as Charlotte turned and watched as a

passing dark sedan slowed, then moved on. Charlotte shook her head and seemed to relax again.

"I'm sorry," she said. "Sometimes I get these feelings and I worry that something's happened to someone I love."

Eric thought he understood Charlotte's concern, despite the peaceful town Doolittle appeared to be. "Do you worry a lot about Pete and your sons?"

She picked up the water wand again and held it over another fern. "I try not to. But yes. And may I say you're very perceptive?"

He nodded. He wanted to tell her who he was, what he did for a living. He wanted, he realized with a touch of self-derision, to be worried about by someone as loving and generous as Charlotte.

And by Jenifer.

What would it be like, coming home at night to a woman who held him forefront and center in her heart and mind? To a woman who cared for him, not just as an escort to the hottest ticket in town, but as the man around whom her life revolved?

He'd never given that depth of bonding a chance.

So why now? Why consider it now?

"Do you and Jenifer have a date?" Charlotte's voice sounded as if it were far away.

Eric nodded. "We're going bowling."

Charlotte smiled and touched him fleetingly on the back of his hand. "Good. Jenifer needs to enjoy her life more."

"Doesn't she usually bowl on Wednesday nights?" He'd gotten that impression from her, anyway.

Charlotte smiled that Cheshire cat grin of hers.

"Oh, yes, but that doesn't mean it's fun. With you there, Eric . . . well, frankly, the presence of a nice young man such as yourself is definitely the ingredient that's been missing in her life." She smiled again, reminding him forcibly of the wink Pete had delivered a few days ago.

"I'll do my best to live up to expectations," Eric said dryly.

"Are you staying through the weekend?" Charlotte asked, catching him off guard.

"I'm not sure. Well, probably."

"Good." She plucked a brown frond from one of the ferns. "Then come with us to church Sunday, since you missed out last week."

"Well, thank you for the invitation," Eric said, realizing he had no gracious way to escape the occasion, especially when he did not wish to offend the mother of the woman he'd love to take to bed.

He glanced at his watch. It was only a little after six. "Mrs. Wright, er, Charlotte," he said, "before I leave, I wanted to straighten out an impression or misimpression I might have made the other evening."

"Yes?" She regarded him calmly, almost fondly.

"There was some discussion about some 'old geezer' coming to town to possibly buy the Horace House."

"Oh, that," Charlotte said, waving one hand. "People do that from time to time, but no one ever reopens it."

"Ah, well, when you and the others were discussing it, I didn't join in to say I'm the person you were talking about."

She smiled. "Of course not."

He didn't quite understand her reaction. "But I am."

"Yes, Pete and I assumed you were, but no buyer in his right mind reveals his interest in advance. It would drive the price right up."

Eric had to snap his lips shut. This woman amazed him. "May I ask why you and Pete reached that conclusion?"

"Eric, really, it's obvious. No one just happens into Doolittle. Well, there was Stacey St. Cyr, two years ago, but her dog got sick so she had to stop. That's how she met Dr. Mike and ended up marrying him. But well-heeled young businessmen such as yourself definitely don't just wander off the interstate and put down stakes."

"Charlotte, you are a treasure," Eric said, thinking that perhaps the staff geniuses who insisted he use the prospective buyer cover deserved a promotion.

She smiled. "Now that you have that off your chest, why don't you run on over to Jenifer's?"

He leaned over and kissed her on the cheek. "Another good idea," he said with a grin.

Walking toward Jenifer's house, he found himself whistling. He also reviewed mentally any possible connections he might have missed between her and Lars and Franco. Other than the two times she'd been seen with the men, he had no indication she'd ever been around them. Given that he now knew Ace was linked to the counterfeit operation and how Jenifer despised him, that gave him further cause to clear her of any collusion. If she'd denied meeting them, he would have gone on alert. But she and her brothers openly discussed her naiveté at having coffee with the guys her brothers knew instinctively were good-for-nothings.

However, he still couldn't account for her reaction at Pamela's house when the topic of making money had come up. So, he'd watch and wait.

And stay out of her bed, Hamilton.

He knocked on the door.

"Who is it?" floated to his ears from somewhere in the house.

"Eric. I know I'm early—"

The door swung open. Jenifer stood there looking as fresh and as young as he imagined her daughter might. He soaked in the sight of her, eyes wide and full of life, her mouth quirked up in a smile, her hair swirling over her shoulders, curling just above her breasts.

She wore a bright turquoise V-neck T-shirt, jeans that followed every curve and line of her legs, and denim wedge sandals.

"You look great," he said, feeling as dumbstruck as he had as a teenager picking up a date.

She smiled. "I'm glad you're early." She turned around, leaning over to pick up a bowling ball case.

If the front view had been great, the sight of those jeans cupping her perfectly rounded butt almost put Eric over the edge. "Let me carry that," he said, reaching for the bag, wishing they could spend the evening right where they were.

"I can do it," she said almost automatically, then stopped.

"Bite your tongue," he said with a grin. "Let me have it."

She let him take the bag. "Thank you," she said.

He stepped back and let her walk out in front of him, admiring her body in the tight, faded Levi's. He'd never been much of a bowling fan, but this night was going to be fun.

He drove, and he didn't even mind when she told him to turn left, then right, then circle around the square and head toward the other side of town. She chatted about her day at the library and who was on her team in the bowling league.

Eric admired the way the deep V of her knit shirt provided a glimpse of the sweetly rounded curves of her breast. She sat turned toward him in the passenger seat, one foot tucked under the other.

"You're a good sport to come tonight," she said as they pulled into the parking lot of Doolittle Lanes.

If only she knew how badly he wanted to do exactly that. Eric flicked a strand of her hair back from her shoulders with one hand. "Thanks for asking me. You have a way of making a stranger feel right at home."

Jenifer smiled, but inwardly she winced. What was wrong with her? She didn't want him to feel at home. That made her sound like an earth mother. She wanted him to see her as a stunning, desirable sexpot, a woman he wanted to ravish. Swallowing a sigh, she swung her car door open.

The familiar jumble of noises inside the bowling alley perked her up. The rolling rumble of heavy balls on the wood lanes, the clang and clatter of the pins and setting mechanism, the mingled scents of the refreshment stand and the rows of bowling shoes, all restored Jenifer's easy good nature.

Eric was looking around as if he didn't have nearly as much fondness for the environment as Jenifer did.

Steering him toward the shoe counter, she said, "When's the last time you did this?"

"Junior high?"

She stopped and he bumped into her. "Are you kidding me?"

He shook his head.

She didn't think this was the time to tell him she'd bribed Junior Wilson, one of the members on her league team, to say he'd pulled a ligament and couldn't bowl so Eric would be able to play instead of just watch and keep score. She'd had to promise him first dibs at the newest Dan Brown thriller, plus an extra two-week renewal to coax him into the deal. "I thought everyone knew how to bowl."

He gave her a crooked grin, and she realized just how silly she sounded. "Well, in Doolittle, anyway," she added, turning toward C.J., the alley proprietor, who was waiting for her request.

"What's your shoe size, Eric?"

"I thought I was keeping score," he said.

"Someone is sick. We need you to fill in." There, she'd said it with a perfectly straight face. Over Eric's shoulder she saw Pamela and Ace stroll in. She waved.

"I wear a twelve," he said, "but I think you might be making a mistake. Anyone would do better than I will as a replacement."

She slapped him on the shoulder, playing the girl next door. "You'll do fine," she said. "I'll give you a few pointers."

Pamela and Ace greeted them. Eric said hello and took the pair of faded and worn shoes the man behind the counter shoved in his direction. Great way to impress a woman. He'd bowled before, yeah, once. As competitive as his nature was, he remembered wanting to be the best. When he'd thrown perfect strikes except for one frame, he decided there wasn't much challenge to the game, and never played again. He doubted whether he could remember now which fingers went where in a bowling ball.

"Let me buy you a beer," Ace said, his attitude practically sunny. "Whatcha drinking?"

"Make it a Bud," Eric said. He could hang with the good old boys. So Ace was buying tonight? He'd probably scored a wad of cash with that delivery. Eric wondered whether Lars and Franco were stupid enough to pay Ace using some of the bogus bills.

Sure enough, when they moved over to the other side of the shoe counter where the drinks were served, Ace tossed down a color-watermarked twenty. Eric glanced at it and noted nothing obviously wrong with it from that distance. The trick was to hold up the bill to the light to check for the vertical strips. Evidently this group of counterfeiters hadn't figured out how to fake that security measure. The last thing he wanted to do was tip Ace off, so he chugged his Budweiser and listened to Ace brag about his bowling score.

"Come on," Jenifer said, popping up between them. "You need to pick out a ball, Eric. And I need my bag."

"Can't you see we're busy?" Ace glared at Jenifer. There was no love lost there, either way around, Eric noted once more.

Jenifer smiled at him, an angelic look that Eric interpreted to mean she would rather wring Ace's neck than share oxygen with him. Eric lifted his beer, thanked

Ace for buying the round, and hoisted the ball bag. "I'm all yours," he said to Jenifer.

She fluttered her lashes at him. That made him smile. He loved her attempts at flirting, almost as much as he did her genuinely natural reactions to him.

He followed her to the ball racks. Oldies blared from speakers overhead, and Eric felt as if he'd been booked on a time travel adventure. She pointed to a large purple and black one. "That looks about your size," she said.

He slipped his fingers into the holes, lifted the ball using his other hand to cradle it, and then tested the feel. "Fine," he said.

"You're sure you're inexperienced?" She looked at him with more than a hint of suspicion. "You handle that like a pro."

Eric leaned over and whispered in her ear, "Thank you. Ever wonder what else I'm good at?"

She laughed, a bit breathlessly. "No. I mean, yes."

"I cause you a lot of uncertainty, don't I?"

Jenifer nodded. "That's something I'm not used to."

"But it's not a bad feeling?"

"Oh, no," she said. "It's rather nice."

He touched his free thumb to her cheek. "Good."

"Jenifer, hurry up!" someone yelled from the lane a few feet away from them.

"Oops," she said, pulling away. "Come on and meet the others."

Eric followed her, said hello to the others on her team, friends she introduced as Kate and Glenn and Judy and Al. Ace and Pamela, it turned out, were on a different team, playing in the lane next to them.

They welcomed him, and Eric found himself at ease in the congenial group. He wondered about the person he'd replaced and made a casual inquiry, gathering enough information to learn that the missing player was male, married, and not at all Jenifer's type. For a fleeting moment he'd experienced a tug of jealousy, something that amazed him.

Eric bowled last in the rotation. The others on the team did well. When it was Jenifer's turn, Eric couldn't take his eyes off her derriere as she reached for her ball, set her stance, and gracefully delivered a strike that set them all to celebrating. Then it was his turn. True to her word, Jenifer had given him a few instructions while the other members were on the line. As he eyed the lane, studied the strips of flooring under his feet and visualized the smooth hurtling approach that would scatter all those pins, it all came back to him. He stepped, his arm coming back then swinging forward, the ball gliding from his hand and sashaying straight down the lane.

The pins scattered and fell.

His teammates applauded.

Jenifer kissed him on the cheek. "And you said you didn't bowl!"

He kissed her back, but on the lips. Right there in the hurly-burly noise-filled room, in front of her friends who no doubt thought she meant it when she insisted she didn't need a man.

The way she kissed him back, Eric knew better.

But it wasn't just any man she needed.

"Hey, lover boy, why don't you pick us up another round?" Ace's voice intruded on his moment with

Jenifer. Eric let her go, stepping back slowly, the look he gave her a promise that they'd take up where the kiss left off.

Rather than rile Ace, Eric headed for the refreshment stand, bought some more beers and some sodas, and returned to the lane. He saw Pamela sitting on the curved plastic bench talking to Jenifer. Every so often they glanced over at Ace. Pamela didn't look at all happy. Well, he couldn't blame her. She'd made a bad mistake, linking up with Ace.

Eric had to admit he enjoyed the evening. He liked to win, and their team did rack up the best score. But frankly, all he could think of was getting back to Jenifer's house and cajoling her into inviting him to stay.

They were wrapping up, stashing their score sheets, shooting the breeze and exchanging their shoes. Ace was clowning around, tossing his ball between his large, hammy hands, when Pamela said something to him that distracted him and he dropped the ball.

It landed on his sock-clad foot. He swore. He grabbed his foot, spewing curses. Pamela tried to help, urging him to sit down so she could look at his foot. And that's when he turned and backhanded her across the face.

She screamed.

Jenifer pulled her away from Ace, urging her toward the ladies' room. Another one of the women ran for ice and followed them to the rest room. The men stood there, glaring at Ace, who'd slumped onto the bench, holding his foot.

The man named Glenn said, "Ace, I don't care if

your foot is broken into a million pieces, you don't hit your wife."

"Leave me alone," Ace said. "I do what I want."

The owner walked over. "You guys settle down. I don't want any trouble. I called the cops, just in case anyone else has any ideas about throwing any more punches."

Eric realized he'd balled his hands into fists. He looked at the other men and saw in their expressions a mirror of his own feelings. Ace needed to be taught a lesson. But first they had to make sure Pamela was safe.

"We're not fighting in here," Glenn said.

Eric leaned over and grabbed Ace by the chin. "Hear that? Not in here, but try that again and all of us are going to come find you."

"Yeah, right," Ace said. "She deserved it, making me break my foot."

"It's not broken," Eric said. "But it's going to be if you touch your wife one more time."

"Who made you the sheriff?" Ace stood up, wiggled his toes, and turned away. He grabbed his shoes and hobbled toward the door. "Any one of you who wants that witch is welcome to her."

They all stood there, staring after him. Eric recovered, said, "I'm going to check on Pamela," and headed toward the sign marked WOMEN, where he'd seen Jenifer rush her friend.

Jenifer stuck her head from the rest room just as Eric approached. "How is she?" he asked.

"Mad as heck," Jenifer said. "And it's about time. She has a bit of a nosebleed. Has the jerk left yet?"

Eric nodded.

"I hope somebody beats him up," she said, looking at him with a hopeful expression.

"He deserves it," Eric said, "but I think we'll let the law take its course."

"Oh, she'll never press charges," Jenifer said sadly. "Though she did agree to spend the night at my place."

"That's a start," Eric said, relieved to hear that she'd opted for safety even if it did put an end to his plans for the evening. But Pamela couldn't go home. "I'll go get your bag."

She nodded, looking troubled.

"What is it, Jeni?" Eric opened his arms and was pleased at the trusting way she stepped into his embrace.

She nuzzled her head against his shoulder. "I feel better when you're around," she said.

"I'm glad." He kissed her on the cheek, touched by her reaching out to him. "Now go get your friend."

Eleven

fter work the next day, Jenifer headed straight to
Doolittle Estates trailer park, where Andie lived.
She'd been up late with Pamela and felt more like going home for a nap than visiting the girl. But during her
talk with Pamela, almost to take Pamela's mind off her
own troubles, she'd told her friend about the suspicious
bill.

That bit of information had opened the floodgates for
Pamela, who told her that she believed Ace was involved
in an illegal activity, possibly involving counterfeiting.
She couldn't prove it, but Ace boasted so frequently now
of making money the old-fashioned way that she'd begun to suspect he had his hand in a broken cookie jar.

Ace had been supposed to leave on an out-of-town
trip that afternoon. Jenifer agreed that Pamela should
search Ace's possessions for any clues while she went
to talk to Andie. Afterward they'd get together and decide when to go to Uncle Pete with their information.

Driving toward Doolittle Estates, Jenifer knew Uncle Pete would be madder than heck with her for holding out, but that was a storm she'd have to weather. This mystery was one she wanted to solve.

Feeling a bit like a foolhardy Nancy Drew, she checked her rearview mirror. For a while she'd had the feeling she was being followed. It was silly, and no doubt caused by an overactive imagination. Several cars whizzed by, and two or three drove behind her. Not surprising, given the size of the trailer park and the fact that its entrance sat off one of the county's busier roads.

Eric, keeping an eye on Jenifer, several cars ahead of his own, checked his watch. She'd wasted no time heading out from the library to the outskirts of town. He yawned, forcing himself to stay alert. After he'd seen Jenifer and Pamela safely to Jenifer's house, he picked up Ace's trail at a country western bar and pool hall. It hadn't been hard to find him. Doolittle wasn't exactly swimming in late night watering holes.

Around two A.M., Ace had lumbered to a fairly recent vintage Chrysler, an automobile Eric assumed belonged to Pamela. He'd driven to the entry road of the Tri-Forest Paper Mill and just sat there.

No one approached in the hour he remained parked. Eric watched from a distance, binoculars trained on Ace. He couldn't figure it out. But then, maybe Ace only wanted to sit there and dream of the ill-gotten riches he hoped to make.

Jenifer quite properly was signaling a turn with her indicator. Eric smiled. Of course she would follow the rules of the road. He fell back, noting the sign over the road's entrance: DOOLITTLE MOBILE ESTATES. Judging by the surroundings, he assumed it was a euphemism for a trailer park.

One fairly shiny recent model car entering this blue-collar neighborhood might not be noticed, but two, especially a Caddy, might draw far too much attention. Eric pulled over on the road, hopped out, locked his car, and hoofed it toward the entrance. He'd stay out of the way, so there would be no reason to explain his presence to Jenifer.

He moved quickly, passing two decently kept mobile homes, then a third that looked like a set piece from a disaster flic, complete with leaning steps, peeling paint, and three scrawny dogs all barking at him at once.

He spotted Jenifer's wagon up ahead. She drove slowly, as if looking for an address. He walked double-time as she turned to the right, but fortunately she halted as he peered around the bend in the road.

The trailer where she'd paused was well-kept. Chrysanthemums bloomed in little clay pots on the steps that led to the front door. The windows gleamed in the afternoon sunshine. From the open doorway, music drifted, music that sounded a lot like opera. Eric had never developed either a fondness or an understanding of that art form, but he did appreciate its presence in this setting. The occupant or occupants strove to rise above their surroundings. Heck, he'd been educated at Harvard, and his music of choice fell somewhere between late sixties rock and roll and whatever music his favorite hangouts happened to have blaring from their speakers. In other words, he didn't fuss over music.

He watched as Jenifer got out of her car and quietly closed the door. She looked around, and Eric knew, as well as he knew his own name, that this visit served as a great source of both excitement and nervousness for her. He'd tucked himself behind a parked car, where he could track her without being seen.

She approached the steps leading to the mobile home and paused, cocking her head to the side. A smile appeared on her face, and Eric guessed that she had identified the opera. Why did that not surprise him? No doubt she could tell him the composer, the year it was first performed, and the biographies of the singers. He grinned. They sure didn't make 'em like Jenifer every day.

She lifted her hand, apparently about to knock, when a car careened around the corner and skidded to a halt in front of her Saturn wagon. Jenifer turned.

Two guys hopped out of the car.

They stood there, staring at her. One of them scratched his crotch, then seemed to catch himself and stuck his hands into his beltline.

Jenifer stared back.

Eric swore softly under his breath as he easily identified the two men. What in the hell were Lars and Franco doing here? He hunkered down, making doubly sure he couldn't be spotted.

Either this was a very big coincidence or the two crooks and Jenifer were at the identical address for a similar purpose.

"Hi, guys," she said. Well, that didn't give him much of a clue.

"Hey," Lars said, looking none too thrilled. So perhaps he hadn't expected to see Jenifer.

A soprano voice trilled, followed by an intense-sounding baritone. Eric wondered whether the person or persons inside the trailer could possibly hear anything other than the highly cultured musical selection. Probably not. Did they even know they had company?

Lars strolled forward, a smile on his pasty face. "Why, if it isn't the librarian."

Jenifer nodded, but she didn't sport any welcoming expression. "Yes. That's me," she said. "The librarian. And you and your partner, the lumber products salesmen."

Lars beamed. "That's right. Two working guys, just trying to earn a living."

Jenifer narrowed her eyes. Oh, no, don't do it, Eric thought. Don't let them know you suspect them of being anything other than what they say.

She smiled. "But it's after five," she said. "You surely don't have to work overtime?"

Lars laughed, and Franco joined in. "No, of course not," he said, his voice rumbling out of his chest. Franco never seemed happy talking, Eric thought, unless he could be threatening some hapless innocent. How in the hell did Jenifer get mixed up with these two?

"Just socializing," Lars said. "How about you?"

"Me?" Jenifer pointed a finger at her chest and giggled. "Now, why would you wonder about little old me?"

Lars advanced a step or two. In a casual enough voice, he said, "Just polite curiosity, that's all."

Jenifer nodded. Eric could tell she was nervous by the way she nibbled on her bottom lip. When her preciously cute tongue darted out to lick her lips, she signaled sexual excitement. This nibbling gesture, well, that meant she didn't know what to do next. And he'd be willing to bet that state didn't make her at all comfortable. No, Jenifer felt a whole heck of a lot better when she knew what shot to call next.

"It does seem kind of odd," Franco said, "that you and us are making the same social call at the same time to the same place."

"Is that so?" Jenifer drew herself up. She had the advantage of holding the top of the stairs leading to the front door. "Well, I just happen to be the librarian, and I just happen to have a business reason to be calling here."

"Ah, business," Lars said, backing off a step or two. "Why didn't you say so?"

Jenifer smiled, a saccharine imitation of one of her genuine bursts of generous humor. "Why didn't you ask?"

Lars nodded. "Good question. Tell you what, my partner and me, we'll just be on our way, and come back to call later."

"Oh," Jenifer said. "Sure."

They nodded, but neither one of the men moved back toward the car.

The operatic frenzy reached a climax and the sound of applause could be heard. Then the music went silent and the front door to the trailer jiggled, opened, and fell shut again.

"Andie?" That was Jenifer, speaking softly, and leaning toward the door.

No one answered, or at least not that Eric could tell.

Lars and Franco edged backward, and Jenifer seemed to ignore them. Instead, she said, "I need to talk to you, Andie."

Then Jenifer turned and said, "See you later, guys. Drop by the library if you want to learn more about the town. I'm always happy to share information on the history of Doolittle."

Lars gave a little wave and a semicheery smile. Franco sneered and said something only he and/or Lars could hear.

Their car moved slowly past, but did not head back to the highway. No doubt they planned to return when Jenifer left. But why? Eric edged closer but couldn't make out what Jenifer said to the young girl who stood in the doorway. Then the door opened and Jenifer stepped inside. Eric glanced around, and still not seeing anyone else, decided to risk a closer view.

He crouched down and headed around the right end of the trailer, planning to get out of sight from the road and find a window to peer through. He'd stay, make sure Jenifer got safely away, then wait for Lars and Franco to return.

Tiptoeing, he spied an open window with a convenient tree stump next to it. He stepped onto it and edged upward for a view into the trailer. There stood Jenifer and perhaps an eleven- or twelve-year-old girl. He balanced on his perch and turned his ear closer to the slightly open window.

"Oh, no, it's okay that you stopped by," the girl was saying, glancing over her shoulder down a hallway, an anxious expression on her face. "My dad had to step out."

Looking serious, Jenifer said, "Do you know those two men?"

The girl shook her head. "No, but they didn't look like they were very nice. I hope my pa isn't in trouble."

"Oh, I don't think they were policemen," Jenifer said.

The girl looked at her—scornfully, Eric thought. "It's not the police I'm afraid of," she said. "I'm sorry. I'm forgetting my manners, Miz Wright. Would you like to sit down?"

"Thanks," Jenifer said, and took a seat on the room's one sofa.

Damn. Her body was turned away from him and he couldn't hear her next words. The girl sat on the opposite end, facing him.

"My library fines, you mean?"

Surely Jenifer hadn't paid a house call to collect for overdue books? Eric grinned. Well, she could do that, he supposed, but no, that did nothing to explain why Lars and Franco were also interested in this address.

The girl lowered her head. Eric strained to hear what she was saying. As he pressed his ear to the window, he felt a sharp tug on his trousers, followed by another one on his other leg. Something wet pressed against his sock, and he looked down and into the eyes of a pair of black and gray goats.

"Hey, fellows," he said very, very softly. "Nice goats." One of them had fairly sharp looking horns. Since when did goats grow horns? he wondered. One of them seemed to favor the taste of his slacks, and the other had started nibbling one of his Cole Haan loafers. Eric attempted to push them gently away and succeeded only in slipping off the tree stump and landing on his butt.

The black goat took this as an invitation to play and butted him on the shoulders.

Eric glanced around. A row of skinny trees backed the tiny yard behind the trailer. Scooting slowly, he edged toward the front of the trailer, the goats playing alongside. In all his years of training and field experience, no one had ever suggested how to handle a goat attack.

One backed off then took a running leap toward him, knocking him in the chest. "Good goat," Eric said, starting to laugh. He knew he looked ridiculous and was also missing the conversation going on inside the trailer, but he couldn't help but find it amusing.

He hoped Chester would see the humor in the situation. Or perhaps he'd leave this episode out of his report.

"There you are!"

Eric jumped as a boy yelled right behind his head. He turned and saw a boy of five or six standing with his hands on his hips, scowling ferociously.

"Bad Billy! Bad Willy!" He stomped toward the goats and pulled the one closest to Eric away, holding him by a dirty rope that Eric saw for the first time around the creature's neck.

"I was playing Billy Goats Gruff and they ran away," the child said. "Hello, who are you?"

"Oh, nobody," Eric said.

The child giggled. "Of course you're not nobody. Hey, you wanna play the troll?"

"Er, not really, but thanks for asking," Eric said,

keeping his voice low, though the child spoke so loudly that even Mrs. Kirtley could have heard him across the yard. "Actually, I need to get going."

The child sighed. "No one ever wants to play with me. Not even my goats." He sank down on his skinny legs, hunkered between his two pets.

Eric felt a twinge of empathy. He'd been an only child, without even goats as companions. "Don't you have any brothers or sisters?"

"Nah." The boy wiped his nose with the back of one grimy hand. "Well, I do, but my sister's grown up and has her own brats and she won't let them come play with me." The boy looked around. "She says we live in a dump, but I don't think so, do you?"

Eric glanced around at the tiny but neatly kept back-yard. It did stand in sharp contrast to the mobile home with the three barking dogs that had more in common with big city tenements than fresh air country living. Then he considered the opera that had greeted his arrival, and he said, "Definitely not."

"So you'll play the troll?"

Oh, what would it hurt? He hadn't heard the front door of the trailer open, so Jenifer still had to be inside. He looked at the boy's hopeful face and said, "Okay, I'll play."

"Wow," the boy said. "You're not like most grown-ups."

Eric propped himself up on his elbows. He'd kept his butt on the ground, thinking it would keep the goats at bay. With a grin, he said, "No, I guess I'm not. At least not today. I know your goats' names, but what's your name?"

The child tugged at the black goat who'd returned to sniffing at Eric's shoes. "Oh, people call me Pooper."

"Pleased to meet you, Pooper. My name is Eric," he said, wishing Jenifer was outside, enjoying this exchange with him. No doubt she'd know exactly what to say, as well as knowing the history of how this child came by such a charming nickname.

The boy nodded, then said, "Let's go out by the bridge and you crawl under it, and me and the goats will start crossing the bridge."

Wondering what he'd gotten himself into, Eric stood up and followed the child toward the front of the mobile home next door.

Twelve

"Would you look at that?" Andie giggled, looking like the child she was for the first time since Jenifer had greeted her at the door fifteen minutes earlier.

The girl had stepped into the small kitchen to pick up two Cokes. She paused on her way back to look out the window.

"What is it?" Jenifer remained seated on the couch. It had taken some effort to put the girl at ease. She seemed to think her dad was in trouble. If Lars and Franco weren't the lumber salesmen they had claimed to be, Jenifer couldn't help but conclude the girl might be right. More mystery to solve, she'd decided, determined to figure it all out.

"Pooper got some man to play with him."

"Who is Pooper?" Jenifer got up from the couch and stepped over to Andie's side. A young boy romped with two goats in the grass between the next trailer and the road. The threesome circled around a massive box, the kind a washer/dryer combo or refrigerator would be delivered in. A pair of feet stuck out of one end.

"He's the little boy who lives next door," Andie said, giggling. "I can't believe he got that man to crawl into the box. Pooper probably pestered him to play Billy Goats Gruff with him. He's always begging people to play that silly game with him but no one ever does."

"Why not?" Jenifer couldn't stand for children to feel lonely or abandoned.

Andie shrugged. "How do you think he got that name?" she said, scrunching up her nose.

"I don't suppose it's on his birth certificate," she said. "Is that his dad in the box?"

Andie rolled her eyes and took a swig of her Coke. "Oh, please. His dad doesn't even get out of bed until the sun goes down, and then he just wakes up long enough to yell at someone to bring him a beer." She clenched the Coke can. "When I grow up, I'm going to live far, far away from Doolittle."

Jenifer wanted to hug the girl. "Your place is very nice," she said, reflecting that as a single unwed mom she might have ended up in a place much worse off than Doolittle Estates if her grandmother hadn't died and left her the house in her will. She could have lived with her parents, but she wanted to be as independent as possible. It was little wonder, though, that Andie hadn't had the money to pay her mounting overdue fines. "It's just you and your dad?"

Andie nodded. "But my dad works hard. He's the janitor at the paper mill. And he's studying computers by correspondence course."

"That's wonderful," Jenifer said. "That's how I earned my college degree."

Andie's eyes bugged out. "You?"

"Yes, me." She smiled. "It's always possible to accomplish any goal you set your mind to." Like finding a man and seducing him into seducing you, she thought. But she needed to stick to her purpose here, not fantasize over Eric Hamilton. Casually, still wondering about the best way to approach the sudden appearance of Andie's colorful cash, she said, "Did your dad get a raise or promotion recently?"

The girl stared at her feet. "What makes you ask that?" She lifted her head, and Jenifer saw that her anxiousness had returned full force.

"You paid your fines all at once," Jenifer said. "And the twenty-dollar bill was a nice crisp new one, the new color bills, too."

"Is that a problem?"

"Not exactly," Jenifer said. "I just wondered about where you earned the money."

Outside the window, the box moved, scooting forward. Now shoes, socks, and trousered legs appeared out of the end. Jenifer looked more closely. Something about those pants looked familiar.

"I got it from my dad," Andie said, "but please don't tell anyone. If it's a problem, maybe I could work at the library after school to pay off the fines."

"Did you take it when your dad wasn't looking?" She figured Andie wouldn't have offered so readily to arrange an alternative means of repaying the fines if all had been on the up and up with her source of funds.

"Sort of," Andie said. "I mean, for one thing, I didn't

think he'd notice 'cause he came home from work the other day all wound up. He had this paper sack under his arm. He didn't think I was paying attention 'cause I had my homework spread out all over the table in the living room. He stashed the sack in the kitchen, behind the wastebasket we keep under the sink. So after he went to bed I sneaked out and looked in there and, Miz Wright, it was full of money!" She looked over her shoulder as she finished her speech, obviously afraid that her dad had somehow returned and would catch her confessing.

"Do you think those men who were here earlier today know about your dad having that cash?"

Andie nodded. "It seemed like a good guess."

"Where's your dad now?"

"Hiding out next door. He went out the back when he spotted them drive up."

"So he could come back in at any time?"

"Yes, Miz Wright. Please don't tell him I took any of the money."

Jenifer nodded. "All right. But do you have any idea where it might have come from?"

Andie shook her head, then very softly said, "Maybe there's something funny going on at the papermill?"

Jenifer stared at the girl. She had begun to think the same thing, but saw no reason to frighten Andie further. "Possibly someone is hiding stolen money at the plant. Cleaning up, your father might have found it."

Andie nodded, looking relieved. "I bet he was hiding it from the bad guys to take it to the police."

"Of course," Jenifer said, hoping that was the case. Another possibility occurred more readily to her—that he had hidden it until he thought it safe to spend it. That would be human nature. Find money, no one claims it, you need it, keep it. She wasn't there to judge, just investigate.

"Look!" Andie giggled and pointed out the window. One of the goats had nosed into the box and the pair of feet flailed wildly, the box shaking. Pooper laughed and slapped his skinny butt.

The occupant of the box backed out and stood.

All six feet of him.

"Eric!" Jenifer said loudly. He must have heard her through the open window, because he paused. Looking straight at her and Andie, he lifted a hand, waved, and began a dialogue with Pooper that Jenifer couldn't hear. It appeared to be a negotiation of some sort that resulted in Pooper climbing into the box to join the goat.

"What in the world is he doing here?" Jenifer said, helping herself to a swallow of Coke as she pondered the chances that Eric's appearance could be attributed to pure coincidence.

"I've never seen him before," Andie offered.

"He had to have followed me," she said.

"Is he sweet on you?" Andie looked interested in that possibility.

Jenifer shook her head.

"Are you sweet on him?"

"No," she said. "I mean, he's interesting, but I'm not looking for a man."

"My dad says he's not looking for a woman, either," Andie said. "I guess not, after the way my ma ran off on us. Is that what happened with your husband, too?"

Jenifer nodded. "I guess you could say so."

Andie sighed, looking far older than her tender years. "Well, Mr. Eric can't be too bad if he's nice enough to play with Pooper."

Jenifer smiled. She'd been thinking the same thing. He looked so out of place in his crisp dress shirt, expensive slacks, and gleaming loafers, climbing butt first out of a broken-down packing box. For whatever reason, he'd taken the time to play with a lonely child, a fact that won him more points with her than he could have scored had he appeared on her doorstep with roses and a magnum of champagne. Of course, no matter how charmingly he played at Billy Goats Gruff, he had some explaining to do about how he'd ended up in Doolittle Estates.

Then she thought of something odd about Andie's reaction. She turned back away from the window and said, "Andie, when those other two men drove up, you said your dad bolted and that you were afraid."

"Yes'm, that's true."

She pointed toward the front yard. "That man's a stranger. Are you afraid of him?"

Andie shook her head. "Nope."

"Hmm," Jenifer said. "Can you explain why not?"

"He's not scary," the girl said. "You can just tell the difference, don't you think, when someone bad is up to no good? And when someone has a good heart, that shows, too." She crumpled her Coke can. "My dad has a good heart," she said, her voice a notch more fierce. "I know he didn't do anything wrong."

Jenifer nodded. She wanted to put her arms around the girl to comfort her, but that didn't seem to be the right thing to do. Instead she said, "I believe you, Andie. I'm also going to figure out what's going on."

"Oh, thank you, Miz Wright," Andie said. "If my dad did want a new wife, I'd want it to be someone like you."

"Thank you, Andie," Jenifer said. "I'm honored." She finished her own soda. Following Andie's lead, she crumpled the can in her hand. "Now let's go have a chat with Mr. Eric."

"Ooh, Pooper, too!" Andie, looking more like the young carefree girl that she should be, giggled, tossed their cans in the trash, and followed Jenifer out the door.

They walked down the steps together. Eric turned as they approached.

"Jenifer, nice to see you again," he said, looking completely suave and unbothered at being caught by her.

"Lovely, Eric," she said. "Who's your friend?"

"I told you his name," Andie said. "That's Pooper."

Eric leaned over and tapped on the big box. "Take a union break," he said. "Come on out from under the bridge."

"That's no bridge," Andie said. "That's a box."

"Artistic license," Eric said. "What's your name?"

"Andie," she said, smiling at him from under her lashes.

Great, Jenifer thought. The man's charm worked its magic again.

Eric shook hands with Andie. "I'm Eric," he said.

The scrawny little boy crawled from the box, goat in tow. His hair stuck out every which way. A Band-Aid decorated one ear. "What's a union break?" Then he scowled. "Girls aren't allowed to play," he said.

"You're so stupid," Andie said. "If I had a hard time

the way you do getting someone to play with me, I wouldn't be so picky about who's a girl and who's a boy." She glared at him.

"That's because you're a girl," the boy said. "You are kinda pretty, though," he said, turning toward Jenifer. "My name's Pooper."

"Pleased to meet you," Jenifer said. "I'm Miz Wright from the library. I don't think I've met you at any of our reading groups."

He stuck a grubby finger down his throat. "Reading! Yuck!"

Eric looked like he had trouble holding down a big grin at Pooper's reaction.

Andie stuck her nose in the air. "I belong to a reading group. We're reading a Nancy Drew adventure right now."

"Are you playing Billy Goats Gruff?" Jenifer asked, hunkering down so she and Pooper were eye-to-eye.

He nodded and sidled closer to Eric. "We're playing. With my goats."

"Did you know that game comes from a book?"

He shook his head, obviously prepared to dispute such a radical concept.

"Well, any dummy knows that," Andie said.

"She shitting me?" Pooper looked up trustingly at Eric.

Eric shook his head, quite solemn.

Now it was Jenifer who had to hold back a smile. "Tell you what, Pooper, you come to the library after school next week and I'll help you get a library card and you can take home the Billy Goats Gruff story and read it to your goats."

He laughed. "They can't read."

"Neither can you, probably," Andie said.

"I can, too," he said. "I'm in first grade."

"That's good," Jenifer said. "Can you come in this week?"

The boy stubbed the toe of his tennis shoe against the cardboard box. It wobbled and fell to one side. "Nah," he said, "I don't need no stinking liberary."

"No stinking library," Eric said gently. "Tell you what. How about if I picked you up and took you there?"

"No shit?"

"Er, that's correct," Eric said. "Maybe next week."

"That's a long ways away," Pooper said. "How about Sunday. That's the day my dad can't buy any beer."

"The library is closed on Sunday," Jenifer said.

"Monday, then," Eric said.

Jenifer blinked her eyes. Eric Hamilton had to be a saint. She lifted her face and smiled at him with gratitude and admiration. "You are a good man, Eric," she said.

"I could have told you that," Andie said. "Matter of fact, I did."

"Andie, get your butt back in this house this minute," a man's voice bellowed from the kitchen window of the mobile home.

"It's my dad," Andie said. "I'd better go. Remember, Miz Wright, secret! Cross your heart and if you lie, never again will you eat pie."

Jenifer nodded, adding the time-honored sign across her chest. "Promise."

Andie scampered toward her home.

"That's an interesting variation on cross my heart," Eric said.

"She's a girl," Pooper volunteered, as if that explained it all. "Prob'ly doesn't like to say 'die.'" He ran around in a circle, firing an imaginary gun. His goats joined him in the energetic display until they knocked him to the ground.

"And they say children are growing up faster these days," Eric said, strolling closer to Jenifer. "What brings you here?" He'd decided the best thing to throw her off guard was to be as brazen as possible.

She practically sputtered as she said, "Me? What brings me here? That's my question!"

He gave her one of his most charming grins, the one designed to clench any deal that involved a female.

Jenifer drew herself up. It was hard to be stern when he looked at her with those dark eyes and that smile lighting his face. "Did you follow me here?"

"I cannot tell a lie," Eric said. "I did follow you."

One of the goats chose that moment to butt Eric on the back of his knees. He dropped in a theatrical slow motion to the ground, ending in a kneeling position in front of Jenifer. She offered him her hand. "I don't think the goat believed you, either."

He rose but didn't let go of her hand. "It's true," he said, and if the heat in his gaze got any hotter, she felt as if she'd melt into a puddle right there, between the mobile home and her station wagon.

"But why would you follow me?"

He shrugged. "Jealous," he mumbled.

She gave his hand a squeeze. "Did I hear that right?"

He nodded and circled his thumb around the palm of her hand. "Thought you'd ditched me for some other guy."

She fluttered her lashes, enjoying a surge of feminine power.

"Aw, poop," Pooper said, staring at them.

"Well, I didn't run out to meet any other man," Jenifer said, trying to remain reasonable even though the way he stroked the delicate flesh of her palm made it hard to breathe.

"Now you're not gonna play with me anymore," Pooper said, kicking the grass.

"We will go to the library," Eric said. "Where do you go to school?"

"It don't matter," the child said. "You won't show up."

Eric let go of Jenifer's hand and knelt beside the child, tipping his chin upward. "You've been let down a lot, haven't you, Pooper?"

"It don't matter none," he said with a shrug.

"It does matter," Eric said. "What time does school let out?"

"Three o'clock."

"And you'll ask permission to go to the library with me?"

"That for sure don't matter," he said, sticking out his lower lip.

"But you'll ask anyway?"

The boy nodded.

Jenifer patted the head of one of the goats that had started to nuzzle her skirt.

"He likes you," Pooper said, smiling again.

"Yeah, he does," Eric said, taking her hand again.

"How about going home now and having dinner with me later?"

Slowly, she pulled her hand free. "Okay, but I'd like to talk to Andie's father first."

"Sure you wouldn't rather do that later?" He looked at her like she was a piece of lemon meringue pie and he hadn't had dessert in a decade.

"Maybe I could," she said. It occurred to her that it might be better to find him at the paper mill. Going back to talk to him would only disturb Andie. "But don't make me believe you walked here from my house."

He grinned. "Nope, but I'll pick up my car where I left it later. Pooper and I are going to finish our game, and he's going to make sure I know where to find him at his school."

"Better not be shitting me," the child said.

Eric crossed his chest with his hand. Then he walked Jenifer to her car. She slid behind the wheel, and he leaned into the open doorway. He kissed her. Jenifer shivered, in a pleasant way, anticipating how he might claim her body and her senses. At least, if all went well and the two of them ever managed to get beyond a kiss without being interrupted.

Even his kisses overwhelmed her sensibilities. She sat there, feeling his nearness, yearning for more, at the same time tempted to drive as fast as she could away from him.

"Jeni?"

She swung her face toward him at his gentle use of her nickname, which only her dad and her best friend Pamela ever called her. "Yes?"

"You'd best start the engine," Eric said, "'cause I really should not kiss you again in front of Pooper. I'm afraid I'd lose way too much face if he catches me playing with a girl."

She laughed, closed the door, and drove away.

When Jenifer was gone, Eric turned back to the scruffy child. "Okay, Pooper, I'm going to crawl back in that box and play a while longer," he said.

"No shit."

"Right," Eric said, dropping to his hands and knees and scooting the box around so he could see out of it but not be seen should Lars and Franco return. He'd no doubt win points with Jenifer for being kindhearted enough to entertain this kid, and he'd clearly made Pooper's day. The crowning victory would be to see what interest Lars and Franco had in the girl's home.

He settled inside the box, rocking it about and making troll noises as Pooper galloped around, laughing as his goats butted against the cardboard. Eric heard a car stop, and he peered out the hole made by the carrying handle of the box. Sure enough, the two goons were back, one knocking on the front screen and one slipping around the side.

No one answered the door. Eric pictured the girl inside, frightened and hiding. He called Pooper over and told him sternly to go inside his own home for the next few minutes. Then Eric rose, holding the oversized box around him, and crab-walked around to the back of the trailer. Franco was peering into the window, standing on the same stump Eric had used earlier. Eric took a running leap and hit the man squarely. Franco shouted.

The goats, not to be left out of the action, romped over Franco's flailing arms and legs. His yelling brought his partner around to see what was going on. Pooper, having disregarded Eric's attempts to shoo him away from potential conflict, laughed and danced around, immensely entertained by the mayhem.

Eric rolled in the box toward the surprised Lars and knocked him off his feet. He hoped Andie and her dad had the good sense to either call the cops or hightail it out of their home while all the confusion was going on. Still keeping the box between him and Lars and Franco, he demanded in a gruff voice that they scram and never return.

"Yeah, like we're scared," Franco said, and just as he did, one of the goats knocked against the back of his knees and sent him tumbling.

"Come on, let's get the hell out of here," Lars said, grabbing his pal by his shirt. "We can catch the janitor later."

They scooted out of sight. Eric heard two car doors slam.

Pooper fell to the ground, laughing. "You play good," he said, running over to Eric and giving him a happy high-five.

"Right," Eric said, climbing free of the cardboard box. "The next time I say go home, go home. It's for your own good."

"Aw, okay," Pooper said. "You're pretty cool about other stuff." He reached for the raggedy strings that served for leashes for his goats. "Come on, Willy and Billy. And don't you forget about that liberary."

"Library," Eric said with a smile.

"No shit," Pooper said, moving away.

Eric caught movement in one of the windows of the mobile home. He loped around to the front door. It inched opened. Andie and a man in his early thirties peered out a crack in the doorway.

"I'm here to help," Eric said.

They let him in, and he set to work figuring out what the paper mill janitor knew.

Thirteen

Jenifer refused to turn around in the pew and look behind her. She fastened her gaze, if not her attention,
on Pastor Roemer. After learning from her mother that
Eric had promised to accompany them to church this
Sunday, she purposely hadn't gone next door to Uncle
Pete's house earlier than it would be time to leave. She
stayed on the phone with her children, catching up during her weekly phone calls with her twins, first with
Autumn and then with Adam.

She didn't want Eric thinking she needed or wanted
to see him. She'd listened to Pamela's male psychol-
ogy advice for years and knew there was no better
means of chasing a man away than chasing after him.
Besides, he hadn't shown up for dinner Thursday and
he'd called her only once since then.

Pastor Roemer had chosen a topic that had to do
with the fall harvest. The main crop around Doolittle—
if it could be called that—were the stands of timber, so

Jenifer didn't find the subject particularly apropros. But no doubt the goodhearted minister had followed some seminary guidebook that recommended seasonal sermons. Last year, Valentine's Day had fallen on a Sunday, and he'd treated the congregation to a discourse on the various Greek terms for love, differentiating between agape, eros, and Philadelphian. Jenifer had enjoyed the topic, but left the service with the distinct feeling that Pastor Roemer had been speaking over the comprehension level of most of the beloved brethren gathered there.

She reflected on that talk now, rather than the harvest theme that did little to keep her mind off wondering whether Eric had indeed shown up for church and if at that very moment was sitting behind her lusting at the sight of the back of her sleek hair, which she'd fashioned in a sophisticated French twist. He wasn't with her mother and Uncle Pete, and she'd slipped in too late to ask them if he'd called them—had she been of a mind to display any interest in his whereabouts.

Eros, as in *erotica,* had been exactly what she'd had in mind when Eric appeared in the library as if by magic sent. To her surprise, he'd also been surprisingly companionable, when he wasn't driving her crazy or sending her through the sensual ceiling. That would relate to the Philadelphian love the pastor had discussed, and how they should treat one another accordingly, as one would a family member. She smiled as she remembered Mrs. Kirtley's confusion over placing which brother Eric was.

Pastor Roemer must have concluded his sermon because all around her there was a rustle of pages turning in hymnals and the shuffling of feet as the congregation rose. Jenifer rose, too, reflecting that the other love he'd discussed, agape—God's love and concern for man—reminded her of the way her parents had loved one another.

Compassionate, caring, and full of life and humor. Her father should not have died, she thought for the nth time. She wondered how God justified that as good and caring toward people, even as she stood with the others and sang the words of the hymn that closed the service. God had a lot to answer for, she reflected, not feeling one bit guilty. One day she'd have a talk with Him, especially about her dad.

She could see her mother standing beside Uncle Pete, a few pews ahead and on the other side of the center aisle. Having come in late, she'd sat closer to the back than usual. Uncle Pete held the hymnal for her mother and smiled down at her as they sang together.

Jenifer's jaw clenched and she looked away. It wasn't fair. She'd lost her father, and her kids had gone away to school. Here she stood, all alone in a sea of people.

A little girl down the row smiled at her, and Jenifer smiled back, kicking herself for indulging in such a fit of self-pity. She might have driven to church alone, but she stood surrounded by men, women, and children she knew by name, by family, and quite a few by their reading habits. She had her friends and family, her community, and if Eric Hamilton would just cooperate, she'd even have sex.

"Hi, Miz Jenifer," the child said as soon as the last amen sounded. "I can't wait till book group!"

"Great, Rita Gayle," she said, "We're starting another Nancy Drew this week."

She clapped her hands together and followed her parents out of the row.

Jenifer turned around, greeted the man and woman in the row behind her, and then said hello to Dr. Mike and his wife Stacey, who looked about ready to give birth at any moment.

Darn. Everyone today appeared to be one half of a couple. Well, that happened to be true every Sunday, didn't it? she asked herself. So why let it prey on her mind now?

Even Ace had dragged his miserable butt out of bed and stood, fairly quietly for Ace, beside Pamela in the back row of the church. He'd been out of town. Pamela had searched through his papers and clothing, but found no evidence she thought linked him to any illegal activities. Jenifer wished her friend hadn't gone back to her house, but Pamela insisted on keeping up appearances until after the school board renewed her contract. Pamela had her head turned, talking to someone who was still seated. Jenifer edged in that direction.

She wanted to make sure her friend had Ace under control.

She hadn't spotted Eric in the crowd—not that she'd looked in particular for him, she assured herself. He did have a way of standing out, with his six-foot height, broad shoulders, and dark hair. He probably hadn't come. When Uncle Pete had said "church" to him at the cookout, he'd looked as if needed a translator. And he'd been happy to escape with her last week when she'd shared her private sanctuary.

Jenifer patted the smooth coil of her hair, figuring she looked as sophisticated as any woman he'd meet in any big city. Eric probably thought only small-town hicks still attended church. She did some of her best thinking during church. Admittedly, she didn't believe in keeping her mind on the sermon if it didn't speak to her, but the peaceful surroundings always helped her relax and think creatively at the same time.

"Jenifer, look who's here."

Looking toward the sound of the unmistakable voice, she saw Pamela beckoning to her. That's when she saw who occupied the seat in front of her.

"Mrs. Kirtley," Jenifer said, astonished to see the woman she'd left sitting in her kitchen all alone last week. "This is wonderful."

She offered her hand to the woman, who patted it and said, "It is so good to be in church again."

"Of course it is," Pamela said. "We've missed you."

Guilt bashed Jenifer right smack in the middle of her gut. "Mrs. Kirtley, have you missed church because you didn't have a ride and not one of us noticed and came and offered to pick you up?"

Mrs. Kirtley looked up at Jenifer, her clouded eyes misty. "It's not Christian to be holding hurt feelings, Jenifer Janey Wright. I could have swallowed my pride and asked the minister or any other Tom, Dick, or Jane for help, but I didn't want to accept charity."

"It's not charity to give someone a ride to church," Pamela said.

"Well, technically it is," Mrs. Kirtley said. "Because charity can mean love."

Love. Someone who cared enough to offer the one

thing the former Sunday school teacher missed more than her sight or hearing, Jenifer suspected. She glanced around in all directions, knowing in her heart the answer to the question she had on the tip of her tongue. "How'd you get here today?"

Mrs. Kirtley smoothed her black silk dress, and as several other people spotted her, their greetings rendered in loud voices by necessity, it drowned out her answer.

The answer had to be Eric. But where had he gone off to?

"Have you seen Eric?" Jenifer asked Pamela.

"Can we go now?" Ace said, tugging on Pamela's jacket. "A deal's a deal, and I kept my end of this one."

"All right," she said. "He was here a few minutes ago," Pamela said.

Jenifer nodded. "So how are things?"

"Fine," Pamela said. "Did you get to use the outfit?"

"Outfit?" Her mind went blank, and then she remembered the lingerie and mules Pamela had packed in the Dillard's bag. "Oh, man," she said, realizing where she'd left the items.

Jenifer backed away as more people heard about Mrs. Kirtley and the circle around her grew. She'd hoped for a glimpse of Eric, to entice him into meeting her later.

"Hi, sweetie," Charlotte said, and Jenifer whirled around. Her mother stood alone, without the ever-present Pete at her elbow. "How are my grandchildren?"

Jenifer smiled. She loved her mother. She loved Uncle Pete, too. It was the two of them together she objected to. "Adam made an A minus on his first chemistry test."

Her mother smiled. "And he's kicking himself for that minus, right?"

Jenifer nodded. "He's so hard on himself."

"That apple doesn't fall far from the tree."

"And Autumn swears she's gained two pounds in the month she's been at school."

"Well, she'll run it off when track practice starts," Charlotte said.

"She'd better," Jenifer said. "I can't afford for her to lose that scholarship. And both of them know better than to screw up their education the way I did."

"Oh, honey," Charlotte said. "You are so hard on yourself."

Jenifer bristled, but before she could fashion a suitable retort, her mother said, "Why don't you bring that nice young man over for Sunday dinner?"

"That nice young man has flown the coop," Jenifer said.

"He called this morning and said something had come up but he'd see us at church," Charlotte said. "You two seemed to hit it off. But as he's not in town to stay, it's just as well. There's no point in you getting your heart broken."

"My heart is not involved," Jenifer said, eyeing the approaching Uncle Pete.

Her mother regarded her, a speculative gleam in her eyes. "Hmm," she said. "Well, are you coming over to join us for Sunday dinner?"

"I don't think so," she said. "I have something to take care of."

Her mother nodded. Uncle Pete gave Jenifer a kiss on the cheek and said, "I'm glad to hear you and that nice young man visited Mrs. Kirtley last week."

"Is nothing a secret in Doolittle?" Jenifer sighed. "What did Randy Robert put in his report?"

Uncle Pete winked. "Just the facts."

"Are you and Eric responsible for Mrs. Kirtley being here today?" Charlotte looked thoughtful. "I just went back and said hello to her. I am feeling so guilty that none of us have visited her in the longest time. I am going to get the Women's Circle together and we are going to check on every shut-in and elderly member to make sure everyone who wants a ride to church gets one."

"That's a wonderful idea," Jenifer said. "Yes, we visited Mrs. Kirtley recently, but no, I am not the person who brought her here. Someone else thought of that."

"Eric?" Charlotte asked.

"That's who I put my money on," Jenifer said, wishing she'd had the idea. Eric had put them all to shame.

"What a nice young man," Charlotte said wistfully.

Oh, no, she didn't want her mother matchmaking. She'd been through these efforts over the years, especially when the twins passed their toddler stage. Before then she'd been too exhausted to even look at a man, let alone think about letting one into her life.

She hadn't even let Lawrence come see them until they reached the age of three, despite the fact that after one missed child support payment, he was on time every month. Jenifer had to admit she knew how to hold a grudge.

"Charlotte. Pete. Good morning."

Eric's voice sounded from behind her left shoulder. She turned, slowly, and just stood there, looking at him.

In his crisply starched white dress shirt, blue blazer, and khaki trousers, he looked better than a root beer float at A&W. His eyes were shining, his short dark hair neatly combed, his luscious mouth smiling.

Jenifer just stopped short of audibly catching her breath. Eric Hamilton, she reflected, had to be too good to be true.

Charlotte gave him a hug. Yes, the Wrights and the Simons sure did hug, Jenifer reflected once again. "You are an angel to have collected Mrs. Kirtley. Why, she's taught Sunday school to probably every member of this congregation, and it took a stranger coming to town to set things right."

Uncle Pete shook Eric's hand and winked. "You're the kind of young man Doolittle would like to have as a resident."

Eric shrugged, looking modestly magnificent. Jenifer almost glared at him, out of sheer frustration, though she couldn't begin to articulate why.

Pastor Roemer walked up and Charlotte introduced Eric to him.

"Nice to have you with us," the pastor said, shaking hands with Eric.

Eric nodded. He looked like he didn't know what to say.

"If you're with us next week, join us for the monthly picnic after church," Pastor Roemer said.

"Thank you," Eric said. "My stay in Doolittle is brief, but I'll keep it in mind in case I'm delayed."

Charlotte looked thoughtful. Jenifer figured her

mother was plotting to remove the distributor cap from Eric's Cadillac.

The pastor smiled and moved on, joining the cluster talking at high volume to Mrs. Kirtley.

"You want to come take your bacon with us? We eat our main meal after church. Don't know why we call it dinner when it's lunchtime, but we do," Uncle Pete said.

Eric smiled. Jenifer did not. Who did he mean by "us"? she wondered.

"I think we both have other plans," Jenifer answered.

"We do?" Eric slanted a look toward her.

"Yes. I'm sure you mentioned an important meeting. I know I have one."

He patted his flat abdomen. "Haven't had bacon in a long, long time."

Uncle Pete laughed. "You have to eat, so it might as well be with us. I'm tossing some chicken on the grill, and Charlotte's already agreed to join me. It'll just be the four of us. Everyone else is going to the Kids Fest."

"I promised Mrs. Kirtley I'd take her home," Eric said.

"Let's invite her to eat with us," Charlotte said. "I have a snow globe she might like to have."

Eric smiled at Jenifer's mother. He couldn't help but like her. She looked almost as young as Jenifer, except for the touches of silver streaking her dark hair and the crinkle lines around her eyes and mouth that Jenifer didn't have. And he'd be willing to bet she'd never harangued her now-deceased husband the way his own mother had berated his dad. Charlotte embodied grace.

"Tell you what," Pete said. "Why don't you two

youngsters take a little time. Go for a drive, then head over to the house. Mrs. Kirtley can come with us."

"I'll go invite her," Charlotte said, moving off with Pete.

Eric got a kick out of Pete's none-too-subtle tactics, but right now he was concerned about Jenifer's emotions relative to her mother. He nodded toward Charlotte. "You feeling any better about that concept today?" he asked.

He could feel her bristle. If her hair hadn't been swept into that tidy, touch-me-not bun, the ends would have sparked electricity.

"I don't know what you're talking about," Jenifer replied.

"Hi, Jenifer," a woman in a navy blue suit said. "Thank you so much for starting that children's book group. My daughter loves reading about Nancy Drew!"

Jenifer smiled and murmured a few words to the woman.

"I think you do, but you don't want to acknowledge it," Eric said as the woman moved away.

She faced him squarely and tapped one slender finger against his chest. "Do me a favor," she said, "and keep out of my family life."

"Ouch," he said. "I'm actually trying to help, though why I'm bothering, I have no idea."

"I don't, either," she said, frustration welling up. She pushed him away when so much of her wanted to embrace him.

"Shhh," he said. He put an arm around her and walked her to the peaceful and now deserted front of the church. "I'm sorry. I didn't mean to upset you. It's just so obvious to an outsider that your mother and your uncle Pete are nuts about each other."

She drew her hands into fists, punched them together, then looked up at him, laughing at herself softly as she did. "You're right," she said, "and I'm wrong. And quick, you'd better record those words 'cause you won't hear them often."

He grinned, pulled her to him and ruffled the top of her hair.

"Hey, you'll mess up my coiffure."

"That's what I'm hoping," he said, reaching around and snagging three of the pins. Her lush, long hair spilled free, and she glared at him.

"Don't fight it," he said softly. "Look pretty for me."

She tossed her head, and her hair fell free, flowing over her shoulders and over her back, curling onto her breasts, which showed to full effect in the simple floral outfit she wore.

"Can we skip the meal?"

She watched him, wary-eyed, her breath coming more quickly. "Why?"

"Dessert," he said. "I'd rather begin with dessert."

He loved the way she moistened her lips with the tip of her tongue. He bet she didn't even realize she'd done it, but the effect devastated his carefully calculated self-control. "Jesus," he said, his voice just above a whisper. "We're in a church. Maybe we ought to leave."

"And abandon Mrs. Kirtley?"

He winked. "You forget. Pete said he'd give her a ride to his house."

"Right," Jenifer said. "Eric, what made you think of bringing her to church?"

She sounded curious, he thought, and breathless, and she looked oh-so-sexy, especially now with her hair curling down and inviting his gaze to the tops of her breasts, hinted at by the V neck of her top. "You," he replied.

"Come on, don't feed me a line." She blushed, and said, "Well, okay, I do appreciate your lines, but right now, the straight truth."

He grinned and flicked a finger lightly across her cheek. "Your mother had it right. Those snow globes got to me, made me think about my grandmother all alone, sitting and waiting for company that didn't come nearly often enough."

"You're a good person," she said, moving closer to him.

"Yeah, well, let's get out of here, and I'll be happy to prove otherwise," he said, wanting one thing and one thing only at that moment.

Pete had handed Jenifer to him on a silver platter. Not for him to lose out on such an opportunity, Eric thought. "A drive sounds like a good idea," he said as they left the church parking lot. He glanced out the window. "Sun's kind of bright. Would you mind if we stopped by my motel so I can get my sunglasses?" That line was almost as bad as, Do you want to see my etchings? but Eric figured it would do in a pinch.

"No problem," Jenifer said, a smile tugging at her lips.

He burst out laughing. She joined in. "Okay, so I'd like a few minutes alone with you. You can't blame a guy for trying, right?"

She ran a hand through her hair, her expression pleased. "No blame coming your way from here," she said with another smile.

"You're very pretty," he said. "I don't think I've told you that."

"Thank you," she said. "Umm . . . er . . ."

"What?" Then he realized what she was trying not to say. "I went the wrong way just now, didn't I?"

She nodded. "You should have turned right at that corner."

"Thank you," he said meekly.

Jenifer grinned. "You're mellowing. But don't worry, it'll be our secret."

He turned the car around and corrected his driving error.

"Which motel are you staying in?" Jenifer asked, talking just to keep her mind off the amazing fact that she was headed to this man's room alone with him.

"I'm disappointed," he said, grinning. "I thought the Doolittle hotline worked better than that."

"Oh, okay," she said. "I know you're at the Highway Express, but I thought it might be, oh, obvious if I remembered that fact."

He leaned toward her and slipped a hand onto her shoulder. "I don't mind obvious," he said. "I'd like nothing more than to spend more time with you, and whether that's your place or mine, I'm happy."

She swallowed and tried to look as sophisticated and nonchalant as possible, as if she spent the afternoon with a sexy guy at a roadside motel more than once in a lifetime. Instead she had a feeling she looked nothing but confused.

If he thought so, he didn't say. For that, she was thankful. He toyed with her hair and watched her through lazy half-lidded eyes. She knew she was about to do something wildly naughty. She ought to run home and stay safely away from this man. She ought to accept her life. After all, she didn't need a man. She had to be out of her mind, going to his motel alone with him.

"Having second thoughts?"

"Did they teach you mind-reading at Harvard?" She laughed nervously.

"Oh, yeah," he said, stretching out more comfortably and drawing little circles on the back of her neck. "How to read the female mind. An invaluable ability."

"Hmm," she said breathily. She spotted the frontage road that paralleled the interstate and the tall sign heralding the Highway Express. They pulled into the parking lot, then drove around to the back, leaving the engine running.

He unfastened his seat belt, slid over, and unloosed hers. Then, pulling her close, he nuzzled her hair, seeming to drink it in. "You drive me out of my mind," he said, his voice deep and enticing. "I feel as if I've known you forever, but also that I'll never know you."

She snuggled against him, tasting his neck with her lips, and feeling very nervy in doing so. "You make me feel very daring," she whispered.

"Funny," he said, "you make me want to be a better person, and that's not something I'm used to feeling."

"You mean like with Mrs. Kirtley and Pooper?"

He kissed the top of her head, then her forehead and the tip of her nose. "I suppose," he said. "But mostly you make me want to make love to you until neither one of us can move an eyelash."

She sucked in a deep breath. How had this happened to her? How had this amazing, sensual, incredibly emotional, not to mention intelligent, man stumbled into Doolittle, Arkansas? Into her life?

Miracles, she decided, definitely did happen. She fluttered her lashes and offered her lips to him.

Fourteen

"**M**ake yourself comfortable," Eric said, opening the door of Room 218. "I'll go get us some ice."

"Sure," Jenifer said, looking very unsure.

He leaned close and held her eyes with his own. "You give the word, and we'll leave and pretend we never came here."

"Thank you," she said, "but I'd like to stay."

Eric nodded, ushered her in, and grabbed the plastic ice bucket. The last thing he needed was ice, since he had no desire to cool down, but he did need an excuse for a few minutes alone. Along with the ice bucket, he'd snagged his cell phone from the Formica-covered table. He punched in the number as he headed down the open-air walkway toward the elevator and the ice compartment.

He wanted to make sure the agent who'd been following Lars and Franco in El Dorado had picked up their trail again. The man confirmed the two were back in the town and promised to alert Eric if they headed his way again.

Now, knowing that the janitor had seen more than he should have at the paper mill, Eric expected Lars and Franco to stir up trouble. That's why they'd never made it big in the crime world—they got too emotional.

He hated to think of the boy and his neighbors caught in any crossfire. They were victims enough without any additional harm. Why he'd told the kid he would take him to the library was beyond him. Well, not really, he thought, punching the black button to set the ice tumbling into the bucket. He'd known Jenifer would be touched by the gesture. Also, he just plain damn wanted to do it.

"Turning into a bleeding heart," he muttered, and pulled the bucket from under the measured cascade of ice. "Must be all this fresh air," he said, turning around, smack into uniformed officer Randy Robert.

"You?" the young policeman said. "What are you doing here?"

"Yes, it's me," Eric said. "I'm about to have some ice water."

Randy Robert looked around, tugging on his collar. His face had turned red. "No need to mention you ran into me here."

A door opened. A pretty woman who had to be ten years older than the young man stuck her head out. "Randy, hon, is everything okay?"

"Close the door!" He ran a hand over his close-cropped hair. "Everything's fine," he said.

The woman seemed to take him at his word.

Eric leaned close and winked. "Your secret is safe with me."

"Yeah?" He looked hopeful.

"Yeah. I guess romance is in the air today." Hoping Jenifer didn't repeat Randy's lover's gesture and pop outside the room, Eric hurried back to 218. He admitted to being confused about his own motivations for inviting her to come to the motel with him. Romance? Lust?

Yeah, he was a guy, and he wanted her in a most elemental way. He also needed to get to know her better, to figure out what she knew about Lars and Franco. But he could have done that in a simple interview. Hell, he'd spent enough time with her already to believe her innocent.

Innocent. Innocent, in the most old-fashioned sense of the word.

Damn if that didn't pose a problem!

So what was a sheltered single woman from a respectable family doing inside his motel room? Jenifer Wright did not fit the profile of a woman who engaged in quickie encounters with a man she barely knew.

No. Not that perky, pert, and oddly innocent, though knowing, brunette.

So why saunter into his room?

Suddenly, his danger sensors sounded. Shit! He whirled around. In the time he'd taken to stroll to the ice machine and back, she could have rifled his room or planted a listening device. What had happened to him? The sleepy little town had lulled him into letting down his guard.

He burst through the door, the ice bucket balanced in

one hand, and halted in his tracks. She stood across the room, in front of the window, next to the air conditioner. Her hair flowed like a river of desire around her shoulders, curling onto her lush breasts.

Breasts that remained demurely tucked beneath the demure floral blouse she wore. She might have unbuttoned the second button from the top, but he couldn't swear to that.

"Hey," he said, standing there, feeling like a cross between a bellboy and a lecher.

"Hey, yourself," she said, giving him a quivering hint of a smile.

Eric moved into the room, plopping the ice container down on the laminated tabletop. He cast a quick glance around. Everything appeared to be in order. If she'd searched, she'd been neat and quick; in short, professional.

She stood there, nibbling on her thumb. He couldn't stand watching that, so he closed the distance between them. Taking her hand gently in his, he lowered it. "You're too pretty to gnaw on yourself."

She smiled in that quirky way of hers, and offered him a half laugh, half gurgle. "Cute," she said. "But it's one of the things I do when I'm about to confess."

Talk about putting him on edge. Forcing a nonchalant attitude, Eric leaned against the edge of one of the two double beds, and said, "Confess? What could you possibly have to confess?"

She laughed, a quick, nervous sound far removed from the sweet sound of a moment before. "You'd be surprised," she said. "Well, I hope you're only surprised and not shocked."

"Try me," he said, crossing his arms on his chest.

She remained where she was, in front of the air conditioner. The air from the vents puffed her skirt around her knees, gifting him with a glimpse of her well-shaped thighs every other gust or so.

"I hope you'll still respect me," she said in a shy voice. "I mean, after I tell you what I'm about to tell you."

He met her gaze. "Let's hear it."

"Right." She edged her thumb back toward her mouth, but caught it with her other hand. "You're probably wondering why someone like me would agree to go to your motel room with you."

She had that right. Eric nodded. "That did cross my mind," he said.

She nodded. "Well, I don't know if you are aware of it, but you are quite attractive, in a classic sense."

"I take it I should say thank you here?"

She shook her head. "That's okay. You can wait until I finish."

He almost grinned, but decided the best reaction would be to nod in a semisage fashion. "Go on."

She twirled a strand of hair between two fingers. "I just want to have sex," she said in a hurry, the words bumping into each other.

"You what?" Eric thought he hadn't heard her correctly.

She tipped her head to one side. "No, that's not it, either. I mean, I want to have sex, but I want to be seduced. Properly. Thoroughly. Expertly." She blushed, and looked down at her hands. "But not just as a means to an end. Oh, I'm getting this explanation all confused. . . ." Her voice trailed off.

Eric didn't know whether to hug her or stare. Clearly she hadn't come to his room to stalk through his possessions to see what she could see. But how could she not understand that she didn't need to invite a seduction? Just watching her, listening to her—hell, even taking driving directions from her—made him want her. Some response appeared to be in order, so he said, "I see."

"I hope you don't mind me being so frank," she said. "It's just that after you left the room, I realized that by coming here with you, you might think my feelings or emotions were somehow involved."

"Excuse me?" Now she had him confused. Sex was all about feeling. Yeah, feeling good. No, great.

"So it's only fair to let you know right up front that's not the case," she said, speaking quickly again.

Eric leaned forward, hands on his knees. "Okay, let's start over. You want me to seduce you but you're not particularly interested in me as a human being. Is that it?"

She wrinkled up her pretty little nose. "That doesn't make it sound so attractive, does it?" She paced to the corner of the room and back. "Things were going so well before I tried to explain, weren't they?"

He nodded. If he could just get her to shut up, he could show her exactly what she wanted. But all this talking was having the wrong effect on him.

"So no explanation is necessary?" She sighed. "Men and women do this all the time, don't they? Get naked with people they don't even know."

Eric patted the bed. "Jenifer," he said, "why don't you come sit down?"

She looked at him, her dark eyes large and luminous. Hell, she was about as skittish as a horse reluctant to enter a starting gate. But she walked toward him, her steps light and graceful as always. She settled primly on the edge of the bed, carefully not touching his leg.

The hint of ginger in her silky hair crept into his senses. He had to hold himself back or he would have buried his face in her hair. He knew better than to make any abrupt moves, though. For a woman asking for seduction, she looked a lot like a prisoner facing the guillotine. Earlier, though, she'd been ready. Several times in the past few days she'd been a malleable mush of sexual desire. But damn if something didn't interrupt them every time. He smiled at her and she smiled back.

"The room's a bit basic, isn't it?" Eric glanced around, leaving his hands on his knees. "Not what you'd call romantic."

"I suppose you're right," she said, sounding surprised at his comment. "I'm not looking for romance, Eric. That's what I'm trying to—"

He cut her off with a kiss. "Can't take any more explaining," he said, his words moving over her warm, soft, kissable mouth. He lifted her onto his lap and she slid easily, cuddling her hips against his groin. He made some noise that had less to do with language than with primal need. Claiming her mouth, he tasted her tongue, her sweetness, her fire, as his hands plundered her hair.

So much for his usual smooth, practiced seduction, he thought somewhere in some dim recess of his mind. He didn't want to pursue her—he wanted to possess her. He moved one hand from her hair to her blouse. The next in her prim little row of buttons slid open easily.

For her part, Jenifer hoped she'd done the right thing by being so up front about her motivation. She'd started to worry she was saying something stupid, because it seemed he almost withdrew from her then, but the moment Eric pulled her onto his lap, her worries evaporated.

Or more precisely, fled in the oncoming rush of sensations. He was literally kissing her senseless. She savored the greedy way his tongue captured hers, and she responded in kind. When he unfastened some of the buttons of her blouse, she pressed her body against his hand, her breasts tingling and aching and needing to be touched in a way she didn't rationally understand.

"Please," she whispered, lifting her mouth from his.

The expression on his face told her she didn't have to ask more than once. He shifted her off his lap and onto the bed. She lay on her back, arms over her head, skirt hiked up almost to her panties. Her legs were bare, and at some point her shoes had dropped off her feet. Her breasts rose and fell with each stormy breath she took, and she knew she appeared every inch the wanton she wanted to be.

And Eric, looming over her, one hand on his belt, looked every inch the conquering sex god hero she'd conjured in her fantasies. His trousers bulged and the outline of his manhood made her feel like a sex-crazed teenager wanting to touch something she'd never seen before. Jenifer reached up with one hand and ever so lightly traced the shape of him with one fingertip.

He groaned, caught her hand and pressed it hard against him. "Teasing is very dangerous," he said, his voice low and rough.

She smiled, feeling very much unlike her typical self. "You're dangerous," she said.

Eric dropped to the bed, lying on his side, still holding her hand against him. "And I guess you're a Girl Scout," he said. Grinning and leaning over, he kissed her again.

She melted. Her bones flowed into the floral polyester bedspread, dissolving beneath the heat he'd stoked within her. He kept saying her name, over and over, as if by forming the word with his lips and tongue, he'd found yet another way to taste and explore her. When he traced the line of her throat and dipped his hand into the curve of her bra, she shivered and pressed her mouth even more hungrily against his, following his example, playing with his tongue, sucking on it softly, then with more force.

He ground his body against her hand, then slipped several fingers beneath her blouse. He reached around to the back and, with an expertise she preferred not to dwell on, loosed the bra from its two-pronged catch.

She supposed she should do the same with the zipper of his trousers and his belt, but she knew she'd never do it half as gracefully. Besides, she didn't see how the zipper would go down past the bulge of his erection.

Eric lifted his mouth from hers. He had one hand cupped around her breast. She whimpered, and he said, "I'm going too fast."

"Oh, no," she said, feeling the dampness between

her thighs and his own arousal. "You're not going fast enough."

"Au contraire," he said, shifting slightly, but leaving his hand touching the fevered curve of her breast.

"But—but—" She couldn't help it. She actually sputtered. "I'm about to explode, and just look at you!"

He laughed. He threw back his head and roared.

Jenifer blushed.

He tucked a strand of hair behind her ear and kissed the tip of her nose. "Do you have any idea how adorable you are?"

"Me?" She tipped her head back. "Are you attempting to seduce me with flattery?"

He grinned and circled his thumb over her nipple, his touch so gentle she almost thought she'd imagined it. But his gaze had moved to her breast. Somehow she could tell from the intense look in his darkened eyes that he knew exactly what he was doing with that drive-me-wild breath of a touch.

He did it again, a whisper of flesh against taut, heated, needy flesh. She made a sound that was a cross between the mew of a kitten and the invitation of a siren. She had no idea where such knowledge came from, but his touch awakened some knowing part of her that she hadn't fathomed existed.

Jenifer eased her legs farther apart and tilted her hips slightly, offering herself, opening to him. He bent and kissed the inside of one leg and then the other, higher up. She wriggled against the bed, arms back, raised over her head.

"Definitely adorable," Eric said, feathering another touch of his thumb over her nipple. That was all he did, repeating the motion until she thought she would scream. He didn't kiss her legs again, or her mouth, or lower his lips to her breast.

She shivered again.

"Cold?" he asked, his hand almost touching her breast but not close enough to feel.

"Hot," she said, straining upward, seeking that incredible contact and the sensations he set off within her.

"Oh, yeah," Eric said, capturing a strand of her hair in his other hand. "We were definitely going too fast. I don't know what came over me. When a lady asks to be seduced, a gentleman doesn't jump her bones."

"No?" She knew she sounded disappointed.

He shook his head, and spread her blouse open. He slipped her bra below her nipples. "Oh, no," he said, dancing the tips of her hair across the nipple he'd been driving to sweet distraction with his almost-touch. He leaned over her, his breath joining with the silky feel of her own hair.

"What does a gentleman do?" she asked, her voice sounding drugged to her own ears.

He touched her nipple with his tongue, a gentle taste, like someone catching the first hint of melting ice cream on a cone. Then he stroked her, and suckled.

Jenifer couldn't catch her breath. Heat rocketed through her, from her breasts to every nerve ending of her quivering body. She licked her lips and tried to lift her head to kiss him, but he only shook his head and smiled like an angelic demon. "Let me do it," he said. "Let me play."

She found it hard to believe he meant that. She thought men wanted to take and conquer and find their own release and satisfaction. She'd hoped for a gratifying sexual encounter, and later—not today, because there wasn't time during this "Sunday drive"—intercourse for the first time in more years than she wanted to count. Orgasms she could handle on her own, but she'd wanted to feel a man's body moving inside her.

She could have achieved that goal and gone away pleased.

But now Eric had shattered that simple objective. Oh, yes, now she understood that she'd definitely undersold her expectations. Still, she knew better than to lie there and do nothing. All the ladies' magazines were stuffed with articles on how to delight your husband and make him smile after a rough week in the corporate jungle. Jenifer lifted her hands and circled his temples with her fingertips. She'd never practiced the techniques she'd studied in between dealing with patrons and reshelving and cataloguing, her magazines disguised behind the covers of library journals, but she'd always been an excellent student. And she had a photographic memory.

"Mmm," Eric said. "That feels good."

"I can make you feel really good," she said, unable to resist a betraying glance at his erection.

"You already have," Eric said, easing her hands from his temples. "But you're talking again. Do you always talk so much during sex?"

"I'm not sure how to respond to that question," she said.

"I am," Eric said, pulling her to him so they lay side by side, fitting perfectly despite their difference in height, or perhaps because of it. He stroked her hair and tucked her blouse more discreetly around her. "First, let me say I probably shouldn't have invited you to my room."

Her lips formed a delightfully inviting pout, but he forced himself to ignore the temptation and go on. "If we don't get to Pete's house fairly soon, I'll no doubt be met by a posse of your brothers once we dare crack open this door."

She smiled. "Oh, I thought of that," she said. "But they're all at the Kids Fest now. And besides, you parked in the back."

"Somehow, that doesn't give me much confidence," Eric said dryly. "Doolittle would appear to be an open book. I'm afraid, my dear, that I've probably ruined your reputation thoroughly."

She wriggled against him with a little moue of satisfaction. "Keep ruining it," she said, enjoying the sound of him calling her "my dear."

"I'd like nothing more," he said. And it was true. Well, no, it wasn't true, and therein lay his dilemma. He, Eric Hamilton, man about town and confirmed womanizer, suffered from qualms of a conscience he hadn't known he possessed. More than sex, he wanted her . . . her what?

Respect? Nah, guys don't think like that, he told himself. You went for the score, the touchdown, the golden ring, the cherry. But somehow he knew that if he forged ahead today, there would be no tomorrow. He might be in Doolittle for only a short while, but he wanted every tomorrow Jenifer would grant him.

What man wouldn't? Jeez, she'd quivered, open and responsive in a way both completely innocent yet totally wanton. Whatever her past experiences had been, he could tell she'd never been spoiled. The word "spoiled" just didn't fit. She'd never been treated to the thrills and wordless satisfaction of total sensual satisfaction. Sex, he knew, wasn't just about sex.

It had more to do with how the sex was perceived than the physical act itself.

"If that's true, then why did we stop?" Jenifer asked, bringing him back to the present.

"You are so damn logical," he said. Against his better judgment, and because when she smiled at him with her laughing eyes he couldn't resist, he pulled her close and kissed her.

The kiss grew and deepened. Before he knew what had happened, she'd rolled over. He found himself on his back, Jenifer straddling him, riding his body, though they were both still clothed, except for her unbuttoned blouse, as he plundered her lips, her tongue, her mouth.

Blood pounded in his ears. He knew if he opened his eyes, he'd be blinded. All his reason told him to slow down, to keep her from undoing his belt buckle. She tugged harder. His betraying greedy self bucked upward, egging her on.

The pounding in his head increased in volume, till the off-white walls of the generic room seemed to reverberate with the pulsing need of his desire.

He had to wait. Hold out. Pleasure Jenifer. Wait until tomorrow. Or the next day. Or the next. He wrapped his arms around her and rolled her over until he lay atop her.

"What's that noise?" she asked just before he lowered his head to her now bare breasts. Her bra had slipped from her body. He almost couldn't stand the anticipation of sucking the tightly pebbled rosy nipples that thrust upward, begging him to taste them.

"I don't hear anything," he said, because he couldn't make out anything other than the rushing that had filled his groin to the explosion point.

He grazed her breasts with his tongue. To his surprise, she lifted her hands against his chest. "Wait. Listen."

He realized then that in addition to the blood pumping in his ears, someone was pounding on the door of the room.

"Shit," he said, forcing himself up and away from Jenifer and off the bed. He didn't need a scene, didn't need attention focused on Jenifer here in his room with him. She had to live in Doolittle. Even though he'd been doing a fairly poor job of it, he owed her the courtesy of protecting her reputation.

"Yoo-hoo," called a voice he recognized only too well. "Open up in there. I just know you're in there."

"That's Mrs. Ball," Jenifer said, sitting bolt upright, tugging her blouse together and fumbling for the buttons. "There's no bigger gossip in town—well, except for Sweet Martha or Crabby Abbie. What's she doing here?"

Eric swore under his breath. Next time someone else offered to create a cover persona for him, he'd thank them politely, then come up with his own solution. "I spoke to her earlier," he said, "about real estate investments. I'm sure she doesn't know you're here. Pop into the bathroom. I'll talk to her until she goes away."

Jenifer nodded. She'd managed to button one of the buttons of her blouse. Her lips were puffy and kiss-swollen. Her hair fluffed around her shoulders, curling on her tingling breasts in a mass of erotic confusion.

Eric leaned over and fastened one more button, then kissed her softly on the lips. "How long can she be?" he said, then shepherded her into the pint-size bathroom and shut the door.

"Coming," he called out, wishing to hell that were true.

Fifteen

Jenifer hurried into the small bathroom carrying her bra. It could have been any bathroom in any one of a thousand roadside motels: standard prefab shower unit, sink without enough counter space, white plastic coffee maker, basic white towels. But this room stood out from all those others. A leather dop kit sat open beside the sink. A razor, a can of Gillette shaving cream, a rumpled tube of basic Crest toothpaste, a packet of dental floss, and a toothbrush with the bristles sticking out every which way—none of these items had found their way back into the bag. Jenifer smiled, feeling oddly comfortable and at home with the scene. Guys never did put things away.

And Eric defined maleness.

Oh, yes. She touched a finger to her lips. She could still taste his mouth and feel the incredible dance of sensations.

She lifted her gaze to the mirror, almost crying out

in amazement. The sultry, ravished creature staring back at her could not possibly be Jenifer Janey Wright.

Her blouse gaped open, revealing breasts and nipples, still taut from the piercing sexual need Eric created in her. Jenifer slipped one finger into her mouth, sucking it as she studied the effect.

A rush of sexual power hit her. At that moment she knew she could try anything with the man who'd unleashed this magic. She moved her hand from her lips to her throbbing breasts, praying to Eros for Mrs. Ball to scram.

At least the knocking had stopped. Noticing that the bathroom door hadn't shut all the way, Jenifer listened while slipping her bra back on over her still-excited breasts.

Evidently, Eric had managed to hold Mrs. Ball off in the doorway. The real estate agent's enthusiasm and persistence would have propelled her past a lesser force and into the room, where she'd remain until the client agreed to go with her.

"But my dear Mr. Hamilton," Mrs. Ball was saying, "it would be so much nicer for you to go in my car. You don't know your way around our little town yet, and I wouldn't want you to get lost." She ended the sentence with her musical laugh.

Jenifer winced. She knew Mrs. Ball possessed a heart of gold. She donated to the library whenever they had a special fund drive; she worked tirelessly to make her business a success. But sometimes Jenifer wished Mrs. Ball wouldn't try quite so hard. Her persistent enthusiasm was hard to take in more than a small dose.

"I'm late for Sunday dinner at Pete Simon's house," Eric replied. "We'll have to reschedule."

"Never put off till tomorrow what can be done today, I always say," Mrs. Ball said.

Jenifer could picture her wagging a finger at Eric. She glanced down at her disheveled skirt and blouse and her bare feet. How much faster Mrs. Ball would wag that finger if she only knew what Eric had been up to when she'd interrupted him!

Bare feet.

Jenifer stared at her toes, painted with a cherry red polish. They stared back at her, and in a flash of imagination, she could have sworn one of them winked at her.

Oh, no, her shoes! They'd slipped off her feet, perhaps after she'd sat on the bed. So they shouldn't be visible from the doorway. Thank goodness she'd snatched her bra!

And what if Mrs. Ball did spot a pair of faux crocodile slides? She had no way of connecting them with Jenifer Janey "I don't need a man" Wright.

"Mrs. Ball, what would you think if I told you I've changed my mind about the Horace House?"

Jenifer stiffened. What did Eric mean?

"I'd listen to every word you have to say," she said. "But first I'd have to ask you if I can come in, sit down, and have a glass of water. I'm not as young as I look."

Nobody beat Mrs. Ball for gumption. Jenifer had to grin despite the fact the last thing she wanted was for Mrs. Ball to stick around. She'd bested Eric on that round. The realtor's voice moved past the door and into the room, and Jenifer's thoughts returned to Horace

House. Eric was an investor. Could he be interested in buying Horace House?

"Oh, I see you already have a nice full bucket of ice," Mrs. Ball was saying, sounding cheery.

"I'll get a glass," Eric said.

He popped into the bathroom. Jenifer barely scooted away from the door in time to avoid being knicked by it. He made a circling sign around his ear, the classic, "kooky crazy" symbol, and then kissed her full on the lips.

"Back soon," he whispered, grabbed a plastic-wrapped cup, tore the cover off, half filled it with tap water, and headed back for more of Mrs. Ball.

"Thank you," Mrs. Ball said. "Water always hits the spot, doesn't it? Now why don't you sit down, too, here at the table with me? This room is rather spartan, isn't it? My my, why you aren't staying at the Schoolhouse Inn, I just don't understand. You are missing out on the charms of Doolittle."

"That's what Pete Simon said, too," Eric said.

Jenifer winced. Strategic mistake. Never engage in conversation with a nonstop talker. She kicked at the bath mat and a towel that lay crumpled on the floor. Evidently the cleaning crew ran late on Sundays, no doubt so they could attend church. A crinkle of paper caught her attention. Bending down, she noticed a square of folded paper on the floor beneath the towel, along with a pair of socks and a pair of men's briefs. Had Eric dropped the paper when he changed clothes?

She picked it up and placed it on the bathroom counter beside his toiletry bag. It looked like a page of printed material, and it might be something he needed.

Thinking of things he needed, Jenifer couldn't help but wonder if he'd packed any condoms for his jaunt into Doolittle. He couldn't have been expecting to pick up any women in such a small town, but perhaps he always traveled prepared. She hoped so. Otherwise, when he did manage to shake Mrs. Ball, the two of them would find themselves at a standstill.

No condoms; no sex.

Jenifer sighed. In the outer room, Mrs. Ball had launched into a tale of the glorious possibilities of the Horace House. Evidently she'd decided to sell Eric on the idea of buying the property. Jenifer didn't know what to think about that. She trusted Eric instinctively, even though she suspected something didn't quite fit about his tale of scouting investment property in Doolittle.

She turned her back to the mirror and leaned against the counter. Her hip jostled the edge of the paper. Her curiosity warred with her conscience. Reading other people's materials definitely crossed the line of propriety. But turning and looking at the folded piece of paper, she spotted the telltale cherry red color of her nail polish, and she remembered the day she'd applied a fresh coat. It had been the Saturday that Eric appeared at the Doolittle Library.

Too anxious to contain herself now, she picked up the page, and unfolded it.

Jenifer stared at the images for a moment, recognizing something she'd printed at the library and then discarded when she'd mistakenly hit the Print button twice. How had Eric gotten hold of it?

Then she remembered. He'd helped her carry the trash outside.

But had he searched her trash?

Why would he do that?

Or had he intended to toss it in the trash and absently stuffed it into his pocket? She preferred to think that, because the page was a printout explaining how to detect counterfeit bills.

She leaned against the counter and tapped the page against her chin, thinking hard. Andie had paid her fine with the crisp twenty-dollar bill from a suspect source shrouded in dangerous mystery, and Eric, a stranger, had appeared in Doolittle at about the same time. Two other strangers had also shown up, she realized—Lars and Franco. Were they in cahoots? Was one or more of them good guys chasing bad guys? Or was none of it connected?

Certainly none of these bits and pieces of information added up.

She could ask him, of course: Eric, what are you doing with my trash?

Mrs. Ball's voice, sounding much louder, intruded. Jenifer folded the sheet of paper into a smaller square and tucked it in the pocket of her skirt.

"Oh, I don't mind a mess," Mrs. Ball was saying. "Goodness knows I've been married to Mr. Ball for thirty-seven years. I've seen everything a man can do to wreck a room, believe you me." She ended her sentence in a trill of laughter.

"No, really," Eric said. "You wouldn't want to go in there."

"But I do," the realtor said. "Also, you don't mind me being just the teeniest bit frank and to the point— after that refreshing glass of water, the need is rather urgent. I promise not to tell anyone what I find." She laughed again.

"I hope to hell that's true," Eric said.

The door swung open.

Jenifer stared.

Mrs. Ball stared back, and slowly a smile appeared on her face, the smile too arch for Jenifer's liking.

"Mrs. Ball," Jenifer said, thinking fast, "what a surprise." She moved into the doorway. "Please, be my guest. You know how it is, when you've got to go, you've got to go." She urged the temporarily speechless realtor into the bathroom and pulled the door shut behind her as she exited.

Eric glared at the closed door. "I am so sorry," he said in a voice just above a whisper.

"No problem," Jenifer replied, speaking in a normal voice. Mrs. Ball wouldn't flush until she listened to every word of their conversation. "Thank you so much for the chance to discuss the history of Horace House. I know you're more than ready—" She glanced at his trousers and saw that Mrs. Ball had managed to cool Eric's ardor. "—to go visit the property with Mrs. Ball. Just drop me at my car and I'll make your excuses to Pete and Charlotte."

"That's a good plan, dear," the realtor called through the door. "You'd make a good realtor. I always say, a realtor is a full-service salesperson. You have a need, I have a solution."

Mrs. Ball had popped out now, and Eric herded her to the door, promising to call her later. Then he turned to Jenifer, intending to apologize.

Mrs. Ball's appearance on the scene had served both

as a nuisance and a gift from the gods. Jenifer didn't need him in her ordered world, he'd decided. What could be a casual exchange for him would have to mean more to her, no matter what she said about wanting to be seduced and not having her emotions involved. She was not the type to have casual sex no matter what she said.

And he didn't want to take advantage of her innocence. Well, that wasn't totally true. He wanted her—warm, yielding, playful, and sensual.

"Jenifer—" he began, but she cut him off.

"I need to go," she said tersely.

"Yes, we do," he said, grabbing his phone and the sunglasses he'd used as the excuse to stop at his room. "But first I need to apologize."

She looked at him. "I'm listening."

"I brought you up here to seduce you, and that was wrong of me. No matter what you may have asked me to do. I've compromised your reputation and I'm sorry. You deserve to be treated like the lady you are."

"Didn't you want to kiss me?"

"Of course I wanted to kiss you. That's not the point. Did you listen to what I just said?"

"So you want to kiss me. You desire me. You're not after me for any other reason?"

"What do you mean?" Her question put him on alert.

"Oh, any ulterior motives? You did mention seeking information the day you came into the library."

Did she suspect him? Interesting. He took a step closer, put his hands on her shoulders and turned her, easing her toward the mirror hung on the wall opposite the foot of the bed. He stood behind her, tangling his fingers in her hair, touching her cheek with the silky tendrils.

"Look at you," he said, nodding toward their images in the mirror. "You're beautiful. Gorgeous. Sexy. What man in his right mind wouldn't want to make love to you?" He stroked her lips, still pouty from his earlier kisses. It was all he could do to keep from turning her around, crushing her close, and starting all over again where they'd left off when Mrs. Ball had so rudely interrupted them.

Jenifer relaxed against him, her fanny teasing him with her closeness. He returned his hands to her shoulders. He whispered in her ear, "I'd love to start undressing you, one button at a time, right here, and show you just how desirable you are, to give you pleasure you've probably never imagined. . . ."

Jenifer shivered and pressed even more closely against him. Her eyes were wide, her lips slightly parted.

"But right now isn't the time," he said.

She moistened her lips, nodding. "No, not right now. But you do swear you're in this room right now because of everything you just said?"

"Anyone ever told you what a single track mind you have?" He said it jokingly.

"All the time."

He nodded, kissed the top of her head. "Yes, I swear it." And it was true. Investigation notwithstanding, he wanted to be with her. More than any other woman he'd ever known.

She regarded him, their gazes meeting in the mirror. "Then don't apologize for kissing me," she said. "I'm a grown woman and I asked you to have your way with me." She slipped from his hold and stepped into her sandals.

"I have my scruples," Eric said, holding the door open for her.

"Me, too," she said. "And my standards. That's why I asked you if you were keeping something from me."

He raised two fingers. "Scout's honor," he said. If all went well, she'd never have to know she'd been a person of interest in the counterfeiting investigation. That might have been what brought him to town, but only Jenifer the woman was what made him want her, and what led him to apologize to her.

Caring for a woman was a lot more complicated than seducing one.

Sixteen

Jenifer had a hard time adjusting from the steamy encounter in Eric's motel room to the normalcy of the Sunday midday meal.

She felt like a different woman than the one who'd gotten out of bed that morning, talked to her children, and then gone to church. In some primal way, she'd been touched by the passion Eric had awakened in her.

She understood for the first time the tale of Adam and Eve. She had tasted the fruit of desire a truly marvelous lover evoked—and she wanted more.

Toying with the melting ice cream on her dessert plate, and casting a glance across the table at Eric, she decided his lips were sweeter. She hadn't forgotten about the mysterious presence of her Internet printout in Eric's bathroom, but she believed him when he said he had no motives for pursuing her—other than desire.

Because what could they possibly be? He'd explained as they drove from the motel that he needed to clarify an impression he'd let go uncorrected at the cookout. He was indeed in town to consider purchasing the historic Horace House, but he hadn't wanted to talk about it earlier. Knowing how zealously Mrs. Ball pounced at the least hint of interest, Jenifer found his statement plausible.

All in all, the only explanation she marveled at was his sensual attraction to her. She took another look at him, sitting between Charlotte and Mrs. Kirtley at the large oval dining room table Pete and his wife had bought after they had gotten married. Jenifer had heard the story many times—of how much his wife had wanted a table large enough to serve a proper Sunday crowd. Even then, before she and Uncle Pete had children, when he was only a patrolman on the police squad, she'd known their home would become a favored gathering place.

Jenifer watched Eric, who appeared so at ease, and wondered whether he always fit in so well with his surroundings, or whether the magic of the Simons' table worked its charms on him, too. Today the five of them clustered at one end of the oval—Uncle Pete, Charlotte, Eric, Mrs. Kirtley, and her.

And everyone except her seemed quite mellow, as befit a relaxing Sunday dinner. Mrs. Kirtley scraped the last crumb off the dessert plate that had held her second helping of Charlotte's apple pie. Jenifer's first slice lay half eaten in front of her and she felt guilty for not chowing down on it as she watched Mrs. Kirtley demonstrate just how good it tasted.

"Miss Charlotte, you sure can bake," Mrs. Kirtley said, laying down her fork with a sigh. "I hope next week you and your family will stop by my house and have some of my next batch of elderberry wine." Her glance bobbed around the table, seeing but not seeing.

She could feel, though, Jenifer thought. And she knew she sat there as part of their extended family. Jenifer peeked at Eric, who was discussing with Uncle Pete the virtues of one caliber of bullet over another for stopping an intruder. Odd conversation for a peaceful Sunday, she thought, but decided for once not to interrupt, contenting herself with the treat of simply watching him.

She noticed that even relaxed, Eric sat upright with an almost military-strict posture. He'd taken off his jacket before the meal, at Uncle Pete's urging, and rolled up his sleeves. His tanned forearms thrust from the crisp white fabric in stark contrast. His arms were chiseled, the muscles evident. His fingers, powerful-looking but slender, wrapped around the coffee mug in a way that tugged at something deep in Jenifer's gut as she pictured them touching her in knowing, gentle ways that were most delightfully wicked.

Ah, yes. Wicked. Was that too much to ask for at least once in a lifetime? Some might say getting pregnant at eighteen and not marrying the man who provided the sperm fell into the category of wicked, but she had been cheated of much excitement that time around. Her darling, wonderful, irreplaceable babies were conceived in a brief tussle in their father's dorm room at the University of Arkansas, when she had been too naive and gullible to insist on using protection. After all, she and Lawrence were in love, so what did all that matter? They were going to spend the rest of their lives together.

Jenifer sighed and picked at her apple pie. Usually she had an excellent appetite.

Lately she'd caught herself thinking back on her life more than made her comfortable. Past equals past, she reminded herself. Now equals now. Future equals who knows, so why fret? After Eric left town, though, she might go to Florida and visit her baby sister Paulette, fondly known as Pickle, as she was always in one fix or another. She didn't think she could stand knowing that no matter who knocked at her door or strolled into the library, it wouldn't be Eric.

She dropped her fork. It hit her plate, bounced and rattled onto the floor.

"Sweetie, are you feeling okay?" Her mother looked at her the way she used to when she was eight and had a fever and didn't want to give into it and climb under the covers.

"I'm fine," she said, the words coming out clipped, almost in one quick word of denial.

Eric turned from his gun talk and looked at her, heat in his eyes, and Jenifer could do nothing but warm slowly, from the inside out, every sensor in her body quivering in response to the message she read in his eyes.

"Fine," she said, a little louder, for Mrs. Kirtley's benefit.

To Jenifer's relief, Uncle Pete's doorbell rang, chiming throughout the house in a startling electronic peal of tones.

"I wonder who that is," Charlotte murmured.

Uncle Pete pushed back from the table. "Nobody rings the bell," he said. "People knock or just walk on in. Forgotten what it sounds like. Pretty darn noisy, isn't it?" The chimes sounded again, and he said, "Hold your horses, I'm coming."

He headed out of the room. Mrs. Kirtley licked her fork again. Charlotte sliced another piece of pie and slipped it onto her plate.

Eric smiled as he watched the refueling action and met Jenifer's eyes. She returned the private look of appreciation of the moment, happy to be exactly where she sat.

"Yoo-hoo, Pete Simon," sang a female voice, growing louder by the second. "I wasn't born yesterday. And there's very little in this town that goes on that doesn't reach my ears."

Jenifer shot a look at Eric. Sure enough, Mrs. Ball rounded the corner, Uncle Pete in her wake. She stood there, one hand on an ample hip, the other grasping a large carryall, surveying the group with her bright eyes. She might have stood only a few inches over five feet, but she dominated any room she occupied.

Jenifer had asked her more than once to lower her voice in the library.

"Hello, Charlotte," Mrs. Ball said as she set down her bag. "And Jenifer, nice to see you so soon again." She winked. "Must be lonesome without those little ones at home. Oh, and Mrs. Kirtley, what a treat. You do let me know when you're ready to move into a nursing home and put that fabulous place of yours on the market!"

Mrs. Kirtley stopped eating. She didn't have to ask Mrs. Ball to speak up. "Is that B-B-Ball?"

"Yes, ma'am," Mrs. Ball said.

"Did I not teach you that Jesus drove the money-changers out of the temple?"

"That does sound vaguely familiar," Mrs. Ball said.

"Is that a yes?" Mrs. Kirtley barked the question, holding her fork like a ruler.

"Yes, Mrs. Kirtley."

Eric sat at the end of the table, grinning. Then, even as she sat there watching him, his grin faded. Instead of amused, he looked concerned. No, he looked downright worried, no doubt concerned that Mrs. Ball would embarrass them by mentioning the motel encounter. But Jenifer thought that despite the earlier wink, Mrs. Ball would put business first. Why, if she couldn't interest him in the Horace House, she might try to sell him a nice little starter house. Mrs. Ball had been selling lots in Doolittle Estates for the past five years, and to her credit, succeeding, despite the fact that the lumber company that owned the development had stripped every tree from every postage-stamp-size lot. Mrs. Ball overcame that objection by offering a coupon good at the local nursery for ten percent off a tree that would reach maturity about the same time as a savings bond.

"So what are you doing working on a Sunday?" Mrs. Kirtley asked in an interrogating voice.

"I'm visiting," Mrs. Ball said, waving one hand.

"Then don't ask me to sell my house again while you're visiting," Mrs. Kirtley rejoined.

Maybe that explained Eric's sudden lack of mirth, Jenifer thought. Maybe he felt concern over Mrs. Kirtley being prodded about moving out of her home, even though both Eric and she knew after their visit that the

Sunday school teacher couldn't keep the house up, let alone look after herself properly.

"Well," Mrs. Ball said, tugging on the sleeves of her suit jacket, "since I'm visiting, I wouldn't say no to a piece of that pie."

"Coffee, too? And some ice cream?" Charlotte asked.

Mrs. Ball patted her rounded tummy and said, "Well, really I shouldn't, but maybe just a teeny slice."

Uncle Pete had taken his seat again, but he didn't look too happy with their visitor. Jenifer had inherited her house from her Wright grandmother, so she'd never had business dealings with Mrs. Ball, but Uncle Pete had, and the real estate lady had never been his favorite person. Not that she was bad-hearted, she'd heard him say more than once, or dishonest, but that she never stopped talking.

Mrs. Ball tasted her pie, made an "isn't it yummy" face, and started talking even before she finished chewing. "My my, aren't you an excellent baker, Charlotte. Anyway, as I was saying, when I heard you had Eric Hamilton over at your house, I said, Millie Ball, why not just slip on over there and surprise him."

Eric managed a smile. Well, she certainly had surprised him. He never would have said they were going to Pete's house if he'd thought she would track him down.

As they continued to talk, Eric felt terrified. Maybe they'd all become entangled in conversation and forget about addressing him.

Mrs. Ball let loose her annoying, tittering laugh. "Oh, yes, Charlotte, I met Mr. Hamilton the other day.

Before that I'd only corresponded with his secretary when we made the arrangements for Mr. Hamilton's visit and tour of the property, and I'm pleased to say he's not at all the old fuddy-duddy we expected." She laughed again and gave him an arch glance.

"Property?" Mrs. Kirtley glared, her rheumy eyes almost bugging from her weathered face. "Are you at it again, working on the Lord's Day?" She shook her head. "First time I'm blessed to make it to services in a coon's age and you want to come along and spoil the peace and pleasure this day has meant to me." She sighed. "I've a good mind to have you stand in the corner."

Eric couldn't help but laugh, though he tried to hide it in a cough. He glanced over at Jenifer and found her smiling, though also showing a faint wrinkle between her brows. No doubt she'd started to analyze his explanation and his silence on the topic of the old hotel. He wondered if she ever stopped analyzing, weighing, thinking. He'd love to help her escape her mind—and live fully in the realm of feeling. Then he realized, with a start, that he wanted the same escape for himself. Just maybe the two of them could help each other achieve a state they'd never known.

"You know, Millie," Pete said, "Mrs. Kirtley's right. You're welcome to sit a spell with us, but no more business talk. Now as we were discussing," Uncle Pete barreled on, and Eric wanted to salute his tactics, "there's no reason for Mrs. Kirtley to ever sit home again and miss church services. Isn't that right, Mrs. Kirtley?"

She patted him on the hand. "What a kind man you are, Pete Simon. If I were a few years younger, I'd think of trying to win your heart. Not that anyone can replace your dear wife, of course." She sighed and folded her hands in her lap. "I thank you."

Jenifer nodded, agreeing a little too vigorously. Eric was willing to bet that Pete and Charlotte would marry in a quiet ceremony before the end of the year.

"We'll pick you up next Sunday," Charlotte said, clearly meaning she and Pete.

"I can do it," Jenifer said.

"You can do it the week after," her mother said.

Eric could tell she wanted to argue. Her mouth wiggled, as if words fought with other words, fighting over her sense of decorum.

Jenifer didn't hold back easily, he realized. When she wanted to do something, she chafed at delay. He thought of the way she'd said the words "I just want to have sex" all in one breath and grinned, remembering her head-on approach.

No, she didn't hold back. He could tell by the heated way she'd responded to his touch in the motel room that she would be a wild, impassioned, unrestrained lover. He bet she would talk a lot, too. Oh, yes, he could hear her now, whispering sweet crazy phrases in a breathy voice. He shifted in his chair, studying the crumbs on his plate, anything to take his mind off the mental image he'd created.

"Would you like a turn, Mrs. Ball?" Charlotte asked, jerking Eric back to the moment.

"Turn at what?" The realtor kept staring at him, practically chomping at the bit to get down to business.

"To offer Mrs. Kirtley a ride to and from church," Charlotte said.

"Oh, well, I'll have to check my calendar," she said, reaching for the large bag she'd set on the floor.

"Hah!" Mrs. Kirtley laughed. "If ever I had a student who didn't mind her Sunday lessons, it had to be you. I think you'd sell your firstborn down the river to close a deal."

"I don't have any children," Mrs. Ball said, flipping open her appointment book.

"Well, now, isn't that a shame," Mrs. Kirtley said. "Who's going to take care of you in your old age?"

"I've already purchased a condominium at Lake Doolittle Retirement Village, plus I have lifetime care insurance. Mrs. Clark, my former business partner, moved there last year to care for her ailing mother. She just adores it."

"Well, aren't you prepared?" Pete said. "I mean, that sounds like sensible planning, Mrs. Ball."

"Oh, I've no plans to retire for years," she replied. "Especially not with the growth I foresee in our little town."

"Most of us live here because we like Doolittle the way it is," Charlotte said.

"Oh, fuddy-duddy," Mrs. Ball said. "The paper mill is expanding, the retirement community is bustling, and once we get Horace House open again, we'll have all sorts of new opportunities in Doolittle."

"I'll believe Horace House is back in business when I see it with my own eyes," Pete said. "That place has been taken back by the bank more times than my golf ball has landed in the rough."

Eric grinned. "We'll have to play a round sometime," he said. "Sounds like my kind of golf."

"Stick around and we'll do that," Pete said. "If you didn't bring your clubs, Busby would probably let you use his."

"Or he could use Shane's," Charlotte said.

"Mother!" It sounded like the word had been strangled from Jenifer's throat. "Those are Daddy's."

"Well, he's not going to be using them, sweetie. Besides, I think he'd approve of Eric."

Jenifer's eyes flashed.

"Using his clubs, I mean," Charlotte added.

"Thank you, Mrs. Wright," Eric said. "I appreciate the offer. And the sentiment." And he did. Their acceptance of him touched him deeply. As a man who drifted in and out of so many settings and who rarely felt he belonged anywhere, he felt at home around this table, surrounded by these people he scarcely knew but already felt close to.

"Well, I can't tell you how pleased I am to find Mr. Hamilton so at home already," Mrs. Ball said. She tugged a long roll of papers from her large bag and eased the rubber band that held them in a tight tube down the length, twisting it around her wrist when it came free. "And, Mrs. Kirtley, think of this as a cultural moment, okay, dearie?"

Eric and the others sat in silence as Mrs. Ball uncurled the long roll of paper. "I just decided to stop by and show you some more ideas, you know, come right straight to the customer. You don't mind, do you, Mr. Hamilton? Or may I call you Eric?"

Eric started to speak but no words came out. He opened his mouth, moved his tongue, then snapped his lips together. Jenifer looked at him, curiosity mingled with what he interpreted as hurt. He should have been more up-front with her, he chided himself.

"Oh, don't tell me you haven't told these good people," Mrs. Ball said. "You have sitting at your table the next owner of Horace House."

Eric cleared his throat. "Mrs. Ball, I haven't reached any decisions. Perhaps we should excuse ourselves and reconvene at your office."

"We suspected as much," Charlotte said, sounding more than pleased. She sounded thrilled.

"You sure kept quiet about that at the cookout," Pete said.

"Yes sir," Eric said, "I did. I don't want to raise anyone's hopes. I'm a prospective buyer. It's not definite."

"Oh, tee-hee-hee," Mrs. Ball said. "Just examine these sketches." She scooted over the pie plate and Pete's centerpiece of garden flowers and anchored the corners of the large paper with her dessert plate, the cream and sugar, and Mrs. Kirtley's empty coffee cup. "Look at the flowing lines of this front elevation. Picture the cash register ringing up hundred-dollar-a-night room sales, and the crystal tinkling in the dining room. This town needs a nice hotel, and you, I can tell, are the very man to bring Horace House into the twenty-first century."

"Now how can you tell that?" Pete had tipped his chair back and regarded Mrs. Ball skeptically.

Mrs. Ball wagged her finger at him. "Don't ask me to give away my business secrets."

"Ha!" Mrs. Kirtley slapped the table with her hand. "I knew these pictures weren't for culture. They're not even pretty. You roll those things up and put them away until Monday. We weren't meant to work seven days a week."

Mrs. Ball glared at the older woman and looked over at Pete and Charlotte, and then to Eric and Jenifer, apparently seeking support to defy the Sunday school teacher. She didn't find it.

With a long-suffering sigh, Mrs. Ball rolled up her sketches, secured them with the rubber band, and placed them back into her carryall. She glanced at her watch and said, "Well, Eric, why don't you come with me and we'll go mosey around the property?"

"Sure would be nice to play the piano again," Mrs. Kirtley said. "But I can't see the keys anymore."

"What would you like to hear?" Jenifer asked, pushing her chair back from the table. "Run along, Eric, with Mrs. Ball. I'll play for Mrs. Kirtley and take her home."

Eric did not figure himself for a fool. If he left now, it would take hours to win Jenifer back to her friendly, kissable self. He wished he'd had Chester Huey and his research staff on the hot seat. They had thought themselves so clever in coming up with the Horace House as a reason for a wealthy stranger to visit the out-of-the-way Arkansas town. None of them had ever set foot in a city with a population less than a million or they would have known that every move a stranger made would be broadcast by the mysterious back fence communications system that flourished in Doolittle. Well, he had his cover, but right now he wanted Jenifer's attentions.

"Mrs. Ball," he said, "I invited Mrs. Kirtley out today and it would be rude of me to run off and leave her.

If you don't mind, why don't we meet later? Better yet, I'll ask Jenifer to show me around the hotel. Jen?"

Eric didn't know who was more surprised, Jenifer or Mrs. Ball.

"You want me to give you a tour of the Horace House?"

He nodded. "Sure, I bet you know the history of the place better than anyone in town."

Charlotte smiled. "I see you've been getting to know our Jenifer Janey."

Eric grinned at Jenifer's mother. "I'm happy to say I have."

"We're happy, too," Pete said, giving him another one of his man-to-man winks.

Jenifer knew when a force superior in numbers had surrounded her. Her family clearly conspired to throw her together with Eric. Well, it was what she wanted, too, wasn't it? Laughingly, she said, "Okay, okay. Of course I'll play tour guide."

"Well," Mrs. Ball said, her eyes almost popping from her face. "I guess that's settled, then. After you've done your look-see, just give me a call. As long as my client's happy, I'm happy." She smiled all around, but she didn't look pleased despite the expression. "Here's my card, Eric. It has my cell phone, my home number, and my pager. So when you're ready to close the deal, you can't miss me." She tee-hee'd a bit.

Eric took the card, tucked it into the front pocket of his dress shirt, and rose from the table. "Mrs. Ball, let me see you out," he said, ushering her from the room.

Pete leaned back in his chair. "Now that's a man who knows how to handle a situation," he said.

"Jenifer, I wouldn't let him wiggle out of town if I were you."

"Uncle Pete!" She glanced toward the door. "Really!"

Charlotte smiled. "It is nice to see you having a good time, Jenifer."

Jenifer wanted to sink through the floor. She felt fifteen again.

Eric reappeared in the doorway, looking pleased with himself. "So where's that piano?"

Seventeen

Jenifer had been surprised when Eric put off Mrs. Ball. Now that his real reason for being in Doolittle was out of the bag, why not go with the agent and visit the property? Yet he'd stayed and seemed to thoroughly enjoy himself, joining in the impromptu singalong with a rich baritone.

She stopped the whirring of her mind long enough to wave good-bye to Mrs. Kirtley from the passenger window of Eric's car as he escorted her to her front door. Eric had insisted on driving and invited Jenifer along, telling her they'd go back to the church and collect her car. Now she faced thinking of a way to excuse herself. This afternoon she wanted to see if she could slip into the paper mill and look around.

Not that the thrill of sleuthing could compare with the excitement she experienced in Eric's company. Still, a plan remained a plan, and she had never allowed herself to be deterred by blood-thumping feelings, so she didn't see any reason to start changing her modus operandi now.

Eric slid back behind the wheel. "That is one happy woman," he said softly, glancing toward the front porch where Mrs. Kirtley stood, waving at them, a smile lighting her face like a sunbeam breaking through a cloud.

"Thanks to you," Jenifer said, resisting an impulse to reach over and touch the back of his hand.

He shrugged and turned the key in the ignition. "It seemed the right thing to do."

"Like planning to buy the Horace House but not saying anything about it?"

He left both his hands on the steering wheel but turned his face toward her. "I am sorry about the, er, double message."

"That's a funny description," Jenifer pointed out; rather rationally, she thought.

"It's only a possibility," he said, sounding defensive.

"And you're not staying in Doolittle?" She needed to get this fact straight.

"Hmm," Eric said, letting the car roll slowly up the block. He grinned. "I know there's a right answer and a wrong answer to that question."

"Just answer honestly," she said. "Turn right."

"That, I remember," Eric said. "And no, I did not undertake this visit to Doolittle with any intentions of taking up residence here."

Jenifer wrinkled her brow as she analyzed his words. "Hmm," she said, mimicking him. "You're sure you didn't graduate from Harvard Law?"

"Cross my heart," he said.

"You do have a way with words. You can just drop me at my car. Turn left here and at the stop sign—"

"Turn left again," he finished. "I'm known for my sense of direction."

"So you must have some wealthy backers, or are you buying the hotel on your own?" She knew the question showed her to be nosy, but she didn't care. Her curiosity won out over polite manners.

"I have a bit saved up," Eric said noncommitally.

Why Doolittle? Jenifer wondered. But she didn't ask that question. Something smelled fishy in his responses, and she decided to treat his presence as her second mystery to be solved. First the funny money, then she'd figure out what lay behind his appearance in town. "Well, I know Mrs. Ball is anxious to sit down and talk serious business with you," she said. "I'll just hop out when we reach my car."

"Have a hot date?"

"Don't be silly," she said, providing a little laugh with her answer. "I do have a few things to take care of, though."

"I can't interest you in a Sunday drive?" He slipped his right arm along the back of the seat as he asked the question. His voice, low and sexy, made her want to cast her plans right out the window and cozy up next to him on the plush seat.

"N-no, thanks," she said. "I have some things I do on the weekend. To get ready for the week ahead, you know."

"Such as?"

She couldn't think of a thing. Usually she relaxed or

went places with her kids, or went swimming at Lake Doolittle. "Ironing," she supplied. "I do my ironing."

He cocked a brow. "Can't you do that later?"

"Don't you need to review your investment plans?"

He flexed his fingers and they grazed the curve of her shoulder. "I'd much rather spend time with you," he said.

"That's nice," she replied, "but not the strongest compliment." She flashed him a smile. "Here we are. Maybe we can take that drive later, if you want me to show you Horace House. Say this evening?"

He pulled over. He watched her more carefully than she liked, since she was sure he didn't believe a word of her excuse. Well, what did that matter? "How's seven sound?" he asked.

"Great," she said. Now that they were pulled up next to her car in the otherwise empty church parking lot, she felt torn about her choice. "About the hotel—don't let Mrs. Ball talk you into anything you're not sure about," she said, looking into his dark eyes and leaning close to him, when she should have had her hand on the door handle and on her way out of his car.

He cupped his hand along her jaw. "Nobody talks me into anything I don't want to do," he said, his voice low and husky.

"Is that right?" She moistened her lips, her breath betraying her by coming too quickly.

"And conversely, I usually get what I want," he said, his darkened eyes and gentle but possessive touch emphasizing his meaning.

"Oh, me, too," Jenifer said, slipping free of his warm hand. Out of the corner of her eye she'd spotted someone looking out the window in the church rectory. "I'd love to continue this moment," she said, "but we're starring in a neighborhood movie right now. Besides, it'll be more private tonight," she said, feeling brazen. Wouldn't Pamela be proud of her?

The thought made her frown, her hand still on the door catch.

"What's the matter, Jenifer?"

"I just remembered that I should check on Pamela."

"She seemed okay at church. Even Ace seemed to be behaving himself."

"But she told me to call her later. That means she has something she needs to tell me."

"Maybe you can talk while you're ironing," Eric said.

"While I'm what?" She didn't catch the reference, then realized her own slip. "Good idea," she said, jumping from the car. She would call Pamela from her cell phone on the way out to the country road leading to the paper mill.

Ironing, my foot, Eric thought, stroking his upper lip and reflecting on the subtle indications of nervous fibbing that Jenifer had been broadcasting. No doubt she didn't realize what a bad liar she was, and those signs of innocence bolstered his conclusion that she had nothing to do with Lars and Franco. Jenifer definitely had something going on that she didn't want to reveal, but he was convinced that she walked on the right side of the law. So what was the mystery? Or did she simply want to ditch him to go for a bikini wax?

Right. In Doolittle, Arkansas, on a Sunday afternoon? Eric grinned as he headed down the street and tucked his car discreetly around the corner, waiting to follow Jenifer to see what she was up to.

Then the image of a bikini wax outlining the delicious center of Jenifer's sweet, sexual self hit him full force. He had to grab the steering wheel and take a few deep breaths to calm his wayward responses. Oh, yeah, a delicately neat trim would lead his hungry mouth to exactly where he wanted to taste, to suckle, to conquer.

"Get a grip, Hamilton," he said out loud. Clearly, his body had overwhelmed his reason. "Down boy," he said, wishing he were in Jenifer's bed rather than sitting in his car waiting to discover her true plans for the rest of the afternoon.

Because she'd given every indication that she had something up her sleeve.

Sure enough. Jeez, I'm good, he thought, as he kept her tidy Saturn in range and she turned in the opposite direction of her house and all that ironing to be done. Luck held with him. She chatted away on a cell phone, heedless of her surroundings. No wonder legislators wanted to pass laws against talking while driving. She'd no more noticed him than she would have an elephant in the road.

Well, maybe that was his ego. He'd hoped not to be spotted even as he'd wanted her to know that he, Eric, the man who lusted after her, was right there in her sights. But no, she talked earnestly as she drove, and he assumed her friend Pamela would be the other party to that conversation. Jenifer had seemed pretty concerned about reaching her friend.

Her distraction allowed him to follow her at a discreet distance without too much concern about being noticed. She headed straight toward the outskirts, taking the county road that led to Doolittle Estates. But she passed the turnoff to the mobile home park without slowing.

In a flash Eric knew her destination. The Tri-Forest Paper Mill sat around the next curve. What in the heck was she doing? Her car was slowing to enter the graveled entrance road.

He didn't want her to be involved.

He wanted her to be innocent.

She had to be. No evidence pointed otherwise, and his own heart certainly had absolved her of any culpability.

Eric pressed on the accelerator, closing the distance he'd left between their cars. He pulled off the road, got out, and moved quietly and quickly on foot to where he could view the parking lot of the paper mill.

The last thing he needed was Jenifer getting in the middle of things. He knew from what the janitor had revealed to him that the paper mill was being used as a production site for the counterfeit bills. The man had turned over a sack of the bills to him, and he and his daughter Andie had been put under another agent's watch after the janitor declined to be relocated for his own protection.

He would have loved to have gone in and busted the operation then and there, but he and his boss knew it was critical to nab the brains behind it, not just the lower level punks like Lars and Franco. Until they had the evidence to connect the Doolittle operation with the international counterfeiter they suspected, he was to lie low.

Jenifer stood next to a guard booth, apparently arguing with a man in uniform who was talking into a radio. She gestured, smiled, then kept on talking.

Eric grinned. No doubt she was trying to wear the man down. But why? Why did she want inside the mill? Then it occurred to him. The janitor's daughter had said something to lead her there, and Jenifer was playing amateur sleuth. If she were involved in the illegal activities, wouldn't she have her own means of bypassing the security?

He watched as she finally gave up, got back in her car, and drove slowly out of the lot.

"It is lovely, isn't it?" Jenifer said, stepping out of the car later that evening in front of the Horace House. Together, they leaned against the passenger side of the car, gazing over the lawns and up the slight rise crowned by the rambling old three-story building.

Eric nodded, taking in the floor-to-ceiling windows that in their heyday would have opened onto the broad, wraparound porch. Now they sat behind plywood, protecting the old building from those who would look in and be tempted to filch what did not belong to them. "Who keeps the yard under control?" he asked.

"The bank."

"Ah, it's been repossessed?" Sad that someone had lost this charming hulk, he thought. He'd never thought of himself as particularly fanciful, but standing there in the moonlight gazing at the house, he could almost hear the tinkling of piano keys, a sweet lilting voice joining in with the music, and picture black-jacketed waiters serving Kentucky bourbon to the men and sherry to the ladies on the porch.

"Repossessed more than once," Jenifer said. "The Horace House first opened in 1878 and flourished until the railroad moved in a different direction, and by the 1890s, instead of a fancy hotel where people came to take the waters, it had been turned into a boardinghouse."

"Waters? I thought Hot Springs filled that order."

"Oh, it's the most famous, but there's actually a spring that bubbles up right around here, in back of the hotel. The bathhouse has since been razed. The boardinghouse operated until the roaring twenties, when someone kicked out the boarders and turned it into a house of not so good repute."

"Somehow I can't imagine a bordello in Doolittle," Eric said, smiling at her.

"Oh, can't you?" Jenifer tossed her hair over her shoulder and said, "I'll have you know there are plenty of hot-blooded people in this town."

Eric knew an invitation when he heard one. He slipped his arm around Jenifer and tucked her against his side. "And they didn't all disappear a century ago," he said, raking a kiss across the top of her hair.

She sighed softly and wiggled closer. Eric heated up with the slight touch. What would she do to him stretched beneath him, beside him, straddling him? He stroked the side of her arm with a slow circling of his fingertips, letting his hand work its way gradually lower, until he oh so softly brushed the side of her breast.

He heard her catch her breath. "The bordello phase ended with the Great Depression," she said, still in her librarian of the year voice, but speaking more breathlessly, he noted with satisfaction. "The hotel remained boarded up until World War Two. Workers for the lum-

ber mills lived there, and during the eighties the last remaining heir of the original owners went bankrupt and
the bank ended up with the building."

"And it's sat there like this since the 1980s?" He circled the lush softness of her arm, skimming to the side
of her breast and then back, almost innocently, as if he
had no clue that his fingers touched her with any se-
ductive purpose.

"Oh, no," Jenifer said, "the bank keeps selling it to a
new owner and it doesn't work out and they take it
back and sell it again. I think it's most profitable for the
bank. I think they actually look for buyers who won't
make it. It's been a music school, a used bookstore,
and a photo studio."

"Interesting," Eric said, reaching for her hand.
"Let's go closer."

Pleased that he liked the historic old hotel, and feeling very alive and amazingly sexy, Jenifer took Eric's
hand and strolled up the wide walkway to the hotel.
The touch of his palm against hers sent warm, skittery
sensations up her arm and down her spine. Those
heated tremors pulsed until they reverberated in the pit
of her tummy. Tummy, shmummy, Jenifer thought,
blushing. As if she didn't know the proper anatomical
term. "Most of the people in Doolittle would like to see
it open as a hotel again."

"But there aren't any takers? It seems the bank
might bankroll the project."

"Yes, but no one who knows anything about the recent history wants to do business with the bank because
they figure any project is jinxed and the bank just
makes its money on interest and reselling the property."

"So someone would need outside financing or be able to purchase it outright without local bank financing?"

"Exactly." Jenifer liked walking up the steps hand in hand with Eric. "Welcome to Horace House," she said when they reached the porch.

And to her utmost surprise, he bent and kissed her, ever so lightly on the lips, so swiftly that she could have sworn she'd fantasized the kiss into being, only he said, "That's for sharing this evening with me."

She nodded, and pressed her lips together, surreptitiously reliving that feather stroke of sensation. And then her mind went to work. Did he mean sharing all the adventures they'd already had, or did he mean the rest of the night, as in, would she spend the night with him? He was guiding her along the porch, stepping carefully over the spots where the floorboards had sprung upward or gone soft with age. She couldn't bring herself to ask for clarification, but she hated imprecision.

"What would you do with Horace House?" he asked.

The question caught her off guard. "Me?" She looked up at him, amazed that he could actually be thinking of urban renewal at that moment. "Well, I like the idea of a hotel," she said slowly. "Downtown Doolittle—I mean, the area around Courthouse Square—only has the Schoolhouse Inn."

"Ah, the place your uncle Pete wants me to move to."

"Yes, and you might think about it because it is charming. It was the old grade school, and the sisters who run it are literally retired schoolteachers. It's a bed and breakfast more than a hotel. The rooms are named after class years, as in First Grade, Second Grade. I've never stayed there, of course, but they have an open house for Doolittle Days, which is when people decorate their homes at Christmastime and give tours. Practically everyone in town has visited it at one time or another."

"It sounds lovely," Eric said, but he didn't sound too convinced.

"Oh, it's probably a little too frou-frou for your taste," Jenifer said.

"Frou-frou?"

"Gingham, ruffles, and lace," she explained.

They'd reached the backside of the porch, where trees grew all around, leaning toward the house and sheltering it from its closest neighbor, a two-story building used for commercial purposes and deserted after five o'clock.

"You know, frilly—" She caught her breath as Eric pulled her toward him, fitting her against the front of his body. "—not masculine," she finished, her voice trailing off as he shifted his body, joining the two of them so perfectly that she couldn't help but sigh with pleasure.

He traced the line of her jaw with his thumb. "You're right. Not my kind of place at all," he said. "I'm edgy—" He breathed against her hair. "—and rough and tumble—" He nipped at her ear, and Jenifer knew she would melt. They'd find her days later, a pool of sensuous liquid trailing off the porch of Horace House. "—and very, very hard." His lips moved over her cheek, not kissing her, but exploring, scenting, tasting.

Jenifer swallowed and tried to breathe. She felt the pounding of the blood that surged within his body as it claimed her through the thin cotton of her shorts. She might as well be naked. "Eric, Eric," she said, not knowing what else to say.

"And hungry, too," he said, following the line of her nose with his little finger and swirling it along the corner of her lips. "And I know just what I want," he said, his voice low and coming almost like a growl from deep within his throat. "You," he said. "I want you."

She nodded, her arms seeming to move of their own willpower till they reached around his neck. She tugged at the short strands of his hair, circled her fingertips over the sun-toughened skin above his collar, and parted her lips in invitation, and in acknowledgment of her desire, and in wonder at this miracle that had happened to her, Jenifer Janey Wright.

His lips slanted over her own, gentle pressure that grew in urgency as she responded hungrily. She moaned and gripped the back of his head, overcome with hot, pure need as he devoured her mouth and parted her lips with his tongue. Jenifer ground against him, unable to remember any delicacy of sensual temptation, unable to remember that she'd planned only to entice him, enjoy a slow seduction, and whet his appetite for her.

No, at that moment she would have lain beneath him on the floorboards of the Horace House until they were both spent and sated.

Giggles erupted from somewhere. Jenifer, in a sensual daze, wondered why Eric was laughing. Had she done something stupid? Couldn't be, because his body remained wedged against hers, his erection hard and hot and heavy even through the layers of his trousers and her shorts. Pulling her mouth from his with great reluctance, she looked up at him. "You're not laughing," she said.

He stared at her, his eyes wide and dark and dangerous. "Oh, no, I'm not laughing." He leaned back and captured her mouth again.

The giggles turned to hoots of laughter.

She gently pushed his shoulders. "Eric," she said in a whisper, "someone is laughing, and that means we're not alone. Listen."

"Don't want to," he said, but he cocked his head and looked over his shoulder.

He remained pressed against her body in a most satisfying way. Well, not the *most* satisfying way, he thought with a grin as he looked around. He found it hard to believe anyone was out there; he'd heard nothing at all but the blood rushing from every part of his body toward his groin. Sweet, Jenifer tasted so sweet. He tasted his mouth, and that's when he heard the high-pitched giggling coming from, of all places, beneath their feet.

"Shit," he said.

"Eric!" Jenifer looked shocked.

"Sorry," he said, "It's just that this moment isn't one I want interrupted." He glanced down to where their bodies meshed. "Too much more delay of gratification and there might be some permanent damage inflicted." He grinned when he said it, but damn, it might be true. He wasn't used to putting off till tomorrow what could be accomplished right at this moment, at least when it came to women. But what had Mrs. Kirtley said? He frowned, remembering how she'd laughed when she told them, "Tomorrow never comes."

Hushed voices drifted in their direction, still coming from beneath the porch. He noticed Jenifer had pulled back and was edging her body out of their clinch. He sighed and said, "I suppose I'd better go see what's going on."

"That's not necessary," Jenifer said, smoothing her shorts and tugging her T-shirt back in place. "You can take me home now."

"Hey, what's wrong?" he asked.

They were both whispering. Jenifer stood on tiptoe and said to him, "I know that most women right now would simply say nothing. 'Oh, nothing's wrong, Eric.' But it's late and I have to get up early for work in the morning, so thank you for a fascinating evening, but good night."

"Uh-oh." Eric crossed his arms over his chest. "Somehow I've screwed up," he said slowly. "Could you give me a hint?"

"I won't gratify that request with a response," Jenifer said, still whispering. "If what you want is sexual release in order to preserve your state of health, go ahead." She pulled one of his hands free and slapped it against his erection. "I won't interrupt you," she said pointedly, and stalked toward the front of the porch.

"Jesus," Eric said, practically shouting. "It was just an expression."

Jenifer kept moving.

"Damn it, I like you! You're not just some mechanical doll!"

"Dig yourself deeper," she called over her shoulder.

Eric followed, moving faster than was wise on the rickety porch. He trod heavily on a weakened board, and before he could scramble sideways, one foot and leg speared through the floor. He tried to pull it free but couldn't budge it.

"Hey, dude, would you look at that?"

Giggling. Now he heard it loud and clear. He also felt a hand touch his ankle.

Jenifer turned and quickly headed back. She stood in front of him, shaking her head, and to his relief, she was laughing. He'd rather see that than her starchy anger.

"Guess you should have asked for directions," she said, hunching down beside him and examining the area where his leg was caught in the boards.

"Yeah, right," he said. "By the way, I found your gigglers." He pointed down. As he did, the fragrant aroma of cigarette smoke drifted up from beneath the porch.

Jenifer wrinkled her nose and looked inquiringly at him. Eric nodded, and said in a low voice, "Get me out of here and I'll make everything up to you."

"Oh, I don't think so," Jenifer said, standing up.

"What do you mean? You can't leave me here!" Eric yanked on his leg. Down below, the midnight revelers had slipped off his deck shoe and were tickling his foot.

Jenifer knelt down again and started manipulating the board next to the one that had given in. "Oh, I'll help you," she said, "but then I'm going home."

"The children down there are trespassing," he said softly. "They are breaking the law and—" He jerked as one of them started tickling the bottom of his foot again. "Oh no, no, stop!" He bent over double, holding his sides.

Jenifer giggled. "I know it's not funny, but it is funny!"

He straightened up and glared at her.

"Tug on this board," she said, still laughing.

Together they yanked it up and Eric rescued his leg. He rose and stood, lopsided, one shoe on, one shoe gone. He looked at Jenifer, her lips quivering. "We're a mess," he said, smiling.

Jenifer kicked her toe against the loosened floorboards, smiling back at him despite her determination not to be sucked in again by his sexy and beguiling ways. She couldn't quite understand why she'd lost her temper. She'd wanted to experience sexual fantasy; she'd practically invited him to have his way with her. And the end result of sexual stimulation would naturally be sexual gratification.

So she could not explain why his straightforward expression of the formula irritated her so intensely.

She knew, though, that she'd been hurt. Disappointed. Embarrassed, too. Only moments before the interruption, she had been living inside his skin, the sensations turning her all whimmy whammy, topsy-turvy, and feeling better than she'd ever felt in her life.

Maybe it had to do with those emotions and wanting them to go on and on and on, not come to an end in some surge of sated lust.

"It's very complicated," she said, thinking out loud. "But speaking of messes, we'd better put something over this hole."

Eric nodded. "I'll grab a hazard flag from my trunk, and then we'll go after my shoe."

"You're prepared for every emergency," Jenifer said.

"Only time will tell if that's true," he said. He kicked his remaining shoe off and moved away, walking carefully toward his car.

Thoughtfully, Jenifer hunched over the hole in the floor and peered into the space below. She knew the hotel had been built with a cellar. Most of the old houses in the area had storm cellars that also served as cool storage for fruits and vegetables and other staples.

A light bobbed below and Jenifer made out three youngsters. The tips of three cigarettes glowed and moved up and then down as she watched. "Hey, dudes," she said, "ever heard of lung cancer?"

"Say what?" Three bodies rose and three young faces stared up at her.

"No?" Jenifer shrugged. "I figure if you're hiding out to smoke, you must have either something to fear or guilty consciences."

"Don't tell her anything, man, she's a snoop."

Jenifer nodded. She'd gotten a good enough look to recognize two of the youngsters. "You know, guys, I'm not in the snitch business, but I think, Sammy, that your parents—and yours, too, Craig Coleman—would like to know about your little clubhouse here."

"Shit," said three young male voices in unison. The cigarettes were stubbed out. Jenifer stuck her hand through the hole in the floorboards. "I'll take that shoe, guys, before you scram."

They handed it up to her. She turned to find Eric watching her, an amused expression on his face. "Well done," he said.

She passed him his shoe, and ignoring the hand he held out to assist her to her feet, scrambled up. "Flattery won't help you," she said, knowing she had to steel herself against the attraction she felt. It was the darnedest thing—the way she'd wanted him to seduce her, but when he spoke in purely physical terms, she got riled at him.

She'd lived this many years without sex, she told herself, so she could live a few more. Maybe she hadn't known it until he spoke of sex in terms of a science experiment, but she knew it now.

Jenifer Janey Wright couldn't do casual sex. Eric had to care for her the way she feared she was coming to care for him.

Eighteen

*I*t had taken some persuasion and persistence, but Jenifer finally agreed to have dinner with him. Not until Friday evening, however. He'd asked her every day from Monday until she'd finally agreed. But she pointedly did not invite him to join her for bowling on Wednesday.

Eric didn't understand where he'd gone wrong. Usually, any woman he wanted tripped over herself when he threw out a lure.

But then, Jenifer wasn't any woman.

During the week, he'd been tracking the movements of Lars and Franco, and noted that Ace had made two more trips to El Dorado. He was getting antsy to round them up before they had too much counterfeit money ready to circulate, but each time he checked in with his boss he was told to hold off. Chester was waiting for the international counterfeit boss to return to Miami from a cruise on his private yacht. Then Eric was to fly down, meet with him in his role as a big money buyer, return to Doolittle and make the buy from Lars and Franco. That's when the feds would move in at both locations. Eric would be arrested along with the others, to maintain his cover.

Meanwhile, Eric found himself more and more at home in the picturesque town. Always a city dweller, he enjoyed the slower pace. The same old men sat on the benches in front of the courthouse every day. The waitress at the coffee shop on the square knew him by name. People said good morning and asked how he was doing as if they truly wanted to hear his answer.

If only Jenifer hadn't been keeping him at a distance, he would have had an enjoyable week.

He went over to Mrs. Kirtley's on bowling night. She shared a glass from her latest batch of elderberry wine and asked after Jenifer. Sitting there in her cluttered living room, Eric had the first inkling of an idea that he grew more excited about as the week wore on.

He couldn't wait to ask Jenifer what she thought of his plan.

Hell, he couldn't wait to see her. He'd resisted dropping by the library. A man had to have his pride.

Yeah, right, he thought, arriving at her house almost forty-five minutes before the appointed time on Friday evening and sitting in the car, across the street. He'd had a picnic hamper put up by the Verandah Restaurant, Doolittle's one claim to fine dining. He wanted Jenifer to himself, all evening long.

He wanted her, but not just for the thrill of the hunt. The usual game didn't interest him now. Perhaps he was changing, growing up at last. Seeing some of his friends settle into a more stable existence had pointed out to him the virtues of coming home to a . . . well, to a home. He lived in a spacious condo with no particular personality to it, or else in a series of anonymous hotel rooms while traveling the many days of the year he put in on his job.

As Eric sat in the car, the door to Pete's house opened and Pete and Jenifer's mother walked out, hand in hand. They smiled at each other as if the rest of the world didn't exist, or if it did, only as a backdrop for the glow that embraced the two of them.

They walked down the stairs from the front porch and crossed the lawn toward Jenifer's house.

Eric knew, as surely as if they'd declared their intentions through a megaphone, that they were on their way to find Jenifer and share their happy news with her.

Only Jenifer wouldn't think of it as happy news.

Eric stepped out of the car and hailed them with a wave. He knew he didn't belong in these people's lives, but he also knew Jenifer needed support. He wanted to be there for her when she received the news, when she grieved all over again the loss of her father, and slowly came to share the joy of what Pete and Charlotte had found with one another.

They waved at him and beckoned him over to their house. As he crossed the street, he wondered what it was about these people that made him feel as if he'd known them for years. Whoa, he chided himself, slow down. Beware. Family equaled trouble in his personal history, and things weren't always what they looked like on the surface.

"Hi, Eric," Pete said. "Looking for Jenifer?" He smiled and winked.

"Well, er, yes," Eric said.

"We are, too," Charlotte said. She glanced at her hand, still resting in Pete's much larger one.

"May I wish you both every happiness?" Eric said.

Charlotte blushed softly, exactly the way Jenifer did when she was pleased but flustered. "Thank you, but how did you know?"

"Sweetheart, we're holding hands," Pete said gently. "And we're both grinning like a bunch of junior high kids with their first crush."

"It's a secret till we tell all our children," Charlotte said. "We wanted to start with Jenifer. . . ."

Eric understood why she let that sentence trail off.

"You two have a date?" Pete asked.

"Yes," Eric answered.

"If you buy the Horace House, will you hire a manager or move here and run it yourself?"

Eric appreciated why she asked the question. Charlotte knew how to get the information she wanted.

"I don't know," he said, and he didn't. He realized that what started as a cover story had taken on a life of its own. He was interested in the idea—for more reasons than one. Sure, the primary attraction here was Jenifer, but he had begun to feel at ease—at home—in Doolittle. He'd let himself picture it as a town where he could belong.

"No need to rush to a decision," Pete said. "Move into the Schoolhouse Inn. Get comfortable. Stick around town for as long as you can. If you need any help holding Mrs. Ball at bay, just give me a call. If you have time now," he added, "why don't we have some iced tea?"

Eric accepted the offer, and took a chair on the front porch next to Charlotte. Pete ambled into the house to get the refreshments.

Charlotte folded her hands on her lap and regarded him with frank curiosity. "Tell me, Eric," she said. "Why are you really in Doolittle?"

So Charlotte suspected things weren't what they appeared to be, Eric realized. He hated to lie to her, but his duty made that necessary, unless he could think of an answer that wasn't an answer but would serve as one.

"It's a long story," he said, buying some time.

The phone rang inside the house, and Eric looked toward the door. He heard the rumble of Pete's voice, and then the older man stuck his head out and said, "Charl, that's Shane. They want us to come to dinner tonight. Want to do that and get everyone together?"

"That's a good idea," she said. "You know nobody keeps a secret in Doolittle."

He grinned and popped back inside.

Eric didn't want to give up his evening with Jenifer but if she chose to join the others, he'd keep his grumbling to himself. Right now he wanted to go to Jenifer's just to see her. It had been a long, lonely week.

"Forgive my curiosity," Charlotte said, "but as I can tell, you and Jenifer have lit up like two firecrackers tied with the same fuse, so I can't help but want to know more about you."

"You think she lights up because of me?"

Charlotte smiled. "My little girl is as transparent as the glass in this house."

He couldn't very well tell the mother that the daughter only wanted to scratch her sexual itch, with him playing the role of scratching post. "I see," he said, wishing Pete would hurry up with the iced tea. Or that Jenifer would come traipsing out her front door.

As it turned out, both wishes came true at the same moment. Pete set down the tray as Jenifer stepped onto her porch.

"I'll go get another glass," Pete said.

"Hi, honey," Charlotte called. "Come over for a glass of tea."

Jenifer waved back at her mother and soaked up the sight of the dark-haired, dark-eyed man lounging in the porch chair next to Charlotte. Eric looked better than ever. How had she held out all week?

She crossed the yard at a sedate pace, aware of Eric watching her with eyes that undressed her as she approached.

She'd need more than iced tea to cool her down. She might have to opt for a dip in Uncle Pete's pool. She'd put him off all week, each time he'd asked her out. But whenever he called, her head leaped at the sound of his voice, and finally she'd given in to the temptation to go out with him.

Evidently, Eric's charms knew no boundaries, Jenifer thought. Certainly, her own mother had come under his spell. She sighed as she crossed the lawn, and as soon as she stepped onto the porch, caught the invisible signals racing between her mother and Uncle Pete. Her senses went on alert. The two of them looked . . . so very much in love? Jenifer wrinkled her nose, considered the accuracy of her conclusion and its implications, and quickly discarded the possibility.

Then the thought flooded her mind again. The two of them looked as if they'd gotten out of bed together not too long ago.

Her mother.

Uncle Pete.

Why did that rankle her? The two people she loved more than any other in the world, except for her son and daughter, yet she couldn't accept that they'd found happiness with one another.

Jenifer dropped into a chair and scowled all around. "No sugar in my tea, please."

Charlotte's glance of gentle reproof shamed her. Jenifer worked at one of the floorboards of the porch with the edge of her shoe, feeling more like an eleven-year-old than a grown-up. Giving herself a mental shake, and letting the floorboard live another day, she sat up straighter in her chair, managing a smile for her mother.

Charlotte returned the smile and passed out the glasses of tea Pete had brought out on a tray. Jenifer accepted her drink, and as she took a sip, glanced over at Eric.

"Shane asked us over for dinner this evening," Charlotte said to her. "We'd like you to come, too."

Jenifer was about to ask who *us* was, but held her tongue. Clearly *us* had become Charlotte and Uncle Pete. She felt Eric watching her. Though she didn't understand why, his presence made it easier for her to respond more appropriately.

"I'd like to," Jenifer said, "but Eric and I have a date."

"You two want to join us? There's always room for

two more," Uncle Pete said. He hoisted his glass in Eric's direction. "Besides, Eric seems like one of the family already."

Eric lifted his glass in return. The ice cubes clinked against the glass, and Jenifer felt as if she could have throttled Uncle Pete. Did any subtlety exist among them?

"What's the occasion?" she asked. Shane and his wife were far more likely to turn up as guests rather than hosts.

"Family news," Uncle Pete said.

"What's new since the cookout?" she asked.

Charlotte and Uncle Pete exchanged a look. Jenifer watched as drops of condensation from her glass soaked into her skirt, darkening the lavender as if night had fallen over it.

Uncle Pete cleared his throat, then said, "I waited until today to pop the question."

Eric got up and walked over to Jenifer's chair. He didn't touch her, but stood beside her, and she knew he intended to show his emotional support. It was funny, but realizing it made her want to cry—not in a feeling sorry for herself way, but because it touched a need deep inside her that she hadn't known she had. She glanced up, smiling shyly at him. To her mother, she said, "So you and Uncle Pete—you're getting married?"

Charlotte nodded. So did Uncle Pete.

And so did Jenifer. "When is the wedding?"

Eric put his hand on her shoulder. She appreciated the sensation of warmth and comfort because she couldn't feel much else at that moment. Her father was dead, and that didn't mean her mother had to live without someone else. The same applied to Uncle Pete and his wife. On paper it all made sense. Still, tears filled her eyes.

Charlotte moved over and Eric stepped back. Her mother took her in her arms, stroked her hair and said, "It's okay, sweetheart. I know you miss your daddy. I do, too. I'll always love him. He'll always be your dad who carried you on his shoulders and changed your diapers and rushed you to the doctor that time you fell off the Coopers' horse."

Jenifer nodded, her tears soaking her mother's shoulder. "I know, but I can't help crying."

Charlotte kept smoothing her hair, exactly as she had when Jenifer was a child and had a fever. Slowly, Jenifer eased her face up and wiped her cheeks. She gave her mother a hug and they both stood up. Uncle Pete watched her, concern in his eyes, and she stepped over and embraced him, giving him a kiss on the cheek. He patted her on the back.

She turned and realized Eric stood right there beside her. She felt almost naked, having shown so much stark emotion in front of him and the others. But she also felt cleansed, as if she could move forward and appreciate her mother's newfound love rather than resent it.

"Let me add my best wishes," Eric said.

"Thank you," Uncle Pete said, moving to put his arm around Charlotte. "Now don't go and spill the beans before the others get to Shane's for dinner."

"You wanted to know when, Jenifer," her mother said. "We're talking about Christmas Eve."

Jenifer nodded. "Autumn and Adam will be home,

on break. You know they won't let you get married without them there." She smiled and suddenly things were looking much brighter than only a few minutes before. "Eric and I had planned to go out. Do you mind if we skip Shane's?"

"You two go on and have a good time," Pete said.

Charlotte nodded.

Eric had put his arms around her, and Jenifer leaned into the comfort of his touch. No, she didn't need a man, but she sure wanted this one.

Nineteen

$\mathcal{E}$ric left the hamper in his car, more concerned over Jenifer's emotional reaction to the news of her mother and Pete's nuptials than the picnic he'd brought to surprise her.

She let him hold her hand as they walked to her house and went inside. Stopping in the entry hall, she said, "I hope I didn't sound petty. I'm just having trouble accepting the idea."

He put an arm around her and led her into the living room. A comfortable-looking sofa faced the wall of windows that opened onto the porch. They sat down there, Eric careful to keep his approach that of a concerned friend, which indeed he felt. This was not the moment for romance.

She kicked her sandals off. Eric smiled. "You do that a lot," he said.

"I only wear shoes when I have to," she replied, dropping her chin into her hands and looking glum.

Then she straightened. "I'm sorry, Eric. You invited me to dinner and I'm moping. That's rude of me."

"There's plenty of time for dinner," he said. "Tell you what, lean back on the arm of the couch—" He rose and tucked some throw pillows behind her. "—and let me give you one of my famous foot massages."

"You don't have to do that," she said.

"I don't have to do anything," Eric countered, "except the usual death and taxes. Come on, let me help you feel better."

She regarded him as if he'd dangled a treat in front of her but might be waiting to snatch it away. "No one's ever given me a foot massage before."

"Then it's about time you had one." He beckoned with his hand. "Lie back and relax and tell me about your dad."

She scooted her bare feet onto the sofa and leaned gingerly against the cushions he'd arranged. Her skirt hiked above her knees and she tucked it daintily around her.

"Why do you ask about my dad?"

He wrapped his hands around her right foot. "Cute toes," he said. "I ask because it's obvious you miss him very much."

Her lower lip trembled. "That's true."

He stroked the bottom of her foot, working from her heel toward her toes.

She sighed and relaxed onto the cushions. "That feels nice," she said. "I wasn't ready for my dad to leave me. I know that sounds incredibly selfish, but he was too young to die, and I'd always been his baby, even though I wasn't the youngest. He always understood, and even when I did something that disappointed him, his love came through."

Eric nodded, massaging her toes.

"He had cancer, but didn't know it until it was too late to do anything to save him. My mother was very, very brave. If I loved someone as much as she loved Daddy, and lost him, I wouldn't know what to do."

Eric thought about that a moment. "You mean a lover or a husband?"

She shrugged. "Yes, I guess so."

"Is that one of the reasons you've stayed single?"

"What do you mean?" She'd sat up against the cushions, looking like a cat about to flee.

"It's hard to feel pain," Eric said, feeling his way through his thoughts. "It's easier to stay locked up inside, not reach out, not risk."

"But Daddy only died this past year," she said. "So your theory doesn't fit."

"Hmm," he said, pulling her other foot onto his lap. "I bet the father of your children hurt you pretty bad."

"He means nothing to me," Jenifer said hotly.

He wiggled her foot gently, circling it at the ankle. "He abandoned you, and your dad did, too. So why would you risk letting anyone get close to you? They end up hurting you, don't they?"

"Hey," she said crossly, "you're supposed to be helping me feel better."

"Yet your mother is willing to risk it all again," Eric said. "Do you understand that?"

Jenifer crossed her arms over her chest. "No. Well, yes, I guess I do. When you're happy in a marriage, I guess it's natural to want to be happy again. That's different from Pamela. She uses relationships as a means to avoid her unhappiness." She tossed a small cushion at him. "And what about you, Eric Hamilton?"

He rolled her foot between the palms of his hands. Wryly, he said, "It's easier to psychoanalyze others." He thought for a minute, continuing his massage. "I avoid relationships because I think of them as a source of pain. If things get dicey, I like to know I can walk away."

"Well," Jenifer said, wiggling her toes. "We're a fine pair."

He grinned, then leaned over and kissed her. "Indeed we are." He tasted her lips, wrapped his arms around her and pulled her close.

She responded, tangling the fingers of one hand in the back of his hair, tracing the line of his shirt collar with the other hand. She kissed him hungrily.

Eric pulled her back to an upright sitting position and reluctantly broke the kiss. Tipping his head toward the open windows, he said, "How about we find a more private spot?"

She smiled and stood up. "My feet feel wonderful," she said. "Thanks for the massage—and the therapy."

He rose, took her hand, and looked into her eyes. "Any time," he said, hoping he'd helped her. Funny how she didn't admit to the pain of her past but kept that wall of toughness around her like a hedge protecting her heart. Maybe, just maybe, she'd let him slip through her defenses.

"Want to go upstairs?" she said, sounding very shy.

He nodded. He wanted to make love to her. "Only if you're sure," he said.

She leaned up and kissed him on the mouth. "Yes," she said.

And that's when his damn cell phone rang, shattering the moment.

He pulled it from his pants pocket and moved into the other room.

Jenifer stood there, feeling abandoned. She couldn't help but wonder who was calling him. The times he'd taken calls in her presence, he'd made sure the conversations were private.

Reasonable enough behavior, she supposed, but he could be hiding something.

Something like . . . a wife tucked away back home?

She studied the strong line of his shoulders, the strength of his back, the tapered hips, and the short hair that showed his neck to advantage. How could a man this attractive and so sensual be single? Add to that the way he'd played with the boy, Pooper, and it added up to one result.

He had a wife. He had to. Probably a wife *and* kids.

You don't know that, she argued with herself. Go ahead. Ask him. Like he'd tell me the truth, came her response. Why not? You only asked him to seduce you one glorious time. You didn't throw yourself at him or fall in love with him or—

He turned back around, his expression unreadable.

No, she hadn't fallen in love with Eric Hamilton.

Only a ninny fell in love at first sight.

And she'd learned her lesson at age eighteen when she thought that she and Lawrence were so in love, and then she discovered who lived under the surface of his beautiful skin. When scratched, he'd proven to be only skin deep. He hadn't risen to the occasion at all. Instead, he'd fled and left her to handle dropping out of college and giving birth to twins as a single mom.

So much for falling in love.

"Jeni?"

His voice reached through her turbulent thoughts and pulled her back to her present.

"Are you okay?" His concern made her want to throw herself into his arms.

"I'm fine," she said.

"I need to run back to the motel for something," he said, tucking the phone into his pocket. "But I'm coming back. I promise."

"Cross your heart?" she said.

He kissed her. Long, slow, lingering. "Promise." He moved toward the door. "Don't eat dinner. I have a surprise."

And then he whisked through the door, almost at a run, before she could ask what kind of surprise.

Intrigued, Jenifer scooted toward the living room window and watched him cross to his car, parked on the opposite side of the street. He had his phone out again, pressed to his ear.

"Busy man," she murmured, hoping he kept his

word and returned. After not seeing him all week, this interruption was enough to drive her nuts.

Jenifer wandered from room to room, the house echoing quietly around her, the creak of a floorboard punctuating the silence. She sat down at the kitchen table. She wasn't hungry, so it wasn't hard for her to wait. What was hard was believing he would come back. She had to hand it to Eric. When he'd pointed out that she'd been abandoned by the twins' father, he'd hit the emotional nail on the head.

Tigger wandered in from wherever he'd been sleeping. The cat rubbed against her ankle, then over to his food bowl. He crunched on the dry niblets of cat food.

"Life is simple for you," she said out loud. "Eat. Sleep. Chase around. Do it all over again."

He twitched his tail, his head planted over his bowl.

Jenifer knew she needed to do something or she might end up feeling undeservedly sorry for herself. She could drop over to Shane's. She could investigate the paper mill. She could call Pamela to check on her.

Instead she sat there doing nothing.

She hated to admit the reason why, but she knew it.

She wanted to be there when Eric returned. "When, not if," she made herself say aloud, and then answered herself. "Idiot," she said.

Tigger lifted his head.

"Not you," Jenifer said, pushing her chair from the table. "Me. Acting like a lovestruck teenager."

Lovestruck? That made her smile. She'd worked up a sexual head of steam that needed release. But hadn't she taken Eric to task at the Horace House for putting things in such mechanical terms?

Jenifer rose. She walked to the sink and looked out the window to her backyard. Hugging her arms around her chest, she acknowledged that nothing Eric made her feel was at all mechanistic.

With Eric, she felt alive. Sensual. Emotional. Not at all practical or sensible.

Her telephone rang. She whirled around, forced herself to wait four rings, then lifted the receiver on the kitchen wall.

"Hey, Jeni, it's me," Pamela said.

Jenifer was pleased to hear her friend sounding pretty chipper while acknowledging her twinge of disappointment that it wasn't Eric on the other end of the line.

"Is Eric there yet?" Pamela asked.

"He was, but he had to leave," Jenifer said, realizing she sounded annoyed.

"You didn't let him slip out of your grasp, did you?"

"He's not in my grasp," Jenifer said.

"Well, he can be. You can have that man eating out of your hand."

"You think so?" Now she sounded downright wistful.

"Honey, is my name Pamela or is it not?"

Jenifer laughed. "So what's your sage advice, queen of Cosmo?"

"Do something for yourself. Something that makes you feel special."

"That's not what I expected you to say," Jenifer said.

"I know. That's why it works. If you hang around your house fretting about when he is going to call you or show up, then when he does, you'll be all tense and self-conscious."

She had that right. "Go on. I'm listening."

"So, take a bubble bath. A nice long frothy one with a tub full of bubbles. You probably haven't opened that bottle I gave you for Christmas, whatever year that was. Light some candles. Do all this just for you. I bet you can't remember the last time you did that."

"True," Jenifer said. "When Autumn and Adam were home, I had to take a number and stand in line just to get in the bathroom to brush my teeth!"

"The benefits of following my advice," Pamela said, "are that you'll feel good whether he's with you or not. If he does come back over, think how ready you'll be for him."

"I'm ready right now," Jenifer said jokingly.

"You think you are, hon, but you're not. I've known you for years and you can't fool Pamela. Just ask any of the kids at school when they get in trouble and land in my office. I can tell from your voice you're not in a good place."

Jenifer wondered how her friend could be so wise for others yet make such a stupid choice for a husband. But she knew better than to divert the conversation to that topic. Pamela would change the subject or hang up. "I should be," Jenifer said. "My mother and Uncle Pete told me they're getting married on Christmas Eve."

"That's wonderful for them," Pamela said, "though it must make you miss your dad so much."

"Exactly." Jenifer closed her eyes briefly.

"I miss Conway terribly," Pamela said in a small

voice. "But life goes on, and it's for us the living to keep on living."

"Oh, Pamela, why do such bad things happen? You and Conway were so happy together." If her friend's second husband hadn't died, Ace would never have entered the picture.

"Don't get all mopey," Pamela said briskly. "Ace and I are going to the movies. I've got to go now, but follow my advice, okay?"

Jenifer nodded. "Thanks, Pamela," she said. "Have fun."

"You bet. Remember, life is to be lived."

Jenifer returned the phone to the cradle. She appreciated her friend's advice even if she couldn't agree with some of the results it brought to Pamela's life. She had a man to go to the movies with, true, so she wasn't sitting home alone.

Wrinkling her nose, she crossed to the refrigerator, pulled out a root beer, and headed upstairs. If she had to choose between a guy like Ace and being single, she'd stay home by herself the rest of her life. Or go see a movie with her girlfriends.

Girlfriends didn't let you down. Or beat you up.

She stopped in front of her hall closet, searching the jumble of jars and bottles for the bubble bath from Pamela. She found it in the back of the bottom shelf, a remnant of Christmas wrapping still clinging to the side of the champagne magnum plastic container.

Root beer in one hand and bubble bath in the other, she plodded into her bathroom. There was a window up high that faced west. The sun had dipped low and a few rays of light scattered through the prism of frosted glass, dappling the white tile walls of the room. The room was immaculately clean, as Jenifer liked it. That reminded her to sort out the hall closet soon. The packing for college had resulted in things thrown every which way.

Deciding she might as well get into the spirit of self-indulgence, she put down the things she held, turned the taps on, and poured the milky bath cream in. The scent of roses ascended from the water. She inhaled deeply. Pamela knew some stuff.

Smiling, and telling herself she could worry about all the things she had to worry about after her treat, she collected several pillar candles, plucked her long silk robe from her closet, and prepared to pamper herself.

She stripped off her skirt and blouse, tossing them into her dirty clothes hamper. Standing there in her bathroom wearing only her panties and bra, she relived the feel of Eric's hands and mouth on her breasts. Her nipples puckered.

She drew in a quick breath, recognition of her need.

Water cascaded into her tub, an old-fashioned, stand-alone, claw-foot type. Watching the bubbles mound and froth, she decided she needed music to finish setting the scene. She carried a boom box, discarded by Adam in favor of his MP3 player, into the bathroom and selected a classical medley CD from her downstairs stereo. By the time the music filled the room, the tub beckoned her.

Stripping naked, she eased one foot, then the other, into the tub.

"Perfect," she said, breathing in the scent as the mu-

sic soothed her senses. She dabbed a handful of bubbles onto her breasts where Eric had kissed her last
weekend.

"Almost perfect," she corrected herself.

Twenty

$\mathcal{E}$ric's boss hated to talk on cell phones. He'd call to summon his agents, then wait for them to return the call on a landline. After leaving Jenifer's house, Eric pulled into the first phone booth he spotted, to save himself a trip back to his motel.

His boss wanted to review their game plan. Eric forced himself to be patient. They'd done this enough times already, but Chester got nervous right before things were due to go down. They'd had word that Newman, their suspect in Miami, had moored his yacht earlier that evening. Due to some things set in motion with another undercover agent in Miami, Eric was told to expect an invitation for "Troy King" to visit.

Before he left for Florida, Chester wanted Eric to check on the agent watching the janitor and his daughter.

Knowing he'd better do that right away, in case the call from Maimi came sooner rather than later, Eric drove toward Doolittle Estates when he left the phone booth. As he expected, everything was quiet there. He reported back to headquarters over another pay phone, then headed back to Jenifer's house.

Eric parked and approached the house. He knocked at the front door, though he knew she never locked it. No one answered. He knocked again, glancing around as he heard music coming from an upstairs room, the sound muffled by the distance and the walls of the solid old house. Maybe she couldn't hear him over the music?

He put his hand on the doorknob, feeling a bit like a burglar. But hey, when in Doolittle . . . everyone had thought it odd when Mrs. Ball rang the doorbell earlier at Pete's house.

Turning the knob, he pushed the door open. No Jenifer. He trod as silently as possible on the aging floorboards, feeling an instinctive need to make sure all was well before revealing his presence.

The only occupant downstairs turned out to be her fat orange cat. It looked up from washing its privates, regarded him coolly, and returned to the job at hand. Eric could appreciate such single-minded concentration. He gave the cat a wide berth and retraced his steps toward the staircase.

Strains of what might be Bach or Beethoven filled the air, growing louder with each step he took toward the second floor.

The floor creaked under his feet and he paused, then realized how silly his reaction was, given the fact that no one had answered his vigorous knocks at the front door. He moved quickly then, checking the bedrooms. Nobody.

At last, he positioned himself outside the door from where he heard the music. The bathroom? He considered the possibilities. Either someone had turned up the music and left it playing, to make it seem that someone was in the house, or Jenifer was in that room.

Doing what?

Taking a bath?

Nah. He couldn't get so lucky. Not even Eric Jay Hamilton could hit such a jackpot.

Naked. Wet. Relaxing to music. He sniffed. The air escaping around the closed door curled around his face, beckoning him with a sweet, heady scent.

It smelled of roses.

It made him think of sex.

His body reacted, responding with heat and need to the fragrance, and to the idea.

Jenifer had to be inside.

Not wanting to scare her, he considered whether he should tap on the door or call her name. What he really wanted to do was open the door, walk in, and soak in the sight of her naked self.

But his imagination had gotten ahead of the facts.

Quietly, he opened the door a crack and peeked inside.

He recognized the curve of her neck, the lush dark tumble of hair pinned atop her head, the dainty yet resilient arms draped over the sides of the funky old-fashioned tub. She sat in the deep water with her back to him, with a boatload of bubble bath froth delicately— yet at the same time suggestively—covering her body.

He had to catch his breath. He hovered there in the doorway, knowing it was wrong to intrude. He should retreat.

Hell, he didn't know the meaning of the word "retreat."

Yet he owed her privacy. He wanted her naked, but not by stealth.

He stood there, barely breathing, unable to decide what to do, incapable of moving forward or backward.

How did this lady librarian tie him up in such knots?

The music built to a crescendo. She lowered one hand to the water, swishing the mounds of bubbles. He opened the door wider, and as she shifted position, he could see the froth covering her breasts. It shimmered and shifted, and two dusky, delicious nipples poked through, pebbled and ripe for sucking.

He groaned.

Jenifer whirled around, eyes wide with alarm. Clasping a hand to her breasts, she said, "Did you ever hear of knocking?"

He grinned, grateful she hadn't said anything harsher. Taking it as a good sign, he leaned into the open doorway, his hand still on the knob, and said, "I did knock. You didn't answer, so I came inside to make sure all was well." His eyes roved the scene in front of him. "I can see all is quite well."

She blushed the faint tinge of pink that he found so delightfully charming. "Yes, well, you can see everything." She sounded cross, but then, he knew that if he'd been caught naked unawares, he might be cross, too.

"I'll step out now," he said, preparing to back into the hallway. "Do you mind if I wait downstairs?"

She caught her lip between her teeth. She'd moved

to the edge of the tub, giving him a beautiful view of the sweep of her back, down to the line that separated her sweetly rounded cheeks.

He waited, figuring his offer to vacate the room would throw her into confusion. She wanted him as much as he wanted her. Did she not know how to admit to those feelings?

If not, he'd gain nothing by moving in too quickly.

"Or I can leave and come back tomorrow?" he said. "I did want to see you again."

"Oh, yes," she said breathlessly. She caught a hand-ful of bubbles in her right hand. "I'd rather you stay, though."

"Here?" Eric glanced around. "You mean wait for you on the porch or in the living room?"

Still with that rosy blush, she shook her head. "I don't mind if you wait here. Right here." She fixed him with a look so full of wide-eyed innocence that Eric could have sworn she had no idea what she was offer-ing. Or did she?

She'd asked him to seduce her. Now she played the role of seductress.

Too damn well.

But he wanted more than sex. He wanted her to let him inside her emotional self—not just her body but her heart and soul.

"Want me to wash your back?" he asked.

"That would be nice," she said, still wide-eyed and looking up at him as if she didn't know whether to ac-cept his offer or take the safe route and shoo him from the room.

"I'd better take my shirt off," Eric said, reaching for the top button. "It's dry-clean only."

She fluttered her lashes and sank back into the sea of bubbles. "That's good thinking," she said, raising her arms over her head and stretching.

Eric thought of leaping into the tub then and there, with all his clothes still on, despite his lofty feeling and desire for a deeper connection. He was a man, after all, and she was a desirable and naked woman. He held back, removing only his shirt.

Jenifer reached up one hand, touching his bare chest, and trailed a finger in the thick mat of hair.

"You look even better half naked," she said, ending her sentence in a giggle worthy of a schoolgirl.

"Thank you," he said. "Give the word and I'll let you compare half naked to fully naked."

"Oh, my," she murmured, glancing down, seeming to realize for the first time exactly the situation she found herself in. "I mean, well, of course I'd like that, but . . ."

He knelt by the side of the tub. Placing one finger over her lips, he said, "Shhh. It's okay. I'm not rushing any fences here, all right?"

She nodded. "Thank you, Eric. I'm not shy, you know, it's just that I'm—"

"Shy," he supplied for her, finishing with a kiss to the tip of her nose. Nothing would be served by making her anxious. "The candles are a nice touch." The sun must have set. The only light in the room came from candles scattered on the side of the sink and the back of the toilet.

"Thanks," she said. She skimmed one hand in the water and held a handful of bubbles up to him. "So indulgent."

Eric picked up a neatly rolled washcloth off the top of a wicker basket full of towels. "Shall I?"

She nodded. Words were hard for her to articulate at that moment. She couldn't quite grasp that she sat naked in her bathtub with a shirtless Eric Hamilton kneeling beside her, gazing at her with desire sparking his dark eyes. Maybe wishes did come true.

He dipped the washcloth into the water, skimming it over her knee and along her thigh. She caught her breath in anticipation of where he might touch her next. He swirled it in a circle just inside her leg, then lifted it from the water, squeezed it lightly, and lay it gently across the back of her neck.

Through the wet, warm cloth, he massaged her neck.

"Mmm," she said. "Nice."

"Very nice," he said, his voice husky, almost ragged.

She glanced at his face. His eyes were half closed. She touched his bottom lip with a fingertip, gingerly, almost testing his reaction.

He opened his lips and sucked in her finger. She gasped and reveled in the sensations that simple touch aroused in her.

Simple?

Anything but. The way he swallowed, suckled, and teased her made her want him to touch her everywhere in the same clever, ravenous way. Jenifer eased closer to the side of the tub.

He released her finger, smiling wickedly at her. He removed the washcloth from her neck and dunked it in the water again. This time he trailed it between her legs, teasing her where she wanted most to feel him. Yet as much as she wanted all of him, she knew she was afraid.

But not of Eric.

Her fears were for her own appetite. Once she experienced sex with Eric, how could she go back to being sensible Jenifer Janey Wright? And what if she let herself care for him and he hurt her?

The washcloth rose from between her thighs, past her tummy, and up to her breasts. Eric wrapped the cloth around one breast and massaged her through the fabric.

Reaching up, she took his face in her hands and pulled him to her for a kiss. There was only so much a woman could stand without going for more! She played his tongue, his lips, his mouth, the back of his teeth, as he had devoured her finger. He moved the cloth over her nipple, teasing her with the same rhythms of her kisses.

Jenifer wasn't sure who broke away first, but they sat, she in the tub, he on his knees, gasping for breath.

And then they laughed. Both of them, wild, uproarious sounds of joy and passion. Jenifer calmed first and smiled. "Wow, Eric, you make life so much more fun."

"Thank you, Jeni," he said. "I think you make me a better man."

She lay her head against the back of the tub, studying him. He meant what he said. She could tell that by the serious expression on his face. Even though they'd been laughing and kissing, she felt a surge of respect and sincerity she hadn't expected.

She'd been looking for a fling, and realized she'd found more. Much more.

"Eric . . ."

"Yes?" He leaned his arms on the side of the tub.

"I think I'd like to get out of the water now."

"Would you like me to help or would you like me to wait downstairs?"

She couldn't believe he'd be so sensitive. No, wait, she could. That was one of the things that made him so special. "I'm not sure," she said. "I don't feel quite as shy as I did when you walked in."

"Understandable," he said promptly. "I took you completely unawares. Speaking of which, maybe one of us should run down and lock that front door."

She knew she blushed, aware of the implication. No point in having any of her friends or family finding her in the throes of passion with Eric.

Because that's what they would find. Jenifer knew they were going to make love.

Have sex.

She frowned. Sex. She wanted sex. Nothing else. No complications. No emotional entanglement. No expectations that could leave her hung out to dry.

"You don't want to lock it?" He looked confused.

"Oh, no. I think it's an excellent idea," she said. "But later."

His eyes darkened. He rose to his feet and held out his hand. "Later? Do you mean after I help you out of the tub?"

"Yes," Jenifer said. Taking his hand, she rose from the bubbly water, froth clinging to her knees, her arms, and one breast. She stood there, open to him, vulnerable and quivering inside with anticipation and desire.

He plucked a towel from the basket and dropped it over her shoulders. "Careful," he said, guiding her as she stepped from the tub. Then he grinned. "Forget careful. You make me feel like a dangerous man."

"Good," she said, kissing his chest.

"You'll find me extremely easy to deal with," Eric said, rubbing her back dry, then toweling her breasts and tummy.

Lowering his body, he followed the line of her waist, her hips, her legs, his hands muffled in the folds of the thick towel. But he might as well have been touching her with his fingertips, so intensely did she experience the contact.

"Now turn around," he said.

She did, moving almost in slow motion. He patted her fanny dry, then the backs of her legs, then let the towel roam between her thighs as he drew it upward again.

"If you do much more of that," Jenifer said, without thinking first, "I'm going to be all wet again."

He laughed softly. "My intentions exactly."

Good thing he still had his pants on, Eric thought, or he wouldn't be able to hold back one second longer.

The towel still around her shoulders, he used it to pull her to him, full body. His erection nudged against her thighs, still warm from the bathwater. "Do you know how good you feel?" he asked.

He drowned her answer with a kiss.

She responded, demanding more. And more. His mouth on hers, he took her in his arms and lowered her gently to the thick bath carpet that stretched alongside the tub. He didn't ask. He didn't inquire as to the direction of the bedroom. He had to have her now.

She lay on the white carpet, her legs spread wide, one hand just below her breast, the other over her head.

"I can't talk while we're kissing," she said, sounding almost surprised.

"Is that a problem?" He grinned when he asked the question. His fingers had gone to rubber, causing him difficulty as he tried to unfasten his belt.

"No," Jenifer said. "It's just that I'm used to talking."

"But not to kissing?" There, he got the damn thing loose. Standing over her, about to drop his pants, he paused.

"Not exactly," she said. "Did you know that kissing is universal? But it's done differently in different cultures. For example, an Eskimo kiss is nose-to-nose, just touching. There's a tribe somewhere, too, where kissing is done elbow-to-elbow."

Eric shook his head. "Wouldn't you rather kiss than talk about kissing?"

She seemed to reflect an awfully long time on what for Eric was a simple question. "With you, yes," she said at last.

He smiled. Kneeling beside her, he took one of her hands in his and said, "Do you talk because I make you nervous?"

"It's not you, per se," Jenifer answered. "It's—" She waved her hand over her beautifully naked body. "—this."

To get comfortable, he eased down next to her, propped on one elbow. That way he could play with her breasts while she explained about "this."

"Facts are much easier to handle than feelings," she said.

"Mmm," Eric answered, enjoying the full weight of her breast against his palm. "But feelings feel so good."

She sighed and smiled and nuzzled against him. "I agree with that statement."

"Tell you what," he said. "Go ahead and recite anything you want to. Start with the Pledge of Allegiance." He dipped his head and kissed the side of her neck. "Then go on to the Declaration of Independence." He kissed her lower, in the hollow of her throat. "Then maybe try the Periodic Table of Elements." He took her nipple in his mouth, wrapping his tongue around her, tugging gently.

She sighed. "I pledge allegiance to the flag . . ."

Her voice trailed off as he rolled from his side, fitting his body over hers. He kissed a path from her breasts to her navel.

"I—I don't feel like talking just now," she said, her voice coming out in breathy tones, music to his ears.

"Then just feel," he said, lowering his mouth from her navel to the innermost curve of her thighs. He tasted her with his tongue. Sweet, salty woman flavor sent his senses rocketing. With a groan, he buried his face between her legs, pulling her up to him, opening and seeking with his lips, his tongue.

"Oh, my God, Eric," she said, bucking slightly, then splaying her legs, giving him access to everything he needed. She was so ready for him that he'd only started to tease her with the delicious torment of his tongue when she went nearly rigid, then shuddered and cried out, giving him what he wanted—more of herself.

More proof she wanted him inside her, sheathed in her hot, slick, secret self.

He wanted more than simply more. He wanted all of her. He leaned over her, smiling at the expression of bliss on her face. He brushed her hair from her cheek and said, "I think you forgot to talk."

She grinned and sat halfway up. "Words cannot describe what you just created inside me."

He sat down on the floor. "I think I know what you mean," he said, eager to join her, wanting to show her how much more he could give to her in the feeling category. He stripped his pants from his legs, thankful he'd had the sense to leave his ankle holster and small pistol in his car, and even more thankful he'd tucked a couple of condoms into his pants pocket. He left his bikini briefs on. He wanted to feel her hungry hands tugging them off his body.

Jenifer gazed up at Eric. From her position on the cozy bath rug, he looked even taller, with parts of him bigger than she remembered. She smiled, embarrassed at her own naughty thoughts. But the incredible ecstasy he'd created inside her made her feel more like a wanton nymph than a staid librarian. "I don't think I can move," she said.

He lowered himself to the rug. Rolling her over on top of him, he said, "You don't have to lift a finger."

She giggled and nuzzled against him. His erection, hot and heavy, seared her thigh through the cotton of his brief. Cocking her hips, she wiggled against him, slowly, up and down. "Some of me can move," she said.

"Oh, yeah." Eric closed his eyes for a moment, and then, as he opened them, he said, "I know I said feelings trump talking, but I need to ask you a question."

She smoothed his forehead with her hand. "Sure, what is it?"

"Well, two things, actually. But I guess they're related."

Continuing her massage of his erection, Jenifer almost shushed him. Just that contact alone had heated her up all over again. Rising slightly, she adjusted him against the V of her thighs.

He gave a moan of satisfaction and need.

"It feels so good to make you want me," she said, marveling at the sensation.

"Good doesn't begin to describe it," Eric muttered. He caught her by the shoulders. "Do I have it right that you've been pretty much on your own for some time now?"

"Of course," she said, surprised at his question. "I've never been married or lived with anyone."

He bucked his hips against hers, and she stroked harder with her own wiggling massaging motions. "So what do you do about sex?"

"Oh," Jenifer said, understanding the point of his question. "Well, actually that's kind of hard to believe, especially when you're making me feel so incredibly sexy, but the answer is I don't do anything about it, except, well, you know. . . ." She blushed from the tips of her toes to her cheeks. She could not say the M word to Eric.

"You mean you give yourself release, right?"

She nodded, grateful that the gesture loosed some of her long hair to fall partially over her face. It was just too embarrassing to admit to such a fabulously attractive man of the world that she hadn't had sex with a guy in half a lifetime. He'd probably make some excuse to head out the door, wondering what kind of freak he'd met. "There aren't a lot of single guys in Doolittle," she said, hoping that would answer the question.

"It's tough to live in a drought," Eric said, "but most of us manage that same way when we need to get through the dry times."

Jenifer nodded. Then she decided she might as well set him straight. He was probably thinking she'd gone without sex for, say, a year at the most. She put her hands on his shoulders. After taking a deep breath, she said, "Eric, I haven't been with a man since the month I got pregnant." There, she'd said it.

He remained exactly where he'd been before she'd said the words. Gazing up at her, he looked like he didn't believe her. Then he tipped her mouth down to his, kissed her gently, and releasing her, said, "That makes me one hell of a lucky guy."

"Oh, Eric." Jenifer couldn't believe he could react so beautifully. "I thought you'd think me some kind of loony."

He smiled. "No, but I think I am. Look at us, on the bathroom floor. You should be on a bed, at least, when you've waited this long."

She laughed. "I don't care where I am, as long as you're right here beside me, or beneath me, or on top of me."

Eric kissed the side of her neck, then rolled her over so they lay side by side. "Point me in the direction of the bedroom. I'll carry you there."

"Didn't you say you had two questions?"

"Oh, right."

"Well?"

"I have a feeling the first answer made my second question irrelevant."

"Try me," Jenifer said, circling her hand in his chest hair, moving her hand lower and lower toward the line that marched into the elastic edging of his brief.

"I was just going to ask what you used for birth control."

Jenifer stilled her hand. "Oh. Good question." Glancing toward the neat stack of his trousers and shoes, she said, "I hope you have what we need."

He smiled and nodded.

She tickled his ribs. "Good—or we'd have to wait."

"That's easy for you to say," Eric said, his voice between a growl and a laugh. He cupped her hand over his erection. "You're not walking around in this condition."

Jenifer felt the size of him, the heat that pulsed through to her palm, sending her own body temperature racing.

He stroked the back of her head, his fingers tangling in her hair. "Any more of this and I won't be sane."

She smiled. Originally, she'd wanted to experience things with Eric she'd never known before. But she'd gone from that simple objective to wanting to lose herself in the way Eric made her feel. Now she wanted to give to him the same sweet, sizzling release he'd given her. "I'd like to help drive you crazy," she said.

He stroked the back of her neck, drawing her closer against his body. "You already do," he said.

"Good," Jenifer answered, and tugged at his briefs. She had to use two hands to draw them out and over his arousal.

He reached down, stripping the briefs from his legs and tossing them to the side.

"Not so neat now," she said, giggling. She touched him with her fingertips. His skin, satin smooth and rock hard, burned against her hand.

He sighed and rolled onto his back.

Jenifer knelt between his legs, dancing her hair over him, teasing him. She'd read every how-to-drive-your-man-wild article in every magazine in the library circulation. Never before had she given herself the opportunity to put any of the suggestions into practice.

He'd half closed his eyes, his features a sweet mixture of pleasure and pain. She understood the look. It was exactly how she'd felt when he'd driven her higher and higher to sexual excitement with his lips and tongue, until she knew she would surely expire if she didn't explode into sweet release.

She bent her head down and then kissed his erection. He groaned. She didn't even get to a second kiss when he pulled her up against the length of his body. "Let's do that another time," he said, his voice raspy. Then with his arms wrapped around her, he swung them both to their feet. "Bedroom?"

She nodded. He turned to the door, then set her down, fished in his pants pocket, pulled out several foil packets, and swept her back in his embrace.

Jenifer nuzzled against him. "Thanks for remembering," she said.

"My job," he said. He kissed her as he carried her down the hall.

Her bedroom was frillier than he'd expected, the four-poster bed covered in lace-edged pillows. Well, why not? he thought. Jenifer was all woman. She wouldn't have a prim and proper twin bed. He sat her down on the bed, and sitting beside her, paused a beat to give her the opportunity to change her mind.

She looked at him, expectant, aroused. "Eric?"

"Yes?" He'd hold off if she said the word, no matter how much he wanted her.

"Let's not stop now," she said, her voice a breathy whisper.

He took her in his arms, gently, as if he might break her if he squeezed too hard. Rolling back on the bed, he drew her close, meshing skin with skin. He felt her heart beating against his own, and that did something funny to his insides. He took her hand and placed it on his chest. "Feel that?"

She nodded.

"That's my heart, beating for you."

Jenifer smiled. Leaning down, she kissed the spot on his chest. She wanted to explode, wanted to cry with sheer happiness, wanted to walk inside Eric's skin. Despite the amazing release he'd given her after he'd taken her from her bath, she quivered inside, trembling with wanting more of him, more of the magic he worked on her.

He patted the pillows at the head of the bed. "Scoot up there," he said.

She did as he asked, feeling marvelously sexy and free, sitting on her own bed completely naked and open and deliriously alive. She lifted an arm and tugged her hair back, sweeping it over one shoulder. "Like this?" she said teasingly.

"Oh, yeah," he said, opening one of the condom packets.

He tugged it on. Jenifer got a little nervous, considering as she watched just how large he was. He caught her watching him.

"Don't worry, sweetheart, nature makes it all work out."

"It's not nature I'm worried about," she said, giggling with a sudden rush of nerves.

He shifted so he lay next to her on the pillows. Opening his arms, he said, "Let me hold you."

She accepted his offer and snuggled against him. "I guess I'm not the woman of the world I've been trying to be," she said.

He kissed her on the tip of her nose. "You don't know how happy that makes me, Jeni."

"Really?"

"Yes," he said. "We'll go just as slow as you want."

"I thought that was hard for guys."

He shrugged. "The longer the buildup, the greater the pleasure, as far as I'm concerned." He stroked her hair and she sighed with pleasure.

"I like everything you do," she said. "Are you sure I didn't dream you up?"

He'd lowered his hand to her lower back and was tracing circles that sent ripples of pleasure through her whole body.

"I'm real," he said.

"And you're sure you're supposed to be here?"

"What do you mean by that?" He kept stroking her back, but she thought his touch hesitated.

"Well, I'm not sure how to ask this, especially when we're lying here naked, but you're not married, are you?"

"Married!" He pulled away and looked into her eyes. "Where did you get that idea?"

"The phone calls," she said. "And you disappear and then show up again. Like you're hiding something."

"That's work," he said. "No, I'm not married, never have been."

And never will be? Jenifer finished the thought in her head. Well, what did it matter to her? She wasn't the marrying kind, so things were much simpler if Eric felt the same way. She was a woman; he was a man. They were in her bed to have sex. Simple, straightforward pleasure, no strings attached.

But that thought gave her little comfort. She outlined his mouth with her pinky finger. "Eric, kiss me so I can't think, okay?"

"With pleasure," he said, and did exactly that.

Not only did he kiss her mouth until her lips ached with wanting him to swallow her up, but he kissed her breasts, her swollen, pebbled nipples, the backs of her thighs, the hollow of her throat . . . and when she thought she would explode, he lifted his body over hers, nudged her knees even more widely apart, and slowly, slowly entered her, claiming her body as she'd never been claimed.

Oh, she'd gotten pregnant, but no man had ever made love to her. She lifted her body to meet Eric's hungry, exploring, exciting thrusts, her breath coming faster and faster, until she thought she'd scream.

And then she did scream, and collapse against the pillows, even as he drove harder and harder, until he too exploded with passion and held her close, hanging on as if he'd never let her go.

* * *

When he could move again, Eric stroked her tangled hair, enjoying the look of sheer bliss on Jenifer's face.

After a few minutes he said, "I'm going to my car to get that surprise I mentioned. Don't move a muscle."

She stretched and sighed. "I'll be right here."

He found his slacks in the bathroom, pulled them on, collected the picnic hamper and returned to the bedroom. Sure enough, Jenifer lay exactly where she'd been when he left, the same contented look on her sweet face.

Her eyes lit up. "A picnic! Eric, how fun!"

He opened the hamper and pulled out a square, checked tablecloth. "The floor or the bed?"

"Ooh, let's be really decadent and have our picnic on the bed," she said.

He set out the treats the Verandah kitchen staff had prepared. He fed her tidbits of Brie on squares of savory bread, and strawberries dipped in chocolate. She dropped sugar-crusted grapes on his tongue, followed by thin shavings of ham.

"Delicious," she said, her eyes glowing.

"It's enough to make me hungry all over again," Eric said. Watching the way she licked her fingers was driving him wild.

"But you're eating right now," she said, and then caught his meaning. She blushed.

He leaned over and kissed her, needing her again, at that moment, as intensely as before.

She wrapped her arms around his neck and drew his mouth to hers.

Later, much later, they fell asleep.

When he woke up, Eric couldn't believe Jenifer lay cradled against his chest. Sleep didn't come easily to him, and comfortable sleep when sharing a bed with another person usually eluded him.

Maybe that's why he'd stayed single, he thought. Nah. He'd never met anyone who had made him consider a lifestyle revolution.

Jenifer sighed softly in her sleep, snuggling against his chest. He felt a surge of protectiveness. Sweet Jenifer who didn't need a man. Smoothing her hair, he realized that he liked that insistence, even if he disagreed with it.

Jenifer did need a man.

Any woman as responsive and sexually expressive as Jenifer Janey Wright should not spend her years with only her vibrator as partner. There ought to be a law against it, he thought.

What man wouldn't desire her? Definitely the guys in Doolittle didn't have their heads—or their male anatomy—on straight.

He couldn't wait until they made love again. He wanted to sink himself inside her, lose himself in her depths, feel her drawing him in, in, in—until they exploded in release together. If he hadn't thought it would spoil the moment, he would have dragged himself away, off to the motel to get more condoms and return to her bed.

But women were funny. Eric knew that as well as he knew his own name. The mood had to be right. Too much thinking about what they were doing and they might not do it. He didn't know if Jenifer fell into that category, but he didn't want to take a chance. Tonight had been perfect.

He slipped his arm out from around her, and she stirred but didn't awaken. He wanted a drink of water. And he knew he had to think about getting back to the motel anyway. He wasn't one to sleep over. He disliked the awkwardness of morning after politeness. Tucking the sheet around Jenifer's naked body, he considered that with Jenifer, morning might be quite pleasant.

He'd have to find out some other time. Tiptoeing from the room, he paused in the bathroom to collect his clothing, then made his way down the stairs. As he cleared the bottom rung, his phone rang. Time to head to Miami.

He wrote a note saying he had to leave town on business and propped it next to a bowl of bananas, then feeling as if he were leaving an important part of himself behind, he walked quietly out of her house.

Twenty-one

Jenifer hated to admit it, but the next two days dragged by. Little things that normally didn't bother her picked at her nerves. Crabby Abbie dropped in, ostensibly to renew the latest Tony Hillerman novel, but since she lingered at the front desk demanding to know from Jenifer why she hadn't sent this new man in town over to the Schoolhouse Inn, Jenifer figured the renewal served as an excuse. With a sniff, she ended her visit with the lugubrious warning that if she and her sister didn't get all the business possible, they might have to shut down.

Jenifer happened to know that the sisters owned the old schoolhouse outright. Since they lived there, too, and were the only employees, she didn't think the bed and breakfast was in any danger of going under.

What she ought to be concerned about, Jenifer thought, annoyed, was what would happen to her if the

Horace House opened as a hotel. Then Abbie would have something to be crabby about. And then she herself would have to come to terms with the role Eric would have in her life, assuming he actually purchased the property and spent a lot of time in Doolittle.

Since he'd disappeared from her bed, the only contact she'd had was the note he'd left. Maddening man! It didn't help that Eric filled her every thought when she went to bed at night. She pictured him there with her. When she took a bath, she felt his presence there, as when he'd pleasured her on the rug.

At three o'clock the only patron still in the library checked out her books and departed. The sun shone brilliantly outside, on one of those fall days determined to cling to summer yet without the humidity that usually made a hot day sheer torment.

A few minutes after the woman left, the library door opened. Good. She needed to keep busy. Eric stepped inside, his head turned away from her, issuing words of encouragement.

Jenifer almost leaped over the counter, then caught herself. All the ladies' magazines preached, "Let the man pursue you." She shuffled some papers, curious who he was talking to outside the door.

She hoped Eric had a good explanation for the time he'd been gone. But she knew that almost any explanation would do, given how badly she wanted him in her bed again.

Eric stood in the doorway, half inside, half out, mustering his patience as Jenifer wondered why he hadn't come in. In fact, the reason was Pooper. The boy did not want to cross the threshold of the library. Eric, on the other hand, wanted very much to see the librarian.

"There's nothing in there but books," Pooper said to him.

"There's lots more than books," Eric replied.

"You're not shittin' me?" The little boy looked up at him, then ducked his head.

Eric's heart went out to the kid. "Pooper, I wouldn't shit you," he said, holding out his hand. "Trust me on this one, okay?"

The boy hesitated, then accepted his hand. "All right, but you better not be—"

"It'll be fine," Eric said, cutting off Pooper's favorite words.

He entered the library half dragging Pooper. Jenifer, sitting behind the checkout desk, saw the boy now and smiled. She looked to Eric even more beautiful than she had the first time he'd stepped through that door. He hoped she had something to show Pooper in addition to the shelves of books or his name would be mud, or something worse.

"Hi, Eric," Jenifer said. "Hello, Pooper. It's nice to see you."

"It is?" The child looked around. "There's nobody to play with here," he said.

"It is a slow day," she agreed. "When the weather is this nice, there aren't as many people inside the library."

"No sh—" Pooper started.

"We always use proper language in the library," Jenifer said, walking around the desk. "For instance, instead of what you were about to say, you might say, 'No wonder' or 'That's not surprising.'"

Eric almost couldn't hold back a shout of laughter. If Jenifer could persuade Pooper to reform his language, she might be able to accomplish any miracle.

The child scratched his skinny backside, looking sideways at Jenifer. "You some kind of teacher?"

"Oh, no. I'm a librarian," Jenifer said.

"Good, 'cause for a minute there I thought the two of you was sh—playing a joke on me, I mean."

"Great word choice," Jenifer said, "but no one is playing a joke." She held out her hand. "Let me show you around. And, Eric, it is nice to see you again."

Eric heard the starch in her voice and knew he'd done the smart thing to bring Pooper with him upon his return from Miami. No woman liked to be left during the night.

Pooper seemed reluctant to let go of Eric, so the three of them moved toward tto Ehe children's section together. Jenifer paused in front of a dictionary stand and a TV/VCR unit set at child height. A computer sat on the same table.

"This is a dictionary," she said, pointing to the open, oversize book on the stand. "This is, too," she said, flicking on all the pieces of electronic equipment.

"What's it do?" He looked curious now, rather than suspicious.

"What's a word you'd like to know the meaning of?"

Pooper shrugged. Then he scratched a scab on his knee. Eric wondered if Jenifer had skipped too far ahead in this lesson, but he had the sense to keep his mouth shut. He marveled at the way she'd been able to engage the child, who had to be six or seven years old at the most.

"Kibosh," he said. "What's that mean?"

Eric smiled at Jenifer's startled expression. Trust the

boy to come up with something unique. "Where'd you hear that, Pooper?" Eric asked.

"From Mrs. Branson. She owns where we live. I heard her tell my dad that if he tried something one more time she'd put the kibosh on him." He made a gagging sound. "I thought she was gonna kiss him."

Jenifer showed Pooper how to find the K words in the dictionary. Together, they ran their fingers along the pages until they found kibosh. Pooper struggled through the definition, his face incredulous when he finished. "That means she was going to stop him, not kiss him!"

Jenifer nodded. She turned to the TV/VCR. "Would you like to watch a movie?"

"Too cool," Pooper said. "Do a lot of people get killed?"

"See for yourself," Jenifer said, pressing the Play button.

Pooper pulled out a chair and plopped down in front of the TV.

Jenifer backed away a step or two. Eric followed her example. "I think he'll be engrossed for a while," she said.

"What's the flick?"

"A Reading Adventure tape. With no one else around, he'll forget it's not cool to learn."

"You're amazing," Eric said, keeping his voice low. "This visit just may change his life."

"You brought him here," Jenifer said. "I'm actually just doing my job. One that I love to do."

He wanted to pull her close, kiss her senseless, drag her into a private space and get next to her skin.

Of course he couldn't, so he contented himself with brushing the back of her hand. "While he's occupied, I need to tell you something."

"You mean apologize?"

"That, too," he said. "I know I ran off the other night."

"Yes, you did. Eric, after what we shared, you left a note!" Hurt brimmed in her eyes.

He caught her hand. "I'm sorry. I had to leave and I just thought that was the best way to handle it."

"Next time you have to disappear, wake me up and kiss me good-bye."

He took those words as a sign of hope. "So you'll see me again?"

She nodded.

"Too cool!" Pooper called out, clapping his hands together. "I'm going to play this again."

"Sure, go ahead," Jenifer said. She left her hand in Eric's. "What was it you wanted to tell me?"

"I may have to go back to D.C. for a while, for business."

"Of course," Jenifer said, her voice growing more formal, distancing herself from him. "I always assumed you would."

"Me, too," Eric said, "but what's different now is I want to return to Doolittle."

"Naturally," she said. "If you invest in the Horace House, you'll want to keep an eye on the property."

"Jenifer, will you please quit agreeing with everything I say?" He pulled her closer to him. "I want to come back because *you're* here."

"Oh."

He wanted to throttle her and kiss her. "Oh? Is that all you can say?"

Jenifer nodded. She didn't trust her voice. Eric was to have been a sexual hit-and-run, a midlife crisis adventure for her. He wasn't supposed to have complicated her feelings or her life, but complicate it he had. She traced his palm with her fingertips, clasped it hard, then let it go. "I'm not looking for a relationship," she said, her voice just above a whisper.

He put his hands on her shoulders. "Are you sure you're not looking *at* one?"

She shook her head.

"I don't think you mean that," he said gently. "That's your fear talking, your fear of being hurt and of being abandoned if you risk caring."

"Maybe it is, Eric," she said, "but it's real."

He tipped her chin up. "So is this," he said, leaning forward to kiss her. "You can take on the world for a cause you believe in. Believe in yourself and in me."

Why did the idea make her so darn nervous? She was tempted by Eric's invitation to trust him, but it was so much safer to rely only on herself. "Don't hurt me, Eric," she said.

"I won't," he said, kissing her again, much more thoroughly.

"Yuck!" Pooper made a gagging sound. "Mr. Eric, you'll get cooties!"

Eric smiled and stepped back. "If I do, Pooper, it'll be worth it." He turned toward the boy. "Let's get that library card now."

"Why do I need that?"

"So you can check books, music, and movies out of the library." Jenifer told him. "You may take them home for two weeks."

"Like they're all mine?"

She nodded. "Yes, but you have to bring them back on time or you'll have to pay a fine."

"I don't got no money," Pooper said, dropping his head. "Guess that means I don't get a card."

Jenifer tipped his chin upward. "That's not what that means at all. The library is free—as long as you return your books and tapes on time."

"Cool," he said. "That goes to show my old man doesn't know it all, 'cause he always says nothing in life is free."

Jenifer walked back to the checkout desk. She'd already prepared most of the paperwork for the card, with one exception. "Pooper," she said, "what's your real name?"

"Aw, you don't have to know that, do you?"

"I think it's a rule," Jenifer said. "Besides, when you get a bit older, you might not want to have the same nickname. You might want another one, like Stud or Jock."

His eyes lit up. "Cool. Okay, my real name is Stanley." He whispered it, looking over his shoulder.

"Thank you, Pooper," Jenifer said, typing in *Stanley* in her desk computer. Noting the twitching of Eric's lips, she shot him a smile. "Stanley is a fine name and will be on your card, but I'll leave it up to you how you wish to be addressed."

"Where's the goat book?" Pooper asked.

"I have it right here," Jenifer said, pulling it from a stack she'd selected for him the other day. "Here's your card. You'll need to keep it somewhere you won't lose it. Do you have a wallet?"

"Nah," he said, picking up the Billy Goats Gruff book. "Don't got no money, so I don't need a wallet."

"Every boy needs a wallet," Eric said. "It helps you plan to make money."

Jenifer watched in amazement as Eric pulled his billfold from his pants pocket. He emptied the contents onto the desk.

"Tell you what, Pooper," he said. "It turns out I have an extra one, so why don't you take this one?" He stuffed a five-dollar bill into it before handing it to the child.

"No sh—I mean, cool!" Pooper ran his fingers over the leather. "Feels nice," he said, "kind of soft, like my goats."

Jenifer gave him the library card. Pooper slid it into the wallet. Rather than putting it in his pants pocket, he clutched it in his hand.

"Want to round off the afternoon with a stop at the A&W?" Eric asked.

"Life is too good," Pooper said. "Thanks, man."

Eric leaned over the desk and kissed her. "May I see you later?" he asked.

Pooper rolled his eyes.

"I thought you'd never ask," she murmured.

"What time do you get off?"

She eyed him impishly. "The library closes at five."

"Go home," he whispered so only he could hear, "relax, draw us a nice bubble bath, and I'll join you around six, okay?"

"Can I come back tomorrow?" Pooper asked.

Eric nodded.

Jenifer watched them leave, feeling fluttery and sexy, yet apprehensive. For some reason, every time she heard someone say "tomorrow," her tummy clutched.

"Silly," she said out loud. "If tomorrow never comes, what is there to worry about?"

She had today to savor. Just the suggestion of sharing a bubble bath with Eric set every nerve to tingling. No woman wrapped in Eric Hamilton's arms could be anxious.

Six o'clock had come and gone by the time Eric made it to Jenifer's house. He'd had to go over arrangements for tomorrow night's sting at the paper mill. He was to be arrested along with Lars and Franco. That way his role as a big money buyer would be protected. After they were all in custody, they'd be separated, Eric supposedly extradited by the feds for some other outstanding charge. If all went well, he'd be back at headquarters in Washington, D.C., in less than thirty-six hours.

Normally he experienced a surge of adrenaline at this point in a job. But now, parking a block away from Jenifer's house, then strolling over carrying the Dillard's bag, he felt desire coupled with a sense of loss.

He'd miss Jenifer. Hell, his days would feel empty without her.

Idiot, told himself. He'd get over her. He'd go on to

the next job, the next amorous adventure. No, that was the old Eric talking. Jenifer had changed all that. But he wouldn't be back in Doolittle for a while.

At least they'd have tonight. Along with the naughty negligee, he'd packed more condoms.

When he'd taken Pooper home, the boy was still drooling over the wallet, almost more than his new library card. Eric knew that he needed someone to look after him. Obviously his dad was nothing but a deadbeat. If he were Pooper's dad, Eric thought as he turned up Jenifer's sidewalk, he'd make sure the kid had every opportunity to improve his lot in life.

Well you're not his dad, he told himself. You're not any kid's dad. He shook his head, chasing away those thoughts, thoughts he'd never had until the last several days. A flash of something caught his attention.

Glancing next door, he saw Pete and Charlotte on the front porch. Oh, great. He didn't feel like visiting right now. But he waved. "Hey, there," he called. He raised the sack. "Just returning something Jenifer left in my car."

Pete nodded, squeezing an imaginary trigger between his thumb and forefinger.

Eric mounted the steps to the porch, feeling like a kid on his first high school date. He knocked on the door, not once but twice, but knew Jenifer wouldn't answer. She'd be upstairs, naked, soaking in the tub, waiting for him.

But to his surprise, the door swung open. To his even greater amazement, the woman who stood there wasn't Jenifer.

It was Pamela.

She seemed even more startled than he did. "Oh, Eric, it's you!"

He nodded as he stood in the doorway. "Everything okay, Pamela?"

She nodded, too. "I was just leaving."

"Don't let me chase you away."

She smiled. "Jeni will hang me by my toes if I keep you from her one more minute."

"You think so?" He smiled, pleased. Didn't girl-friends always know the truth? He heard music, similar to what he'd heard before, drifting from upstairs.

"Most definitely." Pamela curled a hand on his shirtfront. "She's so darn set on insisting she doesn't need a man. I'm putting my money on you to prove otherwise to her."

"Well, I don't know about need," Eric said. "I do recognize desire."

Pamela grinned. "I bet you do, hon. I've got to run. Ace hates it if I'm not there when he gets home."

Eric frowned. "Is he treating you right?"

"As well as he knows how," she answered. "You haven't seen his good side, but I have."

Eric imagined she referred to Ace in bed. He kept that thought to himself, though. "Jenifer doesn't seem to think he has a good side."

"Any man who didn't go to college doesn't stand a chance with Jeni," she said. "Jenifer told me you went to Harvard. Now that makes you a hundred percent desirable."

"And I thought it was my body she wanted," Eric said, laughing.

"She does. So let me get out of here," Pamela said. She winked. "Don't do anything I wouldn't do."

She slipped out the door with a wave. Eric closed the door, turned the lock, and whistling softly, hurried up the stairs.

Twenty-two

*T*heir first night together, Jenifer hadn't been nervous. She'd been startled by Eric's entrance into her bathroom, but then nature—or rather, Eric's sensuality and experience—had taken over.

Now, after her friends' well-intentioned visit, Pamela had turned her, unwittingly, into a quaking, insecure shadow of herself. Jenifer had no idea how to act sexy. She knew only how to be herself. Pammy had brought over a beautiful floor-length sheer silk peignoir, black, with feathery touches all around the neckline and hem. She insisted that Jenifer try it on, and then before Jenifer could take it off and hand it back, Pamela said she had to be going, that Ace liked to have his dinner ready when he got home.

Then, down below, Jenifer had heard her best friend and Eric talking. Torn between showing herself and staying safely hidden upstairs, she opted for the easier of the two choices, hovering outside her bedroom door.

She'd already run the tub. It waited for them, warm and bubbly.

"Jenifer?"

She heard Eric call her name. Feeling like a child playing dress-up, she said in a voice that came out akin to a squeak, "In here." She slipped inside the bedroom as she answered him, lounging against her bed pillows as Pamela had instructed. Really, sex was so much simpler without all these games.

Eric appeared in the doorway. Suddenly, she didn't feel at all silly. She felt only happy to see him. "Hi," she said. "Did you get Pooper home okay?"

He nodded and advanced into the room. She noted that he carried a Dillard's bag, a bag that looked a lot like the one she'd taken from Pamela's closet. Good. She'd rather wear the short, provocative nightie than this bawdyhouse getup.

"You look great," he said.

"You think so?" She heard the disbelief in her voice.

Again he nodded. "Kind of like the cover of a Frederick's of Hollywood catalogue," he said, pretending to lick his lips. "Definitely good enough to munch on."

"Oh," Jenifer said. "Well, I thought I looked kind of like a cross between a madam and a magpie, but Pamela said it was perfect."

Eric grinned. He dropped the Dillard's bag and sat on the edge of the bed. "You'd look great in anything," he said.

"Thank you, Eric," she replied, touched, but not quite believing him. The sheer peignoir had slipped open, revealing her breasts and doing nothing to hide the fact that she wore only her skin beneath it.

He stroked the inside of her calf. "You looked great in that T-shirt you had on the other night."

She laughed. "Don't be silly."

He bent and kissed the inside of one knee, then the other. "I am dead serious."

She shivered, and caught his head in her hands. "Eric . . ."

"Yes?"

She caught her breath. "I'm glad you came over. I did run a bath, if you want to slip into the tub."

He shook his head. Bending over her parted legs, he said, "There's only one thing I want to slip into it. It's hot and wet, but it's definitely not a bubble bath."

"Eric!"

"I can think of a few creative uses for all those feathers you're wearing."

"You can?" Anticipation left her breathless.

He pushed the negligee off her shoulders, baring her breasts and abdomen. Then he lifted one of the many feathers that lined it and stroked her lightly across her cheek. "Feel good?"

"Mmm," she said.

He moved the feather lower, circling her nipples with it, brushing, teasing, until she couldn't stand the intense pleasure and caught at his hand.

"Oh, no," he said. "I get to play all I want to."

"What about me?" Jenifer knew she was putty in his hands. "Don't I get to play with your body?"

He yanked the sash from the negligee. "Time enough for that," he said. With a wicked grin, he captured her hands, tucked them over her head, and wound the sash around them. He tugged at the knot a few times, but Jenifer knew that was more for effect than purpose. Still she shivered.

Spread open for him, she lifted her lips, wanting to feel his mouth on hers.

Instead, he shook his head, trailing the feathers of the negligee across her abdomen, down the inside of one thigh, up another, then across her quivering inner lips.

She bucked against the teasing touch.

He nudged her thighs farther apart, but this time he lowered his lips to hers. He captured them, suckling, nibbling, opening her mouth and claiming all she had to give.

Jenifer quivered everywhere. She wrestled against the silk that held her wrists. She had to touch him, to give to him the pleasure he was gifting to her.

He took her hands in his. "Not yet," he said, then lowered his face, kissing a trail from her neck, past her breasts, down her tummy.

He spread her open, tasted her, and all she could do was give herself up to him. Greedily, he sucked, he teased, he licked. Half screaming, she lifted her hips higher and higher. He caught her buttocks with one hand, then slipped one finger inside her, followed by another. She did cry out then, and every pent-up womanly feeling inside of her flowed free. He drank her in, then lifted his head, a look of pure male satisfaction lighting his face.

"Now that's what I like to see," he said, stripping his clothing from his body. "My baby completely ready for me."

Jenifer moved her hands weakly against the pillow.

"You are amazing," she said, unable to move, still pulsating from the magic he'd wrought.

Naked, Eric poised above her. His erection throbbed. She could feel the heat from the flesh of her thighs. He slid above her, skimming her body with his hard, heated flesh. Unconsciously, she opened her mouth. He let her taste him, then pulled back. He must have opened the condom wrapper earlier, because he yanked it out in one smooth motion, tugging it on with one hand.

With his other hand, he freed her hands from their silken bond. She joined him in pulling the protective sheath along his shaft. Her breath came in quick, shallow gasps, so badly did she want to feel him inside her.

Eric leaned over her, kissed her mouth, eyes, nose, cheeks, lips, and then recaptured her mouth. At the same time, he moved his lower body, gently at first, probing, teasing, withdrawing, letting her feel and accept his size. Then suddenly, as if he could hold back no more, he filled her, plunging into her very being, claiming her as no one ever had or ever would.

Sometime later, they realized they were starving, and made their way to her kitchen.

"We could have an omelet," Jenifer said, looking into the refrigerator. She wore an oversize T-shirt that hung off one shoulder and skimmed the tops of her thighs. When she bent over to peer inside the vegetable bin, she treated him to a lovely view of her bare cheeks.

Eric toyed with a bunch of bananas that sat on the counter. "We could. Do you have any ice cream?"

She turned around, holding a carton of eggs. Her eyes were dreamy, her lips puffy. Her wildly disheveled hair framed her face and trailed over a bare shoulder. "An ice cream omelet?"

Eric grinned. Holding up the bananas, he said, "I have a taste for a banana split."

"Ooh, what a great idea," Jenifer said, putting the eggs back into the refrigerator. In their place, she brought out a carton of Cool Whip. She pulled out a half gallon of ice cream from the freezer. "It's been my favorite treat since I was knee-high to a grasshopper."

"That's me," Eric said with a grin, "the mind of a child."

"There's nothing childlike about you," Jenifer said, placing the items on the counter and kissing his bare chest. She had given him a pair of her son's athletic shorts to wear. Other than that, he was naked.

"Oh, no?" He took the carton of ice cream. "Just give me a spoon and I'll show you what a kid I am."

She smiled. She got dishes, then rummaged in a cupboard for nuts, cherries, and hot fudge sauce. "I thought I had these somewhere," she said. "Adam loved banana splits."

"He did?"

She nodded, her face softening. But it was a different look from the utter bliss of sexual contentment. This expression was more like that of the Madonna and child pictures, Eric realized. She loved her children, and that love showed in her voice, her face, and definitely in her actions.

"Adam is about your height. Skinny as a rail even though he eats constantly."

Eric leaned against the counter, wanting to hear more. "Do you worry about him?"

"Worry?" She smiled softly. "Oh, all the time, but not seriously. Not now. When they were little and I had to juggle so much all at once, I worried about doing everything right for them." She opened the jar of hot fudge and licked a bit from the edge of the lid. "But even then," she said with a smile, "I always believed things would work out. Sometimes I worried that I should have found a dad for them, but my answer to that was to try harder to be a good mom."

"Watching you and your mother together," Eric said, "I'm willing to bet you're a wonderful mom. What about your daughter?"

She shot him a sharp glance. "Do you mean do I worry about her doing what I did?"

"Actually, no, but do you?"

She handed him two dishes. He scooped ice cream into them while he waited for her answer.

"Sometimes I wonder if Autumn didn't go into sports with such passion as a means of convincing me she wouldn't fall into the same situation I did."

"Wouldn't that be too precocious for a child to figure out?"

Jenifer peeled a banana. "When you're one of the only kids in your class who doesn't have a daddy, you figure out some fairly complex matters at an early age."

Eric wanted to give Jenifer a hug, but she had that "don't touch me, I can handle everything" set to her shoulders. "Is their father ever around?" He asked the question casually, but he did want to know.

She shook her head. "Sometimes. Not often. And not until they were ten."

"He waited till they were ten!" Eric found that heartless. "I'm surprised you let him see them after that much absence from their lives."

Jenifer drew a knife lengthwise through a banana. "I had to be persuaded by my parents that it was the right thing to do." She set the knife down. "You see, he waited till he'd finished medical school and started his medical practice before he could be bothered."

Eric did go to her, then. He took her in his arms and rubbed her back. "What a shit," he said. He remembered the story her brother had told him. "Did he keep up support payments?"

"Oh, yes, he sent money," Jenifer said, returning his embrace, then wiggling loose. "There's no need for me to cry on your shoulder, Eric. This stuff is ancient history."

He let her go, reluctantly, understanding that these bruises still hurt her caring heart. "His behavior—that really did turn you away from letting any man into your life."

"I just realized we did these backward," she said. "The banana goes on the bottom and the ice cream on top."

"Let's just fix them side by side," Eric said, understanding she wanted to change the topic. "That makes me think of you and me."

She colored prettily. Eric decided not to press his question about marriage. After all, it wasn't his business. They were two adults having sex; their paths were

about to diverge, and that would be that. He stared
down at the scoop of ice cream he held, watching as
she added a slice of banana to the bowl, then glanced
up to find her watching him, curiosity evident in her
eyes. He added the third mound of ice cream against
the banana. "I just don't understand," he said, "how
someone as wonderful as you is living alone."

Jenifer took the scoop from his hand. He'd given her
the opening she needed to ask something she wanted to
know. "I could ask you the same thing," she said, rinsing the ice cream scoop. "If that is the case."

"I told you I'm not married. Are you asking if I'm
otherwise entangled?"

Jenifer sprinkled chopped nuts across both their
bowls. "I was wondering."

Eric popped open the Cool Whip. "If I were," he
said, "I wouldn't be standing here with you."

"That's a nice sentiment," Jenifer said. "And you've
never been married?"

"Nope. I told you that, too."

"Aha," she said, "so why would you wonder about
me living alone?"

He ran a hand over his short hair. He looked adorably
confused, Jenifer thought. "It's different for me."

"Don't tell me that's because you're a man and I'm a
woman," she said. "It's because you didn't want to
fight the way your parents did."

She'd pegged that right. He held up his hands in
mock surrender. "I confess to that." He leaned over and
kissed her. She wasn't the only one who avoided difficult subjects. "Can we eat now?"

"Drizzle some hot fudge sauce on top."

He did so, quite artistically, drawing a flower to top her whipped cream.

"Beautiful," Jenifer said. "Want to sit in the living room, where you gave me that marvelous foot massage?"

"Lead the way," he said, carrying both bowls.

She got two spoons and some napkins. "I don't spend a lot of time in my living room," she said. "It should be called the 'when company comes over room.'"

"Maybe we should go back to your bedroom," Eric said, halting at the foot of the stairs.

She'd wanted adventure. She'd wanted sexual excitement. Jenifer dipped a finger in her whipped cream, offering it to Eric, knowing he'd understand the invitation implied in the gesture. He licked the cream, a dark randy gleam in his eyes.

"The bedroom it is," she said.

Much later, Eric awoke to the unaccustomed sound of birds singing outside a window. Aside from a random seagull, no birds passed by his penthouse windows, and even if they did, the soundproof seal would have kept the noise at bay.

He remembered a wild evening and night of incredible sex. Not once, not twice, but three times they'd coupled. He'd been so drained that he fell dead asleep, he realized now, blinking, looking around the strange bedroom.

"Hi, sleepyhead," Jenifer said, gazing at him from the pillow tucked against his own.

He smiled. Pulling her against his chest, he asked, "Have you been awake long?"

"A few minutes," she said. "I like watching you sleep."

"You do?" He ruffled her hair. "I never stay over," he said, without thinking about what he'd said.

"Oh," Jenifer said. "I'm not sure how to take that."

He kissed her. "I feel so comfortable with you."

She grinned. "Good. I'd have to say, comfort isn't what comes to mind first when I think of you."

"No?" Had he hurt her? No doubt they'd both feel the effects of their marathon night. "Are you okay?"

"More than okay." She outlined his lips with her pinky finger. "You make me feel soooo sexy."

His body stirred. Rolling her onto his chest, he said, "You're the wordsmith. Forget comfort. Let's go for sexy."

She slipped a hand under the sheet.

The telephone rang, the shrill sound intruding on their private world.

"Awfully early for an interruption," Eric complained.

The phone kept ringing. "It's not that early," she said. "It's almost time to get ready for work." Wiggling her hand back from the covers, Jenifer reached for the bedside telephone.

She put the receiver to her ear. Eric gave in to the temptation to tease her nipple. She giggled as she said, "Hello."

"Mother, hi." She started to sit up, but positioned as she was against his chest, she merely tipped forward.

Eric caught her. Holding her by the waist, he admired the view of her full breasts, her head tossed backward, her long hair cascading around her shoulders, as he listened to her end of the conversation.

"Coffee? This morning?"

His erection nudged against her thigh. She waved a hand as if trying to cool her body as she said, "Well, actually, Mother, I have company . . . Oh, you know?" She blushed.

He looked at Jenifer inquiringly. The last thing he wanted was Pete at the door with a shotgun.

"Let me ask," Jenifer said. Covering the mouthpiece, she said, "My mother says why don't we both come over for coffee. Is that okay?"

Eric couldn't help but smile. Nothing in Doolittle went unnoticed. "Sure," he said.

"See you soon," Jenifer said, then hung up the phone. Straddling him, she said, "I don't think we can play anymore right now. I'll be late for work."

"Too bad she couldn't call an hour from now," Eric said, pulling Jenifer down and cradling her body against his. He'd miss her. More than he wanted to admit. Last night had been different for him. It wasn't just sex. He'd connected with this woman in a way he hadn't thought possible. He wanted to hold on to her and never let go. Yet let go was exactly what he would do.

By tomorrow night Doolittle would represent just another job. He'd be on to Washington, to clean up the details of this case. Then he'd move on to his next assignment.

He held her more tightly, then slowly let her go. "I can almost smell that coffee perking," he said, swinging them up and out of the bed.

Jenifer moved with him, savoring the way their bodies meshed, even when doing something so simple and everyday as getting out of bed. Why, it was even better than the first night. Never in her wildest imaginings had she dreamed of how incredible sex could be. She wondered if it was like that with other people, but doubted it.

Eric made everything special.

They showered quickly. She dressed for work. Eric drew on the clothes he'd worn the evening before. Clearly he hadn't planned to stay the night. But at least he'd packed plenty of condoms, Jenifer thought, smiling at him as they walked out of the house, headed next door.

For the first time, Eric looked uncomfortable.

"What's wrong?" Jenifer asked.

He played with the collar of his shirt. "I feel like a kid taking his date home late from the prom the night before. You know, like I'm going to be called on the carpet and grounded for a month."

She laughed. "You're a good sport to come have coffee, then. Trust me, my mother is so thrilled that I finally—"

"Oh, so that's how it is," Eric said teasingly. "Your mother is happy you found a man."

"She may see it that way," Jenifer said. "But don't worry, I know we understand one another."

He halted and looked into her eyes.

She broke contact first. "I mean, I asked you to seduce me."

Eric tipped her chin upward. "Jeni, it was more than seduction. No matter what happens, I want you to know that for me, you're one of a kind."

She nodded. She didn't want to admit the confusion of her own feelings. She'd spent too many years building up her defenses to confess that Eric had breached them in such a short time. "Thank you," she said, leaving it at that.

The front door of Uncle Pete's house swung open. Charlotte stood there, looking cozy in lounging pajamas. So, Jenifer thought, if she and Uncle Pete were so open about their relationship, there didn't seem any point to be embarrassed about having them know that Eric had spent the night with her.

Perhaps that's why Charlotte had called, she reflected as she and Eric greeted her mother. It would be like her mother to let her know she approved of her.

"Come on into the kitchen," Charlotte said, smiling at both of them.

Uncle Pete was pouring coffee into four mugs. He greeted them and kissed Charlotte on the cheek as if she'd been gone for hours, not minutes.

Jenifer smiled, longing for one poignant moment, for the camaraderie and closeness her mother experienced with Uncle Pete. She felt almost like a traitor to her dad for feeling that way, as her mother's relationship with her dad had seemed more complex, more like a series of negotiations as opposed to the easy understanding she and Pete had. Perhaps that's because she and Uncle Pete had been friends for so long before becoming lovers.

Soon they were all seated around the table. Charlotte passed a basket of muffins and toast.

Jenifer memorized the moment, the four of them, sitting there together so comfortably.

Comfortable.

The very word Eric had used when he woke up.

She smiled at him and sighed with contentment, wishing she could always feel this way.

Twenty-three

*W*hen Eric called her that afternoon at the library and told her he wouldn't be able to see her that night, Jenifer decided she'd visit Andie and then go back to the paper mill. This time she called ahead and asked the plant manager if she could talk to him about a visit for the reading group she wanted to arrange. He didn't sound too thrilled about the idea, but finally agreed to see her.

She drove up to Andie's home, parked, and walked to the door. She didn't see Pooper. He hadn't come to the library after school, but then, she hadn't expected him to be a regular.

Andie opened the door right away, looking pleased to see her. "Hi, Miz Wright," she said. "Come in."

Jenifer stepped in and took the seat Andie offered her. She appeared to be home alone. "Is your dad at work already?"

Andie nodded. "Sometimes he goes early, 'cause he

says he gets more studying done there." She glanced around. "I can see why. It's pretty crowded here and I like to play music."

"So did you work things out with your dad about that money?" Nothing like jumping right into the topic, Jenifer thought, though wincing at her outright question. But she didn't have much time. Rodney the plant manager had grumbled about seeing her, and if she got there late, he probably wouldn't wait for her.

"I'm not supposed to talk about it," the girl said. "But since you know about it, I guess it's okay."

Jenifer nodded.

"A man who said he was with the police came and took the sack of money away with him. My dad told him that he'd found it at the paper mill. He was scared at first, but the man said he'd be okay and if he told him everything he knew, nothing would happen to him."

"I wonder who the man was?"

"Oh, you know him, Miz Wright. He's the man who came here and played with Pooper."

"Eric?" Jenifer stared at Andie.

Andie shrugged. "Yes, I think that's his name."

"Did you tell him about the twenty dollars you took?"

She hung her head. "No, I didn't. I hope that's not wrong of me."

"Don't worry about it, Andie. I have the bill, so no one else will end up with it."

"Should we give it to Mr. Eric?"

Jenifer shook her head, her thoughts whirling. Was Eric a policeman? Or was he involved in the counterfeit operation? No, she refused to believe that of him.

But what was the truth? And what was the truth of his feelings toward her? If he were a cop, had he been spending time with her to see if she knew anything about the case? She recalled the printout she'd found in the bathroom and heard him swearing that he had no ulterior motives for his interest in her.

Right.

She stood up, in a rush to be gone.

"Miz Wright, are you okay?" Andie looked at her with concern.

"I'm fine," she said. "I have an appointment, so I've got to run. I'm glad everything is okay with you and your dad."

"Me, too," Andie said. "It's not fun being scared."

Jenifer gave her a hug and hurried out the door.

Just wait till she saw Eric Hamilton! Did she have some questions to put to him.

Eric prepared for his meeting with Lars and Franco carefully. By the time he'd donned a flashy silk suit, heavy gold chain, alligator shoes, stuffed his Troy King identification in the new wallet he'd picked up in Miami, and slicked his hair with gel, he'd become the big money player the two goons would be expecting.

The buy was set to take place at the Tri-Forest Paper Mill. Eric found this to be an extremely stupid move on their part, but it was their funeral, so to speak. When he'd spoken to Franco on the phone earlier, the man had bragged about having the paper mill in their pocket.

Eric suspected it was simpler for the two men to show up there and hand over the money directly, thus cutting Ace out of whatever they paid him to make another run with a load of cash.

He looked around the motel room, having already paid his bill and left his things with one of the other agents who'd moved into the area for the night's action. He sat down on the bed, where he and Jenifer had kissed.

Stroking the cheerless polyester comforter, Eric hoped Jenifer would welcome him back once he finally returned to Doolittle.

Because he knew he was coming back. He didn't know that he should, but he knew he couldn't stay away from her.

Jenifer pulled into the parking lot of the paper mill. There were a couple of eighteen-wheelers parked in the graveled area outside the guard booth. She walked purposefully forward and explained to the guard that she had an appointment with Rodney, the plant manager.

He didn't look as if he believed her.

She tapped her foot on the floor of the booth while he pushed some buttons on a walkie-talkie and paged the manager.

While she stood there, another truck pulled in. The driver climbed out and stepped toward the entrance. It was Ace.

Jenifer got a bad feeling in the pit of her stomach. She half turned away, hoping he wouldn't notice her.

Luck was not with her.

"Well, if it's not Ms. Know-it-all," Ace said, strolling up to the open doorway of the guard booth. "What are you doing out with us working stiffs?"

"I'm visiting the manager," Jenifer said.

The guard looked from Ace to her. He handed Ace a clipboard. Ace scribbled something on it, then leered at her. "You sure have a habit of messing in what isn't any of your business."

"I beg your pardon?"

He leaned closer. She could smell alcohol on his breath. She winced, and he laughed. "Leave my wife alone," he said. "If you don't, there's going to be trouble."

Jenifer wanted to punch him in the face. She had her fists clenched at her sides. But she knew she couldn't antagonize him further for fear he might take it out on Pamela. If only her friend would hurry up and decide to get a divorce.

"Mr. Rodney's on his way out," the guard said. "You can wait here. I'm going on my rounds now." He looked at Ace, somewhat nervously Jenifer thought, then walked away.

Ace glared at her. "Remember what I told you," he said, then turned and headed into the main building.

Jenifer found it interesting that Ace apparently had free rein. As a truck driver, wouldn't he just pick up and deliver a load? Perhaps they had a break room inside for the drivers.

The manager walked toward the guard booth, a nervous tic fluttering below his right eye. "Jenifer?"

"Hi, Rodney," she said, acting as if she'd seen her high school classmate recently, though she couldn't remember the last time their paths had crossed. She almost didn't recognize him. His hair had thinned dramatically, he had several days of growth on his chin and jowls, and his shirt looked as if he'd slept in it. She remembered Rodney as being much more debonair, almost a man of the world by Doolittle standards.

"You wanted to talk to me about the library?" He laughed nervously. "I don't have any overdue books, do I?"

She smiled. "No. I was thinking of bringing the book group for a tour, if you'd be willing to have someone show them how paper is made."

"Paper? Oh, well, I guess we could do that, but listen, Jenifer, this really isn't a good time." He looked over his shoulder. "Things are kind of rough right now."

Jenifer nodded. She stepped closer to the man. "Rodney, is something wrong?"

"No, no." And then he started crying. He put his hands over his eyes and sobbed.

Jenifer stared. "Rodney?"

He dashed at his eyes. "Sorry. I'm a wreck. You just sounded so sympathetic it got to me."

Jenifer drew him to the guard's chair. "Tell me. Maybe I can help."

"Nobody can help me," he said. "My life is over."

"Are you in trouble?"

Nodding, he pulled a handkerchief from his pocket and blew his nose. "I made a terrible mistake. I've always had a gambling problem, but I got in over my head thinking if I just kept playing, my luck would turn." He shook his head and sighed. "What a fool. Anyway, I ended up owing way too much money to the wrong kind of people, and when they wanted a favor, I couldn't say no."

Jenifer nodded. "Does your wife know?"

He looked horrified. "No! Not about the gambling or the mess I'm in."

"Someone's using the plant as cover for illegal activities, aren't they?"

He nodded. "Hey, wait a minute. How do you know that?"

She shrugged. "Seems like a logical conclusion, based on what you just told me."

He jumped up. "You know something you shouldn't know. You always were a smarty pants, always had to know better than the rest of us."

"Rodney," Jenifer said, her voice soothing, "I'm clueless. Harmless."

He grabbed a flashlight off a desk. "I shouldn't have said a word. What's wrong with me? You tricked me!"

Jenifer's heart was racing. Rodney sounded deranged. "Your secret is safe with me," she said.

He lunged and grabbed her around the waist. "Nobody is safe. You don't understand. These guys will kill me. They'll kill you. All they care about is money. If I let you go and they find out I said anything to you, they'll kill me and my wife." He started crying again, but didn't loosen his hold. Instead, he forced her arms behind her back.

Jenifer fought him off, but despite his ragged appearance, he was far stronger than she was, and perhaps his wild mental state fed his strength. Pushing her forward, he said, "You're coming inside with me."

She kicked back at his ankles, but he forced her out of the guard booth and through the entrance to the paper mill.

The guard had left on his rounds outside the building. Ace was inside. Jenifer took a chance and screamed for help.

Rodney screamed at her to shut up.

Ace raced around a corner of a long hallway. "What in the hell?"

"Help me! Call the police," Jenifer yelled, kicking and struggling.

Ace stared at her and started laughing, the meanest sound Jenifer had ever heard.

At nine o'clock Eric drove up to the paper mill. He carried a large case filled with cash and approached the entrance. The main door was unlocked, as Franco had said it would be. He headed down the hall to the sign that said OFFICE.

He knew there were agents surrounding the facility. He knew this money buy was supposed to go down cleanly. But he also knew better than to assume things would go like clockwork. Something about the building put him on edge. He paused, straining to hear signs of the presence of anyone else.

And then he heard a voice that made his blood freeze. Jenifer.

He edged down the hallway, pausing just before the office door, where he listened.

Several male voices rumbled alongside the unmistakable sound of Jenifer's.

Lars. Franco. Another man, who it took him a moment to recognize. Ace.

Ace? What in the hell was he doing here? He wasn't part of the plan. One look and he'd know Troy King and Eric Hamilton were one and the same.

Had he been wrong about Jenifer?

No. He refused to believe it.

The door shot open, blocking Eric from sight. Through the slit between the door and the frame, he saw Ace standing there, breathing heavily, but thankfully facing away from him. "Bitch, just wait till I get back here. You're going to be sorry your mother ever gave birth to you."

No, Jenifer wasn't one of the bad guys.

But they had her in their clutches.

Ace stomped down the hall, slamming out the door of the building. Saying a silent prayer, Eric waited a long moment, then sauntered into the office.

Jenifer's eyes almost popped out of her head. Eric looked at her dead on, showing no recognition, turning his back on her though it took all his self-control. She was tied to a chair with her hands behind her back. A bruise showed on her cheek. His jaw worked but he played his role. That was the best way to get her safely out of there.

"Hey, Franco, Lars," he said, also glancing at the other man but ignoring him. "What's with the chick? We celebrating our deal with a little party?"

Lars chuckled. The other man looked sick. Behind him, Jenifer gasped. Eric prayed she understood to keep quiet and not call him by his name.

He dropped his briefcase onto the desk. "I've got a better looking babe waiting for me," he said, "so let's do this deal so I can get out of here."

Franco smirked. "This one's real feisty. She made Ace so mad he had to leave to go get some liquor."

Eric shrugged. "Where's my goods?"

Franco prodded the other man. "Get up and earn your keep," he said. "Pull those bags out of the closet."

The man rose and opened the double doors of a storage area. He yanked out two oversized canvas bags. Eric walked over, unzipped each one, rifled the stacks of peach-and-green-hued twenties, and nodded.

Behind him, Jenifer twisted her arms against the ropes that held her to the chair and thought furiously. She thought Eric had signaled to her not to say anything. But had he done so because he was an undercover cop and her recognition of him would compromise him? Or was he truly the slimy criminal he appeared to be?

As she struggled with the ropes, she fought with her heart. She couldn't bear for Eric to be a bad guy. She almost cried with frustration, the binding burning her skin as the possibility of his betrayal wounded her spirit.

It wasn't possible.

Yet she knew it was. She'd loved and trusted Lawrence, the father of her children, and he'd turned against her.

Had Eric abandoned her, too?

She felt one of the ropes jerk free.

Eric turned around, one heavy canvas bag in each hand. He looked her over, his expression unreadable, just as the office door burst open.

"Freeze! Don't move. You're all under arrest!" Men with guns drawn rushed into the room.

One grabbed Eric and threw him to the ground. The

others were tackled and fought back. A man rushed to her, untied her, and hustled her from the room. The last image she had of Eric was of him being driven to his knees, his hands yanked behind his back and thrust roughly into handcuffs.

Twenty-four

*T*hree weeks later, at the first opportunity he had to
take leave from his job, Eric took the turn off the
interstate toward Doolittle, passed the Highway Express, and found his way to the Schoolhouse Inn. He'd
decided to do things right this time.

Two grandmotherly ladies greeted him, hurrying
him inside, explaining that normally they'd sit and
chat a spell, but they had to get to the police picnic.
Eric assured them he understood.

That happened to be his destination as well.

The proprietresses, Abbie and Martha, insisted he
ride with them. He accepted their invitation, thinking
that if all went well, he'd be leaving the affair with
Jenifer. If things didn't go his way, he could always
walk back.

He'd called Jenifer several times during the weeks
he'd been back in Washington. But he couldn't wait until he could see her face-to-face. She'd accepted his ex-

planation of his real job, but had kept him at an emotional distance in their conversations. From her tone of voice, he could tell she didn't believe he'd ever return to Doolittle, no matter what he said.

She expected to be abandoned once again.

When they got to Courthouse Square, the two older ladies pointed him toward the ticket booth, then strode off to their respective volunteer posts. Eric looked around the square. The grounds had been turned into a village fair. Clowns, jugglers, and face painters entertained children and adults. He purchased an admission ticket, looking around for a sight of Jenifer.

He found her working at a collection station by a row of games of chance. She finished a transaction, then looked up to help the next customer. When he'd first seen her photo, he'd been enamored; when he'd first met her at the library he was entranced. And now, seeing her, he felt a rush of tender desire, and longing so strong that it stunned him.

"Hey," he said, the only word he could manage.

"Eric!" She looked as if she wanted to throw her arms around him, and then she said, in a restrained voice, "You're here. In person."

He nodded. "You look great."

She ran the roll of tickets through her hands. "So do you."

"You didn't think I'd show up."

"No," she said, her voice frank even as desire glowed in her eyes and showed in the way her body leaned toward his. "But I'm very glad you did," she added, in that adorable breathless way she spoke when she wanted him.

"What would you say if I told you I'm really buying the Horace House?"

"That's good. I mean, everyone in town will be happy to hear that, especially Rooster, not to mention Mrs. Ball."

"It's not everyone else in town I'm interested in," Eric said.

"It's not?" She had to be teasing him now, he thought.

"But I'm not going to run it as a hotel," he said. "Can you see it as a retirement home?"

"Oh, Eric. You got that idea from Mrs. Kirtley being so lonesome." Her eyes were shining now.

He nodded. Her smile lit him up all over. He would have purchased ten old houses just to see her that happy. "What do you get for those tickets?"

"They're ten for two dollars."

"That's the price," he said. "What do they buy?"

"Any of the games in this row. Or the Photo Fun booth."

"I'll take ten dollars' worth," he said, handing her the money.

"That's a lot," she said.

"I'm buying your time, too," he said, an idea forming. "I'm on duty."

"Take a union break," he said, holding out his hand.

She called another woman over, handed her the roll of tickets and the money bag. "I'll be back in ten minutes," Jenifer said.

"Fifteen," Eric said. "Where's the Photo Fun booth?"

"At the end of the row," Jenifer said, skipping to keep up with him.

He had to hold her close. He needed her skin-to-skin, heart-to-heart, but short of that, cuddled in his lap would have to do. He had to tell her how much he'd missed her, how much hope he had for the future, and dare to ask her if she could possibly feel the same way.

Another couple stood in front of them. They disappeared behind the curtain of the instant photo booth. Giggles sounded from within.

"Tell me you missed me," Eric said.

"Okay. At work I look up every time the door opens, hoping it's you. There, you happy now?"

He kissed her forehead. "Happier," he said. "How is Pamela?"

Jenifer sighed. "She's going to be all right. She's filed for divorce, and the school board renewed her contract. And she's decided not to be in a hurry to find another husband. I couldn't help but think it was Conway she grieved, not Ace."

"Ace should be away a good number of years," Eric said.

"Thanks to you."

The man and woman emerged from the booth, straightening their clothing, laughing over their photos that had spit out the developer window.

Eric held the curtain back. "After you," he said.

Jenifer stepped into the small space. "It was my idea to set up this booth this year," she said. "They promised almost a one hundred percent return on the rental price of—"

He cut off her flow of words with a kiss. "Jeni, you can tell me all about the fair later." He pulled her down on his lap on the tiny bench. "Right now I want to talk about you." He kissed her again. "And me." A blurry mirror faced them across the space of less than two feet. He pointed to their images. "Us."

"Us?" Jenifer asked warily, but at least she didn't pull away from his embrace.

"Us," he repeated. "I've been thinking about the way you asked me to seduce you."

She colored slightly. "Well, yes, that was rather forward of me. . . ."

He kissed her, a brief gesture of reassurance. "Well, you said all you wanted was sex, but I don't think it was just about sex."

"Oh, I don't know," she said, kissing the side of his neck.

"I think it was about you being ready to risk trusting someone again," he said, his voice low and gentle.

"What makes you say that?" She didn't sound as if she disagreed.

"You wanted a stranger, someone who wouldn't stick around, someone you expected to leave you. That was a baby step in risking closeness with a man." He stroked her hair. He'd felt her stiffen.

Jenifer listened hard to what he was saying. That he'd come back to Doolittle thrilled her and at the same time scared the daylights out of her. "Yeah, and when I watched you being handcuffed, I was hating myself for having taken that step," she said.

"I understand that," Eric said. "You weren't supposed to have been there. When I saw you tied to that chair, I almost called the whole operation off, but that might have put you in more danger than keeping to my role and letting the other agents come in and hustle you away to safety." He kissed her on the top of her head. "I hated that you had to be put through that, but I will say you played it just right."

She grinned. "Why, thank you. I have decided to leave the mystery solving to the professionals."

He ruffled her hair. "Somehow I doubt that," he said. They laughed together.

"You two going to be in there forever?" a man called from outside the booth.

Jenifer glanced guiltily at the curtain separating them from the world outside.

"Oh, no, you don't," Eric said. "No worrying about how much profit you might be losing by hogging the photo booth. Not till I've said what I came here to say."

Her heart stilled at those words. Had he come back only to leave again? "And what's that?" she asked, now expecting that he would indeed tell her what she most feared. But she might as well hear it, and then get on with her life. She'd let herself hope, when she first looked up and saw Eric standing in front of her, that he truly had returned to stay.

"I'm not the safest of gambles for someone afraid of risking her heart," he said, brushing her cheek with his thumb. "I've been a wanderer for years. I've avoided settling down out of fear of ending up like my parents."

"Eric, you're not your parents," she said. "You're kind and loving and generous. Just look at what you did for Mrs. Kirtley. And Pooper! I mean Stanley. He's been coming to the reading group I started for boys."

Eric smiled. "Good for him."

It was her turn to give him a hug, a kiss of reassurance. He kissed her back, then said, "Jeni, I've never told a woman these words. . . ."

Her pulse skittered. She gazed into his eyes, hoping he was about to say what she already felt from him, what she felt for him. "Yes, Eric?"

"I love you, Jenifer. I want you, need you, and promise I'll always protect you. I'd get down on my knees right now, but there's no room in here."

She smiled, her eyes misting over. "You've opened up my heart," she said. "I thought I'd never feel like this. I love you," she whispered.

He kissed her, a gentle promise.

"Now about that 'us,'" he said.

"Yes?"

"I know you don't need a man," he said with a grin, "but do you think you could consider wanting a husband?"

"Only if that husband is you, Eric Jay Hamilton," she said.

He smiled, his love for her shining in his eyes. "Thanks for taking a chance on me, Jenifer Janey Wright."

A red light flashed, a camera whirred.

He kissed her again, clasping her close to his heart, the way he would hold her always.

Epilogue

*T*he strains of the organ filtered through to the ante-
room off the vestibule of the Doolittle Community
Church. Jenifer tried to stand still while her mother adjusted the folds of her tea-length white satin dress. Eric
waited for her at the front of the church.

Uncle Pete would be there, too, to claim his wife.

Charlotte stepped back, satisfied. "You are a perfect
bride," she said.

"Oh, Mother, what if I mess it up?" Jenifer said in a
rush of nerves. "I've read every book in the library on
how to make your marriage work, but what if—"

"Shhh," Charlotte said. She kissed her on the cheek.
She tapped her own breastbone. "Never mind those
how-to books. You and Eric may not always agree on
everything, but as long as you both listen to your
hearts, you will live and grow in love."

Autumn danced back into the room. "Mom, it's
time! I just peeked into the church." She paused, glanc-

ing from Jenifer to Charlotte. "Gosh, Gran, it's hard to say which one of you is the prettier bride. But you both sure have handsome husbands."

Jenifer smiled. Autumn and Adam had been home on Christmas break for the past two weeks. They'd gotten along well with Eric, answering the only concern Jenifer had left in her decision to marry. She loved Eric more than she could have believed possible, but she needed her children to accept him, too.

Eric had been in town for the past month, having resigned from his undercover job and turned his attention to the renovation of the Horace House. He still commuted every few weeks to check on his family shoe business, but since he'd had a manager in place for so many years, that arrangement worked out as well from Doolittle as it had when he'd traveled on assignments for weeks at a time. Both he and Jenifer wanted to live in Doolittle, Eric having found the hometown he'd never known. They were also talking about Jenifer realizing her dream of attending law school. She wasn't sure how they'd handle those plans, but she'd learned to trust that with Eric, things worked out.

Adam stuck his head in the door. "Ready?"

Her son looked like a man, Jenifer thought, admiring his tall, lean form, elegant in his first tux. She smiled, took a deep breath, and said, "I'm ready."

He opened the door. Autumn, as maid of honor for both brides, preceded him, and then he turned, offering one arm to his grandmother, the other to his mom.

"This is our best Christmas ever," he said, kissing both of them.

The organ filled the church with the beautiful cadence of the traditional wedding march. The guests rose. Jenifer and her son and her mother stepped forward.

Every pew was filled with friends and family.

But at this moment, she saw only Eric, waiting for her at the end of the white satin runner, love shining in his eyes.

Summer is hot no matter where you are when you're reading an Avon Romance . . .

Look for these sizzling stories coming in July

SO IN LOVE by Karen Ranney
An Avon Romantic Treasure

Though they shared a deep passion, Douglas MacRae and Jeanne du Marchand were cruelly separated when they were young, each one led to believe it was the fault of the other. Years later, they miraculously meet again. With this second chance to love, can they realize that though forgiveness is hard, living without each other is impossible?

IN THE MOOD by Suzanne Macpherson
An Avon Contemporary Romance

Allison, a young divorcee living paycheck to paycheck with her young son, and Dex, a prominent billionaire, have very little in common. Or so they think, until they realize they once shared an anonymous affair that was so amazing that neither has been able to forget it . . .

KISSING THE BRIDE by Sara Bennett
An Avon Romance

Well-favored in looks and fortune, Lord Henry has the ear of the king and any woman he wants, except one—his dear friend Lady Jenova. But when she goes in search of an uncomplicated groom, Henry realizes he cannot let her marry some other man. And when he kisses her, it as if no one else has ever existed.

ONE WICKED NIGHT by Sari Robins
An Avon Romance

Miss Lillian Kane learns quickly that her pretty face isn't enough to get her by when her kindly chaperone is mistakenly carted off to Newgate Prison. To make things right, she needs Nicholas Redford, who will have nothing to do with her. Until one wicked night . . . when he realizes that under all that charm lies a woman he will not be able to resist.

*Avon Romances—
the best in exceptional authors
and unforgettable novels!*

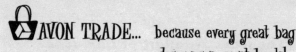

Avon Romantic Treasures

*Unforgettable, enthralling love stories,
sparkling with passion and adventure
from Romance's bestselling authors*

Have you ever dreamed of writing a romance?

*And have you ever wanted
to get a romance published?*

Perhaps you have always wondered how to
become an Avon romance writer?
We are now seeking the best and brightest undiscovered
voices. We invite you to send us your query letter to
avonromance@harpercollins.com

What do you need to do?

Please send no more than two pages telling us
about your book. We'd like to know its setting—is it
contemporary or historical—and a bit about the hero,
heroine, and what happens to them.

Then, if it is right for Avon we'll ask to see part of the
manuscript. Remember, it's important that you have
material to send, in case we want to see your story quickly.

Of course, there are no guarantees of publication,
but you never know unless you try!

*We know there is new talent just waiting
to be found! Don't hesitate . . . send us
your query letter today.*

*The Editors
Avon Romance*